3

FIC
HAN

Handler, David,
1952-

The man who cancelled
himself.

$19.95

MYSTERY

02/28/1995

		TE	

3

DISCARDED

The Man
Who Cancelled
Himself

By the same author

Kiddo

Boss

The Man Who Died Laughing

The Man Who Lived by Night

The Man Who Would Be F. Scott Fitzgerald

The Woman Who Fell from Grace

The Boy Who Never Grew Up

The Man Who Cancelled Himself

A Stewart Hoag Novel

by
David Handler

Doubleday
New York   London   Toronto   Sydney   Auckland

PUBLISHED BY DOUBLEDAY
a division of Bantam Doubleday Dell Publishing Group, Inc.
1540 Broadway, New York, New York 10036

DOUBLEDAY and the portrayal of an anchor with a dolphin are
trademarks of Doubleday, a division of Bantam Doubleday Dell
Publishing Group, Inc.

Book design by Dorothy K. Urlich

Library of Congress Cataloging-in-Publication Data

Handler, David, 1952–
    The man who cancelled himself : a Stewart Hoag novel / by David
Handler. —1st ed.
        p.   cm.
    1. Hoag, Stewart (Fictitious character)—Fiction.   2. Ghostwriters
—United States—Fiction.   I. Title.
PS3558.A4637M29   1995
813'.54—dc20   94-9302
                                                                    CIP

ISBN 0-385-42160-5
Copyright © 1995 by David Handler

For Tab Andrews
(alias Peter Gethers),
the best partner a boy
named Biff could ever ask for

*See, I have this special responsibility
to my kids. Because to them I'm not
just some actor playing Uncle Chubby.
I AM Uncle Chubby. And that means a lot
to me. Heck, that means everything.*
       —from an interview with
       Lyle Hudnut in *TV Guide*,
       two weeks before his arrest

Nobody ever drowned in shallow.
       —old sitcom writers' saying

The Man
Who Cancelled
Himself

One

Lyle Hudnut's beach house may have been the ugliest house I'd ever seen. It was certainly the ugliest house in all of East Hampton. And, trust me, there are a lot of ugly houses in East Hampton. His sat perched atop a choice dune at the end of choice Windmill Lane, right next to the choicest of country clubs, the Maidstone, where Lyle Hudnut was not a member. They wouldn't have his sort. Even before all of the trouble.

My cabbie pulled up at the end of the gravel drive and gaped at the place. So did Lulu, my basset hound, who had her back paws planted firmly in my groin and her large, wet, black nose stuck out the open window. I did some heavy gaping myself. Couldn't help it. It was so huge. It was so hideous. It was so . . . I don't know what you'd call it. Me, I'd call it postmodern blech. Once, maybe forty years back, it had been a modest Nantucket-style beach cottage. Too modest. So, some time during the Stylish Seventies, its then owner had erected a second, much grander house right across the driveway, this one an upended two-story Bauhaus shoe box of white cedar with Palladian windows and a network of queerly angled balconies and sun porches and catwalks with curved pipe railings like you'd see on an ocean liner. Especially if you suffered from migraine headaches. And then Lyle Hudnut got his big, fat hands on it. It was he who had just finished building the third house, this one shoehorned in between the other two so as to misconnect them all into a single, monstrous unit. The new centerpiece, an homage to the *Catalonian Modernisme* school of Antoni Gaudi, was a surrealistic two-story structure of undulating milk chocolate stucco that gave the appearance of melting there in the hot August sun, like one of Dali's clocks. Looked positively edible, if you like milk chocolate. I prefer bitter-sweet.

And then there were the awful grounds. Not so much the plants but the utterly lifelike, utterly kitschy bronze statues all over the damned place. Of a man trying to peek over the fence. Of a gardener crouched before the rose bushes, pruner in hand. Of an Irish setter, male, in the act of peeing on a birch tree. This one Lulu snarfled at with great disapproval. She has pretty strong taste in art.

My cabbie, a sour runt in his fifties, shook his head. "Christ, you'd think with all their money they'd have some taste, y'know?"

"You wouldn't say that if you knew a lot of people who have a lot of money."

"What kind of guy lives here, anyway?"

"I'll let you know when I figure that out."

I paid him and let Lulu out. She made right for the setter, nose quivering. The cab pulled away and left us there. It was quiet, except for the sound of the surf roiling on the beach, and of Lulu mouth-breathing. She doesn't do well in the summer heat, being covered with hair. There was a bit of a breeze, which there hadn't been in the city. Also a hint of fish in the air, though that may have been Lulu's breath.

The front door was a slab of whitewashed wood smack dab in the center of the milk chocolate house. A pair of bronze Halloween trick-or-treaters were there ahead of me. A little girl dressed as a witch, a boy as a ghost. His finger was poised to ring the doorbell. I beat him to it. Though it wasn't a bell at all. It played a little tune, the familiar, insipid nursery ditty that was the theme song to *The Uncle Chubby Show*.

A steamy young blonde in a leopard-patterned string bikini answered it. She was at least five feet ten standing there in her bare feet, and there was nothing delicate or frail about her. She was meaty and big-boned, with a wild, tousled mane of sun-and-bottle-bleached hair, and a pair of hooters so outrageously immense as to defy nature, not to mention gravity. They jutted straight forward through the doorway—no droop, no sag, no way. It was as if she had some kind of double-wishbone suspension hidden there in the top of her bathing suit, though I seriously doubted that. Her string bikini offered no more support than a length of waxed dental floss. She was about twenty-seven and deeply tanned. She smelled of suntan oil and sweat. She wasn't drop-dead gorgeous, but then I'm sure it took people—particularly men—a long time to get to her face. It was a rather blank face. Her blue eyes were set far apart and one of them, the left, drifted slightly, giving her a semizonked appearance. She had a fat little pug nose and too much chin and a mouth wide enough to drive a tractor-trailer through. Other than the bikini she wore a pair of long, heavy, studded necklaces of silver that looked like a collision between Paloma Picasso and Johnny Rotten. They plunged down into the valley to be found between her twin peaks, cleavage so deep and vast a yodeler would get an echo down there. I stared. I tried not to, but I stared.

"I made them with my own two hands," she informed me.

"Made them?"

"The necklaces. They're of my own design."

Now I was trying not to giggle. Because she owned the squeakiest, ootsie-fooeyest widdle baby-doll voice you can imagine. She sounded like Minnie Mouse on helium. It was so unlikely I half believed she was putting me on. She wasn't. She was most serious.

Proprietary as well. She stood planted ripely there in the doorway with her hands on her bare, greased flanks, checking us out. First Lulu, who was wearing the pith helmet I'd had made for her that summer to keep the sun off of her head. It did the job fine, plus she was all set if we ever got invited on a lion hunt. Then me. I had on the double-breasted suit of cream-colored silk and linen I'd just had made for me in Milan. With it I wore a raspberry broadcloth shirt and yellow polka-dot bow tie from Turnbull & Asser, calfskin braces, and the brown-and-white ventilated spectator balmorals from Maxwell's. On my head was the straw trilby.

"I'm here to see Lyle Hudnut."

She tossed her blond tresses at me. "And you are . . . ?"

"Hopelessly depressed. But don't let it bother you. I've learned to live with it."

She nodded at me with recognition. "Oh, sure," she squeaked. "You must be the writer."

"Is it that obvious?"

"I'm Katrina Tingle," she said, sticking out her right hand. It was strong, and it lingered in mine a second longer than it needed to. On her left she wore a diamond engagement ring with a stone big as a chunk of rock candy. "I'm Lyle's fiancée, Mr. Hoag. And manager."

"Make it Hoagy."

"As in Carmichael?"

"As in the cheese steak."

"Lyle doesn't eat cheese or steak anymore," she advised me in her Kewpie-doll voice.

"I'm sorry."

"Don't feel sorry for him," she huffed. "He doesn't want pity. All he's asking for is a little understanding."

"I'm afraid understanding is in much shorter supply than pity."

"People, don't *know* him," she argued with great conviction. "How sensitive and sweet he is. He's just a great, big teddy bear. Believe me, his bark is worse than his bite."

"He bites?" I asked, exchanging a worried look with Lulu.

Katrina frowned at me. "I didn't realize there'd be a dog."

"Nor did I. I assumed she was with you."

"She doesn't have deer ticks, does she?"

Lulu snuffled at this indignantly. I told her to let me handle it. "If she does," I replied, "she hasn't said anything to me about them."

"The reason I ask is that Lyle is deathly afraid of getting Lyme disease. She'll have to keep her distance."

"Not to worry. She never sticks her nose where it's not wanted." I tugged at my ear. "Unlike me."

Katrina bristled. "You're copping an attitude with me, aren't you?"

"I don't mean to," I assured her. "It's this handicap of mine. I'm one of the socially challenged. But I'm getting help. In fact, my doctors think I'm making excellent progress."

Now she took a couple of deep, angry breaths in and out, her hooters heaving. They almost rammed me off of the porch and onto the lawn. "Guys," she squealed defiantly. "They meet me and they think, hey, here's some bimbonic airhead—just because of the size of my zoomers and because of how I happen to sound." Angry, she sounded less like Minnie Mouse and more like Alvin of Alvin and the Chipmunks. "Well, I just let them go ahead and think that. Right up until the moment when they find themselves flat on their back with my foot on their face."

"Careful, I excite easily these days."

"I love Lyle and I love my life!"

"And I'm not here to take either of them away from you."

"Then why *are* you here?"

"I'm beginning to wonder that myself."

She stuck her jaw out at me. "Look, I'm speaking to you as his manager now, okay? Lyle's a man with no sense of personal control. He has to be carefully watched, twenty-four hours a day. If this collaboration is going to work out, then you and I had better see eye to eye. Because you're not working for him. You're working for *me*. Understand?"

"I'm not working for anyone. Not until I decide for myself if I want the job. If I do, I work for the celebrity—not his manager, not his fiancée, not anybody else. And that has nothing whatsoever to do with the size of your zoomers. It has to do with trust. If he thinks I'm going behind his back to somebody else, then I'll lose his trust. The project will fall apart. And I'll have wasted his time and, more importantly, my own." I smiled. "Understand?"

One of my better speeches. I know Lulu was impressed. Even the trick-or-treaters appeared awed.

Katrina panicked. "Oh, shit," she gasped. Abruptly, she bent over at the waist, her blond hair nearly touching the welcome mat. She shook her head violently, her fingers massaging her scalp. I couldn't tell if she was in the process of fainting or searching for head lice. Just as abruptly, she straightened up and tossed her hair back, *thwacking* the side of the house with it. "I've insulted you, haven't I?"

"I don't insult. I'm the writer, remember?"

"You must hate me. You must hate, hate, hate me."

"I don't hate, hate, hate you."

"Gee, I'm so fucking sorry." She laid her hand on my arm. "I really am. See, I'm used to dealing with the network people, the *Uncle Chubby* people. I have to be the blond bitch with them, or they diss me. You're obviously not like them. I can be *me* with you." Her hand was still on my arm. She was playing puddy cat now. "You're totally, totally right. You're working for Lyle, not me. It's his project. I'm just here to help. As a friend. And if I'm somebody's friend, there's *nothing* I won't do for them." She edged a little closer to me, so that her breasts were saying hello to my shirt. Her hand was getting heavy on my arm. "Sure you're not mad at me?" she purred, eyes gleaming at me invitingly. Quite some performance really. Fear will do that to people. And she was clearly afraid. Of what? I wondered.

"I'm not mad at you," I said to Katrina Tingle.

"Oh, good, good, good," she squeaked happily. She was just a big, fun little girl now, all sunshine and lollipops and colored balloons. Me, I wouldn't be turning my back on her. But then I've learned to be careful around a celebrity's loved ones, especially when there's a lot of money at stake. And there was.

"Pinky's doing his laps in the pool," she informed me. "Let's go say hello, okay?"

She took unusually short, mincing steps for such a big woman, almost as if she were balancing on a rubber ball. I followed her wiggles and jiggles and curves along the brick path to the backyard. There was a great deal of Chemlawn, part of it set aside for croquet, where an elderly bronze couple in sun visors was in the process of playing. He was cheating.

"Whew," Katrina complained, crinkling her nose. "Another whale must have washed up on the beach."

"No, that's just Lulu." She was ambling along beside us, panting. "She has rather unusual eating habits."

The house was even uglier from the back, if that's possible. Here the milk chocolate stucco was studded with starbursts of brightly colored bits of broken mosaic tile.

"We finally finished it in May," Katrina confided shyly. "It ended up costing us over four times what we thought it would—nearly ten million dollars. We had to import the whole crew from Barcelona to do the stucco work. Red tape like you wouldn't believe. But it was worth it."

"And who was your architect?" I asked, so I'd remember never to hire him.

"I was," she replied, sneaking a peek at me. "Surprised?"

"Every once in a while."

"I had to let the first two architects go," she explained.

"They just didn't have the same vision I had. The two original wings, they *wanted* to be joined. They cried out to be joined. But the architects, they were just so . . ."

"Hard of hearing?"

"Traditional. I had to battle with them constantly. The second one finally told me, hey, I ought to just design it myself. So I did." She stood there admiring it. "It's not a house for everyone."

"It certainly isn't."

"It's very cerebral."

"It certainly is."

There was a Nantucket-style pool house out back, a blue-stone patio, a redwood picnic table with benches, a built-in brick barbecue pit where Lyle could no longer grill steaks. The lawn gave way to reeds and tall grasses, which separated the property from the beach. The water sparkled in the sun. In the distance there were sailboats. It was all rather nice, considering the rest of the place.

"I haven't gotten around to redesigning the backyard yet," she said, which explained it. "All we did was the lap pool so Lyle could do his workouts."

Lyle Hudnut was no threat to Matt Biondi in the water. He thrashed and snorted and bellowed like a gut-shot hippo, displacing huge quantities of water in the process. But then Lyle Hudnut did nothing in a small or quiet way. Not that anyone in the United States thought of him as Lyle Hudnut. He was Chubby Chance—Uncle Chubby—the immense, gross, unruly sitcom ne'er-do-well who had held forth on network television's No. 1 rated prime-time show for three straight seasons. Uncle Chubby was every little kid's favorite adult, every slob's favorite role model, and every parent's favorite babysitter. Picture a funnier, hipper, and much cruder Mister Rogers and you had Uncle Chubby. Uncle Chubby was television's biggest star. Emphasis on the word *was*. Because Lyle Hudnut was in deep, deep doo-doo. Had been since the spring, when a routine vice squad roundup at a sleazy porn movie house in Times Square had snared him, pickle firmly in hand. His arrest for indecent exposure and public masturbation had sent shock waves through the television industry. Outraged parents' groups had immediately demanded that *Uncle Chubby* be jerked off the air, as it were. The network, horrified, had complied. An equally horrified show business community had rushed to Lyle's defense. His attorney had sued the network. And the controversy had raged for much of the summer, consuming the tabloids and talk radio lines with a passion rivaled only by Mia's split with the Woodman. Disgraced and humiliated, Lyle Hudnut had twice tried to kill himself. But he had survived. And so had his show. The network, not so anxious to lose its ratings leader, was bringing him back for the fall season, angry protestors notwithstanding. And a publishing house was paying him $3 million to tell America what he was doing in the Deuce Theater that afternoon. And how he survived his ordeal. I was there to help him tell it.

When he saw me there, he finished his lap and pulled himself up out of the narrow pool, bringing a hundred gallons or so of water with him. He stood before me, panting and wheezing, wheezing and panting. Lyle Hudnut was a huge man, two or three inches over six feet—about my height—only he had to weigh close to three hundred pounds, most of it pink, hairless blubber. Rolls of fat spilled obscenely over the waistband of his baggy white trunks like scoops of ice cream melting from a triple-decker cone. Each of his mammoth thighs was as big around as I was. His fat feet looked like twin piglets. I was ready for them to sit up and oink at me. Actually, standing there, he looked like some giant freak infant out of a fifties horror movie—*The Baby Who Ate Bakersfield*. For some reason the small screen has often embraced volcanic comics of immense size and appetites, performers noted for their wildness almost as much as their humor. Jackie Gleason, Sid Caesar, and John Belushi come to mind. These days, there was Lyle Hudnut, Belushi's protégé and friend. He was about forty. Had a big round head with short, curly red hair, a bulb nose, jumbo jug ears, and somewhere between seven and nine chins. He looked a lot like Mr. Potato Head, though he had a much livelier personality. His blue eyes twinkled with mischief, his grin was impish and playful. Early on, many critics wrote that he reminded them of Fatty Arbuckle. The comparison had proven to be eerily prophetic.

Katrina handed him a towel and he dabbed at himself with it, his eyes locked on her tits with fascination and pride. They were built to his scale. They were his. She handed him a giant hooded monk's habit of unbleached muslin. He put it on over his head and cinched it at the waist and waddled over to me. I half expected him to cry "Piggyback ride, Da-da. Piggyback." What he said was "Glad you could make it out, pal." His voice was soft and weary, and in it you could hear the streets of working-class Long Island, which is Queens with strip malls. He stared at my extended paw. "I don't believe in shaking hands, if you don't mind."

"I don't mind," I said. "As long as you're not angling for a hug."

He shook his head. "No, no. I just have this thing about germs. I don't like to touch people. Or things people have touched." For punctuation he cleared his sinuses by blowing his nose into his fingers, much like a homeless person.

"Must be rather difficult working around a TV studio," I observed, as he carelessly wiped his fingers on his robe.

"I take precautions. Don't get me wrong, pal. I'm not a nut or nuttin'. I'm just risk adverse."

"That makes two of us."

He grinned at me. Huge grin. There was nothing subtle about Lyle Hudnut. He came right at you, and he had tremendous presence—partly because of his size, but not totally. He also had that *something,* that star quality only a few of them have. He demanded your attention and he got it. Just by being there.

"I've already explained to Hoagy about his dog, Pinky," Katrina squeaked.

Lyle stiffened. "Dog? What dog?" he demanded, his eyes widening with fear. Paranoia seemed to bubble just under the surface with him, like a troubled septic system.

Lulu was curled up in the shade a careful twenty feet away, glowering at him.

"You better keep it away from me," Lyle warned, a whiny edge to his voice.

"*It* is a she," I said. "And she'll stay out of your way."

"She works with you?"

"She does."

"Why?"

"Everyone needs a straight man."

"And she's yours?"

"No, I'm hers."

He drew back and gave me a sidelong scowl, one eyebrow raised. The Scowl. His trademark mannerism. At once sarcastic, mocking, and caustic. Then he snorted and parked his porky self on one of the picnic benches and stuck his fat, pink feet out before him. Katrina fell to her knees like a supplicant and began putting his white cotton socks and his Birkenstock sandals on for him. It was a dirty job, but I guess somebody had to do it—better her than me.

"See, I'm leading a hygienic existence these days," Lyle explained. "No poisons, no germs, no chemicals. This robe, for instance, is totally unbleached, undyed cotton. No formaldehyde. That stuff'll kill ya—right through your pores. I'm off alcohol and caffeine and my diet is one-hunnert-percent macrobiotic. Rice, beans, and veggies. Tastes great—and, Christ, you wouldn't believe the butt music. I can do all of "In-A-Gadda-Da-Vida" . . . I'm gonna be straight up with you, Hoagy. I used to stuff shit into every orifice of my body twenty-four hours a day seven days a week. I devoted my energy to killing myself. These days I'm devoting it to staying alive. I'm *clean*."

He held up a pudgy hand for silence, even though he was the one doing the talking. I could see the fresh scars on the inside of his wrist from when he'd tried to kill himself with a razor blade earlier that summer. A few days later he swallowed the contents of an economy-sized bottle of Uncle Chubby's children's aspirin, 277 tablets in all.

"Time for my readings," he announced, as if this were as momentous as, say, the Israelis giving up their West Bank settlements.

They had a whole little routine. First Katrina grabbed his wrist and strapped a pulse monitoring wristwatch around it. His index finger went inside a sensory cuff. When his rate registered, she dutifully marked it on a chart, then removed the watch and hooked his finger up to a cuff that was attached to a digital blood-pressure monitor. She marked that down as well. She examined the chart a moment, brow furrowed, then gave him an approving nod and a kiss on the forehead. Beaming, he made it into a wet, slurpy kiss, pulling her down onto his lap. I had a feeling this was for my benefit. Proof of ownership.

"Pinky," she squeaked, giggling as he pawed her roughly. "You're an *animal.*"

"Can't help it, Katrina. You do things to me." He winked at me. "This woman saved my life, Hoagy. Her and no one else. Would you believe my blood pressure used to be up over two hundred? I was *dying.*" He reached for a bottle of mineral water and drank greedily from it, much of it streaming down his chest. "God, I love water."

"May I offer you something, Hoagy?" asked Katrina. "Herbal iced tea?"

I said that would be nice. She went wiggling and jiggling off to the house to fetch it.

"Wait'll you taste her tea," Lyle exclaimed jovially. Although now that the two of us were alone, he seemed to have trouble meeting my eyes. "The greatest. She makes it from scratch. She's an extraordinary individual, Hoagy. The perfect woman. She's been a professional dancer, run her own jewelry business, designed this whole place. Plus she happens to be the single greatest fuck in the universe. Of course," he gloated, "she learned *that* under a master." He let loose with his famous laugh, a deep rumble that seemed to start way over in the next county, then build up force until it exploded out of him with a huge *hoo-hah-hah.* "Seriously, I've never met a woman like Katrina. Somebody *real.* Somebody who loves me for who I am. She stuck by me through all of this, y'know. Never complained. She's the only one who did. Mickey Stern, my agent, who I considered one of my two or three closest friends in the entire world, wouldn't even return my phone calls anymore. Ya believe that?"

I did believe that. Of course, you must remember that TV and movie people almost always mistake their business friends for real friends. This is partly because they want to believe that everyone they deal with truly loves them. And partly because they have no real friends.

"My other close friend, Godfrey Daniels, blew my doors off before I even had a chance to defend myself," he said, of the young programming wizard who had engineered his flagging network's turnaround from third to first, mostly on the coattails of *Uncle Chubby. Time* magazine labeled him "a genius." *Newsweek* called him "Mr. Television." Everyone in the industry simply called him God. Lyle shook his head in disgust. "I called him up the day after I sent him the first draft of the *Uncle Chubby* pilot script, and said, 'Well, God, did you like it?' And he said, 'I love it, Lyle. It's brilliant. It's perfect. Don't change a word. I only have one little note: Can you make them robots?' True story, I swear. I'll let you in on a little secret: God is an empty sweater."

"Yes, I seem to recall reading something about that in the Talmud."

"No brains. No taste. No guts. A fucking moron. So's Jazzy Jeff Beckman, who runs the studio that finances me. Another fucking moron. They're all fucking morons." His rage was starting to slip out. He caught it and tucked it back in. "But I've set aside my anger," he vowed. "You have to forgive, and I have."

I nodded, though this one I didn't believe. Something about the decidedly un-Zenlike anger burning in his eyes. And the way he was clenching and unclenching his big fists. Plus there was his reputation to consider. He was supposed to have the most volatile temper in the entire industry, worse than even the legendary Roseanne Arnold. He was a colossal abuser of actors and writers, a screamer, a puncher, a big mean bully. He made people cry. Made them ill. Made them flee. An *Esquire* writer who hung around the set during the show's first season wrote, "If you were to cut off Lyle Hudnut's head, frogs would come jumping out." Reporters had been banned from the *Uncle Chubby* set after that. I don't know about frogs.

"One thing this whole awful experience has taught me," he went on, "is to be grateful for what I have. Because it can all vanish just like that." He snapped his fingers for emphasis, which woke Lulu. She grunted, got up, circled around three times, curled back up and went back to sleep. It doesn't take her long. Not a lot on her mind.

Katrina returned now across the patio with my iced tea and a plate of raw carrots for Lyle. She sat next to him on the bench, watching me like a tigress guarding her one and only cub. Alert. Suspicious. Ready to tear my throat out.

Her cub was waiting anxiously for me to tell him how great the tea was. Lyle Hudnut was one of those—a celebrity in constant need of stroking. Nothing bores me more, except maybe *Jurassic Park.*

I tasted it. "Excellent." And it was—as a bracing rub for razor burn.

He beamed at her happily. "We've been getting me in shape for the season. I gotta be in tip-top condition. I mean, I write the show, direct it, produce it, star in it . . . I'm the show. *Me.* Always have been. Ever since I first put together the Suburbanites back in college. I'm the one who found us that crummy little basement club where we performed for nickels and dimes. I'm the one who held us all together. And I still am. I'm the daddy, Hoagy. Fifty-four people depend on me. And that takes its toll. I had to have a doctor on the set full-time last season to give me oxygen and B-twelve shots." He bit into a carrot. "But that was then. Katrina's involved now, as my coexecutive producer. Second only to me. Which is a huge help." He put his arm around her, his big paw playing with the heavy silver chain that she made with her own two hands. "Naturally, there's been a little resentment from the staff," he allowed. "But anyone who can't deal with it is free to leave. Katrina is part of my life now." He spoke of her as if she were a force of nature. The sun. The wind. Katrina.

"And how did you two crazy kids meet?" I asked.

Lyle's face turned red—faster than any man I'd ever seen. "I don't like to be called crazy!" he roared.

"It's just an expression, Pinky," Katrina said soothingly. "Relax."

"You're right, you're right. Sorry." He calmed down, just as quickly. "Katrina was a production assistant last season, a gofer. Leo Crimp, my line producer, brought her in. Leo's the toughest son of a bitch in the business." Katrina looked away uncomfortably at this mention of her former boss. I wondered about that, too. "First time she came in the control booth I swear it got ten degrees warmer in there."

"Pinky . . ."

He grinned at her. "I mean it. I *felt* her there. Like some kind of animal thing. I stared at her, and she stared at me, and *wham,* we were gone. Went straight in my dressing room and fucked our brains out."

"Pinky!"

"Well, we did!" he boasted.

"And how's the show shaping up for this season?" I asked.

"We're shifting in a slightly different creative direction," Katrina replied delicately, in her Kewpie-doll voice. "There's been some give-and-take between us and God, in terms of Lyle coming back and everything."

He nodded. "Yeah, you'll find this interesting, Hoagy. Being a serious person."

"You must have me confused with someone else."

"Believe it or not," said Lyle, puffing up proudly, "I've talked the network into letting me do more issue-oriented episodes this season. Hey, we're America's living room. It's time for us to deal with what America's dealing with—teen suicide, drug addiction, AIDS."

Quite some shift indeed for a man whose chief claim to comic fame was that he knew 126 different ways to say the word snot.

"We're looking for more of a reality context," Katrina added. "We're also looking more for irony—comedically speaking, of course."

"Of course," I said.

"It's a national shame, Hoagy," he went on. "Kids are now our principal underclass in America. Twenty percent of 'em live in poverty. Six million will go to bed hungry tonight. Sixteen million have no medical coverage of any kind. I tell ya, that's *criminal.*"

I nodded, wondering how it is that show-biz figures can get so worked up about social injustice, yet not have a problem with flushing $10 million down the toilet on an obscene house. Somebody ought to write a book about that someday. Not me, but somebody.

"Those kids are *my* kids," Lyle declared. "The ones who used to look up to me."

"They still do, Pinky."

He waved her off. "Nah, nah. I let 'em down. I know that. So now, I got a responsibility to do good by 'em. From now on, Uncle Chubby is gonna make a difference.''

"Very admirable, Lyle," I said. "And what are you giving up?"

His blue eyes penetrated mine, sizing me up. Or trying. "Giving up?"

"Katrina mentioned there was some give-and-take. What's the give?"

He pressed his lips together and made a short, popping noise which sounded more like flatulence than anything else. "No big deal. We agreed to add a regular love interest for Chubby's sister, Deirdre."

"The testing results showed that our audience would like to see her in a regular relationship," Katrina explained. "Possibly but not necessarily leading to marriage."

"At first, I told God no fucking way," Lyle confessed. "It's my show. I make the creative decisions, not you and certainly not the damned audience. But the more I thought about it, the more I liked it. We can have a lot of fun watching the romance unfold. Really opens up a lotta new possibilities. Chad Roe's gonna play him. Know him?"

"I don't believe we've met," I said, which wasn't exactly true. Merilee did *Streetcar* with him a few years back at the Long Wharf. Chad was one of those aging TV pretty boys who was still trying to prove himself as a serious actor. Mostly, he was a serious clod. "I don't recall him doing a lot of comedy."

"He hasn't," Lyle confirmed. "But God loves him. Or rather his Q-score. He went through the roof in that Judith Krantz miniseries he did with Jackie Smith last season. So I'm working with him. Hasn't been easy so far. Y'know how it is —we've got a certain format that works, and Chad's an outsider. But we'll get there. He's a helluva nice guy." Lyle ran a big pink hand over his big pink face, like he was washing it. "Hey, enough about the show. Let's talk about you and me. You gonna do this book with me?"

I stood up and smoothed my trousers. "I'd like to stretch my legs, Lyle. Can we take a stroll?"

"Sure, sure." Slowly and with great effort, he got to his feet. It was like watching someone trying to get his butt up out of a deep hole. "We'll walk on the beach. C'mon, Katrina. We're walking."

She stayed where she was, eyeing me shrewdly, her left eye drifting slightly. "No," she concluded. "I have some phone calls to make. You boys go ahead."

"Aw, gee, ya sure?" He was whining, like a petulant, jumbo-sized kid.

"I'm sure, Pinky."

"Okay. Oh, hey, that reminds me, Hoagy." He cleared his throat uneasily. "Katrina has something she's busting a gut to ask you. If ya don't mind."

I did mind, but I owed her one now.

"I heard the father of her baby was really Sam Shepard," she blurted out eagerly. "Is that true?"

"I only know what I read in the papers."

She frowned. "You mean Merilee won't even tell *you?*"

"I mean Merilee especially won't tell me."

She tossed her blond mane. "Gee, I don't understand."

"That makes two of us." Lulu let out a low growl from next to me. "Correction—three of us."

And with that we walked down the sandy path to the beach. It was a weekday, and there were very few people out. There was a black nanny in a starched white uniform with a little blond boy, who was crying. There was a teenage girl in a T-shirt and cutoffs sitting on a towel writing someone a letter or a poem. There was us. The tide was out. The Great White Monk wheezed as he clomped through the wet sand, his arms swinging wildly back and forth. I had to walk three feet away from him to keep from getting belted. Lulu scampered down to the water's edge and chased a gull away, arfing gleefully. Some of the happiest days of her puppyhood had been spent here on this very beach. That first summer, when Merilee and I were golden. But that was once upon a time.

"I have the perfect woman, Hoagy," Lyle Hudnut boasted, yet again. "We have unbelievable sex together. Woman's a Hoover, y'know what I'm saying? She sucks up every last drop, is what I'm saying." He had a smug, nasty little smirk on his face. I wanted to wipe it off. I would continue to want that the whole time I knew Lyle Hudnut. "And, whoa, you wouldn't believe the *clam* she's got on her."

"I didn't come all the way out here to talk about Katrina Tingle's clam, Lyle," I said, to shut him up, and because I hadn't.

He stopped cold there in the sand, his face turning bright red again, as if clogged with blood. This time his eyes bugged out, too, and he began to breathe swiftly in and out, his thick lips pulled back from his teeth in a menacing grimace. Quite some intimidating presence, really. I doubted there was anyone in network television he didn't scare the shit out of. "You're one of *them,* aren't you?" he bellowed, fists clenched tightly.

"Which *them* is that, Lyle?"

"Them who are always putting everyone else down. Them who are always criticizing. I can't stand negativism! It's a cancer. It spreads. It *kills.*" He shook a fat finger at me. "I'm totally serious about Katrina. I love her. And she loves me. She's the real thing for me. I even changed my will. Katrina's my sole beneficiary. If that's not love, I'd like to know what is."

"Don't look at me. I'm the wrong person to ask."

He snorted at me. We resumed walking, past the neighboring showplaces tucked back behind the dunes.

"Geez, it's so great here," he observed contentedly. His mood swings were truly awesome. "Can't believe I actually live out here. *Me.* Lyle Hudnut from Bay Shore. Of course, once we go into production I'm in the city full-time. Keep a suite at the Essex House, but all I ever do is crash there for a few hours. Studio's where I live."

"I have to know some things, Lyle."

"Sure, pal," he said easily. "Like what?"

"Like what the hell you were doing in that theater."

He made that popping noise with his lips. "You don't waste any time, do you?"

"It's what everyone wants to know, Lyle."

And absolutely couldn't figure out. After all, the man was living with a major sexpot. After all, the man could have rented an X-rated movie and masturbated in the privacy of his own home if that was what he felt like doing. What was he doing in a Times Square theater with his entire career in his fist? It made no sense. And had been the number one subject of speculation, wonderment, and psychobabble in the tabloid press for months.

"I have to know, Lyle. I have to know you're prepared to deal with this thing openly. Because if all you want is a white-wash, then I'm out of here."

"Fair enough." He considered his reply carefully before he ran his hand through his stubby red curls and said, "I had a headache."

"I understand they have aspirin for that sort of thing."

"Not that kind of headache. I get terrible, terrible migraines. My head feels like it's being cut open with a chain saw. I can barely see. Strictly from doing the show. Fighting with the network, with the writers, with the cast. The pressure's enormous and it's all on me. For years, I coped by snorting coke. Couple thousand bucks' worth a week. But I was trying to get off it, see? On account of Katrina said she'd break it off with me otherwise. She said I was killing myself. Just like Beloosh did. That day . . . that was a bad, bad day. I was stressed out, hadn't slept in three days. Never did, unless I took sleeping pills, and I was off of those, too. See, I was strung out on Halcion for two years. Which they now say can cause major nutsiness. Like I need a drug for that, right?"

"That day, Lyle . . . ?"

"The show wouldn't work," he recalled. "The Munchkins had the flu. The toilet was stopped up. There was a blizzard. I couldn't get hold of the plumber. Sis was coming down with the flu, too."

I tugged at my ear. "You mean in the show."

"Yeah, but it always carries over into real life. I know that sounds weird, but it's true. I was feeling . . . trapped. Like my head was gonna explode. I had to get away. Had to." His voice was insistent and strangely high-pitched over the surf. He sounded almost desperate, like a man who was drowning in deep water, not walking on hard sand. I would think of that often as I got to know Lyle better. "I could just as easily have walked down to the Tenth Street Baths for a shvitz. Believe me, I wish I had. I walked uptown instead. I don't know why I went in that theater. I—I just needed a release. It just happened. That's the truth. The absolute truth." He plowed along through the sand, his eyes out on the sailboats. "I still can't believe how pissed the public got. I really can't. I mean, people went *crazy*. Some parents' group in Alabama said I ought to be castrated. That was my favorite. No, no—my favorite was that shrink in the *Daily News* who said I *wanted* to get caught. Like I was trying to commit professional suicide. Like I'd actually *cancel* myself. I mean, Christ, why would I wanna do that? Chubby's my whole career." He glanced over at me uncertainly. "That open enough for you?"

"Still have these headaches?"

"Haven't since I went on this diet and exercise regimen. Of course, we're not in production yet. That'll be the real test. Whew, let's take a blow, huh?" There was a driftwood log ahead of us, bleached white as bone. He flopped down on it heavily, puffing, drenched with sweat.

I stood there watching him. In some ways he reminded

me of the neighborhood fat kid, the whiny one who always got picked last when you chose up sides for baseball. In some ways he reminded me of the bully who stole smaller kids' lunch money and dangled them headfirst in the boys' room toilets. Uncle Chubby was a bit of both. Was his creator, too?

He squinted up at me. "Wanna know what I'm all about?"

"It would be nice."

"I'm simple," he explained. "If they put out a commemorative stamp of the eighties it would have my picture on it. Gimme, gimme, gimme. Get it all, spend it all, fuck it all."

"The eighties are over," I pointed out.

"Well, I ain't," he said defiantly. "But that me is. All I'm trying to do now is hold myself together, one day at a time. And, believe me, it ain't easy. But I'm doing it. I'm surviving. I'm chemically pure for the first time in practically my whole fucking life. And I'm not in any of that fucking therapy anymore either. No shrink can heal ya, Hoagy. Not if you don't want to be healed. And if you do, you don't need nobody else. I'm through with all of that therapy shit. I'm a grown-up now. The past is the past. Except for one thing . . ." His face darkened. "I can never, ever forgive my parents for what they did to me. Not ever." He poked at the sand with his sandal. "Look, I've never talked much about my childhood in interviews, other than to say it was pretty typical."

"I've yet to run across one that was."

He snorted. "Then you'll get off on this—I'm the star of the number-one family show in America and I haven't spoken to my own family in over twenty years. Pretty fucking weird if you think about it. But some pretty weird shit went down, Hoagy. Shit nobody knows about. Mind-blowing shit. What I'm trying to say is . . . I wanna put it in this book."

"Why now?"

He shrugged. "Because I think it'll lend a certain . . .

perspective to what happened at the Deuce. And because I can't keep a lid on it anymore. Ever since I got busted, the tabloids have been digging into my life like crazy. One of 'em found an old classmate of mine who was willing to talk, for a price. I topped it. For his silence."

"You've been blackmailed?"

"I've been lucky. Next time, I may not be. And there will be a next time. I wanna deal with this myself, in my own way. Not read about it in the *Enquirer*."

I nodded, wondering what was left that could possibly hurt him more than he'd already been hurt. "Your editor said you had new revelations. Is this what he meant?"

He climbed back up to his feet. We resumed walking, Lulu tagging along behind us.

"Mind if I take my turn now?" he asked. "There's some shit I'd like to know about you, too."

This was him seizing back the offensive. Or trying. A collaboration is often this—a battle of wills.

"Such as?"

"Whether I can expect you to be a friend or an enema."

"Are those the only two choices on the menu?"

"They are with me. I've had some pretty negative experiences with people, Hoagy. Too many. So I need absolute loyalty. That's a must. Can I count on you?"

"To do what?"

"Be my friend."

He said it simply and naively. It almost sounded like a plea.

"You can't buy friends, Lyle."

"Sure you can," he said smugly. "I do it all the time."

"What else do you want to know about me?"

"Are you a fan of my show?" He watched me carefully for my answer.

"I've seen it."

He waited for me to say more. He wanted me to say

more. Desperately. TV people always want you to tell them
they're the rare exception, the real thing—genuine quality in
a sea of born-to-be-mild mediocrity. Because they honestly
and truly want to think they are, and because they honestly
and truly know they aren't. Most of them do, anyway. I
wasn't sure about Lyle yet.

When I didn't say more, he said, "I never sweeten,
y'know."

"Sweeten?"

"No laugh track. Not ever. All the laughs you hear on
Uncle Chubby are honest laughs. I earn 'em. I do quality,
every single fucking week. Because I care. Because I won't
do that brain-dead *shitcom* they do out in L.A. My show is
New York. It's alive. It's unique. *I'm* unique." He proclaimed
this grandly, for all the birds and fishes to hear. "Face it, I'm
the funniest man on television."

"If you say so."

He gave me The Scowl. "Okay, who's funnier?!"

"Do politicians count?"

"*I'm* the funniest," he insisted, jabbing himself in the
chest with a fat, blunt thumb. "Me. Get this, pal—*Uncle
Chubby* matters to me, okay? My people there, those are the
people who count in my life. They're my family. I'm not just
talking about Katrina. I'm talking about Muck and Meyer, The
Boys, who been writing for me since college. They're like the
brothers I never had. I mean, Christ, Marty Muck was one of
the original Suburbanites. So was Fiona." He meant Fiona
Shrike, the actress who played his sister, Deirdre, in the
show. And who Lyle was once married to. "I'm talking about
The Kids, Annabelle and Bobby, my young writers. I'm so
fucking proud of 'em. And The Munchkins, Casey and Caitlin," he added, referring to the real-life brother and sister
who played Chubby's on-camera nephew and niece.
"They're like my own flesh and blood, those two. And their
mom, Amber. Her and me go way back. Amber was my assistant director. And Marjorie Daw, my network supervisor.

She's the greatest. I gave her her start in the business." He cackled. "Also her first orgasm."

I was beginning to think I would detest Lyle Hudnut. Which didn't exactly thrill me, but didn't surprise me either. I was used to working for people I didn't like. "I think I understand what you're saying, Lyle. Believe me, I intend to interview everyone who—"

"No, ya *don't* understand what I'm saying," he snapped.

"Okay, then, what are you saying?"

"I'm saying we go into production next week. And once we do, we become totally cut off from the outside world. We're a classic closed society. We got our own pecking order, our own laws, our own loves and hates and beliefs. I'm saying that you're an outsider. And the only possible way you can comprehend my world, comprehend *me,* is to be one of us. I'm saying I want ya on staff."

I tugged at my ear. "As what, Lyle?"

"As a writer, whattaya think? A fucking prop master?"

"Thank you, no."

"Why not?" he demanded, waddling along.

"I don't do windows or sitcoms."

He waved this off. "The Boys'll teach you in no time flat. They're walking, talking sitcom encyclopedias. Know every episode of every show that's ever been done. You'll hang out, you'll listen, you'll learn. And most importantly, you'll be accepted as part of the family. That's the only way you'll get to know 'em. Believe me, they're very sensitive people."

"I didn't know it was possible to work on a sitcom and be sensitive."

"Hey, we're all human beings."

"I didn't know it was possible to work on a sitcom and be a human being."

"I want you by my side," he insisted stubbornly. "Look, pal, I'm gonna be major-league busy. I can't be blocking out time for you. You gotta catch me on the run. Over lunch, in editing . . . Only way you can do that is to be around. Tell ya what—I'll make you an executive story consultant, okay? Seventy-five hundred a week. On top of what you're getting to do the book, which is already the highest fee of any ghost in the business."

"I give good value."

"I wouldn't call a third of my royalties good value," he growled.

"No one's complained yet. At least not by the time it was over." Of course, a number were dead by the time it was over, but there was no use telling him that. He had enough on his mind. And I needed the job.

We walked in silence a moment.

He broke it. "All right, I'll make it ten grand. If it's money that's bothering ya."

"It isn't."

"Then what is?"

"I don't write jokes—at least, not intentionally."

He let out his huge *hoo-hah-hah* of a laugh. "Christ, nobody's gonna expect you to be funny. Half the sitcom writers in the business can't break a pane of glass with their best fast ball. Besides, I don't need ya for gags. The Boys are my shtickticians. No, you . . ." He scratched his chin thoughtfully. "You'll be my feelings specialist."

Lulu stopped cold in the sand and began to cough violently, sending her pith helmet toppling down over her eyes, blinding her. I bent down and straightened it.

Lyle frowned at her. "Swallow a shell or something?"

"No, she just can't believe her ears," I explained. "And neither can I." Now she showed me her teeth. She's rather sensitive about the subject of her flappers. "Your feelings specialist, Lyle?"

"My feelings specialist," he confirmed. "Everybody's a specialist of some kind nowadays. Nobody's good at doing everything. That's why you gotta have a staff. Me, I come up with the story ideas and break 'em down into scenes. The

Boys, they bang out the best first drafts in the business. Table-ready in three days. All that's missing is the texture and the depth. That's when the group takes over. Annabelle, she services The Munchkins and Rusty. There's nobody better at kids and dogs. Bobby, he's our angry young playwright. A real head-banger. Plus he's deep—which The Boys, God bless 'em, ain't. Then we get it up on its feet. Me, I rewrite most of my own lines on the floor as we rehearse. Fiona's the same way. She's a master of improv. The Boys punch up the gags as we go along. We're a small, tight group. Real efficient. But I been thinking we need a feelings specialist this season, what with Deirdre's new romance and all. You have feelings, don't ya?"

"Why, is that a prerequisite?"

"Your job is to keep each character's emotional arc straight, vis-à-vis the story. Which ain't always easy. I mean, I always know where Chubby is. But with the other characters I can use someone at the table with a clear eye to say, 'That's a funny line, Lyle, but Deirdre wouldn't say that just yet because she's not ready to forgive Chubby.' And I'll go, 'Okay, you're right.' And change it. Or say we get stuck and we can't figure out what the fuck Deirdre's supposed to say next. I can turn to you and you'll say, 'Okay, what is Deirdre feeling right now?' And we'll talk it through."

"And for that I get paid ten thousand a week?"

"Every week. It's right up your alley."

"I try to stay out of alleys. How much writing is involved?"

"None. You're strictly a consultant. Unless you wanna try your hand at a first draft, in which case you'll get paid the Writers' Guild half-hour minimum just like everyone else, fifteen thou and change. Plus all the residuals you can eat." We walked on in silence. "So whattaya say, pal?"

"Exactly what I said before, Lyle. I'm not a sitcom writer."

"I don't get you, man!" he fumed angrily.

"I'm complex," I acknowledged. "But I'm not deep. Tell me about these new revelations of yours."

He stopped, shaking his head slowly. "No way, Hoagy. Uh-uh. Not unless you agree to my terms. Take it or leave it."

"This is a deal-buster?"

"This is a deal-buster," he promised me, jowly chin stuck out. "I'm drawing a line in the sand."

He actually did, too, with his sandal. Right there between us. TV people tend to be rather heavy-handed. Or footed, as the case may be.

"Sorry we couldn't do business, Lyle." I was about to stick out my hand until I remembered his thing about cooties. I pulled it back and thanked him for the tea. Then I started back up the beach to his awful house without looking back. Lulu followed me. She likes my cooties.

"Would it make any difference if I told you that one of 'em set me up?!" he called after me.

I stopped. "One of who?"

"My family. I was done in by one of my own people. That whole bust was a setup, from start to finish."

"How do you mean?" I walked back toward him. He was still planted there beside his line in the sand.

"All I know," he replied, "is what my lawyer told me—the Public Morals Division of the New York City Police Department doesn't do routine roundups. They got better things to do than sweep porn theaters for beaters. They only follow up specific complaints. Which means somebody tipped 'em off that I was there that day."

"I see," I said doubtfully.

"The whole scene was weird," he said heatedly. "They *knew*. I mean, the van was *waiting* there out front to take me in. And, get this, the press was out there, too. Ready to nail me."

"You have to admit it was not lacking in news value."

"No, no, you're missing my point—they were *already* there. Practically before the cops. How did they know about *me?* Unless they were tipped off, too?"

"By who?"

"Hey, not everybody loves me. This is me admitting it. Some of my people even hate me. One of 'em enough to try and ruin me. I wanna know who, Hoagy. I have to know who."

"Why didn't any of this come out before?"

"Because everybody wanted to get it over and done with. The district attorney, my lawyer, God, me . . . I was a wreck. It was a fucking circus, for Chrissakes. So I pleaded no contest, and the DA agreed not to push it. A fair deal for everybody, and I'm back on the air. But I'm not satsified. How can I be? One of my own people tried to ruin me. I wanna know who did it to me. I wanna deal with it in this book. I got to. Because . . ." He broke off, lips quivering with rage. "Because it's driving me crazy!"

"How do you know it's one of your own people? Have you got any proof?"

He snorted derisively at me.

"How do you know?"

"I *know*, dammit!" he roared, over the sound of the waves. "Christ, don't you ever believe what people tell ya?"

"Not lately," I said quietly.

He glanced at me sharply. "That's no way to live, man. You gotta have faith. I know where you're coming from. Trusting no one. Holding everyone at arm's length. I been there. And it sucks. It's no way to go through life, believe me."

I watched a jogger pass by us, wondering why it is that celebrities who are trying to clean up their act always try to run mine through the rinse cycle as well. Why can't they just shut up? Why can't they pick another writer? I took a deep breath and let it out slowly. "If you're serious about this—"

"I'm totally serious," he fired back.

"Then I suggest you hire yourself a good private detective. Someone who knows what he's doing."

"I don't want someone who knows what he's doing. I want you!"

"Careful. I flatter easily."

"Look, I can't hire a detective. I need someone who can function as a real member of my family. An insider. *You.* Besides, you're supposed to have a certain . . . knack. I mean, my editor said if anyone could get to the bottom of it, you could."

I had worked for this editor before. His gleeful taste for high-profile tell-alls by convicted serial killers, drug-addicted teen prostitutes, and would-be presidential assassins had earned him the nickname The Merchant of Menace. He bothered a lot of the highbrow brigade. Me he had never bothered. He paid on time and he left me alone, which is all I ever ask.

"I write books, Lyle. I don't solve crimes."

"He said it was a perfect fit, you and me," Lyle argued stubbornly.

"Never be fooled by a perfect fit. There's at least three-percent shrinkage to take into account—particularly when I'm thrown in hot water."

Lyle Hudnut clasped his hands before him, as if in prayer. "This isn't just about a show, Hoagy. Or money. Or endorsements. Uncle Chubby is my *life.* Somebody tried to take him away from me. That's murder, is what it is. You take a performer's character away from him and you're committing murder. Nobody should be allowed to get away with that. Nobody. I have to know who it is. I got a right to know who it is. You're the one person who can help me. I'm begging you, Hoagy. I'm down on my knees."

And he was, with a thud. Right where he'd drawn that line between us in the sand.

Only the line in the sand was gone. The waves had

erased it. There was only smooth, wet sand there between us now. A corny and obvious symbol, to be sure. But I wasn't surprised by it. Not in the least. Because it had already happened. I had already entered the world of prime-time television.

I never thought I'd ever stoop so low as to be a sitcom writer. Not me. No way. But my life had been full of surprises lately, few of them pleasant. Still, my story was cherry pie compared to Lyle Hudnut's. What had happened to Lyle Hudnut shouldn't happen to anyone.

He was an unlikely candidate for stardom, this round-faced pink elephant from Bay Shore, Long Island. It was while he was part of a scruffy Greenwich Village comedy troupe in the midseventies, the Surburbanites, that Lyle Hudnut first stumbled on Chubby Chance, his nasty, dirty, and thoroughly off-the-wall send-up of Mister Rogers. Dressed in a moth-eaten cardigan and sipping from a hot cup of what he claimed was Ovaltine, Chubby advised kids on how to get the family dog stoned, how to steal money from their dad's trousers, how to get the most fun out of playing doctor with that cute little redhead next door. Chubby Chance on proper nutrition: "What's the big difference between boogers and broccoli? Kids won't eat their broccoli."

Stardom did, in fact, elude him at first. Lyle Hudnut was still just another fringe performer kicking around the comedy clubs a decade later when he hit upon the idea of Uncle Chubby's Bedtime Stories, his own hip and caustic version of old childhood favorites. Like "Tom Thumb," in which poor, tormented little Tom moves to West Hollywood and becomes involved with an older man who is into chains and whips. Like "Henny Penny," in which Henny Penny, Cocky Locky, Ducky Duddles, Goosey Poosey and Turkey Lurky *do* tell the king that the sky is falling, for which he has them slaughtered, dressed, and eaten. Chubby's bedtime stories caught on with savvy college audiences. Soon Lyle Hudnut was reciting them on David Letterman and campuses around the country. Cult success led to his own HBO special, *Uncle Chubby's Story Hour,* and a best-selling book, *Uncle Chubby's Storybook.* All of which caught the attention of Godfrey Daniels, enterprising new programming chief of America's third-place network. Daniels saw Uncle Chubby as a way to pull in both the kids who had outgrown Mister Rogers and their baby-boomer parents as well. He convinced Lyle Hudnut to sand down Chubby's rougher edges and to move him into the tidy, surburban New Rochelle home of his sister, Deirdre, a prim, no-nonsense lawyer—as well as a divorcée with two little kids and a not-so-gentle rottweiler. It was there that Stanley Chance, an irresponsible, beer-swilling slob who listed his last full-time employment as "high school," found a home. And a career—as Deirdre's live-in housekeeper, babysitter, and nemesis—the latter a role he had thoroughly enjoyed since age five.

The show's premiere at eight P.M. on Monday, September 24, 1991, was the highest-rated sitcom premiere in the history of network television. *Uncle Chubby* was an instant phenomenon, a No. 1 breakout hit that left *Roseanne, The Cosby Show,* and *Cheers* choking on its dust. Over its first season it averaged a 40 share in the Nielsens—as in 40 percent of the televisions in use when it was on. *Roseanne,* the previous champ in the weekly ratings, had pulled in a mere 33. *Uncle Chubby* held the No. 1 spot for a record 127 weeks in a row. So potent was it that it shot the rest of the network's Monday night lineup through the roof, too, making top-ten hits out of *Master President,* a sitcom about a twelve-year-old boy who we know is going to become president of the United States in 2032, *The Abdul-Salaams,* which one critic described as a "black *Cosby Show,*" and *Hammer & Tongs,* a cop show set in San Francisco's Chinatown. So potent was it that it turned the third-place network into America's leader, often by more than three ratings points per week, generating an estimated

$500 million in new annual profits. All of which made God-
frey Daniels a genius, and Lyle Hudnut a very, very wealthy
man. He was soon being paid an estimated $400,000 per
episode to dispense to his on-screen niece and nephew pat-
ented Chubbyisms like "Life is short and so are you," and "I
got a real problem with all of this sex and violence on MTV—
there ain't enough of it." There was another volume of his
bedtime stories, this one a No. 1 best-seller for nearly a year,
its sales rivaling those of Dr. Seuss at his peak. There were
Uncle Chubby dolls and Halloween costumes and comic
books and instructional videos. There was Uncle Chubby ce-
real and vitamins and cough syrup. His ratty old cardigan
became better known than Columbo's trench coat, his easy
chair more familiar than Archie Bunker's. Kids *loved* Uncle
Chubby. He was one of them—messy and funny and always
in trouble. He was so popular that, inevitably, they began
looking to him for genuine advice, the kind that Mister Rogers had given them when they were younger. Their parents
did, too. When Magic Johnson turned up HIV-positive, it was
Uncle Chubby who parents turned to for help. "Heroes are
people, too," Uncle Chubby told little Erin and Trevor, in the
historic AIDS episode—a show which the Laker star personally endorsed. "And all people get sick."

And so the surreal evolution was complete. Uncle
Chubby was no longer a send-up. He was the semireal thing,
trusted by kids and parents alike. And Lyle Hudnut was no
longer a comic-actor playing a role. He *was* Uncle Chubby.

Until that day he strolled into the Deuce Theater in
Times Square to see *Of Human Blondage,* a hard-core porn
film starring one Tamarra Wett. That day when it all came
tumbling down. They placed him in a holding cell. He was
freed within hours on three hundred dollars' bail but, as his
lawyer candidly put it, "The man's career is over. Uncle
Chubby is dead." Both the *New York Post* and *Daily News*
devoted their front pages to his grim-faced mug shots.
"BOOKED & COOKED" screamed the *News*'s banner headline. "FAT

CHANCE," cried the *Post.* America's parents were horrified and furious. Because they had trusted Uncle Chubby, and because they didn't know how the hell to explain this to their kids. Oprah and Sally Jessy and Phil rode quickly to the rescue with special programs devoted to the subject. But the bad jokes rode up even quicker, and made a far more lasting impression: *Hear about the new Uncle Chubby doll? Wind him up and he plays with himself. Hear what Uncle Chubby is doing next? Coming back in a remake of* Diff'rent Strokes. *Know what Uncle Chubby's favorite restaurant is? The Palm.* Don Imus, the popular New York radio personality, even campaigned for a concert to benefit the Uncle Chubby defense effort called Fists Around America. Its anthem: "All we are saying is give Chance a piece."

Toys "R" Us, the nation's largest toy retailer, announced it was pulling the popular Uncle Chubby doll from its shelves immediately. Mattel, the doll's maker, discontinued its production, even though it had generated an astounding $52 million in the past two years. Librarians across the country yanked Uncle Chubby's storybooks from their shelves. Pressure groups advocating so-called family values demanded that the network remove this supposed role model from the air, vowing to boycott the products of any and all companies which continued to sponsor it. The network promptly complied, shelving *The Uncle Chubby Show* until, stated Godfrey Daniels, "this unfortunate episode can be resolved in a court of law, rather than the court of public opinion." The American Civil Liberties Union, as well as many high-profile show business figures, promptly blasted the network—for finding the man guilty until proven innocent, and for just plain knuckling under to pressure from so-called guardians of public morality. A Performers' Coalition headed by Kevin Costner, Susan Sarandon, Glenn Close, and Sting organized a protest march on network headquarters on Sixth Avenue in support of Lyle Hudnut. Forty thousand marchers joined them, some clashing with anti-Lyle Hudnut forces. Dozens were arrested.

The nation's newspapers devoted countless editorials to the question of whether Lyle Hudnut had or had not committed a victimless crime. Some argued the man was being hounded unfairly. It wasn't as if he'd committed rape or murder or vehicular manslaughter while intoxicated. He hadn't, in fact, hurt anyone. Others felt that there was indeed a victim here—America's children. A role model like Lyle Hudnut, they argued, had to be held to a higher standard of personal conduct than someone else did. On and on it went. When *Entertainment Tonight* conducted a phone poll on whether or not the TV series should be reinstated, fourteen million people called in, the highest response ever. Fifty-four percent said yes, forty-six percent no. Everyone, it seemed, had an opinion on Uncle Chubby—even Tamarra Wett. "I don't see what everybody's so worked up about. The man kept his hand to himself," sniffed the *Of Human Blondage* star, who herself landed on the cover of *People* magazine when she was discovered to be the runaway daughter of an Evansville, Indiana, Methodist minister. And fifteen years old. In fact, she was still peddling a memoir of her own, *Slippery When Wett.* I turned it down, if you must know.

The Manhattan DA chose to prosecute Lyle Hudnut. But to avoid the circus of a trial, he offered him a plea bargain—a five-hundred-dollar fine and a year's probation if Lyle pleaded guilty to indecent exposure. Lyle refused it. He was innocent of any criminal conduct, he insisted, and vowed to fight all the way to the U.S. Supreme Court if that's what it took. Legal experts debated the merits of his case on *Larry King Live.* Several believed he had a strong case, arguing that exposing one's sexual organs in a theater designated for the express purpose of showing pornography did not necessarily constitute indecent exposure. The DA came back with a new offer: Lyle Hudnut would agree to plead no contest, pay a one-hundred-dollar fine and all court costs, in exchange for which all criminal charges would be expunged from his record. A pale and shaken Lyle Hudnut appeared in court to accept this offer. It was his first public appearance since his arrest. The hearing was televised live on CNN. It was over very fast. Then a limo whisked him away.

God elected to reinstate the nation's No. 1 show, a decision for which he was widely applauded within the show biz community. Not that his decision had anything whatsoever to do with bravery. It had to do with money, and with the extremely deep financial soup his network was drowning in. His and the other two networks as well. None of them, as it happens, had ever learned how to swim.

America's three-network system was dying. In 1976, the big three could claim nine out of ten prime-time viewers as their own. These days, they could claim only six. Cable TV and home video were to blame. Viewers were channel surfing now. They had more viewing choices—lots of choices. And they weren't choosing the calculated blandness and sheer vapidity of network programming. Shrinking audiences meant shrinking advertising revenues. And that meant the networks had to cut back. News and sports divisions were going fast, virtually conceding defeat to the new cable rivals like CNN and ESPN. Meanwhile, Godfrey Daniels was even predicting that one or more of the networks might soon have to scale back their hours of prime-time programming. Maybe get out of prime time altogether one or two nights per week. Maybe go out of business, period.

A hit show like *Uncle Chubby* could still turn a network's entire fortunes around. But not one of the three networks had found a hit in the past three years. Snap, crackle, flop was the painful norm now. Fickle audiences were thumbing their noses at one new show after another. Losing *Uncle Chubby* because of Lyle's arrest had cost the network an estimated 13 percent of its viewers, viewers it could ill afford to lose. Its aggregate weekly ratings share fell from 21 percent to 18, dropping it from first to second place. And dangerously close to third. The network had wanted *Uncle Chubby* back on. The network had needed it back on.

So did Panorama City Communications, the film and TV studio that was financially partnered with Lyle in producing the show. The studio was his bank. It absorbed the rather punishing weekly budget overages that are common practice in network series production. In the case of *Uncle Chubby*, the licensing fee was $800,000 per week against an actual production budget of just over $1 million. Spread out over a season of twenty-two episodes, this amounted to a shortfall of $5 million. Panorama City was willing to take such a hit—a practice known as deficit financing—because they, not the network, owned the show's syndication rights. That's when a long-running series is sold into rerun heaven on local stations all over the country—all over the world. A sitcom was presently earning its producers and distributor around $1 million per episode. A hundred episodes means a $100-million pot of cash at the end of the rainbow. Of course, there is some risk involved. You can't syndicate a show until you have that pool of a hundred episodes, which means at least four seasons' worth of shows. Most series don't stay on that long. Only the hits. *Uncle Chubby* was just such a hit. A lock. A studio's wet dream. There was just one problem—it had only been on three seasons. Sixty-six episodes. Not enough. So the studio was out $15 million and *very* anxious to see it get back on the air. They had a huge financial stake in it.

As did Lyle Hudnut, who stood to take home a third of that syndication pie. More than the man's dignity was at stake. Thirty million dollars was involved. And that buys a lot of dignity.

So *Uncle Chubby* was back on the air—with a few changes. And its season premiere would be a big-time happening, the biggest since *Murphy Brown* squared off against Danny Quayle. That meant big-time bucks, too. The leading sneaker manufacturer in the world had already signed on at an astounding $350,000 per thirty seconds of commercial airtime—a record for a sitcom. So had a new diet soft drink and one of the Detroit automakers.

Lyle Hudnut was back.

That made one of us.

Like I said, the past few months hadn't exactly been swell for me either. If you were around and semialive you've been reading all about it. All about Merilee and me. Once, she and I had been something. She was Merilee Nash, fabulous star of stage and screen, two-time Tony award winner, Oscar winner, glamorous, respected, admired, the woman who had it all. I was Stewart Hoag, that tall, dashing author of that brilliantly successful first novel, *Our Family Enterprise,* the man who *The New York Times* called "the first great new literary voice of the 1980's." We were New York's hottest, cutest people. Hands down. Until it all fell apart. That was my doing. Writer's block is what they call it. I lost my juices, lost my voice, lost my wife. Merilee got it all—the seven rooms overlooking Central Park, the red 1958 Jaguar XK–150 drop-head, marriage to that fabulously successful new Southern playwright, Zack something. I got my drafty old fifth-floor walk-up on West Ninety-third Street, and Lulu. The juices did finally come back to me, in fits and starts, only the second novel was a thermonuclear dud. Novel number three was, as we say in the trade, in progress. Had been for nearly four years. It was not, as we also say in the trade, under contract. Neither was Merilee. She came back to me in fits and starts, too, after the Zack thing fell apart. We got semiinvolved all over again. Separate addresses. No commitments. No promises. But for me, there was no one else. There was only Merilee. Same with her, or so I had thought. See, it all blew up in my face over the winter when she politely informed me by phone from Fiji that she was pregnant. She said she knew I didn't want kids, but she did, and since she was forty it was now or never so she was going to have this one. And, by the way, I was not the father. She wouldn't tell me who was. She wouldn't tell anyone. I can't tell you why. I don't know why.

I only know that when word got out that Merilee Nash was with love child, everybody, but everybody, wanted to know who Daddy was. The *National Enquirer,* convinced that all leading ladies fuck their leading men—because they do—deduced that the father was her costar in the black comedy she'd been filming at the time the dirty deed took place. I doubted this—Danny DeVito is happily married, and a borderline dwarf. Merilee is six feet tall in her size ten bare feet. *Hard Copy* was sure that the father was hubby number two, Zack something. I doubted this, too. Zack had been in India for the past two years trying to find himself. Not that it should be such a big fucking discovery. David Letterman chipped in with his own top ten candidates, including Colonel Muammar al-Qaddafi, Wile E. Coyote, Frank Perdue, and Spiderman.

As Merilee got bigger, the story got bigger. It simply wouldn't go away. So I did. Fled to Provence with Lulu. Being a writer means you aren't tied to any one place. You're free to be unhappy anywhere in the world. I rented a two-hundred-year-old stone *mas* in the countryside outside of Joucas with a pool and six hectares of olive trees and grapevines. There I'd spent the past six months living in splendid, morbid isolation. I worked on the third novel. I swam. I ate the sun-ripened melons and cold roasted peppers, the garlicky pink *saucisson* and the *tapenade,* a native paste of black olives and anchovies that Lulu loves nearly as much as caviar. I drank the new Côtes du Rhône and found it every bit as amusing as the old Côtes du Rhône. It wasn't a terrible life. Lulu did keep wondering where her mommy was. She didn't understand what had gone wrong. The little ones never do. But it wasn't a terrible life. I think I could have stayed there forever if it hadn't cost money. And if mine hadn't run out.

I didn't call Merilee when I got back to town. I did catch a glimpse of her, but that was on the front page of the *Star,* a photo of her waddling down Central Park West in maternity clothes and sunglasses, very pregnant. The headline: WHERE'S POPPA?

Damned if I knew.

You're probably beginning to wonder exactly what it is I do when the money runs out. Let me tell you about my not-chosen field. I'm a pen for hire, an invisible man, a ghost. In my own defense, I'm not one of those "As Told To" lunch-pailers who routinely run some doddering ex-movie star's self-congratulatory twaddle through the word processor. Or maybe it's the food processor. No, I am *the* ghost. The reigning champ, if there can be such a thing as an invisible champ. Four number-one best-selling memoirs to my noncredit, as well as someone else's best-selling novel. Unlike the lunch-pailers, I know how to handle stars. Used to be one myself, and I was married to one and am not, repeat not, the father of her child. I also happen to be a former lion of American literature, a master of the finer nuances of character, tone, structure—which is to say I know how to make up better stories than they do. Sorry if this is disillusioning you, but you should never, ever confuse a celebrity memoir with Truth. And you're old enough to know this by now.

Of course, there's one other reason why my celebrity memoirs tend to be breakout hits. Things—how shall I put it —have this way of heating up when I arrive. I don't mean the way Lyle said the control room heated up when Katrina wiggled in. I mean the way famous people have this unpleasant way of turning up dead. By other than natural causes. Ghosting, you see, isn't just about making up stories. It's about dishing dirt on friends and foes. It's about secrets, past and present. Usually, there's someone around who wants them to stay quietly buried. Most ghosts say fine, 'nuff said. Not me. I rise to the challenge. At least my ego does, and my ego is executive producer of this particular long-running sitcom.

Not that I look for trouble. I don't. Trouble just has this uncanny knack for searching me out, like a pig nosing around in the dirt for truffles.

I told you I never thought I'd be a sitcom writer. Well, I never thought I'd be a ghost, either. Same as I never thought Merilee Nash would be pregnant with another man's child. "Just another one of those little surprises that make life so interesting," as Ozzie used to tell Dave and little Ricky on *The Adventures of Ozzie and Harriet*. Of course, Ozzie is history now, and father no longer knows best. Nobody knows best. I sure don't. I used to think I did, but that was the old me. The me who knew everything. The new me knows next to nothing. The new me is growing dumber every single day.

TWO

Hudson Studio, where *The Uncle Chubby Show* was taped before a studio audience every Friday evening during the season, was located down on West Twenty-sixth Street, on the edge of the garment district. It was a street lined with wholesalers and sweatshops and shops that did nothing but service sewing machines or sell body parts for mannequins of the nonhuman variety. Trucks were double-parked everywhere, loading and unloading dresses, furs, and leather jackets. The studio itself offered little in the way of curbside appeal. It was a converted warehouse, six stories high, with its upstairs windows bricked over. There was a two-bay loading dock for trucks. There was no fancy sign. Just the words Hudson Studio stenciled on the double doors of smoked glass. Not that those doors were easy to get to.

There was a blue police barricade on either side of them and a knot of uniformed cops stopping everybody. This because about two hundred angry protestors from Citizens for Moral Television had rolled out the unwelcome mat. They carried signs saying "CHUBBY MUST GO!" and "JUST SAY NO TO PERVERTS!" They chanted, "Shame, shame, shame on you!" for all to hear. Especially the news crews from local TV stations and *Entertainment Tonight*. The protestors were plenty worked up. A few were even stretched out in the middle of Twenty-sixth Street with the hope of getting arrested for blocking traffic. Had to be from out of town. That tactic doesn't play in New York, where nine out of ten cab drivers would just as soon go over you as around you. One of the cops let me inside.

There was a tiny reception area with a desk where a young black kid in a Hudson Studio T-shirt sat reading about last night's sorry performance by the Mets in the *Post.* A phone, a walkie-talkie, and his feet were on the desk before him. After he'd checked my name against a list I asked him how long the protestors had been out there.

"Since eight o'clock this morning. Said they won't go away til they take the man off the air. Don't they have nothin' better to do than stand out there in the hot sun all day?"

"If they did they'd be doing it."

He flashed me a grin. "Have a good one."

Lulu growled at him. It's her least favorite expression. I've never known why.

She ambled along beside me, snuffling, as I went down a long, narrow corridor past a rabbit warren of offices, storerooms, and conference rooms. I passed through the double fire doors at the end of the hall, then climbed a wide steel staircase vaguely reminiscent of one in an inner city high school. It was actually used as such when they filmed *Fame* there several years before. After two flights I reached a landing. Here there was an open door marked "PRODUCTION OFFICES" and a closed door marked "DRESSING ROOMS—NO ENTRANCE—PRIVATE." There was a big padlock on it in case you couldn't read. There was also a men's room, which smelled like it hadn't been cleaned since the glory days of John V. Lindsay, a water fountain, which was out of order, and a bank of grimy windows overlooking a rather repulsive air shaft. If you're looking for luxury, TV production is not for you. The glamor is on camera, not behind it.

I went in the open door. There was a narrow alcove immediately inside the door with private offices on the left—first Lyle's, then Katrina's. Both doors were shut. A couple of desks were positioned just outside them. The alcove opened onto a big room that had the hastily assembled look of a campaign headquarters. Dented, mismatched steel desks were set up here, there, everywhere. Several had computer terminals parked on them. Production assistants, most of them young women in various states of grunge, were frantically working the phones and bustling about with armloads of office supplies and scripts. There was tremendous energy in the air. Everyone was moving, moving, moving. Everyone except for a trio of strapping young men who sat on the dog-eared sofa in the corner, sipping coffee. Actors. I could tell by the bulging nylon shoulder bags that lay at their feet. They live out of those bags. From nine to five, they are like the homeless. I also recognized one of them from a singing muffler commercial. It was the muffler that sang, not him. There was a mammoth photocopier at the far end of the office, where two P.A.'s were running off copies, and a kitchen where two more were making coffee. Also a corridor that led to the stars' dressing rooms and to the makeup and costume rooms. A second corridor, next to Katrina's office, led to the writers' offices.

I stood there a moment, taking it all in, until an officious young woman in an *Uncle Chubby* T-shirt and crew cap buttonholed me. "Yeah, who are you playing?" she demanded brusquely.

"I'm masquerading as one of the writers."

Her manner changed instantly—all the way from *Get lost, loser,* to *Hold me, touch me, feel me, heal me.* "Oh, gee, I'm so-o sorry." Big smile. "You must be Hoagy."

"Somebody has to be."

"I'm Naomi Leight, your P.A. I work for all the writers, but I'm especially looking forward to working for you."

Naomi Leight had the single worst nose job I'd ever seen. It looked like she'd gotten it slammed in a car door. Otherwise she was not unattractive. Her black hair was lustrous, her lips pouty, her complexion creamy. She wore rings on all of her fingers and one of those heavy studded necklaces of Katrina's. She was on the tall side in cowboy boots, and her skintight jeans, artfully ripped at the knees, clung for dear life to her every curve. Her eyes bothered me, though. They had an eager, sneaky glint in them. They were the eyes of a born conspirator.

She was still smiling at me. "I'm *really* sorry. See, I thought you were an actor."

"Now there's a truly horrifying thought."

"C'mon, let's get you settled . . . Oh, *hi*, sweetie," she exclaimed, stopping to pat Lulu, who glowered up at her. Lulu can smell a predatory female from a mile away. And still clings to the feeble hope that Merilee and I will kiss and make up and all will be well again in Lululand.

Naomi led me down the short, L-shaped corridor to the writers' offices, swinging her hips big-time. All the doors were closed. I was early. Mine was the office at the end of the hall. The door was unlocked.

"There are no locks on any of the office doors," she informed me. "Lyle had them removed. He believes in open doors. He wants people to feel at home."

"I guess he and I grew up in different kinds of homes."

"The outside door to the dressing rooms is kept locked. Maybe you noticed. That's for traffic control and to ensure the stars their privacy when the audience comes in. Everything else is open."

She turned on the light. My office had a small student's desk and chair. There wasn't room for any other furniture. At some point in show-biz history it had served as a performer's dressing room. There was a mirror with light bulbs around it and a narrow shelf for cosmetics. Prior to that, I'm fairly certain it had been a broom closet.

"Now if there's anything you need," Naomi offered. "Anything at all . . ."

"A window would be nice."

She giggled, a practiced, insincere giggle. Major suck-up. "Sorry. Lyle has the only office with a window."

"Then how about a hanger?"

"There's a hook on the back of the door."

"Worst thing you can do to a jacket. Ruins the drape."

"Then I'll see you get one right away," she promised me with heartfelt sincerity. My hanger was the most important thing in her life. "Wire or wood?"

"Didn't you see *Mommie Dearest?*"

"Wood it is." She sashayed out, giggling.

I helped Lulu off with her pith helmet. She cased our new digs, nose to the floor, which took all of seven seconds. Then she curled up under the desk. I opened my battered Il Bisonte briefcase and unpacked my notepads and took off my jacket. By this time another young woman, this one bovine and plain as milk, had come scuffing around the corner with a stack of scripts and my hanger. The hanger she handed me. The script she dropped on my desk with a *thwack.* Then she was gone.

I hung up my jacket and sat at the desk with the script. A sitcom script is quite short—this one was forty-six pages— and almost all dialogue. Description and stage direction are minimal, even less than a screenplay. Several production sheets, green, were on top. One glance at a sitcom production schedule will tell you a whole lot about why prime-time TV is what it is. Every minute of every day is accounted for. Rehearsals, run-throughs, rewrites. More rehearsals, more run-throughs, more rewrites. Camera blocking, pretaping, taping, pickups . . . It's a tight, tight, schedule, and there is no margin for error. No one can be late. No one can be sick. No one can be difficult. Because there's barely enough time to get the show done at all—let alone done well—before you're already on to the next show. And the next one. And the next.

Another young woman appeared in my doorway, this one round and very short.

"No way!" she exclaimed. "I'm, like, I see!"

"You see what?"

"Why the women are all going, 'Ow, mommy-mommy'

over you. But I'm, like, huh? Which new tall, totally excellent babe? And then—okay, wait—I remember you're the new writer. The one who's helping Lyle. I'm, like, Annabelle."

Annabelle Gamba was a cross between a hyperactive New Jersey mall teenager and a troll doll. She was well under five feet tall, with a cute little face and black button eyes and a deep passion for purple. Purple lipstick and eye shadow. Purple nail polish on her soft, childlike hands. She had on an oversized cotton sweater, purple, and knit leggings, purple again. Her tiny patent leather pumps were black. So was her hair, which she evidently teased with an egg beater. It towered in chaotic splendor a full eighteen inches above her head. Whole gallons of mousse held it in place up there like some kind of ceremonial headdress.

"Okay, wait," she jabbered on. "So, like, are you?"

"Are I what?"

"Gay. They begged me to find out."

"Not in any known sense of the word. I'm divorced, actually."

"I *know* all about that. Hurt?"

"Only when I laugh, which hasn't been a big problem lately."

"No, no. I meant, is Bill Hurt the baby's father?"

I sighed inwardly. "I only know what I read in the papers."

"No way! Merilee won't even tell *you?*"

"Merilee especially won't tell me."

"So, like, are you in play? There are a lot of women here who would—"

"No, I'm afraid I've been kicked clear out of bounds. You'll find me out in the parking lot under the team bus, covered with cleat marks."

She nodded animatedly, her big hair nodding right along with her. Forget about mousse. This girl used epoxy cement. "Cool. I'll pass it along. See, there aren't many eligible men around this place. They've all been after Bobby for years. He's a major bunny, even if he is full of blah-blah-blah."

"Blah-blah-blah?"

"Anger. Plus he's kind of wocka-wocka in the commitment area." Her glance fell under my desk on Lulu. "No way! You have a dog!"

"I understand you're the staff pet specialist."

Annabelle fell to her knees and began to stroke Lulu. "Pets and kids. And I'm, like, desperate for new material. Mind if I follow her around and take notes?"

"That's really up to her."

Lulu yawned in Annabelle's face. Possibly her most definitive response. Certainly her most noxious.

Annabelle jumped back from her. "Shit, her breath!"

"She has rather strange eating habits."

"Okay, wait. What about Rusty?"

"I'm not familiar with his eating habits."

She shook her head at me. "No, no. I mean does she get along with other dogs?"

"They've never complained before. Why?"

"Because Rusty's built like a truck and I'm, like, he's *vicious.*"

"I assumed that was just his character in the show."

Annabelle let out a playful shriek, the sort you'd hear coming from a thirteen-year-old's slumber party. "No way! Haven't you noticed he never does any scenes with The Munchkins? Just Lyle? That's because their mom, Amber, is scared shitless he'll eat them. For, like, real. That dog's *mean.* Also superterritorial. Rusty may not be cool about another dog being around the studio. That's why I asked."

"Well, we'll just have to play it by ears."

Under the desk, Lulu snuffled at me indignantly.

Annabelle frowned at her. "Now why's she doing that?"

"She's a bit sensitive about her appearance."

"Oh. Well, Rusty won't be around anyway until we do blocking on Thursday. Lyle doesn't like having him here because of ticks and—'' She stopped. "Whoa! I'm, like, wait a minute. She *understands* you?''

"She likes to think so. I prefer to think she misses my subtler nuances. And there are many.''

She shook her head at me in disbelief. "I love this!''

"You won't after a while, believe me.''

"But I can *use* this!'' She stuck her purple lower lip out. "If Rusty can play it. He has his limits—his forte is chasing Lyle into the laundry room and barking at him menacingly.''

"How are The Munchkins to write for?''

"A snap. They just play themselves, which is all any munchkin can do. You like kids?''

"In very small portions. Shish kabob is ideal.''

"Well, Casey and Caitlin are real sweet. Real normal. Not like stage kids at all. Amber won't let them get swelled heads. She's a totally gifted director herself. She did that biker *Hamlet* with Luke Perry for Shakespeare in the Park.''

"I understand Amber was Lyle's assistant director for a while.''

"Second season,'' Annabelle confirmed. "So she could learn the technical side of sitcoms. And be around her kids. Plus Lyle promised her he'd eventually let her direct some episodes for him. I'm, like, fer shure. They were getting it on, was what that was about. Amber was nuts for Lyle. Even wanted to marry him after she and her husband split. Only Lyle dumped her cold. Fired her, too. A classic double boning. But that's nothing unusual. Lyle's exes are all over this place. His ex-wife, Fiona, is his costar. And then every season he picks out a new babe to doink.'' She counted them off on her tiny fingers. "First season was Marjorie Daw from the network. She's real sweet and an unlikelier pair you never saw. Second season was Amber. Last season was Katrina, who's already, like, history. Count on it. New season, new babe. My money's on Naomi Leight. She's ready, willing and doable. Major snoop, too, which he gets off on, being that he's so paranoid.'' She glanced at her wristwatch, one of those with the cat chasing the mouse around the dial that they sell on late-night TV. "I don't know what it is about the man, but for six months he's a total goner. He's found the greatest woman in the world. She's perfect. He loves her. They move in together, start talking about doing a family together. And then, wham, he breaks it right off. And starts all over again with someone else."

"He seems to have no shortage of takers," I observed.

"Hey, most men are dull," she explained. "If there's one thing Lyle isn't it's dull. Plus he's a star. And you do get a house."

I tugged at my ear. "A house?"

"Yeah. When he breaks it off I'm, like, he feels so guilty he moves out and lets you stay. Other guys give jewelry or a car, maybe a mink. Lyle gives a house. The man must be broke. He's given away millions in property. Fiona got their duplex on West Tenth Street. Worth over a mil. Marjorie got the penthouse on Riverside. Another mil, easy. Amber got the loft in Tribeca. Katrina'll get that humongous dump out in East Hampton, guaranteed. She knows it, too. That's why she doinked him in the first place. Not a bad gig, considering. But I'm, like, no way. He's too terrible a person."

"In what way?"

There was a rustling noise out in the hall. Annabelle shot a glance that way, instantly on alert. No relaxed place this. "So you do feelings, huh?"

"Feelings," I affirmed. "Nothing more than feelings."

"I've always admired feelings specialists," she confessed. "Wouldn't mind being one myself when I'm older. How'd you get there? By doing a lot of living? Having your heart stepped on a few dozen times?"

"Something like that."

"And you're doing Lyle's book, too."

"I am."

She lowered her voice. "We'll have to do lunch today

while The Boys are in rewrites. I'll give you the straight dope on everybody. I can't keep my mouth shut, in case you didn't notice. Bobby'll join us, too, if he gets here. He's usually late on Mondays. You'll like Bobby. He's real perceptive." She glanced down the hall again. "Ah, good. The Boys are here. Let's go say hello. "C'mon, Lulu. Come meet The Boys." Lulu stirred under the desk. "God, she's so *great!*"

"Careful," I cautioned. "Her head swells easily."

"But, I mean, she looks so profound."

"Just a profound case of gas. Trust me, I know about these things."

"Because you're a feelings specialist?"

"Because she sleeps on my head."

The Boys' office was a lot bigger than mine. Big enough for a pair of desks set back to back, a sofa, two chairs, a TV monitor, and a human skeleton, which hung from the ceiling with a gorilla mask over its head. The Boys were going over the script at their desks. Both of them were short. Both of them were clad in Ralph Lauren polo shirts, pleated khakis, and moccasins. Preppy-casual is the standard sitcom uniform. Has been since the heyday of Grant Tinker, who was half-hour television's answer to Babe Paley. Muck and Meyer were not boys. They were in their forties. But comedy writing teams are always called The Boys. Have been since the first caveman delivered the first spit take. Just as young writers like Annabelle and the absent Bobby would always be The Kids, though I'd heard that that one was currently being edged out by the New Yids on the Block.

"Say hello to Stewart Hoag," Annabelle commanded them. "And be nice!"

Marty Muck jumped to his feet and shook my hand, all smiles and geniality. He was tanned and fit and robust, with wiry black hair and even white teeth and a prosperous, contented air about him. Marty seemed very West Coast to me, possibly because he reminded me of a Beverly Hills dentist who once had both of his hands in my mouth. That guy never stopped smiling either. "Glad to have you, Stewy."

"Make it Hoagy," I said.

"As in Carmichael?" he asked.

"As in the cheese steak."

"Cheese is a funny word," he declared, veteran shticktician to novice. "You can always get a laugh with the word cheese. Also goulash, guacamole, spackle, argyle, and Rosemary Clooney. Say hello to my partner Tommy."

"Hello to my partner Tommy," I said.

"Now *that* particular gag," Marty advised, "got a laugh *all* the time for Burns and Allen. But then *Laugh-In* used it a hundred times in three months and killed it stone dead." He paused, pondering it. "Of course, that was twenty-five years ago. Maybe it's coming back and you're ahead of the curve."

"I generally am."

He turned to his partner. "What do you say, Tommy?"

Tommy Meyer didn't say anything. Or crack a smile. Or get up. Just slumped there in his chair, sizing me up with a suspicion that bordered on outright hostility. Tommy was a sour, cadaverous, dead fish of a fellow, his skin translucent and faintly bluish, as if he'd been left dead out in the snow for several days. He had chalky lips and limp gray hair with a vivid patch of white at the forelock, like a tuft of cotton. He looked uncommonly frail and brittle and ill-nourished next to his partner. It was as if one were feeding off of the flesh of the other—the writing partner of Dorian Gray. He gave me a brief nod, then turned stiffly back to his script, his joints creaking arthritically. "You're helping Lyle with his book," he said. More an accusation than a question.

"That's correct," I said. "An examination of his life and career. His arrest, too, of course." I tugged at my ear. "Lyle contends he was set up."

Tommy's eyes flickered at me.

Marty motioned for Annabelle to shut the door. She did. He said, "Set up how?"

I sat on the sofa. Lulu explored. The skeleton she steered clear of. "He says someone called the police on him."

"I'm, like, who?" wondered Annabelle.

"Someone who wanted to ruin him," I replied. "Someone from the show, to be exact. Possibly even one of you."

The Boys exchanged a look. Marty shook his head sadly. "He's lost it. The man has totally lost it."

"How so?" I asked.

"Hoagy, no one purposely sets out to get their own show thrown off the air," he reasoned. "No one *wants* to be unemployed. Christ, he can't really think that's what happened."

"What do you think happened?" I asked.

"I think," Tommy replied, "the man went to a dirty, disgusting movie that had a lot of dirty, disgusting people doing dirty, disgusting things to each other. I think that he got horny and pulled out his chicken so as to choke it and he got caught. Face it, he's your basic skeegee guy. I ought to know—I'm your basic skeegee guy." And drier than dry. The man was the Gobi Desert. He positively exuded bleakness. It was an odor not unlike stale beer.

"He says he's living clean now," I mentioned.

"When a comic says he's living clean," said Tommy, "he means he's no longer injecting directly into the vein."

"He says he's off coke."

"Hey, you're not actually *buying* him, are you?" asked Marty, brow furrowing with concern.

"No, he's buying me. Though I prefer to think he's renting me, month to month."

"Well, you jump in when you feel comfortable," said Marty with a reassuring grin. "We're all friends here."

"A common enemy will do that to an otherwise diverse group of people," Tommy explained.

"Tommy's overselling a bit," Marty apologized. "We're actually kind of divided in our feelings about Lyle. Some of us dislike him—"

"And the rest of us can't stand him," Tommy cracked. "A lot of writers just plain hate him on sight."

"Why is that?" I asked.

"Saves time," Tommy fired back bluntly.

"One time," recalled Annabelle, "I'm, like, he actually stuck a table draft down his pants and farted on it in front of the whole cast and crew."

"I still haven't decided if that improved it or not," muttered Tommy.

"I suppose you feel sorry for him, Hoagy," Marty suggested tactfully.

"I don't feel anything," I said. Though I was starting to feel Marty overplaying the nice guy bit. "I'm here so I can get to know him."

"I wish you luck," said Marty. "I don't think anyone's ever been able to *know* Lyle. Not really. You reach a point with him and he pushes you away. Christ, I've known him, it must be twenty-two years, and he's never been to my house. Never given me a birthday present. He doesn't even know when my birthday is."

"Because he doesn't care." Tommy shifted in his chair, joints creaking. He sounded like a bowl of Rice Krispies when he moved. He pointed a crooked finger at me. "You worry me."

"I worry myself."

"We tell you what we really think about Lyle and he'll just use it against us. The man's been known to pull some major vindictive shit on people."

"We can make it off the record."

"How do we know we can trust you?" Tommy demanded.

"You don't," I replied. "But you can."

"Of course you can," echoed Annabelle. "Would those eyes lie to you?"

She was referring to Lulu's eyes, not mine. But I'll take support wherever I can get it.

Tommy Meyer peered at me skeptically. I had expected this. Because I was one of them, but I wasn't. An awkward role, no question.

"Okay, wait, do we dish or don't we?" Annabelle wondered.

The partners made silent eye contact with each other. Before Tommy turned back to me and said, "Main thing you should know about our grand-high-exalted mystic ruler is that he's big, he's fat, and he turns everything into a major battle."

We do dish. I had expected this, too. Because when it comes to dishing I've found most people can't help themselves.

"It's a battle you can never win," Tommy continued. "It's his ball, his court, and his game. Lyle always has to get his way. Always. He won't listen to anybody else. He won't take criticism—"

"I'm like, he doesn't even *hear* it," said Annabelle. "He has this screen that filters out anything negative."

"He has to feel like he's in total charge at all times," said Tommy. "If he doesn't, he feels threatened. And when Lyle feels threatened you'd better duck—he wigs out big-time. So nobody challenges him. Not ever."

"Not even you?" I asked.

"We used to," said Marty, a bit defensively. "First season. It bothered us the way he kept changing our scripts in rehearsal. He'd throw out half our gags, schlock everything up. So we'd fight."

"Creative differences," Tommy recalled sourly. "We wanted to do something creative and he wanted to do something different."

"But the fight's gone out of us," admitted Marty. "We have zero clout. We can never change his mind. So what's the point? Besides, who are we to tell the man he's wrong? He has the top-rated show in America. We just give him what he wants and try to stay out of his way."

Tommy: "Think of us as master furniture makers laboring in a chair factory."

Marty: *"Formica* factory. Formica says fake. Plus it's a funnier word."

Tommy: "You're right. Formica factory it is."

Now here were two guys who had been writing together a long time. They even punched up each other's conversations.

"I'm, like, you guys are being so negative," objected Annabelle.

"Okay, okay, maybe we do sound like total cynical hacks," acknowledged Marty. "But at least we have no illusions about what we're doing here."

"Unlike Bobby." Tommy sneered unpleasantly. "Where is the Bobster anyway? The Boston shuttle running late again?"

"Naomi was looking for him," said Annabelle.

"Why, she need servicing?" he cracked.

"No, the copier does," Annabelle fired back. To me she said, "Bobby's the only one around here who's handy."

"Another thing you're going to discover, Hoagy," Marty went on, choosing his words carefully, "is that Lyle changes directions on you a lot. The man's completely unpredictable. Which means a lot of our time is spent stabbing around in the dark—"

"Or, if possible, in Lyle's back," chipped in Tommy.

"For a gag that pleases him. And that's a nonstop adventure, because what he says he loves one minute he may hate five minutes later. We never know why. We only know it's out. So a lot of what we do is . . ."

"Trial and terror?" I suggested.

Marty nodded approvingly. "Not bad. You're going to be okay."

"So I keep telling myself."

"Okay, wait, why's she doing *that?*" wondered Annabelle, intently observing Lulu, who was snarfling at the wall next to the couch, tail thumping. "Is it a mouse?"

"No, she'd be cowering between my legs if it were any form of rodent life." Now Lulu was growling at the baseboard. "Offhand, I'd say there's a person listening on the other side of the wall."

"Lyle," Marty whispered. "He's in Katrina's office eavesdropping on us with his Super Ear. Some stupid James Bond gadget he bought at this spook supply shop on Madison Avenue. He can hear through walls with it. Show him, Tommy."

Tommy got up out of his chair and creaked over next to the wall. "Just remember, Hoagy," he exclaimed, voice raised. "No matter what happens we know we can always count on Lyle to come in at the last minute and *pull it out!*"

There was a brief moment of silence. Followed by a tremendous crash on the other side of the wall.

"See?" chuckled Marty.

"And so another Uncle Chubby mug bites the dust," intoned Tommy, clipping off the words like David Brinkley. He bent and gave Lulu a pat on the head. "You, Lulu, are okay."

"I love her deadpan, too," Marty observed, inspecting her. "Reminds me of Lady Macbeth."

"Marty's first wife," explained Tommy. "Actually, she looks a lot like Beth. Especially around the nose."

"She does," Marty agreed. "Does she get PMS?"

Lulu let out a low moan of outrage. She has a rather Victorian sense of propriety. Picked it up from her mommy. Or so I'd once believed.

"Does Lyle often eavesdrop on you?"

"One of his favorite hobbies," Tommy confirmed with dry dismay. "The man likes to go through our trash, too. He thinks people are constantly plotting behind his back to overthrow him. We're talking serious paranoia here."

I nodded. I wondered if that's what all his talk about

being set up at the Deuce was: paranoia. I wondered indeed.

"Tommy and I also happen to be in the middle of a rather ugly contract dispute with him," Marty confessed.

"No way!" exclaimed Annabelle. "Not again!"

"Stick around, Hoagy," said Tommy. "You may be head writer within the hour."

"See, we found out last night from our agent that he's trying to chisel us out of ten grand a week," said Marty.

I tugged at my ear. "I'm afraid that may be my doing, indirectly."

Tommy peered at me bleakly. "That what he's paying you?"

"It is," I replied. "And, believe me, if I'd known it was coming out of your—"

"Oh, hey, hey," Marty cautioned me, with a raised hand. "Don't you feel responsible, Hoagy. Not your doing. It's *her* salary that's killing us."

"Katrina," said Tommy distastefully. "He's paying her thirty grand a week this season to be his coexec producer. Christ, she was Leo's runner last season, making three hundred a week. Now she gets to sit in on writers' meetings. She even gets to *speak.*"

"I hate, hate, hate this scene," squeaked Annabelle. It was a drop-dead imitation. Her eye even drifted. "Where's the irony, guys, comedically speaking?"

"The woman," said Marty, "has Lyle's ear."

"In addition to various other parts of his disgustingly gross anatomy," added Tommy.

"The woman," said Marty, "knows very little about comedy."

"The woman," snapped Tommy, "is a stupid, nasty twat and we all hate her stupid, nasty fucking guts."

No one disagreed. Tommy's designated role, it appeared, was to give voice to what the others were too afraid to say out loud. It was a role he seemed to savor as much as he did his sourness.

"You notice that rock on her finger? The show paid for it —twenty grand easy. She wanted a john for her office—the show paid for it. Hey, if it's for us, no way. Nickels and dimes. He even charges us for our long-distance calls. But if it's for him and his bim, the money's there. Would you believe the show paid for all his coke last season? It was right there in the budget, under car and driver. Hell, the show pays for half a dozen extras every week who don't even exist. He pockets their wages himself. He must pull in thirty grand a week under the table."

"And then he pockets the table," Annabelle chimed in. "Him and Leo. I'm, like, one time last season our art director, Randy, needed to build a set, last minute, and discovered there was no money left for it in that week's budget—even though he hadn't even built one set! I'm, like, so he went out to the prop warehouse in New Jersey to see what he could beg and borrow and, guess what, he discovers an antique dining table and chairs being loaded onto a truck headed for Leo's place in the Berkshires. Leo sells the stuff up there to dealers and then splits the proceeds with Lyle. They're thick as thieves, those two."

"That's why Lyle insists on personally supervising the entire production," Tommy explained. "If there were a lot of lawyers and business affairs people around he'd never get away with all the shit he pulls. Or he'd have to cut them in on it. That's also why he insists on doing the show here instead of in L.A. God and Jazzy Jeff are three thousand miles away. And with Marjorie he can play human bulldozer."

The office door suddenly burst open. And there stood the human bulldozer, filling the doorway shoulder to shoulder in his unbleached caftan. He wasn't kidding about taking precautions against germs in the studio. Over his mouth and nose he wore a surgical mask, on his hands latex gloves. He

looked like he was on his way to the O.R. to take out somebody's spleen. The man was boiling. His face, what little of it
showed, was a deep shade of crimson. His eyes were high
beams of intense light, the whites huge. They looked like a
pair of poached eggs. He slammed the door shut behind him,
shaking the whole office. Papers flew from the desks. "Your
agent is *scum!*" he raged at The Boys. "Your agent is *filth*.
Your agent is—!"

"Why do you say that, Lyle?" Marty asked him calmly.
"Because he's trying to hold you to a deal you already agreed
to?"

"Human pollution!" Lyle roared on. "That's what he is—
human pollution! He's *everything* that's wrong with the
television business! I *won't* speak to him again! I *won't* let
him destroy my show! I won't . . . !" He trailed off, chest
heaving. He'd noticed me there. "Hiya, pal," he said pleasantly. Total mood change. He may have even been smiling—
hard to tell with the mask. "Getting settled in?"

"In a manner of speaking."

"Good, good. Knew you'd fit right in. We're all family
here." He glanced around the office. "Where's Bobby?"

"Not here yet," replied Annabelle, cowering. The man
clearly terrified her.

He turned back to The Boys, who were glaring at him.
He softened. "Now, guys, you gotta be reasonable. That's all
I'm asking. Agents, they make it about money. They make it
about threats. He even said you guys were gonna walk out on
me. Christ, if you did that I'd die. I *need* you. We're not about
money. We're about doing what we love doing, with people
we care about. What do we need agents for, huh? Let's us
settle this thing between ourselves, like family, okay? Whattaya say?"

"We say no, Lyle," Marty replied, quietly but firmly. "We
are *not* going to negotiate our contract with you. That's why
we have an agent. You'll have to go through him."

"I refuse!" Lyle bellowed. "I won't talk to him! I won't! I'll fire you if it comes to that! You hear me?! I'll fire you!"

"You can't fire us, Lyle," Tommy said scornfully.

"I can, too!" screamed Lyle. "I don't need you hacks! I've never needed you!"

"You *can't* fire us!" Tommy repeated.

"We *quit!*" screamed Marty.

"Bullshit!" yelled Lyle. "You don't have the nerve!"

The Boys sat there in tight-lipped silence a moment.

"All right, we'll listen," Marty allowed grimly. "But we're saying nothing, and we're agreeing to nothing."

"Totally cool," said Lyle. "That's all I ask."

Annabelle made for the door. Lulu and I joined her. I did not slam it behind me.

Outside, all was quiet. Everyone in the production office was staring at us, examining our faces for a clue as to what was going on in there. Particularly the occupants of the two desks in the alcove outside of Lyle and Katrina's offices. Naomi Leight, Annabelle's designated babe-in-waiting, sat at one, sneaky eyes gleaming. At the other sat a woman in her fifties with close-cropped silver hair and olive bags under her eyes. She got up and came charging right at me, clutching a handful of papers. She was a bunched fist of a woman, in a gray gymnasium T-shirt and fatigue pants. She had a pair of glasses on a chain around her neck. Stuck behind her right ear was a Sherman, one of those dark brown cigarettes that come in the red box.

"Stewart Stafford Hoag," she boomed in a deep, authoritative voice. "Do you wish to get paid at any time in the near future?"

"It would be nice," I replied.

Somehow, she seemed to be looking down her nose at me, even though I had a solid ten inches on her. I guess it was her manner, something of a cross between a women's prison guard and David Frye doing Bill Buckley. She moistened her thin, dry lips. "Then would you like to sign your payroll forms?" she demanded.

"By all means."

We went to my office. Lulu was already there, curled up under my desk.

"I'm Leo Crimp, your line producer," she announced gruffly. "You got a question, you come to me. You got a complaint about the P.A.'s, you come to me. You got a problem with Lyle, you don't come to me—but you will anyway."

I sat at my desk. "I was expecting a man—from the name."

"Leo's short for Leona," she growled impatiently. "But if by that you mean you were expecting somebody with balls, you got somebody with balls."

"I'll remember that."

"No problem if you don't. I'll remind you."

Leo laid the payroll forms out on my desk and offered me her Bic pen. I used my gold-nibbed Waterman. I've found that true luxury is found in the little things, not the big ones. Especially when you can no longer afford the big ones. When I was done Leo snatched the forms back from me. She tried to take my Waterman, too, but I was too fast for her.

"You've joined the Writers' Guild, correct?" she asked.

"Correct."

"Good. Remember—they're the only protection you got."

"From what?"

"Not what," she snapped. *"Who.* Lyle, naturally. From when he tries to fuck you out of the credits on any episodes you write. Don't let him get away with any of it. Fight him. Because it's residuals money out of your own pocket, and because he's full of shit. *He* doesn't write the show—*you* do."

This from Lyle's own partner in crime. There wasn't a lot of warmth around this place. In that sense it was like the house I grew up in.

Leo took the Sherman out from behind her ear and stuck it in her mouth. She didn't light it. Smoking was prohibited in the production offices. "Just telling it like it is," she explained brusquely. "I admire writers, but most of you are babes in the woods when it comes to money and what people will do to get it."

"Thank you, Leo. I appreciate the advice."

"You know good from evil?" she demanded, removing the unlit cigarette from her mouth.

I tugged at my ear. "Does anyone?"

"Watch out for Katrina," she said vehemently. "She's the worst kind of evil."

"And which kind is that?"

"She's a user."

"Aren't we all?"

"Steer clear of her, Stewart Hoag," Leo Crimp warned. "I mean it."

I thanked her for this bit of advice as well. I was getting real curious about what had gone on between the tough producer and her former runner. She stood there twirling her Sherman around in her fingers.

"Ever smoke that thing?" I asked her.

She stuck it back behind her ear. "Only in the ladies' room."

"Sounds a little like high school here."

She considered this. "No, it's more like a four-car pileup. Horrifying, yet at the same time so fascinating you can't tear your eyes away from it. Welcome to my place, Stewart Hoag," she said. And then she went barging out.

My phone rang. It was Annabelle.

"All clear, Hoagy," she reported. "Their door's open and I'm, like, Lyle's safely back in his own cage."

"Did they quit?"

She let out a shriek. "No way! The three of them go through this every season. He chisels them out of what he promised them, they threaten to walk, then they back down and take whatever he gives them. It's an opening day ritual of theirs."

"Like throwing out the first ball at Yankee Stadium?"

"I'm, like, they're total wusses, in case you haven't figured it out. Wait, hang on—" She covered the phone a second before she said, "C'mon, they're calling for you."

Lulu stayed behind this time. The better to focus on her morning nap.

Tommy and Marty were calmly reading over the script. Annabelle was seated on the sofa.

"Ah, there you are, Hoagy," said Marty, smiling pleasantly. "Where were we?"

"As I recall, you two were in the middle of changing careers."

Marty shrugged his shoulders. "That's just Lyle being Lyle," he said with mild resignation.

Tommy slumped in his chair, fuming. "I hate that man," he said savagely. "I really do. I fantasize about him dying in painful, horrible ways. It's how I get to sleep at night, instead of taking Sominex."

Marty said, "We've got an assignment for you, Hoagy."

"Feelings," I said. "Nothing more than feelings."

"We're not happy with how Deirdre's new beau turned out in this draft. He's a total yutz."

Tommy: "Straight out of a Grecian Formula commercial."

Marty: "We ought to know—we made him up."

"To Lyle's exact specifications," pointed out Annabelle, in their defense.

"Yutzy's how Lyle wants him," Marty acknowledged. "Even the guy's name—Rob Roy Fruitwell. Is that a yutzy name or what? See, Lyle's being . . . *Lyle* about this. He hates the whole idea. Because it wasn't his. Because it's being forced on him by God. And because—"

"He's scared shitless," Tommy said bluntly. "He figures God's master plan is to phase him out. Deirdre gets involved with Rob. Deirdre marries Rob. Zap, you've got yourself a solid franchise than can function fine without the Chubster. End result: God gets what he really wants, which is *The Uncle Chubby Show* back on the air, and Lyle Hudnut *off* the air. And out."

"Him and Katrina both," added Marty. "Which would also make the studio very happy. They'd save close to half a million an episode on their combined salaries."

"Is this just Lyle's paranoia?" I asked. "Or is it actually the network's plan?"

"We don't know," Tommy replied quickly.

Marty weighed his response more carefully. "It could be," he allowed. "Lyle's a loose cannon. And he's controversial. God hates controversy. Pickets make him crazy."

"And who would run the show?" I asked.

The Boys made eye contact with each other.

"That's strictly idle speculation at this point," Marty replied evasively.

"Bullshit," Tommy snapped. "We would. Muck and Meyer. Sure we would. Which would make us very happy, too. We'd be able to digest our food again."

"I can't remember what that's like," confessed Marty.

"I'm, like, it could be a totally excellent show," gushed Annabelle, egging them on.

"It could be cute," Marty admitted guardedly.

"And good for The Munchkins, too," she added. "We can let them have their own stories for a change. They can grow up as characters."

And she, I mused, could grow up as a writer—into a baby producer. "And who would direct?"

"Amber," Annabelle suggested. "She's ready."

"But it's strictly idle speculation at this point," Marty insisted. "Like I said."

Or was it? The pieces were all in place. Something for everyone. Except for Lyle, of course. Was this real? Had they been approached by the network? Or were they simply dreaming of what it would be like to get out from under the man's thumb?

"What we need from you, Hoagy," said Marty, "is a way to make Rob more likeable that won't freak Lyle out. We can't get a thing by him."

"If you can do that," said Tommy, "I'll kiss you on the mouth."

"That's not a good line," Marty told him.

"You're right—it needs work," he admitted, turning to me. "I'll get back to you."

"Do you know Chad?" Marty asked me.

"I don't believe we've met."

"Well, watch out for him. The man's a major suck-up."

"He may even lick your face," added Tommy, with great distaste.

"All the actors lobby us for good material," Annabelle explained. "It's kind of an occupational drag thing."

There was a faint tapping at the door. A scrawny nebish in his late twenties stuck his head in. "Morning," he said, bashfully.

"Come in, darling!" Annabelle sang out warmly. "I'm like, did Naomi . . . ?"

"Just needed a k-kicking," he stammered, blinking furiously. "Feeder was jammed. I-I miss anything?"

"Strictly a minor eruption," reported Marty. "A three point two on the Lyle wig-o-meter."

"Bring us any brisket sandwiches, Bobby?" needled Tommy, brightening. Although I'm sure an electrocardiogram would still have classified him as comatose.

"Be nice, Tommy!" Annabelle ordered, with motherly protectiveness. "Now, Bobby, dear, come meet Hoagy."

Bobby Ackerman came over to me with his hand stuck out. He had a head of soft, curly blond hair and an innocent, almost angelic face. He looked like a lamb—a really intense lamb. The kid was tightly wrapped. Typical writer in that regard—timid on the outside, simmering on the inside. Most of us are shy egomaniacs, myself excluded. I have never been shy. Bobby wasn't overly tidy. His blue oxford button-down was frayed at the neck, his gray twill trousers stained and wrinkled, his Rockports scuffed. He needed a shave. He needed a haircut. He needed to stop blinking.

"It's an honor to m-meet you," he said to me. Actually, he didn't so much stammer as he did speak in choked, over-heated bursts. "I really admire y-you."

"You won't once you get to know me better." I casually laid my hand on the sofa to air dry. His had been wet as a fresh caught flounder.

"But you do novels," he said, blinking at me incessantly. "That takes such g-guts. You're on your own. N-No other writers. No director. No actors. You do it all. J-Just you."

"There is a down side," I cautioned.

"W-Which is what?"

"There's no one else to blame. Just you."

"Now that must be weird," said Marty. "Life without Lyle to blame for everything."

"Now that must be nice," quipped Tommy.

"Have a seat, Bobster," said Marty. "We were just about to give Hoagy The Three Rules."

"Which Three Rules are those?" I asked.

"D-Don't listen to this shit, Hoagy," Bobby warned, with great urgency. "This isn't your kind of d-deal at all. I mean it. You're m-much too fine a—"

"Feel free *not* to have a seat, Bobby," Tommy snarled.

"F-Fine," Bobby retorted angrily. "I'll be in my office." And he split.

Annabelle watched him go, sadly.

"Don't mind Bobby," Marty said to me. "He's still living under the illusion that he's going to be the next Arthur Miller."

"Or the next Bea Arthur," added Tommy. "Now then, Hoagy, you'll want to write these down. Got a pen, pencil, quill?"

"I'll remember them."

"Rule Number One," Marty intoned grandly. "There are no new gags—only new setups."

"Don't ever be afraid of a joke just because you've heard it before," explained Tommy. "If it works once, it'll work again."

Marty said, "Here's a joke I heard the other day: Guy gives a Jewish blind man a piece of matzo, and the blind man runs his fingers over it and he says, 'Who wrote this shit?' Cute joke, right? I heard the exact same joke fifteen years ago —exact same joke—only it was Stevie Wonder and a cheese grater."

"And what was the punch line?" asked Annabelle.

" 'This is the most violent book I've read in years.' " Marty grinned at me. "See? Same joke. Different setup. And it's still funny. Got it?"

"What's Rule Number Two?" I wasn't that anxious to hear it. But my head was starting to throb.

"Rule Number Two," declared Marty. "Attributed to the late Carl Reiner—"

"Wait, Carl Reiner's still alive," objected Annabelle.

"I know—but he's always late," Marty shot back. "Rule Number Two: Write 'em Yiddish, but make 'em British."

"All comedy's Jewish," Tommy said flatly. "If a character has personality and foibles and quirks—in other words, if he's funny—he's Jewish. For television, you gentile him out. You make him black. You make him brown. You make him whatever." He broke off, narrowing his eyes at me. "This is valuable stuff, Hoagy. Took us years and years to learn. Sure you don't want to write it down?"

"I'll remember every word."

He shrugged his bony shoulders. "Okay. Rule Number Three. The oldest rule of them all, and the most important one to shtickle by . . . Relax, this isn't brain surgery."

Marty turned to him. "I can't believe I forgot to tell you

this—I met my wife's cousin, Phil, at a family barbecue on Saturday. He's actually a brain surgeon—"

"Oh, yeah?" Tommy said. "Maybe he should have a look at Lyle."

"And I was telling him all about Rule Number Three," Marty continued. "I said to him: Phil, what do *you* guys say when you screw up and can't figure out which nerve attaches to which? Or whatever the hell it is those guys do . . ."

"And what did he say?" asked Annabelle, raptly attentive.

Marty replied, "He told me they say, 'Relax—this isn't sitcom writing.' "

Little Annabelle let out a huge donkey bray of laughter.

There was a brisk tapping at the door. Naomi Leight stuck her head in. "Five minutes to reading, everyone!" the P.A. announced excitedly.

We all got to our feet, Tommy moving like he was three hundred years old. Bobby appeared in the doorway, blinking, blinking, script under his arm.

"One other thing, Hoagy," said Marty, with evident concern. "Can you fake an orgasm?"

"Excuse me?"

"Can you laugh even when something isn't funny?"

"No."

"Learn how," Tommy advised gravely. "Fast."

The rehearsal room was at the end of the hall where the actors' dressing rooms were found. Their doors were open. Not that there was a whole lot to see. Each was small and plain, though this was Sutton Place compared to my own digs. Fiona had a quilt hanging on one wall of hers to give it that homey, Amish feeling. Chad had a Joe Weider pressing bench and a full-size three-way mirror to give his that he-guy, look-at-me feeling. The Munchkins' own artwork adorned their walls. One watercolor portrait of Lyle made him look like something you'd find half submerged in a pond at the Bronx Zoo. Splendid likeness, actually. Wardrobe and makeup were next to the dressing rooms. Those doors were not open.

The rehearsal room was large and brightly lit and very cold. Conference tables had been set end to end to form a large rectangle with chairs for thirty people or so around it. Naomi was busy laying out scripts and pencils before each of them. Everyone else, some three dozen cast, crew, and production people, was drinking coffee and chatting gaily. The mood was very up. People were genuinely happy to be back working. Bagels and doughnuts and coffee were to be found at one end of the room, as well as a gigantic fruit basket. Lyle and Katrina were not to be found. Nor was Fiona Shrike. Chad Roe was. The actor was speaking urgently to Leo Crimp, who was trying just as urgently to get away from him. Common response.

The writers arrived together. I was to discover that they often moved about the studio as a group. They seemed to feel safer in numbers.

Lulu headed directly for the coffee table. Where there are bagels there are often lox.

Tommy Meyer, not one of your smiling, happy people, stopped cold in the doorway and sniffed the air disagreeably. "Ugh. Actors."

Marty Muck waded right in, patting backs, cracking jokes, one of the gang. He was the social one. Tommy exchanged only curt greetings as he oozed through to the coffee pot, shoulders hunched. Bobby Ackerman wouldn't even do that much. He went right for his place at the big table and sat and began studying the script, head down, defiantly standoffish. Annabelle Gamba, meanwhile, was a born schmoozer. She hugged, she kissed, she called everybody honey and darling and I'm, like, sweetheart. Annabelle was the one who introduced me around, clutching me tightly by the arm with her tiny fist. I met Phil, the thirtyish stage manager, who shaved his head. I met Sam, the grizzled old control room rat who was Lyle's current assistant director. I met Randy, the tubby little art director, who crinkled his nose, and Gwen, a too-fat older woman in a too-tight sailor suit who was, believe it or not, the costumer. It was Gwen whom I was most interested in.

It seemed she was having a real bad morning.

It seemed someone had just stolen Chubby's famed cardigan out of Wardrobe.

"Any idea who?" I asked her.

"One of the crew, naturally," she huffed. "If it's not nailed down they take it." Gwen had very bad false teeth. They angled outward, like a half-open garage door, and were the color of old piano keys. "Makes my life pure hell, too. I keep a spare, naturally. I have to. But now I have to break in a new spare. Distress it, stain it, unravel it, sew on the patches. And it all has to be just so, or people will notice it's wrong. After all, Chubby's sweater *is* Chubby."

"Have you had one stolen before?"

"No, never," she replied, peering out at me from behind a pair of thick glasses. "I keep them locked up tight."

"I thought Lyle didn't believe in locks."

"Lyle doesn't, but I do. The wardrobe room is *locked.* Has to be. Otherwise it would be like leaving a small fortune lying around."

"Who has keys?"

"To what, dear?" Gwen fumed impatiently.

"The wardrobe room."

"Stephen, my assistant," she replied. "Lyle, of course. And Katrina and Leo. But people are always in and out when we're in there working. Common pilfering happens all the time. A real pain, but there's no way to avoid it."

Annabelle introduced me to six or eight others as well. Too many to remember. All of them hoping that someone, anyone, knew how to turn down the air-conditioning. Leo did, but her departure, I'm sorry to say, freed up Chad Roe. The actor nailed me at the coffee pot.

"Hoagy, nice to see you again, man," he said warmly and earnestly.

"I don't believe we've met."

"I did *Streetcar* with Merilee at the Long Wharf," he reminded me, moving in for the kill. "But, hey, I guess that was years ago, huh? How's your novel coming?"

Possibly I'm not being fair to Chad Roe. He really wasn't a terrible guy. He was sincere, decent, politically and environmentally correct, solid, nice. It's just that he was, well, too much of all of those things. A big oaf. A clod. Early in his career, he had been dubbed the next Redford. Never happened. He didn't have the talent, just the looks. Still had them. Even at forty-whatever he remained maddeningly perfect looking—big and strapping and boyish in his blue chambray work shirt, faded jeans, and running shoes. The posture was perfect, the tummy flat, the hair still blond. Possibly it was thinning a bit at the temples and crown, but that may just have been my imagination. Or wishful thinking. The camera always liked Chad a lot. He had a jaw you could chop wood with and one of those automatic matinee-idol smiles that was all sparkling white teeth—sixty of them at least—and sincere blue eyes. And then there was his dimple. It was in his right cheek, and it showed whenever he smiled just so. Which he did with calculated regularity. *Working the dimp* was what Merilee had called it. It was a habit with him. So was clinging. He always stood just a little bit too close when he was talking to you, forcing you to back away from him. No use—he'd just keep coming. He was always anxious to talk. He was always needy. He was, let us not forget, an actor.

"Hoagy, I want you to know, straight out, that it's not me," he informed me solemnly.

I started backing away. He stayed chest to chest with me. "What's not you, Chad?"

"I'm not the father. Merilee and I were, *are,* friends. But that's all we are. Were. I mean, we've never—"

"I see." Chad was married to an actress himself. Brenda something. They had twins. "I appreciate hearing that from you, Chad. Means a lot."

"Sure, man. Sure." He moved in closer.

I moved back, until something ugly happened—I hit wall. I was trapped now. Doomed.

Chad worked the dimp. "It changed everything for me when I heard you were joining the show. Lyle kept telling me about all of the serious things he wanted to do this season, but I have to admit I was skeptical—until I heard about you. I was genuinely surprised."

"As I was."

"Pleasantly, I mean."

"As I wasn't."

"I mean, you're . . . how else can I put this—you're a *guy.*"

"Seem to be, so far."

"You're somebody I can *talk* to about Rob. Have lunch with, go to Mets games with—"

"I'm more of a Yankee fan, actually."

"I have so many ideas for him." Chad plowed on, undeterred. Nothing could stop this man, short of a sharp blow to the skull from a ball peen hammer. "He needs humanizing. He needs to be, I don't know, more of a . . ."

"A guy?" I suggested.

"Exactly. What do you think about rock climbing?"

"I suppose it's fine for some people. Me, I've always preferred the relative safety of the lobby of the Algonquin and a nice glass of—"

A huge cheer interrupted me. The King had arrived, masked and gloved, along with his beloved queen, Katrina, who was decked out in a sleeveless leopard-skin leotard, hot pink tights, and gold-colored spiked heels. Her hair was done up in a rather severe bun and she wore a pair of heavy black-framed glasses. All of which made her look a little like Mamie Van Doren showing up for her first day of law school.

"I meant for Rob," Chad said doggedly, barely noticing their entrance. "His hobby is rock climbing. It might give him that inner calm those guys have. Guys who stare death in the face. I once played a test pilot on *The Love Boat,* and he was like that. *Calm.* A climber'd have those strong hands, too. And wear the boots and stuff. What do you think, Hoagy?" He worked the dimp. "Want to talk about it over sushi today?"

"I'm afraid Hoagy can't," Lyle replied for me. He'd worked his way over to us, and was clearly peeved. "He'll be in rewrites. Would you excuse us a moment, Chad?"

"Sure, sure," said Chad pleasantly. "Say, Lyle, I still have some questions about my character."

"Later," Lyle blustered. "We'll talk about it later."

"But that's what you said on the phone last—"

"We'll talk about it later!" he roared.

"Okay, Lyle," said Chad, backing off. "Later." Mercifully, he moved away.

"You don't wanna talk to that guy," Lyle growled at me through his mask.

"Hey, tell me something I don't already know."

"I'm serious, pal," he insisted. "I don't want you talking to him. I want him speaking to me and me only. Got it?"

"No, I'm afraid not, Lyle. I speak to whomever I want to. Last I heard there was still a Constitution, and this was still American soil."

"You're not on American soil. You're on *my* soil."

"I may have to quote you on that one."

"Help yourself," he snapped.

"I generally do." I couldn't believe it—I was actually standing there fighting for my inalienable right to speak with Chad Roe.

Lyle's chest rose and fell. "Look, I want you involved. I

do. I just want your input filtered through me, that's all. So he gets one clear signal." Lyle glanced around at the others, then edged in closer to me. Everyone, it seemed, wanted to get close to me that morning. "What do you think about my sweater, huh?" he asked, his voice hushed.

"Gwen figures one of the crew took it. Big collector's item."

Lyle shook his huge, round head. "Don't kid yourself, man. That was no robbery."

"What was it then?"

"A warning," he replied, with total certainty. "I'm right and this proves it."

"Proves what, Lyle?"

"Somebody in this fucking room wants me off the air. And they aren't giving up." He stabbed himself in the chest with a fat, gloved thumb. "Well, neither am I, Hoagy. They *aren't* gonna win. I won't let 'em, ya hear me? I *won't* give 'em the satisfaction. They'll never, ever—"

"I need you, Lyle," Leo broke in gruffly. "I have a problem—with Chad."

Lyle rolled his eyes. "Now what?"

"It's about the john in his dressing room," she replied.

Lyle stared at her. "He hasn't *got* a john in his dressing room."

"Exactly," she responded wearily. "He has to use the same men's room out by the stairs that the crew uses. He says it's filthy. Actually, the word he used was revolting. Plus all of the extras dress in there on tape day and he's really uncomfortable about that, because he'll be spending a lot of time in there." She lowered her voice. "It seems the man has a . . . nervous colon."

"Why is Chad Roe's colon my problem?"

"He claims it'll affect his performance," she said. "He needs privacy to collect himself before he goes on. If he has to share a bathroom with everyone he won't get it."

Lyle ran a gloved hand through his red curls, exasperated. "I can't do anything about that. No one has their own john."

"Fiona has her own," Leo pointed out.

"Fiona's been here three seasons."

"You have your own."

"Well, I'm not installing one for him."

"You installed one for Katrina."

"Katrina's different," fumed Lyle. "She's an executive."

"Then how about sharing yours with him?" she asked.

"What?!"

"You won't even see him," she pressed. "He can use the outside door—it opens right out into the main office. He won't have to go inside your dressing room at all."

"It's *my* john!" Lyle raged. "Mine! I don't want *his* germs all over it. Why would I want that, huh?" He shuddered. *"No!* I forbid it!"

"Fine," Leo said shortly. "I'll tell him."

"Wait," he commanded, glancing at the breakfast buffet. "Who sent that fruit basket?"

"God did," she replied.

"Get rid of it—microbe city."

"Yes, Lyle." She carried it off.

Lyle shook his head in disgust. "Totally unreal. Where does it stop, huh? What next?" He shot me a cold look. "Remember what I told you, Hoagy. Don't talk to him."

"What if we run into each other in the men's room?"

He didn't answer me. Annabelle was right—whatever Lyle didn't want to hear he didn't hear. He wandered off.

Katrina was busy playing hostess. Each and every person got a hug, a kiss, and a squeaky "We're gonna have *so* much fun!" Randy, the art director, also got a paper napkin with a drawing on it. "My ideas for the set of Rob's apartment," she informed him. "Just in case we ever build one." She left him staring at it in wide-eyed horror.

When she got over to the writers she steered around Tommy, who was busy curling his lip at her. Not a major fan.

Bobby, on the other hand, was a goner. He gaped at Katrina Tingle like a lovestruck fourteen-year-old. She dragged him to his feet and hugged him and squeaked, "God, you're so cute!" All he could do was give her a feeble grin. And blush.

"Ba-boom, ba-boom, ba-boom," Tommy muttered as she went ootsie-fooing off, hooters heaving. Then he turned to Bobby and said, "That a yardstick in your pocket, Bobster, or are you just glad to see me?"

Bobby dove back into his script, blinking furiously.

Katrina carefully sidestepped Leo Crimp, refusing to so much as make eye contact with her former boss. When she got to me she lit up and cried, "It's Hoagy!"

Hugging her was somewhat like running smack into a pair of leopard-skin water balloons. I practically bounced off the woman.

"Lyle is so glad you're here," she whispered. "He's incredibly nervous about this episode. It's *so* personal." She deposited a wet kiss on my neck. "And I'm glad you're here, too."

There was another big cheer when The Munchkins, Casey and Caitlin, arrived with Amber. They were an impossibly cute little pair of moppets with soft blond hair, tiny noses, and huge brown eyes. Casey was six, his sister five. Both reacted with pure delight at the sight of Lulu. She let out a low moan when she spotted them scampering her way, and skittered under the table. They went under there with her, tugging at her ears and making a big fuss, all of which she suffered in stoic silence. Amber, a taut, toothy Park Avenue blonde in her early forties, came over, too. Amber wore her hair back in a ponytail and no makeup or nail polish. Her face and hands were weathered by the outdoors, nearly leathery. But it was good leather, the kind that ages well. And there were strong bones underneath. She was dressed in jodhpurs and gleaming black riding boots and a white silk blouse buttoned at the throat. I wasn't sure if she was affecting the severe Claremont Riding Academy look or the severe Erich von Stroheim look. I do know she carried herself with great authority and confidence, and wore no monocle. And I felt quite certain she owned a Range Rover.

"You used to play squash at the Racquet Club with Niles," she informed me, gripping my hand. Hers was firm and a helluva lot drier than Bobby's. "Niles Walloon. I was married to him. I'm not anymore."

"That makes us even," I said. "I'm not a member of the Racquet Club anymore." Largely because of dullards just like Niles Walloon, a stiff-necked commodities trader, very old money. Everyone called him Walloon the buffoon.

"Do you belong anywhere now?" she asked, faintly condescendingly.

"I try not to."

Amber nodded her approval. "Tony, my new husband, isn't a club sort of person at all. He sculpts. Couldn't care less about the social world." She glanced down at her kids, who were still playing with Lulu. "I've never been lucky enough to work with Merilee, but I admire her work enormously."

"Are you working on anything now?" I asked.

She flared her nostrils at me slightly. "No, I'm afraid a lot of the money for good, innovative theater has dried up recently."

"I understand you'd like to direct TV."

"If I could get the opportunity. The sitcom form is so full of potential, such a marvelous, marvelous platform. My kids love it here. They have a wonderful time." She gazed around at the staff with an air of fond, patrician benevolence, the same kind of look she might get while observing a busload of welfare kids on their first trip to a petting zoo. "These are not very mature people. I sometimes think Casey and Caitlin are the two oldest people here. But they absolutely adore Lyle."

"And you?"

She raised an eyebrow at me. "I think Lyle Hudnut is a genius. Don't you?"

I left that one alone. When I hear the word genius I tend to think of Edison, Picasso, Gershwin, me. Not Lyle Hudnut. My silence made Amber uncomfortable. She poured herself coffee. "Don't believe what you hear about me. I'm completely over Lyle. Unlike someone else around this place."

"Meaning who?"

She let that one slide on by. "I was at sea after Niles and I split up. Lyle was, for a time, a life preserver. But I've taken control of my own life now. I have Tony. I have the kids. I have *me*." She forced a smile. "Everything is fine now."

"I see." People who keep trying to convince you that everything is fine are trying even harder to convince themselves. And failing. "That must be nice," I added.

"Oh, it is. It most definitely is." And with that she went off to chat with Gwen, the costumer. They seemed to be good pals.

Fiona Shrike showed up last. Leading ladies always do, so they can make an entrance. They have to cause a fuss. Have to be noticed. Don't believe what you read—aging isn't what actresses fear most in life. Being ignored is. Fiona made a great show of greeting Chad first so as to let him—and everyone else—know just how thrilled she was that he was on board. Then she made her way over toward me. Fiona was a small, extremely slender woman. I doubt she weighed more than ninety-five pounds. Her *Uncle Chubby* character, Deirdre, was demanding and fierce. Much of the show's comedy came from her ability to intimidate Chubby, even though Lyle was a foot taller and outweighed her by two hundred pounds. In so-called real life, Fiona was no toughie. She was quite dithery and otherworldly, the kind of woman who would keep pet snakes and paint her fingernails black. If she had any. She didn't. What she had were ten chewed stumps. Also an amazing repertoire of involuntary shudders and gurgles. The woman was as squirmy as a chihuahua. Remarkably, she was able to shut it all off when she performed. Her face was delicate and fine-boned. Without makeup she looked fragile and a great deal older, the lines in her face etched deep. She was, after all, no kid. She was a twenty-year veteran of improv, Broadway, and television. Most recently, she had spent the summer touring in a much-publicized all-girl *Odd Couple* with Delta Burke. She had on a white silk camp shirt, flowered linen vest, jeans, and bedroom slippers. Her hair, which was henna-colored, fell to her chin in a sort of blunt pageboy.

"You're the new feelings writer," she said to me softly, tipping her head forward so that her hair shielded her face, rather like a curtain. She didn't do that on camera, either.

"Feelings," I affirmed. "Nothing more than feelings."

"They're so very important." She shuddered, as if someone had just dropped something very cold or very alive down her bare back. "We all have to find our emotional cores." She began to claw at the cuticles of her left hand with the nails of her right. They were already puffy and red, and she wore Band-Aids on two of them. "Noble believes that's what's wrong with us. That we haven't."

"So that's it," I said. She had recently married her spiritual advisor, a touchy-feely yogi-to-the-stars named Noble Gesture, who previously had developed condos in Arizona under the name Sherman Finkel. "Have you found yours?"

"I have. And it's ugly. I'm selfish. A total bitch." She paused, clawing at herself. "You seem very . . . spiritual."

"I'm not, and your hand is bleeding."

She had drawn blood. A vampire would go crazy around this woman. "Oh, it always does that," she said casually, ignoring it. "No, you *do,* Hoagy. You have a strong aura. You're so . . . *you.*"

"Better me than some guy with an inferior wardrobe."

"A piece of advice about Lyle." She tipped her hair in front of her face. "The line between performer and character has been erased. Lyle *is* Chubby—a big lonely slob who desperately wants to belong. A failure."

"I'd hardly call Lyle a failure."

"In his own eyes he is." Fiona glanced over at him. He was talking to Sam, his A.D. "Believe me, that is not a happy man."

"You know him better than anyone." And what a fun, relaxing couple they must have been to hang out with.

"I know him too well," Fiona said. "And I hate him."

"Yet you stick around."

"I'm also very fond of the man. Is that so strange?"

"I guess I'm old-fashioned. I believe in not liking the people I hate. I hope you and I will be able to talk about his past for the book."

She frowned. "That's not in my contract."

"It would make Lyle happy."

"That's not in my contract either." She gurgled. Not pleasant. Sounded like a death rattle. "Will you listen to me? What a bitch. Let me ask Noble about it, okay? He's *so* evolved. I clear everything with him. This morning, for instance, he said today was a really good day for me to release my spontaneous side. Which is *so* perfect, being that it's the first day of rehearsal. Amazing timing, isn't it?"

"Amazing. And how do you feel about Deirdre getting herself a boyfriend?"

"Thrilled," she answered, without hesitation. "I've been after Lyle to let her date for the past two seasons. She never, ever dates. She's this weird, pent-up nun. But he wouldn't do it because it would take attention away from him. For me, Rob is a godsend. I can show Deirdre vulnerable. Show her girlish. I can *stretch.*"

"And how do you feel about Chad?"

"I love Chad. We were in *The Ritz* together on Broadway ages ago. He's solid as can be, as long as he stays within himself. Y'know, doesn't try to do too much." She leaned in to me, voice hushed. "Just remember to throw me the funny lines and him the straight ones. He's death when he tries to get a laugh."

"ALL RIGHT EVERYBODY!" Lyle called out, clapping his gloved hands together. *"LET'S GET STARTED!"*

"Marjorie's not here yet, Lyle," Leo pointed out.

"Hey, I'm not holding up my rehearsal for some lousy network," he grumbled. "C'mon, let's take our places."

It was like taking your place at a huge dining table. Lyle sat at one end, his bulk occupying space for three. His two lieutenants, Leo and Katrina, sat on either side of him. His writing staff—The Boys, The Kids, and the first major new literary voice of the 1980's—sat at the opposite end, Lulu under me with her head on my right foot. Fiona, Chad, and The Munchkins were seated across from each other so they could make eye contact while they read. The assorted guest players, including the guy from the singing muffler commercial, were grouped around them. Production people filled the remaining seats at the table, as well as a row of folding chairs that had been set up against one wall. Naomi closed the door.

"Welcome back," Lyle began, playing genial host. "I hope you all had a good summer. Smelled the flowers and soaked up the sun and ate corn on the cob and all that good stuff." He paused, for comic effect. "On account of not one of ya is gonna see daylight again until *February!*"

This drew a rousing laugh from his minions. Muck and Meyer dutifully faked their orgasms. So did Annabelle, who possessed a hearty *huh-huh-huh* that came up like a hiccough. Bobby sat there in tight-lipped silence. Me, I just wanted to go back to France.

Lyle turned to Casey and Caitlin. "Did you have a good summer, Munchkins?" he asked, blue eyes twinkling.

"We sure did, Lyle," they replied, in unison.

"What'd you do?" he wondered, doting on them.

"I learned how to ride a horse," said Casey. "His name was Ghost."

Lyle shook his head in amazement. "You kids aren't real. You're straight out of a Norman Rockwell painting."

Amber sat against the wall with the runners, beaming. "And how about you, Caitlin?" Lyle asked. "What'd you do?"

"I played with Archie, my new kitten," Caitlin replied. Innocently, she asked, "What did *you* do, Lyle?"

Everyone in the room froze, instantly uncomfortable.

Lyle cleared his throat. "Me?" He scratched his chin under his mask. "I mostly played with myself."

It was all a setup. A prearranged ice-breaker. And a triumph. The entire *Uncle Chubby* family roared its appreciation, applauded. Because their fallen hero was back—bloodied but on his feet. And able to laugh at himself. He winked at Caitlin, who happily returned the wink, pleased that their little gag had worked so well. She didn't understand it, of course. Too young. She only knew that everyone laughed and that Lyle was pleased.

"We've got some changes around here this season," announced Lyle, getting down to business. "First off, we got ourselves a new coexecutive producer, and she's somebody all of ya already know—Katrina Tingle." He put his arm around her. "Fast rise up the ladder, kid," he teased. "You must be doing something right."

"Or someone," Tommy Meyer muttered under his breath.

Leo was suddenly very busy with her script and her stopwatch. She would not look up.

Katrina folded her hands before her on the table and raised her chin. She reminded me of a little girl about to introduce her experiment at a science fair. "I'm really looking forward to working with all of you this season," she began.

Tommy let out a small squeak, barely audible. Marty snickered. Annabelle kicked Marty under the table. Marty kicked her back. The three of them had gone back to their roots—class clowns. Bobby, on my right, would have none of it. He sat there burning with artistic purity, and blinking. I could hear his eyelids flutter. It was like sitting next to a moth.

"Titles don't mean a thing to artists," Katrina squealed. "And that's what all of us are—artists. What matters is we care about what we do, and we care about each other. I personally hate divisiveness. I hate, hate, hate it. We have to treat each other with respect and love. If we don't, we can't win. If we do, we can't lose!" She paused. "I just hope we can all stay friends. Thank you." It was a bizarre little pep talk, something of a cross between Knute Rockne and Shannen Doherty.

Lyle patted her hand. "Nice going, kid. And I think I speak for everyone when I say you've definitely got the biggest pair of cazongas of any producer in network television history. Moving right along . . ." he said, over the laugh. "Say hello to the newest member of our writing staff, Stewart Hoag."

Everyone smiled at me. I smiled back. Not one of the things I'm best at.

"Frankly," Lyle confessed, "Hoagy was forced on us. We're an equal opportunity employer and the law says we gotta have someone on the writing staff who's over five feet six." More laughter. "I'd also like to welcome those cast members who are here with us for the week," said Lyle, glancing around the table at them. "You're in for a unique experience. We hope you enjoy being a part of our family. Anything we can do to make you feel more comfortable, let us know."

"You could pay us," joked the singing muffler actor.

Which got a big laugh, though not from Lyle. He shot him The Scowl. Before he relaxed and whined, "I do the jokes around here."

Which got an even bigger laugh, naturally.

"I've saved our most significant new addition for last,"

Lyle declared. "Someone who I'm very, very excited about. As I'm sure we all are."

Chad smiled warmly at everyone. He was better at it than me. That damned dimp helped.

"Contrary to what you may have heard," Lyle said, a bit defensively, "it was *my* idea to introduce a new character to our show. A fella for Deirdre. I've always known exactly who I wanted for the part—an actor whose strength and intelligence and basic human decency have shined through every single performance he's ever given . . . Unfortunately, Donald Sutherland wasn't available." He waved off the laugh. "Seriously, I'm so thrilled to have this man here. And when I told God he was my first and only choice, God was just as excited as I was. Please welcome a man who's going to make a major, major contribution to *Uncle Chubby* for years to come. Joining us in the role of Rob Roy Fruitwell is . . ." Lyle frowned. "What's your name again . . . ?" More laughs. "Chad Roe, everybody!"

Major applause. Chad acknowledged it gratefully, working the dimp. The man was really something. A political future was not out of the question.

"I'd just like to say one more thing," Lyle added. "On a personal note. Maybe it's not necessary . . ."

"But I'm gonna do it anyway," muttered Tommy, running a gelid hand through his white tuft of forelock.

"But I'm gonna do it anyway," Lyle stated. "Because, well, you all know that we almost didn't make it back this season. And you all know why." It got very quiet in the rehearsal room. The only sound was Fiona gurgling. "A lot of people thought we were finished. For a while there, I was one of those people." His eyes welled up with tears. "Your support was the only thing that kept me going through the hardest few months I've ever had in my life. You people, you're the only ones who stood by me. . . ."

"Because you pay us to," Marty murmured quietly.

"Knowing you were pulling for me kept me *alive,*" Lyle went on, emotionally. "And I'd like to thank each and every one of you from the bottom of my heart. It's because of you that we're back." He paused significantly, holding everyone's attention. Knowing he would. "And now that we are, boys and girls, *we are gonna make us some noise!* We're gonna do television like nobody's done it before. Important television. Gutsy television. We're holding *nothing* back. And America is gonna sit up and take notice. Because this . . . this is *our Emmy season!*" The man was working the room now, directing his ass off. "Is that okay with you, people? Huh?"

They answered him with cheers. They clapped their hands. Stomped their feet. Pounded the table. Though it wasn't a table at all anymore. It was a balloon, and Lyle was lifting it up into the air with his words and his willpower. Almost like a form of creative levitation. A common preproduction ritual. In cruder circles, they call it the circle jerk.

"I'm very, very proud of the episode we're about to read," Lyle said, when it was quiet again. "It was written by The Boys, Muck and Meyer. And I'm not exaggerating when I say it's the best first draft I've ever read in my entire career. It's not just howlingly funny. It has taste, it has humanity. It's *real,* and I consider it a privilege to—"

The door burst open. An uncommonly tall and slender and leggy young woman came striding in.

"Shit, it's Chuckles," grunted Tommy.

"Sorry I'm late, Lyle," she apologized coolly. "I was in a daytime programming meeting and simply couldn't get out of it."

"Class, say good morning to Marjorie," commanded Lyle, adopting the tone of a stern schoolmaster.

"Good morning, Marjorie!" everyone sang out, as she took her seat next to The Munchkins.

Marjorie Daw of the network had large, liquid green

eyes, a swanlike neck, and ash blond hair cut in a short, bouncy style *Seventeen* magazine would no doubt call "spunk 'n' sass." She handled herself as if she'd spent her formative years walking around with a book balanced on top of her head. Every inch of her was erect and under control. Perfect posture. Perfect poise. Perfect grooming. She was your classic goody-goody, the kind who looked like she hadn't done a single spontaneous, reckless, or fun thing in her entire life. The kind whom little boys of all ages like to splatter mud on. All that was missing was the white gloves, and I wouldn't have been shocked if she had a pair in her bone-colored Coach bag, which went with the bone-colored career-girl pumps, the double-breasted ivory gabardine Brooks Brothers blazer, the long, slim, glen plaid skirt, the demure white silk blouse and the single strand of pearls— faux, judging by the way the light hit them. Or didn't. She wore clear nail lacquer on her fingernails. No lipstick or other makeup. Her complexion was flawless, her features young and softly defined, as if there were no bones underneath the skin. She looked very familiar to me, though I couldn't imagine why.

"The woman never laughs," Marty advised me under his breath. "The ideal network exec to supervise a comedy."

"Which, fortunately, isn't a problem with this show," cracked Tommy.

"How's God, Marjorie?" Lyle asked her, his eyes twinkling with mischief. He was going out of his way to make her uncomfortable.

"Godfrey is very well, thank you, Lyle," she replied, steadfastly refusing to employ her boss's nickname. "Number two son had an ear infection, but it cleared up." She had an unusually precise way of speaking, each word carefully weighed as if she were delivering a valedictory address. She reached into her briefcase and removed a Cross pencil. Also her reading copy of the script, which she'd marked up heavily.

The Boys shot each other a look of fear and loathing.

"All set, Marjorie?" asked Lyle.

"Yes, Lyle. Thank you." She whispered hi to Annabelle. They were evidently chummy. Me she smiled at. I smiled back. Lulu immediately let out a low, threatening growl at my feet. She sensed trouble. Possibly it was those green eyes. Merilee has green eyes.

"Okay, start the stopwatch, Leo," Lyle commanded briskly. "Let's take this baby for a little spin and see how she handles. . . ."

Three

I love this script!" Lyle exulted afterward, when everyone but the writers, Marjorie, and Katrina had filed out. "Every beat is absolutely, totally perfect. Neil Simon would be proud to have his name on it. We're not changing a word." He shot a fierce look down the table at Marjorie, defying her to contradict him. "Not one word."

In fact, the reading had gone quite well. Everyone had laughed at all of the right places. Chad's handling of Rob Roy Fruitwell had been surprisingly charming. All of which meant nothing. What mattered was how it played before an audience that wasn't on the *Uncle Chubby* payroll. What mattered were those notes that were scrawled all over Marjorie's script. God's envoy had sat there impassively throughout the entire reading, her emerald eyes betraying nothing. She would make an excellent poker player. Most network executives would. They only lack for one element—nerve.

"I thought there were a few minor dents," said Marty, glancing down at his notepad.

Lyle waved him off with a gloved hand. "We'll fix those on the floor. No point in—"

"I'd like to hear what the writers have to say, Lyle," Marjorie interrupted, quietly but firmly.

Lyle gave her The Scowl from behind his surgical mask. Disgustedly, he threw down his pencil and crossed his huge arms. "Okay, fine. Go ahead."

"First act, end of scene one," began Marty. "We need a

stronger beat when he gets stuck out on the porch in the rain. 'I hate my life' doesn't play."

"I'm, like, we could move the Chia Pet gag there," suggested Annabelle. "It got a huge laugh."

Marty: "What's funnier than a Chia Pet?"

Tommy: "A Thighmaster?"

Marty: "We'll work on it."

Bobby said nothing. Just gripped his script tightly, blinking.

Marty leafed through his script. "I'd also like to take another whack at the scene where Chubby and Rob fix the dishwasher together. We've got our Ruth Gordon gag and not much else. Rob needs more attitude."

"I didn't *get* your Ruth Gordon gag," Katrina squeaked. "I mean, where's the irony, comedically speaking?"

"It's a guy thing," growled Tommy, his complexion turning bluer. "You'd get it if you had a penis."

"It's a reference to *Harold and Maude,*" Marty replied pleasantly, smiling his smile at her. Clearly, the man went home and whipped small animals. Kittens, maybe.

"I think we should explain that," she maintained doggedly. "So people will get it."

Tommy rolled his eyes. "It won't be funny if we stick the title of the movie in there."

"It's not funny now," she insisted, her little voice trembling.

"I know what's funny, Katrina!" Tommy snarled, furious. "That's why I get paid! To know what's funny! If I say it's funny, it's *funny!*"

Katrina swallowed, struggling to control herself. "Look, I don't think you guys are addressing yourselves to what's really wrong with this script."

"Gee, I could have sworn I just heard Lyle say it was perfect," Tommy pointed out bitterly.

"Well, *I* say you're totally missing the point of what *Uncle Chubby* is about now," she argued.

The Boys exchanged a look.

"Which is what, Katrina?" Marty's voice was husky, with dread.

"It's about the six million American kids who will go to bed hungry tonight." She was back up on the soapbox. "It's about the sixteen million who have no medical coverage of any kind. It's about teen suicide and drug addiction and—"

"I'm, like, don't get me wrongola, but where do the jokes come in?" wondered Annabelle with fish-eyed confusion.

Katrina considered this, Lyle beaming at her like a proud parent. "We're past jokes," she replied. "We have a public responsibility here. And from now on, we're going to meet it. That's what we're about. We're not about *comedy* anymore. We're about *dramedy*. Understood?"

The Boys stared at her in horror. Annabelle's mouth was open, but nothing was coming out.

It was Bobby who broke the silence. "I-I think that's g-great," he blurted out.

The Boys shot him a look. So did Katrina. Hers was grateful. Theirs wasn't.

"I-I for one will be thrilled to t-tackle serious issues," he sputtered. "In fact, I-I already have an idea for a story that would be perfect for—"

"Don't pitch in front of the network, Bobby," commanded Lyle harshly. "You're not good enough."

Bobby froze for an instant. Then he jumped to his feet, kicking his chair over, and stormed out of the rehearsal room. Annabelle watched him go with motherly concern. Lyle cackled.

Tommy stabbed his finger at Lyle. "Exactly who is doing the talking here, Lyle? Is this you talking or is it her? We better get this straight right now. Because the last I heard this was supposed to be a sitcom, not Bill fucking Moyers!"

"Yeah, Lyle," Marty chimed in. "What the hell is this?"

Annabelle nodded in agreement, her lacquered head-dress nodding right along with her. "I'm, like, yeah!"

Sensing mutiny, Lyle held out his gloved hands, palms up. A placating gesture. "What this is is normal, healthy, creative give-and-take," he replied soothingly. "Something for us folks to work out among ourselves. No sense keeping Marjorie tied up here for it." He got to his feet with a loud grunt. "We'll pick this up again later. Right, Katrina?"

"But, Pinky," she whined. "You promised me I'd get to—"

"*Right,* Katrina?" he thundered, his eyes turning into murderous blue slits.

Her own eyes widened with fear. Too much fear. She was terrified of the man. I wondered why. "Right, Lyle," she whispered in her little girl voice. "Whatever you say."

"All right," he said cheerily. "If that's all, we can break for lunch now and then we'll—"

"That is not all, Lyle," Marjorie Daw stated stiffly. "I still have Godfrey's notes, as well as my own."

"Just give 'em to me after tomorrow's run-through," he said, brushing her aside. A bullying maneuver. "That way you'll be able to visualize it better."

"We have serious problems with this script, Lyle," she insisted, holding her ground. "And they have to be addressed *now.*"

He glared down at her. Marjorie glared right back up at him, her jaw firmly set, her back straight. She would not be steamrolled. No cupcake she.

Lyle plopped back down into his chair. "Okay, fine," he said with weary condescension. "Let's hear the word of God. By all means."

"On the positive side," Marjorie reported, enunciating each word clearly and carefully, "we feel very good about that scene in Act Two when the kids are watching TV together. Their scenes test very high with audiences. They would like to see even more of them if that's possible."

Lyle said nothing. Just sat glaring at her like a petulant child. I had no doubt that behind his mask his lower lip was stuck out in a belligerent pout.

Marjorie turned a page in her script. She had lovely hands, her fingers long and gracefully tapered. She clasped them before her on the table, as if she were in prayer. I wondered if she always did this when she was delivering the word of God. "We're also high on the final scene, when Deirdre accepts Chubby for who he is. That's a very sweet scene."

"*I* wrote that scene," boasted Lyle. "Every word of it."

The Boys stared at him in stone-faced silence. Obviously, they did not agree.

"But we don't like how the story gets there," Marjorie continued. "We feel it's pitched much too heavily toward Chubby." At this Lyle began to redden. "Rob doesn't even arrive on camera until the second act. That seems awfully late."

"We can move the act break back a scene," offered Marty.

"We want him in much earlier, Marty," Marjorie said. "We want to see them spend the whole evening together."

The door opened. Bobby returned, his eyes red. He had been weeping. But he had his composure back now. He took his seat next to me. Lyle ignored him.

Tommy scratched his head. "You mean you want to see them eating dinner before the pool hall scene?"

"We don't feel good about the pool hall scene, Tommy," she replied primly. "In fact, we feel there's altogether too much emphasis on gambling. First, you have Chubby losing forty dollars to Jimmy the milkman on a horse. Then you have Deirdre, who's our moral compass, hustling the money out of Jimmy at pool. It's simply not appropriate for an eight o'clock show. Particularly for your return episode."

"So, what, the pool hall's out?" Marty wondered.

"Godfrey wondered if Rob could take her to a video arcade at the mall," Marjorie replied, with a perky smile.

"This is what, the nineties?" Tommy cracked sourly.

"We also feel *how* they meet should be more memorable," Marjorie plowed on determinedly. "Something of an event. What if it's not a blind date? What if they meet by accident?"

"I'm, like, you mean a meet cute?" asked Annabelle.

"I don't *do* meet cutes," Lyle said vehemently, as if he were discussing one of his bedrock personal beliefs, like the right to vote or bear arms. "I don't do chance encounters of any kind. That's shitcom." He shook his head at Marjorie, his anger mounting. "Okay, so far you *don't* like the gambling, you *don't* like how they meet, you *don't* like where they go. What else don't you people like, huh?"

Marjorie laid her hands out flat on the table, palms down, fingers spread. She looked down at them. "We're not happy with Rob. He doesn't fit in. Marty is right—he needs more attitude. There's simply nobody there, at least not on paper."

"Or in the flesh," cracked Tommy.

Lyle's fists were clenched now.

"Godfrey feels Rob's job doesn't give us enough," she added. "We'd like him to have one that can bring in stories. A wood shop teacher doesn't do a thing for us."

"Anything else, Marjorie?" asked Lyle, his voice now low and threatening.

"That about covers it, Lyle." Swiftly, Marjorie closed her pencil, took a deep breath, and held it, clenching her jaw. She was nailing sheets of plywood over her windows, preparing for the coming storm. It blew in right away. She knew her man.

"Okay, *fine!*" he roared. "Now *I'm* gonna say something! Now it's *my* turn! You people are *unreal*. Totally, absolutely unreal! You take all of the joy out of this business. Every bit of it! Rob Roy Fruitwell was *your* idea, not mine. *You* stuck me with him. Now you say he doesn't fit. Hey, guess what? I *told* you he didn't fit! I *told* you there was no place for him. But did you listen to me? *No!"*

"We're committed to Rob, Lyle," Marjorie said sternly, rising to his challenge. "Rob is here to stay. Accept him. Grow with him. I believe he can be an excellent addition to this show."

"Don't tell me what you believe," Lyle huffed at her. "My plumber knows more about good TV than you do. Know what you are, Marjorie? You're somebody who fucked her way to the middle."

Annabelle gasped. There was no other sound in the room.

The skin on Marjorie's face seemed to draw tighter against the bone, sharpening her soft features. Red splotches formed on her cheeks. But she held her ground. "I have a job to do, Lyle. And I am going to do it. You are not going to bully me. I am not going to run sobbing from this table. So you can just forget it. What we want is—"

"What you want is a page one rewrite," Lyle blustered.

"We want changes," she maintained.

"Or *what?"*

"We want changes," she repeated.

The two of them stared at each other in charged silence.

Marty stepped into it. "Okay, let's break it down. See where we are. How do they meet? Do we keep the blind date or don't we?"

"Let's hear from our new guy," commanded Lyle. "Let's hear from Hoagy."

They all turned to me anxiously. Lulu stirred at my feet. Even she wanted to hear this.

I tugged at my ear. "Well, what's Deirdre feeling?"

"Nausea, if she's watching this show," Tommy fired back instantly.

"A-Anger," Bobby replied, his voice a choked spasm. "I-I think she hates the whole idea of being fixed up with someone. L-Listen to those words—*fixed up.* She's not b-broken. She's fine. She's attractive, she's s-successful, she's . . ." He sputtered out, gasping for breath.

"I *like* that, Bobby," Katrina squealed approvingly. "That's very astute. And *so* ironic."

Bobby ducked his head bashfully.

"I like it, too," agreed Marjorie. "Blind dates make you feel ugly and unwanted. I know I hate going out on them."

Tommy said, "Well, as it happens, this is a show about Deirdre, not you." He sat up suddenly, turned to his partner. "Of course, we *could* do the ultimate blind date gag."

"Which is what?" asked Katrina.

"Hasn't been used since *Taxi.*" Marty was warming to the idea. "And that was twelve, fourteen years ago."

"What is it?" asked Marjorie.

"Rob's genuinely blind," Marty replied enthusiastically, pitching his ass off. "He's a *blind* blind date. Great gag, and it gives Rob just the kind of spin you're looking for. Plus it gets us into all sorts of serious issues about the handicapped, like Katrina wants."

"On the downside," cautioned Tommy, "we'll be locked into it."

"Unless we want to do an operation at the end of the season to restore his sight," countered Marty.

"This coming Monday," intoned Tommy gravely, "a very special *Uncle Chubby* . . .*"

"I love this!" squealed Katrina.

"We don't find out until next fall what happens," Marty went on excitedly. "Helluva summer cliffhanger. What do you think, Chief?"

Lyle considered it a moment, brow furrowed. "Let's not do that."

"Too limiting," agreed Tommy instantly.

"Snap-crackle-flop," admitted Marty, retreating from it.

"Okay, he works for the Internal Revenue Service," pitched Tommy, moving right along. Neither of The Boys was the least bit fazed by Lyle's turndown. Their job was simply to offer up possibilities, not to believe in one of them. Or in anything. It was scary. It was like being a lawyer. "And Deirdre gets this letter summoning her to headquarters. She thinks she's gonna get audited. She freaks, because she's such a stickler for keeping precise records. So she barges in with ten shoe boxes full of papers and really lets the IRS agent have it and—"

"Rob's the agent?" asked Marjorie.

Tommy nodded. "Turns out she just forgot to sign her return. After she apologizes for screaming at him, he asks her out."

"Or she asks him out," suggested Marty, playing to Marjorie's presence at the table.

"I *don't* wanna do a meet cute!" bellowed Lyle. "How many times do I gotta say it?! Besides, an IRS agent does even less for us than a shop teacher."

"Audiences do tend to dislike characters who work for the government," Marjorie pointed out, as if a survey had been commissioned on the very subject. Very likely one had been.

"He c-could be an old friend," sputtered Bobby. "Someone D-Dierdre and Chubby grew up with. She maybe went out with h-him once or twice in high school. They l-lost contact through the years, and now he's back in town and . . . and . . ."

Lyle started snoring loudly. He was a man who needed a whipping boy. Bobby was it. "I swear to God, Bobby, every time you open your mouth I feel like I'm listening to National Public Radio," he cracked, taunting him.

Bobby just gripped his script tightly, blinking, blinking.

I *got* it!" cried Marty, smacking the table triumphantly. "It's a natural! It's staring us in the face!"

"The only thing staring us in the face is cancellation," muttered Tommy.

"What is it?" asked Marjorie anxiously.

"We make *him* the milkman!" declared Marty. "Natural, right?"

Total silence. Deafening silence.

"Then again," Marty quipped, with admirable aplomb, "shit is natural, too. And you wouldn't want to watch it for thirty minutes a week."

"Whatta we do, Hoagy?" wailed Lyle mournfully. "Tell us. Don't hold nuttin' back."

They all looked at me again, beseechingly this time. They were hoping I somehow had it—the magic solution that would somehow make the network happy, Lyle happy, Katrina and The Boys all happy at the same time. Something each of them could live with—for better or wurst.

"I think there's absolutely nothing wrong with doing a blind date," I replied. "Provided you explore Deirdre's feelings about it ahead of time, as Bobby suggested. It might also be nice to hear how Rob feels about it, too. We'd like him more if we knew he was feeling insecure, possibly even intimidated—she is, after all, a lawyer. And she has children. That would scare a lot of men off."

"That plays," Marty said. "That would also give him something to do if we want to get him in the show earlier."

"Who does he unload on?" asked Marjorie, musing aloud. "Does he have a friend?"

"He's a yutz," replied Tommy. "How could he?"

"There's always Jimmy," suggested Marty.

"Again with the milkman," moaned Tommy.

"No, wait!" exclaimed Annabelle. "I love that. Check it out—I'm, like, Jimmy is literally delivering the story from one house to the other, like the milk. That's *extreme.*"

"W-Wonderful resonance," agreed Bobby. "Shades of Odets."

"That's Bernie Odets," cracked Tommy. "Used to write for the Skelton show."

Marty shook his head. "What are we saying? He lays it on

Chubby when the two of them are fixing the dishwasher together. *Chubby* is his friend. *He's* who Rob confides in."

"Mo' better," said Lyle approvingly.

"Okay, okay . . ." Marty started scribbling notes on a long yellow legal pad. "We stay with the blind date, but we still have to get Master Fruitwell in earlier. . . ."

Tommy: "We open the night before, instead of that morning. It's suppertime, okay? We do the usual domestic shit. . . ."

Marty: "Dishwasher's not working . . ."

Tommy: "Dishwasher's not working. . . . The phone rings . . . It's Rob. Chubby thinks he's a solicitor, hangs up on him. Rob calls back . . ."

Marty: "And we do the phone call. There's sparks. There's flirting. There's heat."

Tommy: "He asks her out for tomorrow night. She says yes."

"We can pretape his end," Lyle added, for Marjorie's benefit. "Won't even have to build a set. Randy can whip up a piece of backdrop in two seconds flat. Go on, Tommy, you're on a roll."

"That's a Kaiser roll," cracked Marty. "Lightly seeded."

"We cut to next morning," Tommy continued. "We still do Chubby losing Deirdre's forty bucks to Jimmy."

"Stop," objected Marjorie. "I told you that the gambling is—"

"We'll kill the pool hall," offered Marty, negotiating. "She and Rob can go somewhere else. But Chubby's got to blow the money on the horse. We need that. You can let us have it, can't you, Marjorie?"

She considered this gravely, lips pursed, her head cocked slightly to one side. Again I thought she looked familiar, and again I wondered why—I so seldom ran into her type anymore. Or at least I tried very hard not to. "Where do they go on their date?" she asked.

"I know where," Lyle replied. "We got a set for a Japanese restaurant left over from last season we never used. It's in the warehouse, all built and paid for. Can have it here by the end of the day."

"We'd have to hire Asian actors, Lyle," Katrina pointed out. "And pay off the ones we already have."

"Keep 'em around. No reason they can't be eating sukiyaki."

"We'll still need waitresses," she contended. "And costumes."

Lyle sat there making these short, flatulent noises with his lips behind his mask. "We make it into a bonus—it *was* a Japanese restaurant, now it's a Tex-Mex joint. Just opened. They haven't changed the decor yet. We can get in a joke about a Japanese business going broke, huh?"

"And what about the forty dollars Deirdre wins back from Jimmy?" Marjorie wondered doubtfully.

"She doesn't," Tommy replied. "Chubby loses it, period. Typical Chubby behavior. And she's genuinely pissed at him. Also typical."

"Whattaya say, Marjorie dear?" asked Lyle. "Can you live with it?"

Marjorie clasped her hands and gazed up at the ceiling, mulling it over in silence. Or maybe she was looking to Him for an answer. The silence grew longer, The Boys more anxious. Finally she shifted in her chair and cleared her throat. "We can live with it, Lyle."

"Yesss!" exclaimed Marty, jumping to his feet. "Let's go, pardner, we got rewrites." He was halfway to the door before he stopped cold. "Shit."

Tommy was still struggling to get up out of his chair. "Shit what?"

"Shit, we still haven't got a job for Rob," Marty said miserably.

"Shit." Tommy slumped back into his seat.

Marty sat back down. Silence followed. Now a number

of people were gazing up at the ceiling. Until, slowly, they began looking you-know-where again.

I tugged at my ear. "Would someone tell me what's wrong with Rob being a wood shop teacher?"

"It doesn't give us enough," said Marty.

"He can't bring any stories in," said Tommy.

"Unless he cuts off a finger," said Marty.

"And we can only do that, what, ten times," said Tommy.

"I'm, like, it's boring."

"B-Bland."

"What if he taught health education?" I proposed. "That covers a lot of ground in a typical suburban high school—sex education, AIDS awareness, drugs, alcohol—"

"N-Nutrition," added Bobby, with great intensity. "Kids don't know how to eat right any more. We have an entire g-generation being raised on the Taco Bell instead of the L-Liberty Bell."

"I swear to God, Bobby," jeered Lyle, "one more line like that outta you and I'm taking out a gun."

"I *liked* that," protested Katrina.

"So, what, he's Mr. Novak?" asked Tommy.

"If you like," I replied.

"Who's that?" asked Katrina.

"A sixties classroom show starring the late Jimmy Franciscus," replied Marty.

"Wait, wait," said Annabelle. "You call him that because he's always late, right?"

"No, I call him that because he's dead." Marty thumbed his chin. "So Rob's the cool guy. The one that they can turn to when they're in trouble. He listens. He cares. He gets involved. All of which means he can drag a million stories in the door with him. I like this, Hoagy."

"Extreme!" cried Annabelle. "It'll even bring in the *Beverly Hills 90210* crowd!"

"Slam dunk," conceded Tommy.

"B-Brilliant."

"God was searching for a positive new direction," Marjorie responded cautiously. "We may have found it." Her way of voicing approval.

"I love it, I love it, I love it!" squealed Katrina. *Her* way. She got up and ran toward me with her arms outstretched and her hooters ajiggle, shades of Morgana, The Kissing Bandit. I didn't know whether to duck or run. Before I could do either she'd planted a hard, wet kiss on my right ear, temporarily deafening me.

Yes, everyone loved it. Everyone except for the one person who hadn't said a word. "Last time I looked I was still running this show," Lyle growled irritably.

Which chilled things considerably.

"What do you say, Chief?" asked Marty. "Great, huh?"

Lyle ran a fat gloved hand through his red curls and leaned back in his chair, which groaned under him. He glanced balefully around the table at everyone. "Try it," he said grudgingly. "Only don't get carried away. Remember we're not doing *To Mr. Fruitwell, With Love.* We're doing *The Uncle Chubby Show.*"

"For now," muttered Tommy under his breath.

The protestors were still out there on the sidewalk in front of the studio with their pickets. They seemed quieter and limper than they had that morning. Maybe it was the hot white summer sun and foul, heavy air. Maybe it was that the news cameras had bagged their footage for the day and moved on. I don't know. The cops just looked bored.

The Kids took me around the corner to Big Mama Thornton's for lunch, Chelsea's version of a shit-kicking Southern roadhouse. The walls were of aged barn siding and studded with dented hubcaps and chrome bumpers and old Louisiana license plates. There was sawdust on the floor, and Michael Bolton was not, happily, blasting over the stereo. John Lee

Hooker was—"Streets Is Filled with Women," from the Detroit sessions produced by Bernie Besman in the late forties.

Our waitress wore jackboots and a T-shirt and a great deal of crust around the edges. "Okay, don't tell me," she said hoarsely as she stomped over to us. To Annabelle she said, "Diet Coke." To Bobby she said, "Regular Coke, no ice." To me she said, "Gibson?"

"Never touch them. Make it an iced tea."

"I meant," she said, "is Mel Gibson the father?"

"With lemon," I added wearily. Lulu wanted to tear her throat out. "No sugar."

We all ordered pork barbecue with cole slaw and hush puppies. Lulu went for the fried catfish.

"Now, does she always eat with you in restaurants?" Annabelle asked, keenly interested.

"If that's where I happen to be eating."

"And what if you're at home? What does she eat then?"

"You don't want to know."

Bobby sat there quietly twisting his paper napkin around one knuckle, again and again, tighter and tighter. Origami for the clinically hostile.

"Was that a fairly typical notes session?" I asked him.

"P-Par for the course," he replied bitterly. "Most shows g-get ripped apart and thrown back together that way. That's w-why they don't make any sense half the time."

"Today's gang bang was maybe a bit more amped out than usual," Annabelle said, sucking on her Diet Coke through a straw. "I'm, like, now that Katrina's sitting in."

"Leo told me she thinks Katrina is pure evil."

"No way!" shrieked Annabelle. "Leo *would* say that."

"Why?"

"Because she let Leo love her."

"Y-You don't know that," Bobby blurted out.

Annabelle batted her eyes at him. "You are such a bunny."

"That's gossip," he insisted vehemently.

"I'm, like, Leo is gay," Annabelle explained for my benefit. "I'm not putting her down or anything. Just explaining. Katrina came in as an extra for a party scene last season. She was one of the dancers. She can dance for real. Used to be on *Club MTV,* I mean. And I'm, like, she still works out two hours a day just to hold onto her shape, which would go *so fast* if she let it. Anyway, Leo fell for her *extreme.* Gave her a full-time job. Got Gwen to buy some of her stupid jewelry for the show. And when the sublet ran out on Katrina's apartment, Leo let her move in with her. Bought her clothes, gave her extra spending money. I'm talking love here, okay?"

"Did the two of them—?"

"No!" replied Bobby, sharply.

"Nobody knows fer sure if they did the wild thing or not," said Annabelle. "Me, I wouldn't put it past Katrina. On account of, that woman is full of blah-blah-blah."

"Blah-blah-blah?"

"Shit. She led Leo on. Let her believe whatever she wanted to about her, okay? When the whole time she was just using Leo to get in the door. Soon as she spotted something better—Lyle—she went for it. Dumped Leo cold. Wham, zoom. Told her never to call her again. I heard she's done it before, too. With this musician she used to live with. She treats people like sponges, okay? Squeezes every last drop out of them. Check it out—Leo loved her. She *let* Leo love her. And that's a pretty shitty thing to do when you don't love a person back, if you ask me. Not that I'm a feelings specialist like you are, Hoagy. I do know Leo *hates* her. And hates Lyle for stealing her. And that's not gossip. That's fact."

"I'm surprised Leo has stayed around," I observed. "Why doesn't she quit?"

"Too illegit to quit," Annabelle replied. "She and Lyle have *so* many crooked deals cooked up together. No way she'd pull down those kind of bucks anywhere else. Besides, she's not the type to walk. She's the type to get even, if you know what I'm saying."

Our waitress brought our food. The barbecue was tangy and peppery and I was starved. Bobby ate his with his fork held underhanded and his face over his plate, like a little kid shoveling down a bowl of Maypo. Annabelle just nibbled.

"B-Boys will be halfway through their rewrite of Act One already," Bobby mentioned between forkfuls, glancing at his watch.

"They're awesome how fast they are," Annabelle agreed, nodding her headdress.

"They're total hacks," he sniffed. "B-Body-and-fender men. No commitment to their art."

"This isn't art," I reminded him. "It's television."

"T-Too damned cynical for their own good," he went on, with mounting intensity. "Tommy especially. I mean, Tommy's a really smart guy. And talented. But he b-believes in *nothing.*"

"And why do they stay around? Same reason as Leo?"

Annabelle shook her head. "It runs deeper than money," she hinted darkly.

"How much deeper?"

"D-Don't listen to her," Bobby argued, blinking at me. "It's strictly the money. They both have m-monster overheads. Marty's ex-wife, Beth, lives in West Nyack with their three teenage kids. And then he and his new wife, B-Brandy, have a baby and a four-year-old. Plus they just bought a house in the West V-Village. Tommy's oldest son, Ronnie, goes to Harvard. His daughter starts college next year. He's got a big house in Tarrytown. . . ."

"He commutes?" I asked.

"He never goes home," Annabelle replied. "At least not during the week. I'm, like, Tommy hates his wife. She is, after all, a woman. He stays in town at a really, really grungy hotel in Times Square. He likes to fuck hookers and go to porn movies. He and Lyle used to go to them together all the time." She made a face. "Tommy is . . . Tommy is . . ."

"Skeegee," I said. "He mentioned something about that." He had not, however, mentioned anything about how he and Lyle used to go to porn movies together. Not one word.

Bobby took a gulp of his Coke. "The point is there's nothing else that would p-pay them this kind of money. Especially in New York. Lyle's got the only sitcom going here. Everything else is done out of Los Angeles."

"And if they moved out there," Annabelle said, "they'd have to uproot their families and—"

"They'd get drop-kicked right out the door," said Bobby bluntly. "They're shlockmeisters. No style or vision of their own. Which is f-fine if you're twenty-five and working your way up, but they're over forty. Forty is *old* for TV."

"If you're forty you're part of the past," Annabelle concurred. "Forty is ancient. Forty is—"

"You can pull over and stop any time on this one." I sipped my tea. "You've staffed out there?" I asked Bobby.

He shoveled more barbecue. "I was on a N-Norman Lear show for a season. Hated it. I'm no sitcom writer. I'm a p-playwright. My first play, *Cold Storage,* was produced three years ago at Playwrights Horizons. Amber Walloon directed it. It was about a m-man who puts himself in cold storage when he can't figure out what to do with his l-life."

"It was brilliant," said Annabelle, nibbling at her corn bread.

"Lear's people saw it and flew me out there—paid me a shitload of money, too." He was starting to puff up, his arrogance seeping out as he got more relaxed. Bobby was not, I felt sure, someone I'd want to go out drinking with. "There were eight of us. They'd sit us all down in a room with the first draft and say, 'Okay, kids, we need t-twelve new punch lines.' We'd each write two or three per gag and initial them, then the executive producer would p-pick one. It was about as human as taking an SAT exam. And the *p-people*. They spend twelve hours a day on the lot talking about their show, their d-deal, other people's shows, other people's deals . . . I c-couldn't handle it. I was miserable. P-Plus it's way too far away from Boston."

"Got a girlfriend up there?" I asked.

"M-Morris Helfein, my shrink." He went back to twisting his napkin over his knuckle. "He's been helping me deal with my anger ever since I was thirteen. Like when I walked out of the notes session this morning. That was p-positive. I didn't let L-Lyle get to me. I went to the men's room, I controlled my feelings, and then I came back. I'd be lost without Dr. Helfein. I see him Saturday, Monday, and Tuesday mornings. I'll f-fly back up tonight and be back here before noon tomorrow for rewrites. I can do that from New York, but when I was in L.A., I c-could only see him Saturdays and Mondays. I had to fly back out and skip my Tuesday session, which was really tough."

"Expensive, too, I imagine."

"Still is. The shuttle c-costs a fortune." He reddened, blinking furiously. "To save money I stay with my m-m-mom when I'm up there."

"Lyle gives you a pretty hard time," I observed.

Bobby let out a short, humorless laugh. "Lyle thinks he's being nothing but good to me. He d-did give me a job, after all. I have Amber to thank for that. And he *is* trying to teach me the sitcom ropes, in his own cruel, abusive way. Maybe . . . Maybe I'm just not cut out for this business. B-Because all it's about is learning how to pitch. I want to learn how to write. I-I want to grow, and you don't from TV. You get much too used to reducing life to simple problems with simple, feel-good solutions that can be reached in twenty-two simple, feel-good minutes."

"Lyle seems to feel *Uncle Chubby* is the exception."

"That's his standard line," Annabelle scoffed. "That and about how he never sweetens."

"He does?"

"I'm, like, of course he does. He just won't call it sweetening. Because that would be him admitting a joke bombed. He can't. Check it out, he figures the laugh *belongs* there, okay? He *hears* it, okay? As long as he does, to him that's not sweetening."

"He always g-goes on and on about how he's d-doing a unique show," Bobby sputtered angrily. "B-Better than Neil Simon. Total bullshit. He knows *Uncle Chubby* sucks. He only says it t-to psych everyone up for the grind."

"Including himself?" I asked.

"Especially himself," Bobby replied. "If he ever stopped t-to think about how bad it was he'd b-burn out in a second." Bobby drained his Coke and smacked his glass down hard on the table, startling Lulu. "I should be doing g-good work," he groaned. "I should be doing theater."

"So why aren't you?" I asked him roughly. His self-pity was getting to me.

"You write a p-play and maybe a couple of hundred people hear your words," he replied bitterly. "If you're lucky and it runs a while, a f-few thousand. You live in a c-crummy studio apartment with roaches and no heat. Women won't have anything to do with you. Your family wonders what's wrong with you. You're a f-failure. You write a TV show and tens of millions of people hear your words and see your name on the screen. I made a hundred and ninety-seven thousand d-dollars last year, Hoagy. I have a two-bedroom apartment with a d-doorman and built-in bookshelves. Women want to go out with me. I've got everything a person could ask for— except for p-pride and self-respect. Because those *aren't* my words they're hearing. L-Lyle has rewritten them. Or The Boys have. Or the network has. They've been twisted, m-made cute . . . I've sold them away, for money. If I were stronger, I'd do nothing but plays. My words. My way. Only, I-I'm not that strong."

I turned to Annabelle. "And how about you?"

"Me, I'm, like, clam happy," she answered brightly. "Everyone I went to school with bageled out in the job world. Took meaningless, low-paying McJobs. They all sit around talking about downscaling, lessness. I'm, like, making more in one year than my father makes in five selling Oldsmobiles in Paramus. Plus, I *love* being in production. I get a buzz from it."

"And what do you get from Lyle?"

She pulled a pocket mirror out of her black leather drawstring bag and began to swab purple lipstick all over her mouth. She reminded me of a little girl playing at her mom's dressing table. "Lyle gave me my start, okay? I mean, I wrote a spec script and submitted it and next thing I know I'm on staff, okay? I'm, like, no way! I was about to take a job selling sportswear at Nordstrom's. So, I'm, like, totally grateful to him. Only, he's *so* extreme. Like last season he hired and fired me three times in the same week, okay? He's, like, 'You're too young and immature to get the show.' So I'm, like, out the door in tears, and he's, like, 'Hey, sit down—I just thought of the perfect story for you to write.' So I'm, like, 'You fired me.' And he's, like, 'You can't fire family.' So I scene it out and go in to pitch it to him and he's, like, 'Annabelle, what are *you* still doing here? I thought I fired you.' I mean, fer sure. Still, I can deal with that head shit, okay? What I can't deal with," she confessed, her dark button eyes flashing with anger, "is the way he's all the time in my face. Like he's my father. I can never forgive him for Lorenzo. That was *low*. We fell in love last season, Lorenzo and me. We met on the show. And when Lyle heard about it he called me into his office and he, like, *ordered* me to stop seeing him, strictly because Lorenzo's below the line."

"That's production jargon for blue collar," Bobby explained.

"Lorenzo's a cameraman, like his father," she went on. "Like that's not good enough for me or something. Like it's any of Lyle's goddamned business or something. I'm, like,

Lorenzo's the great love of my life. He sucks on my toes. He writes poetry. He cooks. And I'm, like, he's not a pinhead. He has his degree in pharmacology, F.U.''

"Excuse me?''

"Fairfield University. When he and I moved in together, Lyle *freaked.* Fired him from the show—for being 'difficult,' which he isn't. No way.''

"What is Lorenzo doing now?''

"He got on a soap for a while, filling in for a guy who was on sick leave.'' Annabelle looked away uncomfortably. "I'm, like, he's kind of free-lancing now, y'know? I mean, steady gigs are hard to find, especially if you've developed a bad rep. Which is totally unfair. Lorenzo's still bumming about Lyle. Hates him. I mean, the man's ruined his career. Or tried to. But, hey, as long as I'm working, we're cool.''

"And if you're not working?''

"I can always go out to L.A. and get a job.''

"Can he?''

"No,'' she confessed unhappily. "He's not in the L.A. union. He pretty much can't leave New York.''

"So you need *Uncle Chubby,* too, don't you?''

Annabelle shot a glance at Bobby. "Cut to the chase, Hoagy. We all need *Uncle Chubby.* It's our lifeline. The writers, the actors, everyone.''

"Including Marjorie?''

"Supervising *Uncle Chubby* is Marjorie's whole reason for being here,'' Annabelle replied. "She has some daytime stuff she oversees, but nothing that couldn't be handled by the West Coast. If *Uncle Chubby* goes off, she'll probably get the ax. If she can keep it on the air for another year or two, running smooth, she'll be made a vice president. Maybe even develop some new shows out of New York.'' Annabelle patted Bobby's hand. Her way of telling him to signal our waitress for the check. He tried, but the waitress ignored him. "Marjorie loved Lyle major, y'know. And he broke her poor little heart. She still isn't over him.''

"Yes, I believe Amber mentioned something about that."
For the third time Bobby tried to catch our waitress's eye
and failed. He was starting to blink and squirm in anguished
frustration. I couldn't take any more of it, so I honked Lulu's
big black nose with my shoe. She promptly sneezed, causing
our waitress to glance our way. Bobby signaled her, relaxed,
mission accomplished. Lulu snuffled in protest. She doesn't
like anyone to touch her nose. I assured her that it was an
accident. She bought it. Sometimes it's a plus having a partner whose brain is the size of a chick pea.

"Me, I never understood why Marjorie fell so hard for
Lyle," Annabelle confided, leaning forward over the table inti-
mately. "I'm, like, the man got off on being cruel to her. Still
does. She deserves better. Only, she scares most guys off. I
mean, she's a stone fox—in a wholesome, drop-dead sort of
way. Plus, she's kind of six or eight inches too tall for most of
the guys in television." Her eyes glittered at me. "But for the
right guy, she's Ms. Right."

"Any particular reason you're looking directly at me?"
"I'm, like, you do happen to be tall."
"I also happen to be Mr. Wrong."
"Positive you're not in play?" she pressed.
At my feet, Lulu growled.
"Now why did she do that?" Annabelle wondered.
"Because she's positive. Does Marjorie confide in you?"
Annabelle shrugged. "We're pals. I don't know if she
tells me everything."
"Has she told you God wants to ease Lyle out?"
Annabelle and Bobby exchanged a guarded look.
"I'm, like, there's no telling what they're planning to
do," she replied evasively. "I mean, we never know."
"Because *they* n-never know," Bobby added, his eyes
avoiding mine. "Until they d-do it. They just aren't that
t-together."
"She hasn't said anything." Annabelle forced a smile.
"Not to me, anyway."

"I see." They were playing it cagey. I didn't blame them. But I also didn't think they were very good liars. It wasn't speculation. It wasn't paranoia. It was for real—Chad Roe was in and Lyle Hudnut was out. For the second time. The first time had been last spring, after that day he went to the Deuce Theater. Only who had been behind that? Who set him up? The Boys? They certainly stood to gain the most. "Let me ask you this—is there anyone who *doesn't* want Lyle ousted?"

"His fans," Annabelle replied. "They love him. By the millions."

"I mean anyone who actually knows him."

"K-Katrina," Bobby said, blushing at the mention of her name. "First thing The Boys would do is fire her."

"And what's the second thing they'd do?"

"The second thing they'd do," answered Annabelle, "is fire Leo."

The soundstage where *The Uncle Chubby Show* was taped was one floor up from the production offices. It was not a large soundstage by West Coast standards. Space is more precious in Manhattan than it is in Burbank. It was more like a really large padded cell. In more ways than one. Just inside the steel fire door was the control booth, one wall of it nothing but television monitors and speakers. Six chairs were parked before a console facing it, each equipped with a microphone and control panel. There was a second row of controls situated behind it with six more chairs and mikes. Against the back wall there was a black leather sofa and a pair of armchairs where network and studio people could watch the taping in comfort. Later in the week, the booth would be command central. Right now all of the activity was out on the studio floor, where three burly stagehands were dismantling the set for the pool hall and carting it away to the freight elevator while three more were unloading the flats for the

Japanese restaurant set. Two others hastily assembled a bookcase that would serve as the backdrop when Rob phoned Deirdre in the new opening scene.

Chad and Fiona were running lines on the sofa in Deirdre's living room. Chad wore reading glasses, either because his eyes were starting to go or because he thought they made him look deep. Lyle was on the kitchen set walking through Chubby's scene with Jimmy the milkman, one of the few scenes that wasn't undergoing a radical change. Unless you count casting. The actor from the singing muffler commercial was out. The actor who'd originally been hired to play Jimmy's friend, Tony, was now playing Jimmy. The living room and kitchen sets, which were much smaller than they appeared on TV, were lit from overhead and faced a tier of bleachers that would hold three hundred people on tape day. The four cameras were presently parked out of the way, covered, as was the sound equipment. There were coils of cable everywhere. Microphones and TV monitors were suspended from the ceiling over the bleachers, along with a big APPLAUSE sign. A few crew members and extras were sitting up there in the bleachers, watching and waiting. So were The Munchkins, whispering to each other like they were at a school assembly. So were Amber and Gwen, who abruptly stopped talking when they spotted me. I took a seat in the front row. Lulu had elected to hang with The Boys and The Kids, who were downstairs working on rewrites and making a huge fuss over her.

"Okay, pal, I'll be over at the sink doing the dishes," Lyle told his new Jimmy. "You'll knock and . . ." Lyle stared at the script, rubbing his tight curls with a gloved hand. "Nah, that's no good. I got it—I'm trying to get the pilot light going in the oven. It's out, see? So when you walk in I got my head stuck in the oven. Much funnier, right?"

"Yessir," the actor chuckled. "Much funnier."

Lyle opened the oven door and knelt before it with a grunt. "Okay, go ahead and knock."

The actor went ahead and knocked.

"Yo, Jimbo," Lyle called out, head in the oven.

"Yo, Chubbo," read the actor. "How's by you?"

Lyle sat back on his immense haunches, wheezing slightly. "Okay, wait. What's your name, pal?"

His name was Bart.

"Bart, instead of saying 'How's by you?' say . . . 'Don't do it!' Remember, my head's in the oven." He turned to a P.A., who sat at a table nearby with a laptop computer. "You getting these changes, honey?"

"Yes, Lyle," she said.

"Great. Then I'll say, 'Jimbo, what the heck are you talking about?' And you'll say—"

Naomi Leight came clomping onto the set in her cowboy boots, interrupting him. "God's on the phone, Lyle. He wants to know how the show is coming."

"How the fuck should I know?" fumed Lyle. "I'm still making it up."

Another P.A. was trailing a few steps behind her, clutching an armload of pink pages. "Scene one rewrites," she announced, passing them out.

"About fucking time," snarled Lyle, snatching one from her.

"What should I tell him, Lyle?" Naomi asked.

"Tell him I was in rehearsal and couldn't be disturbed. And where's Katrina with my macro-fucking-biotic lunch? I'm hungry enough to eat my foot."

"I'll get right on it, Lyle," she vowed.

Lyle's blue eyes twinkled at her impishly. "Thanks, kid. Y'know, that's kind of a nice little ass you've got on," he observed, admiring the curve of her tight jeans. "Been wearing it long?" Subtle he wasn't.

Naomi giggled invitingly. Subtle he didn't have to be. "As long as I can remember."

"Don't know why I never noticed it before."

"Maybe you had your mind on other things," she said coyly.

He cackled. "You go ahead and do *your* thing. I wanna watch."

She headed off with her tail twitching, knowing he was watching her. Which he was. And from the look in his eyes it wasn't just his foot he was ready to devour. She was next in line, definitely.

He moved over to the living room with Fiona and Chad and flopped down into Chubby's easy chair, where he scanned the new pages, making those flatulent noises with his lips while he read. Chad and Fiona were reading them, too. When Lyle finished he tossed the new scene aside and said "Okay, whatta we think?"

Fiona tipped her head forward so her hair shielded her face. "I'd like to be a little more in the moment," she replied, gurgling. "I'm always so centered all the time."

"You have to be," Lyle pointed out firmly. "You hold the place together."

"But no one holds *me* together," she countered, glancing down at the script. "Like Rob asks her how she feels about dinner. She says, 'I happen to be a big supporter of the food pyramid.' She has to have some vulnerability under that, like . . . 'I happen to be a big supporter of the food pyramid—of course, I also supported Jerry Brown.' Or—"

Lyle let out his *hoo-hah-hah* of a laugh. "I love that. Get it down," he commanded the typist. "How about you, Chadster?"

Chad took off his glasses, thumbed his big, square chin thoughtfully. "Who am I? That's my gut reaction, Lyle. Who the hell am I? I've been asking you and asking you. You kept telling me it would all become clear to me when I saw the script. Well, I've seen the script. And it's not clear. All I am is a passenger. I need some direction here, Lyle. We have to talk about this. And we have to talk about it *now*."

Lyle shifted his bulk in the chair, staring at him. "Sure, okay. Whatever you say, pal. You wanna talk, we talk. You excuse us a minute, Fee?"

Fiona got to her feet. "I'll be in my dressing room." She slipped off the set and across the soundstage. As she neared the bleachers she spotted the first major new literary voice of the 1980's, and came on over.

"Chad has a stage background," she informed me. "He needs to talk things through, *feel* his character evolve."

"And Lyle?"

She shuddered and began to claw at her cuticles. "Lyle goes more by instinct. He's not very good at analyzing. Way too impatient." She glanced over at Amber a few rows away. "Amber's much more Chad's kind of director," she murmured. "But if he talked to her Lyle would freak. He's very easily threatened."

"Does he have reason to be?" I asked her, wondering how much she knew.

She hesitated, tipping her head forward. "This is TV."

"Meaning what?" I asked, tipping my own head forward. I could barely hear her.

"Meaning," Fiona replied, "we're all replaceable parts."

"Speaking of which, what happened to the milkman?"

"Lyle didn't care for his delivery."

"I see." Or for someone else making jokes at his table.

"Oh, I spoke to Noble. About your book. He said it would be a positive thing for me to talk to you. He thought it would help me to get in touch with my inner core."

"Glad to hear it."

She headed off to her dressing room. Or possibly her inner core. On her way out she passed Naomi, who was on her way in with Lyle's macro-fucking-biotic lunch. Lyle lit up at the sight of it. Or possibly her. Off came his mask, better to attack his plate of brown rice and beans and steamed veggies. He ate greedily, food spraying from his open mouth as he chewed.

"Okay, let's talk," he said to Chad, pausing to gulp down some mineral water. "Wait, where's the Hoagster?" He spotted me in the bleachers. "Get your bony ass down here, man! Conference time! *Now!*"

I stayed where I was.

"Hey, come here!" Lyle commanded, louder.

Phil, the stage manager, scampered over to me. "Uh, Hoagster? Lyle wants you on the set."

I stayed where I was. The crew was staring at me now.

Lyle frowned at me, then heaved an exasperated sigh. "Uh, Hoagy, would you mind joining us for a moment, *please?*"

"Be glad to, Lyle," I replied cheerfully. I strode onto the set and sat next to Chad on the living room sofa.

"So you're one of *those,*" Lyle growled at me.

"One of those what, Lyle?"

"People with *manners,*" he replied scornfully. "I bet people in your family say please and thank you and shit like that to each other all the time, right?"

"Actually, we don't speak to each other at all. But we are very polite about not doing it. And Lyle? Don't ever call me the Hoagster again. It makes me sound like some three-in-one garden gadget."

He roared with laughter, just a great big jolly fat man. This was him trying to loosen up Chad. Maybe get him off of his back. It wasn't working. Chad sat there with his script, totally focused. No dimp.

"Now what do you mean when you say you're a passenger, Chad?" Lyle asked.

"I mean that I have no personality," Chad replied earnestly. "I mean that I'm a consummate wienie. Even the kids think so. It's right here in black and white." Chad searched through the script. "Here when they're watching TV. Erin says, 'I think he's a wienie.' And Trevor says, 'He seems okay to me—for a wienie.' I *hate* being called that. Frank Rich called me that once in the *Times.*"

"Would you feel better if we changed the word?" asked Lyle patiently.

Chad considered this. "That's a start."

"To what?"

"How should I know?" Chad demanded petulantly. "I'm not a writer."

Lyle looked around for his stage manager. "Phil?! Get The Boys, will ya?!" Phil promptly skedaddled off. Lyle cleaned his plate and belched and wiped his mouth with the sleeve of his caftan. The mask went back on. I think I liked him better with it on. "Okay, what else is on your mind, pal?"

"Camera angles," Chad replied, somewhat uncomfortably.

"What about 'em?"

"I, uh, have certain specific angles that I can't be shot from. When I'm seated, I mean. At least I'd rather not be." Gingerly, he tapped the crown of his blond head. So it wasn't my imagination after all. The man actually had a bald spot. "It's nothing major, but sometimes if the light hits me wrong there's, well, a . . . shine."

"Say no more, pal," Lyle assured him soothingly. "No way I want you to look bad. You look bad, we look bad. Just remind me when we do the camera blocking on Thursday."

"Thanks, Lyle," Chad said gratefully.

Muck and Meyer came charging onto the set now, Lulu waddling along behind them. They had her dressed up in an Uncle Chubby T-shirt and crew cap, which was turned around backwards. She was one of the gang, and loving every minute of it.

"Trouble with the new pages, Chief?" asked Marty.

"Trouble with wienie," Lyle replied. "Chad doesn't feel good about it. What can the kids call him that isn't so negative?"

"If it's not negative it won't be funny," Tommy said with a pained expression on his face.

"What is it about wienie that bothers you?" Marty asked the actor.

"I'm trying to get a handle on this guy," Chad explained, working the dimp. "I need to figure out who he is. About all I have to go on is that Erin and Trevor think he's a wienie. And to me, a wienie is—"

"A dick," snapped Tommy. "Commonly accepted sitcom euphemism."

"Or schmuck," added Marty, nodding.

"Well, I don't want to play a dick or a schmuck."

Marty crouched before us, his elbows on the coffee table. "Okay, so what we need is a new word. . . ."

"Erin did call him a stud in the kitchen," I mentioned. Never let it be said I don't earn my paycheck.

Chad brightened. "Now stud's a word I can—"

"Much too positive for here," said Marty, trying it: " 'He seems okay to me—for a stud.' No, definitely not. What we need's a word like stud, only negative. *Slightly* negative," he added hastily, before Chad could object.

Tommy tugged at his white forelock. "Pretty boy . . . Hunk . . ."

Marty: " 'He seems okay to me. For a hunk.' Nah."

"Beefcake. Stiff. Drip." Tommy was whipping through them now. "Dork. Bozo. Gonzo. Yutz. Putz—"

"They won't let us use putz at eight o'clock," Marty said.

"Putz and a half. Putz and seven eighths—"

"Will you stop with the putz?"

"Sissy. Wimp—"

"Wimp means the same thing as wienie."

"Not necessarily," interrupted Chad, stroking his chin.

The Boys exchanged a hopeful look.

"You *like* wimp?" Marty asked him.

"Well, yeah," replied Chad. "Because I'm obviously not one. To me, wimp says weakling. It's a physical put-down. Whereas, you call a guy a wienie you're attacking his manhood. Wimp is different. Because people will look at me and they'll know I'm not one. Especially if I'm a rock climber.''

"Who's a rock climber?" growled Lyle.

"Actually, we were thinking of making you a champion swimmer," said Marty.

"We were?" asked Lyle.

"Ooh, I like that," exclaimed Chad. "A guy who's competitive, in great shape . . ." He frowned. "I don't have to shave my chest, do I?"

"Not on my account," replied Tommy.

"I had to shave it when I did *Tender Is the Night* with Debbie Raffin. Got this rash all over that took three weeks to go away."

"From Debbie Raffin?" asked Tommy, with keen interest.

"No, from shaving my—"

"Is wimp okay with you, Chad?" Lyle broke in irritably.

"I feel good about wimp," Chad affirmed.

Lyle heaved a huge sigh of relief. "Fine. If you feel good about wimp then I feel good about wimp. Thanks, boys. You saved the show."

"Come on, Lulu. Let's go." Marty gathered her up in his arms and tickled her tummy, which made her leg twitch, her tongue lolling out the side of her mouth. She was in basset hound heaven. "Lulu's our new Team Chubby mascot, Hoagy."

"Her deadpan inspires us," explained Tommy.

"Can we keep her?" asked Marty.

"I'm sure we can work something out."

Off the three of them went, leaving me there with Lyle and Chad.

"What else, pal?" Lyle asked him with mounting impatience.

"Balls," said Chad. "Rob needs some balls. Like when the two guys are fixing the dishwasher together. Chubby nails him about why he's not married. Rob should nail him right back. He should say, 'What are *you* doing sponging off of your sister, fatty?' " Lyle's eyes widened. "Maybe not those exact words," said Chad, beating a hasty retreat, "but he should be a *guy.*"

"He *is* a guy," Lyle argued. "Look, Chad, I understand what you're going through here. You're an outsider coming into a close-knit family. You're not sure how you fit in. Rob's in the same boat. He doesn't know where he fits either. He's feeling what you're feeling."

Chad listened intently, head bowed like a fighter soaking up last-minute advice from his trainer.

"So don't block those feelings out," Lyle continued. "Use 'em. Be yourself. Be the terrific guy you are. You're a health ed teacher now. That was Hoagy's idea. You're hip. You're relevant. The girls all wanna fuck ya. You're hot."

"I don't feel hot," Chad confessed.

"Why the hell not?"

"It's this business about my bathroom. Leo told me that you said no way. I just can't believe it."

"There's nothing I can do about that, pal." A hard edge crept into Lyle's voice. "The studio won't spring for it. Times are tough."

"That's just not acceptable, Lyle," Chad declared angrily. "You can't treat me this way. I've worked with Spielberg. I've worked with DePalma. I've done three series. And I've never, ever not had my own toilet. Not once. I want a toilet. I have to have one. Or I'm having my agent call God."

"Fair enough, Chadster," Lyle said pleasantly. "If that's how you want it. Only answer me this: When was your last successful series?"

"What do you mean?" Chad's voice quavered slightly.

"Lemme see now . . ." Lyle said, counting them off on his gloved fingers. "There was that piece-of-shit Indiana Jones rip-off you did for ABC. Then there was that piece-of-shit *Bull Durham* rip-off you did for NBC. Then there was that thing you did with Valerie Bertinelli where you were the alien."

"I wasn't the alien," Chad retorted. "She was."

Lyle suddenly turned vicious. "Who's fooling who here, huh?" he snarled. "This show is *it* for you—your last series shot. You know it, I know it, and God sure as hell knows it. You're, what, forty-five?"

Chad swallowed. He looked like he was about to be sick. "I'm forty-two."

"Bullshit!" Lyle exploded. "You're forty-seven. Your hair's falling out by the handful and you're fucking lucky to be here! So don't go copping a fucking attitude with me, you fucking bastard, or so help me *I'll* call up God and get you axed! This is *my* show! *I'm* the director! *I'm* the star! You'll play the character I tell you to play and you'll piss where I tell you to piss! Got it?!"

Everyone on the soundstage had stopped what they were doing. They were all staring at Lyle, transfixed. In the bleachers, Casey and Caitlin were gaping at him as if he were the monster in a real-life horror film.

Chad was too angry to speak. The man just sat there a moment, quivering, before he lunged for Lyle's empty lunch plate and hurled it at him. It bounced harmlessly off Lyle's big chest. Lyle jumped to his feet. They both did, Lyle towering massively over his new leading man.

"Wienie!" Lyle sneered like a schoolyard bully.

"Pervert!" raged Chad.

Lyle started breathing hard. Sweat formed on his brow. Menacingly, he moved in on Chad, his huge fists clenched.

"Not my face!" cried Chad, his voice unpleasantly high-pitched and shrill. "Don't hit my face!"

I slipped in between them. "Gentlemen, please. Think of the children."

Lyle turned to look at them, his chest heaving. "Hiya, Munchkins!" he sang out, waving to them. "How ya doing?"

"Fine, Lyle," they answered, their eyes huge with terror.

He turned back to Chad, the spell broken. "Go chill out for ten minutes," he barked. "Go on. Get outta here!"

Chad charged off the set and across the stage, slamming the steel stage door behind him. The crew watched him go. Slowly, they went back to work.

Lyle ran a gloved hand through his tight red curls, disgusted. "See what I gotta live with?"

"I'm certainly getting an up-close-and-personal view, all right."

He shot me The Scowl. "What's that supposed to mean?"

"It means I see what everyone else has to live with, too."

"Hey, nice people don't keep a hit show on the air."

"Then you should stay number one for many weeks to come, Lyle."

He dropped down heavily into Chubby's easy chair. "If he'd just put himself in my hands, he could be a terrific straight man. Christ, Fiona's the funniest woman on television. And I'm—"

"The funniest man on television. I know. You already told me."

Lyle peered up at me, as if he'd only just remembered who I was. "You helped out big-time with Marjorie this morning."

"Don't remind me."

"I mean it. You really poured oil over troubled waters."

"I'm a major slick, all right. Number two crude."

He guffawed. "You ask me, I see you around here permanent."

"I don't recall asking you."

"Television may be your true calling. That ever occur to you?"

"In the night sometimes. But then I start screaming and that wakes me up."

Lyle raised his chin at me, eyes narrowing. "About before—sorry if I was being rude bellowing for you like that. Just the way I am. You'll get used to it."

"No, I won't."

He rolled his eyes, exasperated. "You always this way?"

"What way is that, Lyle?"

"Thin-skinned."

"My skin is plenty thick. I just don't like you."

"Well, hell, don't let that bother you, Hoagster. Nobody does."

"What I mean is, you'll either learn to love me or to hate me. That's the way it is with me. Right, Katrina?"

"Right, Pinky," she squealed dutifully.

The three of us were in his combination office-dressing room. Rehearsal was over for the day and one of us, Pinky, was naked. He lay flat on his stomach on a rubdown table, mask off, gloves on, while Katrina expertly massaged the huge, hairless globes of his ass, her zoomers whomping up and down inside of her leotard.

"Why is that, Lyle?" I asked.

He stuck out his lower lip. Gloved and naked, he looked a lot like a Disney cartoon character. "We working on the book now?"

"Do you mind?"

"Hell, no. Just checking."

Lyle's inner sanctum was sumptuous. Also overbaked, overripe, and over the top. Animal magnetism was its theme, Katrina-style. The walls and ceiling were covered with woven zebra-print wallpaper, the floor with a faux tiger-skin rug. The sofa, the throw pillows on the sofa, and the two easy chairs facing the sofa were leopard skin. Lyle's desk was of clear Lucite. There was a red phone on it, and a lamp with a cheetah-print shade. Behind the desk chair (ocelot), the drapes (more leopard skin) were partly open on the only window in the entire place, which came with a deep granite ledge and a perfectly splendid view of the air shaft. One wall of Lyle's office was given over to the worship of Uncle

Chubby. An antique glass case contained a reverent display of Uncle Chubby dolls, games, books, nourishing microwave meals, the works. Hanging above this were the many awards and citations Lyle had received from the many parents' and children's groups. Before his arrest. A framed photograph of Magic Johnson was signed "For the *real* big fella, with thanks." Still more leopard-skin drapery separated the office from Lyle's dressing area, where there was a makeup mirror and dressing table and wardrobe cupboard. A door led to his much-contested private bath, which also had a door that opened out into the main office.

"Why is that?" Lyle wondered aloud. "Okay, I know why —it's because I'm too honest with people."

This one I had to sit down for. I chose one of the leopard-skin easy chairs. "Oh?"

Katrina dug her fingers into the muscles in his lower back. He yelped in protest. "Pinky, you're *soooo* tense."

"See, I don't believe in holding back. Anybody gets in the way of my own personal happiness, I gotta let 'em know, is what I'm saying. I hold nuttin' back. Not ever. Some people can deal with that. Some can't. They get hurt. But, hey, I'm cool with that. Because I'm not the one with the problem— they are. I mean, you can't deal with the truth, you got yourself a problem, let's face it." He raised his huge head so that he could look up at me. "How's that for a deep fucking philosophy of life?"

"Sounds more like a self-serving justification for being a complete asshole."

Katrina froze. Her lazy eye gave her a somewhat glassy expression.

Lyle grinned at me expansively. This was him being in a deep fucking philosophical mood. "Hey, lemme tell ya something, Hoagy. Probably the only fucking thing I ever learned in life—I can either hold things in and beat up on myself, or I can let 'em out and—"

"Beat up on other people?"

He pointed a fat index finger at me. This was him being cautioning. "I feel good about me, Hoagy. Best I've ever felt. I 'like' me. Don't fuck with that."

"Wouldn't dream of it, Lyle."

Katrina handed him his caftan, thus earning my eternal gratitude. Then she began to gather up her things. "Okay, I'm going to leave you guys," she announced.

"Where are you going, Cookie?" he whined, like a sorrowful little boy.

"To the health club. I'm *soooo* flabby."

"Who you kidding?" he asked, looking her up and down lasciviously.

"Pinky, you're awful!" she squealed. "Besides, you two need time alone."

"Okay," he said grudgingly. "But don't use the shower there. No telling what kind of fungus you might pick up."

"Not to worry. I'll shower when I get back to the hotel. How late will you be?"

"Dunno. Hoagy'll want some din-din."

She stroked his forehead. There was genuine affection in the way she did it. "That's fair. But don't you eat the food, Pinky. Remember your diet. I'll have a special meal ready for you when you get home, okay?"

"Okay, baby." He buried his face in her neck. "God, I love you. You're the *greatest.*"

"*You're* the greatest," she cooed, kissing him on the forehead. Then she left us, closing the door softly behind her.

He turned and winked at me, gloating. "Is that the greatest pussy in New York or what?"

I left that one alone.

He glowered. "How is it you manage to register so much disapproval without saying a word?"

"I do special facial exercises every morning. I thought we'd begin with the early stuff."

"How early?" he asked, turning sullen.

"As early as you can remember."

"Anything in particular?"

"You just go ahead and talk. I'll pick out what I need. And stop you if I'm not getting it."

"Yeah, I don't doubt that," he muttered, flopping onto the sofa like a big, unbleached muslin whale. "Fair enough. The early shit. I was born in '53, April the eighteenth, in Bay Shore, Long Island—Queens by the Sea. You catch the Fire Island ferry there. So every summer there's this swarm of yammering, horny singles from Manhattan tromping through. Otherwise it's strictly working-class hell. Block after block of raised ranches with above-ground pools, power boats in the driveway . . . Herb bought into a dry cleaning business out there when he got out of the navy in '46. He's from Queens. Elmhurst. So's my ma. They met in high school. Aileen waited for him the whole time he was in the Pacific. Four fucking years." Lyle paused, gazing out the window at a pair of pigeons roosting there on the ledge. "When I was going through my darkest periods I used to think if only he'd been blown out of the water I wouldn't have been born. I used to be damned sorry he wasn't." His eyes flicked back to me. "He and ma ran that same dry cleaning store until they sold out two years ago. They sent me a letter about it, right here to the show. Not that I answered 'em. Forty-five fucking years they ran it. Lived in the same house the whole time. Can ya imagine that, Hoagy? Together behind that counter every single fucking day for forty-five years, stinking of dry cleaning fluid. Together in that same crummy little house every single night. Christ, what a miserable life. His dad was a garbageman, so maybe it seemed like a step up to him. Hers was a doorman at a hotel in midtown. He was a big, tall Irishman. I got my size and coloring from him. Aileen's Irish through and through. I was their second kid." The red phone on his desk rang. He ignored it. "First one died a few weeks after it was born. They didn't have no more kids after they had me." He let out a laugh. "I kind of spoiled 'em." His phone rang again. It was past six—no one was answering it.

He cursed, struggled to his feet, and got it. "Mr. Hudnut's office . . . I'm sorry, Mr. Daniels, Mr. Hudnut's in rehearsal right now. . . . Yessir, I'll have him call you just as soon as he's free. . . . Yessir, I'll be sure to tell him. . . . Good-bye, sir." He hung up and sat in his desk chair. "God himself. He's *very* anxious to hear how the show's coming."

"Didn't he recognize your voice?"

"Nah, I got me one of these voice-changer phones," he replied proudly, swiveling it around to show me. "Looks totally ordinary, but it ain't. Can disguise your voice sixteen different ways at the push of a button. Make you sound like a secretary, a kid, whatever. Digital voice modification, they call it. Greatest invention in the world." He opened a small refrigerator behind the desk, removed a half-empty bottle of mineral water, and took a swig from it. He watched the pigeons some more. "My earliest memory is biting the mailman when I was three. Sunk my teeth right into the dude's leg. Drew blood. Poor fucker had to get stitches and a tetanus shot." He cackled gleefully. "Damn, was I a little rockhead or what?" Now there was a knock on his door. "Christ, it never stops," he complained. "Yeah?!"

It was Chad. He had a tan leather knapsack slung over one shoulder and a penitent look on his ruggedly handsome face. "Just wanted to say good night, Lyle," he said meekly.

Lyle crossed his heavy arms. "G'night, Chad," he said coldly.

Chad lingered there in the doorway. "Look, I'm real upset about what happened before. And real sorry."

Lyle's face broke into a wide grin. "Hey, don't be, man," he said easily. "Nothing bad happened. We both care. We're both trying to find our way, and we will. I know it. Now you go on home. Have a glass of wine. Make love to your beautiful wife. We'll tackle it in the morning, okay?"

Chad lit up. He was an actor like any other—hungry for approval, especially from his director. "Okay! See you tomorrow!" The man practically flew out the door.

Lyle nodded contentedly. "He just showed me a lot of class, doing that. I'm starting to like what I see. I think the Chadster's gonna be okay. Yup, I have a mo' better feeling about him now." He struggled to his feet with a grunt and padded off to his bathroom. "Much mo' better."

I sat there, wondering how long it would take me to get used to Lyle Hudnut's mood changes. Maybe you never did. Maybe you just got used to being continually off balance. They say you can get used to anything—if you have to.

"Where were we, pal?" he called out. He was taking a pee in there with the door open.

"You just bit the mailman."

"Oh, right." He cackled. "Like I said, I was a rockhead—right outta the gate." There was the roar of a urinal being flushed. He returned. "Dunno why. Just came natural to me. I was *baaaad,*" he boasted. "Always fighting with the other neighborhood kids in the sandbox. If one of 'em wanted to play with my shovel, I'd fight him. If I wanted to play with his shovel, I'd fight him. I was constantly having to be dragged off of somebody, biting, scratching, kicking. None of their moms would let 'em near me after a while. Especially on account of I was so big for my age." He flopped back down on the sofa. "They thought I was some kind of bully."

"And were you?"

He considered this. "What I was . . . I was born to be a rebel, y'know? Born to be wild. Bad to the bone."

"Slow down, I think there's a song in there somewhere."

"Just born too soon, that's all. I mean, we're talking fifties suburbia, here. The age of conformity. Me, I was a free spirit. Too hip for their games and their bullshit. Nursery school, kindergarten . . . forget about it. I wouldn't go along. Any kind of authority made me *crazy.* I'd call the teacher names. I'd make 'em *sorry.* First two nursery schools called up Aileen after one day and said get this whacko little motherfucker out of here. Another time and place, they'd have let me be free to be made. Not then. Then they tried to make me toe the line." His voice had a hard edge now. "Because I was *different*. And because different was *bad*. That's sure how Herb and Aileen saw it. I freaked 'em out, totally. Bay Shore was a small town. They ran a local business, belonged to the Chamber of Commerce. They wanted to fit in. They didn't want to be known as the people whose kid bit the mailman." He took a gulp of water. "So they had my head examined," he recalled fiercely. "When I was five."

"What was that like?"

"They were both with me. Must have closed the store for the day. Took me to the child guidance center at the children's hospital in Central Islip. Got me checked out, top to bottom. For hyperactivity—not. For brain damage—not. They gave me all of these tests—IQ, Rorschach. Know what they figured out? I was a fucking genius. My IQ was like a hundred and ninety-something. That's what was 'wrong' with me. I was too fucking smart for my age. They figured once I started school and had a way to channel myself, I'd be cool. They attributed my problem to frustration."

"And to what do you attribute your problem?"

"I had no problem," he snarled. "They had the problem."

Whoops of laughter came from the direction of The Boys' office. They were still in there working on rewrites with The Kids and Lulu. Lyle glanced at the wall, clearly hankering to run into Katrina's office so he could stick his Super Ear against the wall and hear what they were saying about him. Instead he stuck a huge, fat foot up on the coffee table and crossed his arms tightly against his chest.

"How did you do once you started school?"

"Shitty," he snapped. "Academically, I was fine. Straight A's. But I just couldn't stand it, having to sit there all of those hours, doing what I was told. So I'd make 'em pay. If there were guinea pigs in a cage, I'd let 'em out. If there were pots of paint, I'd pour 'em out. If they said to draw an apple, I'd draw a car. I was a contrary fucking rockhead. I remember one time my second-grade teacher, Mrs. Kellam, told me to close the window. I said no, I was hot. She said close it or she'd send me to the principal's office. So I closed it. And then I put my fist through it. Took twenty-seven stitches to close me up." He showed me the faint white scars across the knuckles of his right hand, proudly, as if they were earned in battle.

"Did you get along better with the other kids?"

"Didn't want to," he sniffed. "They were brainless sheep. Didn't interest me, except to pick on. If they were playing dodgeball at recess I'd take their ball away, to piss 'em off. I remember there was this one little goody-goody, Nancy Linden. A real teacher's pet, y'know? She called me a 'big penis' for spoiling everyone else's fun. So I spit on her, just to see what she'd do."

"What did she do?"

"Wimped out. Told the teacher on me, who told the principal, who called my parents to come get me. They were always coming to get me. My behavior was a source of great shame to them."

"Is that why you kept doing it?"

He grinned at me. "Maybe."

"That's not a strong enough answer, Lyle."

He snorted. "You sound just like God sometimes."

"Your readers want to understand you. Help them out. Tell them what was going on inside your head."

He heaved a big sigh. "I don't know if I can, Hoagy. I just had this . . . this *energy* boiling inside me. Remember when you were a little kid sitting in church, squirming, bored to death, choking from your necktie, ready to run screaming up the aisle? Well, I felt that way *all* the time. At school, at home, everywhere. I felt trapped. I felt like I was gonna go crazy if I had to keep quiet for one more second. I had to *do* something. Make some noise. There was never a time I didn't feel that way—except for when I was acting up, making a scene. A born rebel, like I said."

"And a born performer."

"You got that right." His eyes twinkled at me. "Sometimes I'd just escape. Take off from school at recess and not come back. Scared the shit out of the big people, which was part of the fun, no question. I'd prowl around town on my bike. Go down to the beach, or the movies. I loved to sit in movie theaters by myself. Didn't care what the movie was. It was the dark that drew me, the images of somewhere else, anywhere else, flickering away up on the screen. I felt swallowed up by it. I felt free."

"Is that how you felt that day in the Deuce Theater?"

He stared at me. "Christ, Hoagy," he said hoarsely. "You're absolutely right. That was me doing just what I did when I cut school thirty years ago. And for basically the same reason. Wow, that's twisted, really bent. Let's put it in the book."

"It's in."

He rubbed a gloved hand over his round moon-face. His whole face seemed to be made of rubber when he did that. "Since my IQ was so high, the school figured my 'problem' was I wasn't being challenged enough by the curriculum. So they tried skipping me a year, directly to the fourth grade. But I fooled 'em. I was still the same old rockhead, nuttin' but trouble. So they called in Herb and Aileen and said, hey, do something with this kid. We can't handle him anymore. He needs too much attention. Not fair to the other kids. Which meant another trip to the child guidance center, and more tests. And guess what they discovered? I had trouble interacting with people—particularly my parents."

"Did you hate your parents?"

He turned evasive. "Not then, no."

"Did you love them?"

"They were there, that's all."

"Did you think they loved you?"

"I had no idea. I didn't know what love was."

"Did you blame them?"

"For what?"

"For how you were."

He scratched his head. "Lemme think about that one."

"Take your time. I'm not going anywhere."

He gazed out the window. The pigeons were gone, and it was getting dark. Lights were on in the windows across the air shaft. "I accepted the way I was," he said slowly. "I liked the way I was. The only thing I didn't *get* was how come I was never happy."

"Happy how?"

"I never laughed when I was a little kid," he confided. "Not ever. I had no comprehension of humor."

Still don't, I could almost hear Tommy Meyer crack. The man's nasty wit was contagious.

"It was years before I learned how to laugh," Lyle confessed. "Maybe that's why it means so damned much to me now to make kids happy. Because I wasn't." He reddened. His intimacy had made him uncomfortable. "Sorry. Didn't mean to turn corny on you."

"You can turn any way you want on me, Lyle. I'm your collaborator, not your audience."

"Thanks, Hoagy. That's nice of you to say." He coughed and cleared his throat. "The shrinks said I should start therapy. They would, being shrinks."

"Did you?"

"Yeah."

"And how did your parents react to that?"

"They freaked. Working people didn't *go* to shrinks, not in those days. Especially not ten-year-old kids. Not unless they were fucked-up big-time. To the parents, it was like there was some stigma attached to it. Shame. Me, I thought it was a complete bust. Twice a week Aileen would take me to some doctor's office. He'd ask me a bunch of stupid questions, like what I did that day and how I liked it and what I dreamt about. He was a total bozo. His glasses were crooked, and he smelled like rotten eggs. I called him Doctor Buttwipe. Once a week all three of us had to go see him together after dinner. Family therapy, they called it. Doctor Buttwipe would tell us all to be more patient with each other and communicate our feelings better. Aileen would get real defensive, like he was judging her or something. Herb would hardly say a word. Although I think Buttwipe must have told him to do more things with me. Because he was suddenly in my face a lot.''

"In your face how?''

"Herb's big thing was tinkering. Man was a major do-it-yourselfer. He was always installing his own lawn sprinklers or putting together a hi-fi or fucking around under the hood of the car. All of which I hated. Still do. Can't stand any of that suburban handyman shit. Won't touch a screwdriver.'' He gulped down some more mineral water, wiping his mouth with the sleeve of his caftan. "Plus I got zero aptitude for it.''

"We tend not to be good at things we don't want to be good at.''

"Not true.'' He grinned at me. "You're good at TV.''

"I asked you not to remind me.''

"I'm pleased. Can't I be pleased?''

"You can be anything you want. It's your show.''

"You got that right,'' he said defiantly. "All I wanted to do was read comic books and eat Fudgsicles, but suddenly Herb wouldn't leave me the fuck alone. He even started dragging me out to his ham shack. He was one of them ham radio enthusiasts. Built his own Heathkit shortwave. Converted part of the garage into his workshop. He'd lock himself in there after dinner, talk to his ham radio buddies all over the free world. I guess it was his way of getting away from Aileen.''

"And what was she doing with herself?''

Lyle tugged at his fleshy lower lip. "To tell ya the truth, I don't have much memory of what Aileen was up to. Other than staring at the TV. She always went to bed early, I remember. She got tired. 'Your mom's not strong, Lyle,' Herb would say to me. 'Not like we are.' He bought me a Heathkit of my very own for the two of us to build together. Tell me, did yours ever pull that gung ho father-son shit on you?''

"He tried."

Lyle raised his chin. "You two get along?"

"Not yet."

He nodded approvingly. "My fingers were so thick and clumsy, and I had zero patience for reading all of those stupid directions. I mean, none. Finally one night I just swept the whole damned thing off the workbench onto the floor and stormed into my bedroom. Herb followed me right in there and said, 'You *will* build this radio with me, Lyle.' He turned it into a real battle of wills, which was a major mistake. He wasn't in my league. No way. I won hands down."

"How?"

"I burned down the ham shack," he replied, cackling proudly. "Right to the ground. Got me some lighter fluid, some crumpled newspapers, and *wham!* Whole fucking garage went up like kindling—with our car inside. It blew up. Neighbor's porch caught on fire. I practically torched the whole neighborhood. Ya shoulda seen it. Took three fire trucks to put the thing out."

"Why did you do it, Lyle?"

He stared at me blankly. "To get my way, of course. I think that was the first time Herb and Aileen realized that they couldn't control me."

"And what did you realize?"

"The true definition of power."

"And what's that?"

"Make people realize you're dangerous if you don't get your way," he replied, with an eerie calm that made my stomach muscles tighten. "Doctor Buttwipe's response was to put me on Thorazine, which is probably my biggest problem in life, Hoagy. Because every time I didn't toe the line, every time I got a little uppity, they'd solve it by doping me. Doctors have been getting me stoned forever. You name it, I've been on it—Thorazine, lithium, Prozac. I've had 'em all. I'm a really addictive personality, okay? I can get hooked on work, food, sex. They got me hooked on drugs. They always doped me. *Always.''* He was getting louder now, and waving his arms. "When I got old enough, I just went right ahead and doped myself. Any kind of dope I could get my hands on. Alcohol, grass, hash, coke . . . That's what I was *conditioned* to do. The Deuce Theater, that was me *not* drugging. Finding a positive way of dealing with my anxiety. At least compared to drugs it was. I didn't hurt myself. I didn't hurt anyone else. But did anyone understand that?"

"Did you honestly expect they would?"

That caught him short. He glared at me angrily. "I expected them to try." He heaved a sigh, calmed himself. "They checked me into a psychiatric hospital after that little incident. The bin. Spent two weeks there in a dormitory with a bunch of other rockheads. They gave me the usual tests. Then they stroked their beards and told the parents that maybe I belonged in some kind of full-time residential treatment facility—a boarding school for wackoes. Now this really appealed to Herb and Aileen," he recalled sardonically. "Because it meant they could get me the hell away *and* do it with a clean conscience. For my own good, was how they put it. Bullshit. They wanted me gone. No matter the price. And it wasn't cheap. We're talking ten, fifteen thou a year. Major bucks in those days. They didn't care. No price was too high. They wanted me *away.''* His voice was husky now, his eyes remote. "They tried to make me into somebody I wasn't. They couldn't. I was too tough for 'em. So they threw me in a dungeon."

"Is that why you hate them?"

He let out a short, harsh laugh. "I ain't even getting

warmed up yet." He broke off. "You were asking me before about love. I'm sure, in their own sick way, Herb and Aileen thought they loved me." He kept speaking of them in the past tense, as if they were dead. I had to keep reminding myself they weren't. "But they didn't. They were ashamed of me, Hoagy. Ashamed of what I represented—their own failure as parents. If they'd really loved me they would have accepted me for who I was. Instead, they bailed out on me. Sent me far, far away. That's not what love is. Love is Katrina telling me, 'Don't you eat the food, Pinky.' That's what love is. Love is . . ." Lyle's eyes widened. He struggled to his feet, towering over me. "Geez, we gotta hear that!" And with that he went barreling out the door. I followed.

He made straight for The Boys' office, burst inside, and roared, "We need it in the script! We need to hear him say, 'Don't you eat the food, Pinky'!"

There was very little reaction to this pronouncement. The Boys just kept right on gazing at their computer screen, Marty seated at the keyboard, Tommy perched on his right shoulder with a pencil between his teeth. Bobby kept right on pacing. Annabelle, who was stretched out on the sofa, kept right on scribbling on a yellow legal pad. Lulu, who was curled up at her feet, didn't so much as stir.

"Don't eat which food, Lyle?" Tommy finally asked, wearily, after several long seconds of silence.

"When Rob and Chubby are fixing the dishwasher," Lyle explained excitedly, waving his arms for emphasis. "And they're talking about why he's not married. We need to say—"

" 'Don't you eat the food, Pinky'?" Marty quoted, mystified.

"Don't ya get it?" whined Lyle, exasperated. "I mean he's gotta . . . they gotta . . . Shit, it made total sense a second ago. Tell 'em, Hoagmeister. Tell 'em what I mean."

Great, now I sounded like a home beer-brewing kit. I

tugged at my ear. "I think he means that what a man misses when he's not in a good relationship is someone who's looking out for him."

"Exactly!" cried Lyle.

" 'Don't you eat the food, Pinky'?" Tommy repeated, still perplexed. Not that I blamed him.

Lyle nodded. "Put it in the dishwasher scene," he commanded. "When we're talking about finding the perfect girl. Those exact words. And give 'em to Chubby, not Rob. I want Katrina to hear me say 'em. As a gift from me to her. I wanna see her face when I do. Okay?"

The Boys just stared at him in bewildered silence. All four writers did, Bobby blinking furiously.

"Aw, Christ," Lyle growled, stung by their lack of enthusiasm. "Do whatever the fuck you want. We're going to dinner."

"Enjoy," exclaimed Marty, greatly relieved.

"I'm, like, yeah," Annabelle chimed in, happily.

Lulu yawned and jumped down from the couch, ready for dinner herself. Or maybe she'd just had enough shpritzing for one day.

"Have you made her laugh yet?" I asked Marty.

"Not even close."

"She's killing us," Tommy confessed. "Has she ever laughed?"

"Never in my presence," I said. "But we have much different senses of humor. Martin and Lewis, for example."

"What about them?" asked Tommy.

"She doesn't get them."

"This is hopeless," he muttered. "Totally hopeless."

The picketers had gone home for the day. The blue barricades and a lone cop were all that remained. The night air was sticky and still. It smelled like rain. We walked, Lyle waddling along beside me, sandals clopping, his arms swinging mightily. Lulu ambled along ahead of us, nose to the pavement.

I suggested Periyali, a Greek place on Twentieth, where it was quiet, and the fried octopus wasn't terrible.

Lyle shook his head. "Nah, I'm more in the mood for pasta. Lotsa pasta."

I glanced at him. "You're joining me?"

"Dinner time, ain't it? I'm starved."

"What about 'Don't you eat the food, Pinky'?" I asked.

"Hey, it's not like I'm married to the cunt," he snarled viciously. "And I sure as hell ain't married to *you!* So back the fuck off!"

"My mistake," I said stiffly.

"Hey, no sweat," he said cheerfully. "Can happen to anybody."

I suggested Umberto's on Seventeenth. We walked in silence. I don't know what he was thinking about. I was thinking what an asshole he was. I was thinking about Herb and Aileen, wondering what they'd done to make him hate them so much. I was thinking. Lulu, she just wanted to get to the restaurant.

Umberto's is ultramodern, Milanese sleek. High ceilings. Lots of tile. The dinner crowd was the usual media mix of fashion, publishing, and advertising. Most of the tables were full. We got noticed as we stood there waiting for the maître d'. Lyle was hard to miss. And, as we were led to a non-smoking table in the back, he got a reaction, too. It started small—a smattering of applause. A few lusty cheers. But it didn't let up. By the time we reached our table everyone in the restaurant was on their feet cheering Lyle Hudnut. They cheered him because he was a victim. They cheered him because he was a survivor. It was downright stirring to witness, until I recalled that people had also cheered John Gotti, David Begelman, and Ollie North.

"Never been in this place before in my life," Lyle blubbered, deeply moved. He blew his nose loudly in his napkin and asked the maître d' to give every table in the place a bottle of his best wine and to put it on our tab, which came to three thousand and change, in case you're interested. The show paid for it. I ordered the angel's hair pasta puttanesca followed by a grilled veal chop. Lulu had fried calamari. Lyle ordered two different bowls of pasta for starters, two more for his main course, and another for a side order. It was the largest quantity of pasta I've ever seen an individual shovel away in a single sitting, though I must admit I've never eaten Italian with Dom DeLuise. Lyle drank only Pellegrino water, two big bottles. I had a bottle of Chianti Classico.

"Exactly where did Herb and Aileen send you?" I asked him, as we ate.

"Place called the Allen School on the north shore of the island," he replied, his mouth and both cheeks full of pasta. Oil and tomato sauce flew, splattering the white table cloth, his arms, gloves. "It was this humongous Locust Valley estate that had been converted into a 'special' school for 'special' kids. Had a red brick manor house with something like thirty-seven bedrooms. Stables, tennis courts, pool, twenty acres of grounds. Like a fucking country club. Some rich dead guy left it to 'em. The kids were ages twelve to seventeen. Me, I'd just turned eleven, but they let me in anyway. A lot of 'em were rich kids from Manhattan. But they were all rockheads just like me. Kids who didn't fit in. Kids whose parents had decided they were bad news and needed to be stuck somewhere. The headmaster, Mr. Mitchell, was a shrink. So was his wife. They ran it together. Actually, I dug it there, if you can believe that. The Mitchells were totally righteous people. Their attitude was, hey, there's nothing wrong with you. Be yourself. It was nice to hear that for once. I never had before. They taught us how to express ourselves, instead of shutting it all inside. Not a lot of that boring classroom shit either. At Allen, I learned about photography by developing pictures in a darkroom. I learned about music by playing the drums. I loved banging on them drums. A few of us even used to jam together. Of course, they kept us real busy. We all had to pitch in. Do the dishes, clean the stables, make the beds. Plus we had therapy, individual and group. But I never felt any desire to run away from Allen. I never felt trapped. I guess because I was finally someplace where people weren't coming down on me just because they were too narrow-minded to hear where I was coming from. I didn't feel strange or wrong. None of us did. The teachers understood us. And we all understood each other. And that was really cool. First time I made friends, really. No, we were more than friends. We were brothers and sisters. We watched out for each other. We were there for each other. Because, hey, our parents sure as hell weren't.''

A young couple all dressed in black stopped by our table to thank Lyle for the wine and get his autograph. They lingered a bit too long, but he was extremely gracious about it. His recollections of Allen seemed to have put him in a jovial mood. Or maybe he just got contented when he was fed.

"Tell me about your friends," I said.

He wiped his pasta bowls clean with the heel of our second loaf of bread, then stuffed that in his mouth and pushed the bowls away. "I made 'em for life," he said, sitting back from the splattered table. It looked like it was left over from a mob rubout in Ozone Park. "There was Erin Sudbury, who was my first fuck. Her mother had committed suicide and her stepmother hated her. Erin was sixteen. I was fourteen. She was the one who taught me how to laugh. Had a totally twisted sense of humor. Ended up marrying an ear, nose, and throat man out in Northern California. We're still in touch. Then there was Trevor Bernstein. Trev was a great, great sculptor. Gay, which his parents couldn't deal with. I have a couple of his pieces at the beach. He died of AIDS three years ago. I guess he and Erin were the best friends I've ever had. I named the *Uncle Chubby* munchkins after them. I mean, we were *close*. Holidays, I'd have to go home to Herb and Aileen, but I'd feel trapped the second I walked in the door. I couldn't wait to leave. Allen was home now, and Erin and Trevor were my family. Herb and Aileen never gave me what I got from them. I was happy there. The happiest I'd ever been." He cackled. "Especially after Trev's older brother, Joel, started sending him grass and hash from the city. This was, what, maybe '66, '67. The three of us would sit up all night getting stoned and rapping on the true meaning of life."

"And what did you decide it was?"

"Be yourself," Lyle replied. "No matter what other people think. No matter if it puts you against the flow. Be who *you* wanna be. I still believe that," he declared, punctuating it with a loud fart. "Ahh . . . that was a good one."

Lulu let out a low, unhappy moan of dissent from under the table.

"Allen was the best four years of my life. I was totally bummed when I had to leave. Man, that was hard."

"Why did you?"

"Because I was ready to start high school, and they decided I was 'well' enough to go to my regular high school back home in Bay Shore. Time to plug me back into their repressive system. Time for me to be Herb and Aileen's good little boy."

"And were you?"

He guffawed hugely, turning heads at neighboring tables. "No way, pal. Once a rockhead, always a rockhead." He gulped down some water. "They were scared of me, Herb and Aileen. Physically scared. Because I was a big fucker now. Much bigger than they were. And they were just really afraid to piss me off. So they kind of tiptoed around me, avoiding confrontations. Which was cool. And I had to admit the setup was cool. Herb had redone part of the garage as a bedroom for me, so I could come and go as I pleased. He soundproofed it, bought me a drum set. He wanted me to feel like my own man, he said. They steered clear of me, pretty much. They were at the store all day, and in the house at night. I went to school when I felt like it. Saw a therapist three afternoons a week—another geek without a clue. Mostly, I hung out. Banged my drums half the night. Played my stereo ultraloud. I loved Jimi Hendrix." He was growing more animated. "I was a major Grateful Deadhead, too. The early shit-kicker stuff, when they were still a Hell's Angels biker band. My idol in life was Pigpen. Had posters of that ugly dude plastered all over the garage. I even dressed like him—black leather jacket, black T-shirt and jeans, steel-toed jackboots, bandanna over my head. . . . Couldn't wait until I turned eighteen so I could get a chopper. My favorite movie was *Easy Rider*. Saw it two hundred times. That was me, man. An *outlaw*."

"How did you get along at school?"

"The coaches wanted me to go out for football, because I was so big. But I wasn't having any of that. What I got into was drama. They had this really cool drama teacher, Mr. Schoen, who was into expressing yourself, like the teachers at Allen had been. Improv was his thing. First day, he says to me, okay, you're an ape. And to this girl, he says, you're a lion, and you two are in a cage together. Get it on. Right away I start sniffing her bum, like I figure an ape would, right? And the kids in class totally lose it. That's when I discovered that performing for people, making them laugh, was a real high for me. It was a license for me to be *me* and get away with it. . . . The whole atmosphere around school was different. I mean, I hadn't changed, but the times had. It was '68. Revolution was in the air. Being a rockhead like me, anti-everything, was now considered *okay*. Hip, even. I mean, I wasn't alone anymore. There were other kids around who were like me. Antiwar people, flower people, stoners, greasers. My garage, it became the neighborhood place to hang out, get stoned, fuck your girlfriend. Especially over the summer. Couple of guys started bringing guitars by. We'd play "Louie, Louie," shit like that. Called ourselves the World's Worst Garage Band, because we were. We didn't care. We were stoned all the time. I was still getting dope from Trevor's brother, Joel, in New York. Pounds of grass, chunks of hash. He mailed it to me disguised as books—he worked in the mailroom at one of the big publishing houses. Runs the whole company now. I dealt around the neighborhood. Not to make a fortune. Just enough to break even on what I smoked with a little money left over for records and concerts. The most amazing thing was when the straight kids started knocking on my garage door, wanting to buy weed for the prom. I thought that was really cool." He crackled. "I know Herb and Aileen were pleased to see how well I was starting to fit in."

"Did they have any idea what was going on back there?"

"None," he recalled gleefully. "Joel sent me sheets of windowpane acid, too, but I took most of that myself. I really got into dropping acid. I'd put on my headphones and trip my brains out. A bunch of times I even went to school on acid. Just sat there in class all day, quietly tripping away behind my shades like the Frito Bandito. I was feeling really good about things. Good enough to skip therapy even, which pissed off the parents. But I didn't give a fuck. My head was together. Life was beautiful." Lyle broke off, his face darkening. "Until I got busted."

Our waiter came by to clear the table. I ordered a profiterole and a double espresso. Lyle asked only for more mineral water. Most of the tables around us were empty now. Lulu was asleep under me with her head on my foot, snoring softly.

"What happened, Lyle?" I asked, after the waiter had gone.

"Nothing," Lyle grunted, sticking his chin out. "Some teacher caught me junior year selling a gram of hash to a kid in the boys' room. Big fucking deal, right? But the principal freaked and called the police. They dragged me down to the station. Major, major shame for Herb and Aileen, getting that call from the law. I'm talking *disgrace*. The look on their faces when they came to get me, man, I'll never forget it. It was hate, Hoagy. Total hate." Lyle sat there in hurt silence a moment. He ran a hand over his face. "It was a lousy gram of hash, Hoagy. No big deal. The law was willing to put me on probation, since it was my first offense and I was supposedly seeing a shrink and all. The high school was willing to take me back after a one-week suspension. It was *no big deal.* Everybody was cool about it. Everybody except for Herb and Aileen. They weren't about to forgive me. No way. I was a bad boy and bad boys get punished. I shamed them, Hoagy. So they came down on me. They buried me. They . . . They . . ." His eyes filled with tears. He choked them back and began to shake all over, as if he were going to explode.

"They what, Lyle?"

He couldn't answer me. A huge sob came out of him. Tears streamed down his face.

"What did they do?" I pressed.

Quietly, he said, "They had me jumped, Hoagy."

"Jumped?" I leaned forward. "Jumped how?"

"Like a car battery, that's how," he cried. "They had the doctors give me shock treatments, man. They hooked me up and they zapped me, okay? You got it?" He was sweating heavily, now, greatly agitated. "My own parents had it done to me. To their son. Like I was a fucking rat in a lab."

My profiterole came. I pushed it away. "Tell me what you remember, Lyle," I said.

He snorted. "Not much. That's one of the things about it. There's shit you don't ever remember. It's *gone.* I know they checked me back into the psychiatric hospital. Beyond that, I remember very little. They knock you out when they're doing it to you. It's not like they wanna give you a chance to just say no or nuttin'. So I was unconscious a lot of the time. I think they did it to me every day for a week. But I ain't sure."

"And how did you feel when it was all over?" I asked, sipping my espresso.

"Blank," he replied woodenly.

"That's not a good enough answer."

"Look, it's supposed to chill you out, okay?" he elaborated, impatiently. "Turn you into a nice, docile little boy. That's why they do it. What it did . . . It made me somebody who got shook easily. I wasn't before. I was cocky. You couldn't touch me. But once somebody's done something like that to you, you lose your nerve, your cool. It took me a long, long time to get that back. Maybe I never have. Not all of it. Part of me . . . Part of me felt brand-new, like I was tasting everything for the first time. A simple glass of water was the best glass of water I'd ever had in my life. I'd never been so thirsty. Or so grateful for the chance to drink that water. One thing didn't change though. The hate didn't go away. I still hated Herb and Aileen—more, in fact." He paused, weighing his words carefully. "This is something that's never come out before. I've never told anyone. Just Fiona. And she's never betrayed my confidence. And I ain't looking for sympathy now. Or excuses. I'm bringing it up because I wanna be understood, okay? As somebody who'd had some weird, strange shit done to him." He glanced hungrily at my uneaten dessert, licking his lips. "I think the treatment also gave me this incredible need to be in control of my life. Because they took it from me. I need to be in control. And I am."

"That's an illusion—no one is."

"*I* am," he insisted, stabbing the table with a fat index finger.

"Bullshit. A car could crash into this building right now and kill all of us." At my feet, Lulu began to tremble. She's always been rather literal. "Just an example, girl," I assured her.

"Okay, okay," Lyle conceded. "I need to control what I *can* control."

"And who you can control?"

The Scowl. "Yeah, maybe."

"What happened when you went home?"

"I went back to school after a few weeks. And it was

totally weird. Kids would come up to me and say, 'Hey, Lyle, what's happening?!' And I wouldn't quite remember who they were. I'd start talking about some album I liked, only I couldn't think of the name of the band. Or who was in it. I couldn't remember which classes I was in, or where the rooms were. I didn't feel like I was totally, one-hundred-percent *me*, which shook me. It also made me want to get away. Start over someplace where no one remembered something that I didn't remember. More than anything, I wanted to get away from Herb and Aileen, and the hate I felt for them morning, noon, and night. Because they *did* it to me, Hoagy. Their own son. They fucked with my head. Nobody has a right to do that to somebody else. Especially their own child. There should be *laws*. Who knows how I would have turned out if only they'd let me be? Maybe I'd have been a great writer like you."

"Now there's a truly horrifying thought. Did you get away?"

His eyes were on my dessert again. "The day I graduated from high school—and I did graduate. I'm very proud of that, considering my fucking brains had been rearranged. I took off. Caught a train for New York. Got a room at the Chelsea Hotel. And I started over. I was seventeen years old." He shifted his bulk in the chair. He seemed drained by our session. "What the fuck, now you know my deep, dark secret. And why I haven't spoken to the parents in over twenty years, and never will. I don't hold a grudge. Ask anyone. But that's one grudge I'll hold until the day I die. So how is that?" He meant the profiterole.

I tasted it. "Not terrible."

"Gonna finish it?"

"Help yourself."

He devoured it in great, starved mouthfuls. "Man, I love chocolate," he exclaimed, as some of it dribbled down his chin. "It's my favorite thing in the whole world to eat— except for pussy."

"You're all class, Lyle."

"Class is strictly for phonies," he snarled. "And if there's one thing I'm not, it's a phony. I am who I am. The real me. And proud of it." He sneered at me across the table. "Besides, you got no class either. Know why?"

"Do tell."

"Because if you were as classy as you think you are you wouldn't be working for me." He smirked at me. "Would ya, *Hoagster?!*"

I had to hand it to Lyle Hudnut. He knew which buttons to push. This was a singular gift he had. I told him so. I also suggested he get fucked. I said it in a classy way, of course. Then I walked out of the restaurant.

Papa Bear was sitting in my chair.

He was drinking my Bass Ale and leafing through an old volume of newspaper columns by Jimmy Cannon, which is something I read every couple of years just to remind myself what good writing is. I didn't bother to ask him how he got in. Vic Early was always good with locks. He was a balding, sandy-haired giant in a knit shirt and slacks, six feet six, about two hundred fifty pounds and quite mild-mannered, provided you didn't get him mad. Once, he had anchored the offensive line for the UCLA Bruins. Would have been a first-round NFL draft pick, too, if he hadn't come back from Vietnam with a steel plate in his head. By trade he was a celebrity bodyguard. I brought him to New York to protect Cameron Sheffield Noyes, the best-selling novelist. Maybe you read about that one. Lately, he'd been keeping an eye on Merilee and her farm in Connecticut. Lulu whooped and jumped into his lap, happy to see him. Me, I wondered what the hell he wanted. I didn't bother to ask him that either. He would tell me.

The air conditioner was wheezing away in the window, but the living room was still stuffy and smelled more than faintly of Nine Lives canned mackerel for cats and very strange dogs. I stripped off my jacket and went to the refrigerator for a beer. There was none left. I poured myself two fingers of twelve-year-old Macallan instead. My sofa was buried under a pile of newspapers and unpaid bills and chew toys. Those were Lulu's. I sat. I waited.

"She has a favor to ask of you, Hoag."

I waited some more.

"She's having a pretty rough time of it, emotionally," Vic went on, in his droning monotone. "And she could really stand to spend some time around someone who loves her."

"Why doesn't she try calling the father of her child?" I suggested, trying to sound casual about it.

He raised an eyebrow at me. "Hurt?"

"No, it's not Bill Hurt," I snapped. "Or John Hurt. Or John Heard. Or Garfield Heard. Or—"

"I meant, does it hurt?"

"Oh." I sipped my drink.

"I don't know who it is, Hoag. Honest, I don't. Neither does Pam." Vic was referring to Merilee's elderly British housekeeper. Another of my choice finds. "Merilee won't say a word to either one of us. We're baffled. Nobody, but nobody's been around. She's had no dates. No phone calls from men. No messages."

"Flowers?"

"The occasional bouquet. I figured those were from her agent."

"You ever know an agent to send flowers?"

"I never had an agent," Vic replied gravely. "This one guy was maybe going to represent me when I turned pro, only he sent me a Pontiac Firebird and two tickets to the Hula Bowl."

"I don't think I qualify anymore, Vic."

"As what, Hoag?"

"As someone who loves her."

"Actually, I wasn't referring to you," he confessed, shifting uncomfortably.

I stared at him a second. "Oh, no, you don't . . ."

"She needs her, Hoag."

"She can't have her. Lulu's my dog."

"Merilee feels she belongs to both of you."

"She does not belong to both of us. She belongs to me."
Lulu let out a low moan of consternation and slunk into
the bedroom. And very likely under the bed with the dust
bunnies. She hates being fought over. It's true what they say
—divorce is always hardest on the little ones.

"Merilee tried pulling this on me once before, Vic," I
explained. That was in London. She succeeded, too. "Lulu is
mine. Merilee got the apartment, the Jag, the furniture. I got
Lulu." I drained my single malt and got up and poured myself
another. "And she has a lot of nerve asking for her after all of
this shit she's put us through."

Vic's eyes widened. "Wait, she doesn't even know I'm
here, Hoag. Honest. This was all my idea. See, I was around
the corner at Sometimes A Great Lotion picking up some
stuff to rub on her feet and I just thought I'd . . . I'm worried about her, Hoag. The publicity's been a real strain, and
it's been a rough pregnancy. She's no kid, and it's her first.
She's got the heavy ankles, the bloating, the heartburn, the
hemorrhoids. Plus, she's still vomiting every morning."

"Glad to hear it."

"You sound bitter, Hoag." His brow furrowed with concern. "That's not like you."

"Say hello to the new me."

"It would just be for a few weeks."

"Forget it, Vic."

"Oh, well," he said heavily. "I tried." He got to his feet,
filling the small, dingy room. Lulu reemerged to oversee his
departure.

"We'll walk you back."

"That's not necessary, Hoag."

"Yes, it is. You drank my last beer."

Broadway was almost totally quiet, empty cabs prowling

up and down the street for fares. It was barely eleven, but a light rain was starting to fall in warm, greasy drops, and Yushies can't go out in the rain. They melt if they get wet. Even in good weather I was seeing fewer and fewer of the young urban shitheads around than I had back in the go-go years, when they had overrun my neighborhood and nearly ruined it. The crash had hacked a lot of them off at the knees, sending them scuttling back under the baseboards from whence they came. Only a handful of their trendoid boutiques and garish, overrated eateries were still in business. The rest were shuttered. Happily, my neighborhood was even starting to recover. The old merchants who had been crowded out were moving back in. I could buy fresh fruit again. Possibly someday soon I'd even be able to get my shoes resoled without having to walk sixteen blocks. That's one of the best things about New York. You can't kill it. You can't kill something that doesn't have a heart.

"Hear you're doing the Lyle Hudnut book," Vic mentioned as we walked, Lulu ambling along ahead of us.

"I am."

"What do you make of him?"

"He's an eight-hundred-pound sitcom gorilla. He sits wherever he wants and on whomever he wants. He's crude, abusive, belligerent, and erratic as hell. I haven't known him for long, but I hate him intensely. He has that effect on most people. In his defense, he told me some extraordinary stuff about his childhood tonight. He had it rough."

"Standard celebrity cop-out," Vic said gruffly. "They all say, 'You have to put up with my selfishness and cruelty because I had it rough when I was a kid.' I've heard that from a million stars, and it's self-indulgent bull. We all had it rough as kids. But we learn how to deal with it, and we get on with our lives. There's no excuse for their rotten behavior. Either somebody's got class or they haven't."

"I'd rather not talk about class anymore tonight."

"A bully like that," Vic droned on, "that's a guy who is

trying to prove he's not vulnerable. So he goes and makes everyone else feel like wimps so he'll feel better. I hate guys like that.''

"Like I said, he has that effect on most people.''

We waited for the light to change at Amsterdam, where there was traffic, the cars' tires hissing on the wet pavement. The rain was falling more steadily now. Thunder rumbled in the distance. Or it may have been a subway train. It's always hard to tell in the city.

"What do you know about shock treatment, Vic?''

He glanced at me sharply. He had done heavy trank time twice at the Veterans Administration hospital. Sometimes he just sees red and wigs out. I don't know if it's the steel plate or the pieces of shrapnel that are still in there. He looked back at the street. "They don't call it that, Hoag,'' he said quietly. "They call it ECT, short for electroconvulsive therapy. Know a couple of fellows who had it. Did Hudnut?''

"When he was seventeen.''

"That's young. That's very young.''

The light changed. We resumed walking.

"He claims his parents had it done to him because he was a rockhead.''

"A what?''

"A rebel. Always in trouble, from day one.''

"Tell me more.''

I told him about Lyle biting the mailman when he was three. About his fights with the other little kids, his trouble with authority. About burning down Herb's ham shack. About Allen. About the drugs he'd been put on, and put himself on, and sold. I told him what I knew. "What do you think?'' I asked him when I was done.

"I think it makes for a very nice story,'' he replied. "I myself am a big fan of *One Flew Over the Cuckoo's Nest.* Terrific book, and the movie is one of my all-time favorites. Nicholson's best performance, in my opinion. Only, that's fiction, Hoag. In reality, they don't administer ECT as a disciplinary tool. It's not there to zap the rebellion out of people. It's strictly for patients who aren't responding to any other forms of therapy. And in teenagers it's a last resort. Used only in the most acute cases."

"What kind of acute cases, Vic? What are we talking about?"

"I'm no shrink," he replied grimly.

"He said his head was fine. Totally together."

"No way, Hoag. Not if they gave him ECT."

"He also said they knocked him out so he couldn't object."

"They knocked him out because they have to," Vic countered. "We're talking about a massive convulsive seizure. If he wasn't put under and given heavy doses of muscle relaxants, he'd have broken bones from all of the twitching that goes on. Sounds horrible, I know. But like I said, it's only used when all else fails."

"He mentioned something about memory loss."

Vic nodded. "The guys I know, their memories were definitely scrambled. Especially about recent events. But a lot of that comes back. Or it's supposed to."

The newsstand at Seventy-ninth and Amsterdam was bustling. "MY DADDY IS AN ALIEN" screamed the current *Weekly World News,* which was claiming that the father of Merilee's love child was, well, a Martian. They even had a photograph of him. Or it. Complete with tentacles.

Vic's jaw muscles tightened as he lumbered past it, but he didn't mention it. "What did Hudnut tell you about his parents?"

"That he hated them. Why?"

"Because the kind of incorrigible behavior you're describing, that just doesn't happen in a kid on its own. Lyle Hudnut is a product of the household he grew up in. You ask me, he's not telling you the whole story."

"Possibly he doesn't remember the whole story," I suggested.

Vic shook his head. "No way. You're not dealing with memory loss here. You're dealing with fabrication and denial."

"This is, after all, a memoir."

"How does this connect up with him getting caught waving his wienie in Times Square?"

"He claims that was done to him, too. That he was set up."

"More persecution, huh?"

"That part's not so farfetched. A lot of people would like to see him get dumped from the air."

"Count me in," said Vic. "I've never understood his appeal. There's nothing funny about being gross. At least that's my opinion."

Vic Early always had a lot of those.

Central Park West hadn't changed a bit. It never does. Lulu speeded up when we got to Merilee's block. She always does. The lights were on in the eight windows overlooking the park, and the Jag was parked out front by the awning with its top up, beads of rain glistening on it in the streetlights. Happily, there were no paparazzi about.

Ned, the doorman, got all excited when he spotted us. "Why, Mr. Hoag," he exclaimed. "What a delight to see you again, sir." He bent and patted Lulu. "The both of you."

A kid delivering pizza pulled up on a bike. Ned intercepted him and rang upstairs.

I stood there under the awning, gazing at the Jag. If it's possible to love a machine, I loved that one. It seemed to glow. "Do you rub them for her, Vic?"

"Rub what, Hoag?"

"Her feet."

"Who, me? Heck, no. Pam rubs them. Pam and no one else. She's real upset about this whole business, Pam is. She's taking it hard. Hey, why don't you come up and say hello?" Vic offered. "She'd love to see you. She misses you."

"Are we still talking about Pam?"

"You know who we're talking about," he said softly, pawing at the ground with his size fifteen-EEE black brogan. He was a bit large to be a matchmaker, but I guess there's no height or weight requirement.

"Look, I know you mean well, Vic," I said gently, "but she's messed up my whole life. I'm not going to let her ruin my day, too."

Lulu had other ideas. She was scampering toward the elevator with the pizza delivery man. I asked her not to. She ignored me. I told her not to. She ignored me. She wanted to see her mommy. She even started to get in the elevator.

"Lulu, get your ass back here *now!!*"

She froze, shocked and terrified. I usually didn't raise my voice at her that way. Didn't have to. Slowly, she skulked back to me with her tail between her legs. She slithered the last few yards until she was between my feet, trembling, a soft whimper of hurt and confusion coming from her throat. She didn't know what she'd done wrong. She hadn't had an accident on the rug. She hadn't stayed out past her curfew. She didn't understand. How could she?

I picked her up. "Sorry, girl. I'll explain it to you someday when we all grow up."

She brightened and nosed my left ear. I put her down and said, "Good night, Vic. Good to see you."

"Same here, Hoag."

I started back home in the warm rain, my mind on Lyle Hudnut. By his own admission, the man was a total control freak. How much of the truth about his own life story was he trying to control? How much hadn't he told me? How much was I prepared to fight him over it? Lots of questions, and no easy answers. I expected this. This was why they paid me the big bucks. Not for banging out the words. That part's easy. The hard part is separating the truth from the bullshit. To do that means wading around inside my celebrity's head, hip boots required. Particularly with actors, who are the most gifted liars on the face of the earth. That's what they do for a living—they make us believe in make-believe. A trait they share with most politicians and heads of Fortune 500 companies.

Why had Lyle Hudnut undergone ECT? What wasn't he telling me? And what, if anything, did this have to do with his arrest at the Deuce Theater? Questions. I had lots of them.

I stopped at the Red Apple on Broadway for a six-pack of Bass Ale. There was a deep, ominous rumble of thunder as I got closer to home. Lightning crackled over the Hudson and the rain started coming down harder. Lulu speeded up the last hundred yards or so. We both did. My building has no doorman or lobby. Just a vestibule between the outside door and locked door, large enough for the mailboxes, the buzzers, and one person.

There was one person in there. The person was Marjorie Daw. She was ringing my buzzer.

Four

She was clutching a flat bakery box and a dripping umbrella emblazoned with the network logo.

"Oh, here you are," she said calmly, as we stood there nose to nose in the vestibule. Marjorie was as tall as I am, lean and cool and spotless in a crisp white broadcloth shirt and faded jeans.

"In living black and white," I said, smiling at her.

She lowered her eyes demurely. Though clearly she was not shy. Shy women don't ring my buzzer at eleven-thirty on a school night, not even if I know them well. Her I barely knew. "I was out walking—I live around the corner on Riverside," she explained in that poised, practiced voice she had. "And I wanted to thank you."

"Thank me for what?" I asked, Lulu panting away damply at my feet.

"For saving this week's show. Your health ed idea was brilliant. If you hadn't been there this morning I don't know what would have happened. Good thing Lyle listens to you."

"I can't imagine why he does."

"He thinks you're smart."

"I'll soon break him of that."

"I told Godfrey all about you," she continued. "And he's glad you're on staff. We both are. You're a valuable addition."

"If you're going to stand there insulting me I'm going upstairs." I was going upstairs anyway. It smelled too much like damp basset hound in the tiny space. Marjorie was starting to look positively ill. Lulu, wet, can be a real assault on the senses. I unlocked the door to usher in some air.

"Anyway, I brought this for you," she said gamely, holding out the bakery box to me. "My way of saying thanks."

I opened the lid. It was a peach pie, still warm. "Smells great. Where did you get it?"

"I made it."

"You baked me a pie?"

"The peaches are fresh."

"You baked me a pie?" I said it a little louder this time.

She drew back from me, coloring slightly. "I suppose it does seem a little old-fashioned. That's just the way we do things back home."

"Where's that—Oz?"

"No, a little town in Wisconsin. Rhinelander." She hesitated, brushed her short, frisky blonde hair back from her forehead with her fingers. "Ordinarily, Lyle doesn't listen to anyone."

"Not even you?" I asked.

"Especially not me," she replied coolly. "No one there does. They call me Miss Priss, The Iron Maiden. . . ."

"Chuckles," I added.

"They call me Chuckles!?" Quickly, she regained her composure. "They can go ahead and call me whatever they like. I'm not there to be their pal. I'm there to represent the network's interests."

"Everyone has to represent something."

"Do you have any idea what it's like to be hated by fifty-four people?"

"Fifty-three. I don't hate you."

This one brought a disapproving response from my protector.

Marjorie looked down at her warily. "Why is she growling at me like that?"

"You have green eyes."

Large, liquid ones. They locked onto mine. And lingered,

softening. "Something wrong with that?" Marjorie asked, with a slight catch in her throat.

"No, something right," I said, my own voice huskier than I expected. Too many nights alone. Or maybe it was just the rain. Sure, that's what it was. The rain.

I walked her back home in it, holding her umbrella over the two of us. She glided along beside me, chin high, back straight, light and graceful on her feet. Lulu splashed gleefully ahead of us in the puddles. She loves the rain, which has always amazed me, considering how squeamish she is. But she's a dog full of surprises. She even likes the new *New Yorker.*

"I keep thinking you look familiar."

Marjorie nodded. "You probably saw me on TV."

"You've acted?"

"Not exactly. I did consider acting at one point, but I wanted to do something a bit more intellectually fulfilling." Hastily, she added, "Not that I mean to insult Merilee Nash."

"You go right ahead. I won't stand in your way."

"What I really mean," she said thoughtfully, "is that I didn't possess the inner talent or fire or—"

"Madness?"

"Whatever it is that makes a person truly great at it."

"It's madness, trust me."

"Maybe I'm just too repressed."

"Maybe you're just too normal."

"I figured I could never be anything but average at it, and I'm sorry to say I'm much too obsessed with achievement to settle for that."

"Do you always apologize for yourself so much?"

She bit her lower lip. "I guess it's not a very appealing habit."

"Not very."

"I've been finding that if I'm too confident I scare most men."

"I'm not most men."

"That's true, you're not," she conceded. "You're much more . . . secure."

"You'll discover there's a great deal of security that comes from having no illusions left."

"Is there any joy in that?" she asked, as if we were sampling an exotic new dessert.

"There isn't so far. I'll let you know if I stumble upon any."

She shot a sideways glance at me. "You don't look like a writer." A faint smile crossed her lips.

"Thank you. That's the first nice thing anyone's said to me in a long time."

Marjorie Daw lived in a swank, art deco building with a doorman, on the corner of Riverside and 90th Street. Lulu was already there waiting under the awning. Don't ask me how she knew where Marjorie lived. She always knows these things. I gave Marjorie her umbrella back, and stood there in the rain holding her peach pie.

"Care to come up for a slice of that?" she offered. "I'll even put a scoop of vanilla on it."

"Did you make that yourself, too?"

"No. Ben and Jerry did."

"All right. If you'll join me."

"I'm watching my figure."

"So am I," I said, grinning at her.

She wrinkled her small, upturned nose. "Now you *do* sound like most men."

"I have to sometimes. We're an endangered species."

The apartment that Marjorie Daw had received as payment for sleeping with Lyle Hudnut was a vast, airy penthouse with high ceilings and a terrace overlooking the Hudson. Her taste in decor ran to barren. There was a tweed sofa all by itself in the center of the living room. A black lacquered side table against one wall of the dining room. There was nothing else. No dining table. No chairs. No rugs on the floor. No art on the walls. No flowers or books or magazines or letters. It was as if no one lived there at all. Our footsteps echoed on the parquet floor.

"I haven't had much time to furnish it yet," she explained.

"How long have you been here?" I asked, as Lulu went prowling about, nose to the floor.

"Two years," she replied. When she caught me staring she added, "My taste isn't totally defined. So I'm sort of waiting."

She was waiting, all right. For Mr. Right. It would be *their* place. They would furnish it together, holding hands in the display rooms at Bloomies. There would be flowers then, and books and life. I found that incredibly sad. I also found the bare walls starting to close in on me. I went out on the terrace while she sliced the pie. There were a couple of canvas director's chairs out there under an awning. The rain was running off it in sheets. The river was barely visible below, enveloped by the storm clouds and the glow of lights on the West Side Highway. It reminded me a little of a Hopper nightscape. Or maybe it was just the mood I was in. The air was starting to feel a bit cooler and fresher, though not much. Marjorie came striding out a few moments later with two peach pie à la modes on a serving tray and Lulu on her heel.

"Tropical depression," she observed, sniffing at the air. "It drifted up the coast from the Carolinas, brought all of this moisture with it. An Alberta Clipper is on the way though. Jet stream will send all of this packing in the morning. We can sit inside if you'd rather."

"No, I like it out here."

She smiled. "Good. I like it, too."

She sat, crossing her uncommonly long, slender legs. Lulu stretched out between us, watching us carefully. I tasted the pie. The crust was flaky and light, the filling juicy and flavorful. The ice cream did it no harm either. Altogether superior. I told her so. Then I said, "So why did I?"

She ate in small, delicate mouthfuls and spoke only between bites. "Why did you what?"

"See you on TV. If you're not an actress."

"I used to do the weather on Channel Five news."

"Wait, you're not the one who had the hand puppet, are you?"

"No, no. She was on Channel Nine."

"You're a meteorologist?"

"Not exactly. I studied botany at Wisconsin. I wanted to save our virgin forests. Still do, for that matter. I used to earn money for my tuition by entering these, well, contests, and . . ." She broke off. "I made us coffee. Would you care for some?"

"What kind of contests?"

"Beauty contests," she replied uncomfortably. "See, I was . . ." She took a deep breath. "I was Miss Teen U.S.A. when I was sixteen. My strengths were congeniality and the environment."

I stared at her. "You're kidding."

"I never kid."

"It's not so hard. I'll teach you how."

"Wait, it gets even more ridiculous."

"It generally does."

"I was also Miss Wisconsin. I represented my state in the Miss America Pageant and—"

"Don't tell me you're a former Miss America."

"Third runner-up," she confessed sheepishly.

That explained the poise, the polish, the practiced voice. That explained plenty. Everything except for Lyle Hudnut.

"I think I'll have some of that coffee now," I said. "May I . . . ?"

"No, I'll get it," she said, leaping nimbly to her feet. "But thank you for offering."

She went inside with the tray, returned with two bone-colored mugs, cream and sugar. I had mine black. A slug of calvados wouldn't have hurt it, but she didn't offer me any. She used cream, no sugar.

She took a sip and continued with the story of her brief life. "After I graduated I didn't know what I felt like doing next. I drifted out to Los Angeles to visit friends, and one of them suggested I go on *Star Search.* I ended up winning—in the spokesperson category—which led to my landing a feminine hygiene spray commercial. I also filled in for Vanna White on *Wheel of Fortune* for two weeks when she was out sick. But that didn't exactly engage me intellectually. I mean, I already knew the alphabet. And the *clothes*—they were practically Saran Wrap. From there I got a job as a weather bunny on a station in San Diego. They also made me ride the elephant."

"Ride the elephant?"

"When the circus came to town. Every station has one girl who they make do all of those puff pieces with large animals and small kids. That was me. After two years there I got the job here in New York on Channel Five. Lyle saw me on the air one night doing live updates on Hurricane Al. Remember Al? The winds topped out at one hundred forty miles per hour on the Sound? Anyway, he—Lyle, that is—hired me to do a bit as a weather girl in one of the early episodes of *Uncle Chubby.* And he and I got to talking on the set and he was so thrilled to discover I had a brain that he convinced Godfrey to hire me as the network's production and development person here in New York. I've been with the network for two and a half years now, mostly supervising *Uncle Chubby.*"

"Lyle's pretty hard to supervise."

"I can stand it," she said bravely.

"Plenty tough, are you?"

"I have to be. That's my job. And I'm darned good at it."

"I understand the two of you were lovers."

Marjorie stiffened. "He *told* you about us?"

"I heard something about it."

She was silent a moment, her eyes on the rain. "He'd scream, I'd cry. We'd kiss and make up. He'd scream some more. That was our entire relationship. He berated me, tormented me, saw other women behind my back. Once, I walked in on him and that—that bitch Amber going at it together right there in the control booth. His pants were down, his thing was out—it was horrifying."

"I can imagine."

"Lyle Hudnut practically destroyed me," she said, her voice flat. "I was a complete mess. I had colitis, hand tremors, T.M.J. spasms from clenching my jaw in my sleep." Her big green eyes searched my face for a moment, then darted back out to the rain. "I also miscarried during my seventh week. From stress, my doctor said."

"You were pregnant with his child?"

Her eyes filled with tears. A couple of them spilled down her cheeks, shimmering in the soft light from outside. She nodded briefly. "He didn't know about it at the time. He still doesn't know. I wouldn't give him the satisfaction. Promise me you won't ever tell him."

"Of course not." Though I couldn't help from wondering why she'd told me. I handed her my linen handkerchief. "Were you planning to have the child?"

"I was seriously considering it," she replied, dabbing at her eyes. "I was so madly in love with that man."

"May I get personal?"

She turned her gaze on me. "What is it?"

"Why?"

"Why what?"

"Why were you in love with him?"

She thought about it a moment. "He's exciting. There's just this incredible buzz around Lyle, this appetite for life. He's alive. Most of the men I've ever known are so . . ."

"Nonalive?"

"Guarded," she replied. "Careful. They hold themselves

back. Not Lyle. He's ill-mannered, but he's *real*. He comes right at you. Plus, he happens to be very sexy."

"He does?"

"Oh, my, yes. Talent is very sexy. At least I think so. I've always been much more attracted by talent than by looks. Of course, like most funny men, he's very sad."

"Me, I'm happy all the time."

Marjorie glanced at me curiously. "You like to flirt, don't you?"

"It's still the ultimate definition of safe sex."

She took a sip of her coffee. "He was also very edgy and unpredictable. Disordered, almost. The cocaine was a big part of that. He was stoned a lot of the time in those days. I wanted him to get help. I felt he needed it. He felt he didn't. Not then, anyway. And you can never, ever make Lyle do something he doesn't want to do. When you're with Lyle it's very much *his* life on his terms. And you simply hop aboard for a while. Or not."

"Did he ever talk to you about his childhood?"

"Never. Other than to say his parents were horrible people and that he hated them. I go home to Rhinelander every Christmas to be with mine. We all do—my sister, my two older brothers, their wives, all of their kids . . . I look forward to it. We're all very close. Since Lyle was the man in my life, I invited him to come with me."

"He refused?"

"He wigged out. He not only wouldn't go but he didn't want me to go either. He insisted I fly down to St. Bart's with him instead. I wouldn't. So he dropped me cold. From that moment on, he treated me like the enemy. All because I'd tried to include him in my family." She shook her head. "I thought he needed me. I thought I could—"

"Change him?"

"Sounds a little pathetic, I guess," she said ruefully.

"No more so than most relationships. Are you still in love with him?"

She pursed her lips primly and glanced down at her coffee mug. "I don't think people ever get over something like that. They simply move on."

"Why haven't you?"

Her eyes flashed at me. "Because *Uncle Chubby* is my shot. If I can keep it on the air, Godfrey promised he'll make me a vice president."

"That means a lot?"

"That means everything. Vice presidents are taken seriously."

"And *that* means a lot?"

"It does if you want to develop your own projects, which is my ultimate goal in life." She put her mug down on the tray and folded her lovely hands neatly in her lap. "It used to be that finding a man was. My traditional upbringing. But I've gotten over being a woman who defines herself by the man she's with. See, I don't have particularly good luck that way. My first boyfriend, Curtis, who is employed by the Securities and Exchange Commission, decided after two years and much soul-searching that he preferred having sex with his secretary, Gerald. My second boyfriend was Lyle. I've dated a lot of men, but I've only been involved twice in my entire life. Curtis and Lyle." She glanced at me nervously. "I suppose to a feelings specialist that doesn't sound like a lot."

"It does to a feelings specialist who's only been involved once."

"Are you still?" she asked me, more than casually.

Lulu didn't care for this at all. She got up and sat on my foot with a grunt, glowering at Marjorie.

"Merilee and I are finished, if that was your question."

"It wasn't," Marjorie said, watching Lulu carefully.

"How soon are you easing Lyle out?" That was mine.

"How soon am I *what?*" She was shocked, or giving a very good impression of it.

"Look, I know the network brought in Chad Roe so you

can drop Lyle. You'll have The Boys run the show and Amber direct it." Not that Marjorie sounded like a major Amber fan. But Lyle had gone on to dump Amber, too. Maybe the two of them were allies now. A common enemy, as Tommy had pointed out, can do a lot to unite people. "My question is, when? Is there a specific time frame?"

"I'm not at liberty to comment on anything as speculative or conjectural as that," she replied. Quite the official spokesperson. *Star Search* wasn't wrong.

I tugged at my ear. "I'll take that as a yes."

Her eyes widened. "It most certainly was *not* a yes."

"It wasn't a no either," I pointed out.

She went silent on me. At least she didn't lie. I'll give her that much.

"Dumping him from his own show will be a nice, sweet bit of revenge for you, won't it?" I suggested.

"I'm not a vengeful person," she said curtly.

"Don't kid yourself—we're all vengeful people. Some of us just don't get the opportunity to prove it."

"And you'd call this an opportunity?"

"Of the twenty-four-karat variety."

"You're not being very nice," she scolded me with prissy disdain, as I've been getting fresh with her in the front seat of my car outside the sorority house.

"Just doing my job."

"Then it's not a very nice job."

"It's not a very nice world."

"It can be," she asserted, vintage Doris Day.

"Not as long as people are living in it."

Her brow creased fretfully. "Are you always so negative? Or is it just some kind of act?"

"Isn't everything?"

She shook her head. "I don't think I follow you."

"The secret is not to think too much."

She narrowed her green eyes at me coolly, then looked back out at the rain.

"Lyle is convinced someone tried to push him out last spring. He claims the Deuce was a setup."

She didn't respond for a moment, just stared out at the night, as if her mind were on something else. Slowly, she turned her head to me. "I really wouldn't know anything about that," she said with weary resignation. "As for the show, I honestly don't know what will happen in the long run."

"As John Maynard Keynes once wrote, in the long run we are all dead."

"Was he a comedy writer?"

"Economist. Same thing."

She stared at me blankly.

I was starting to understand how The Boys felt around Lulu. Also to realize why Marjorie Daw had looked so familiar to me. It wasn't because I'd seen her on the news. It wasn't even her looks, per se. It was her personality, or lack thereof.

"You remind me of someone I was married to a long time ago."

"Merilee Nash?" she asked, surprised and pleased.

"I'm afraid no one reminds me of Merilee. I was referring to my first wife, Patrice."

"I didn't know you were married before."

"It doesn't come up very often. The subject, I mean."

"But . . . you just told me you'd only been involved once."

"I didn't say Patrice and I were involved. I said we were married. Just out of college. She thought she could turn me into someone serious. I thought I could turn her into someone fun. We were both wrong."

"I can be fun," Marjorie Daw insisted, her chin stuck out defensively.

"I didn't say you couldn't. I just said you reminded me of her." I stood up, smoothing my trousers. Lulu stirred. "I've had a long day at the laugh factory. That sound I keep hearing is my brains oozing out my ears. Thank you for the pie. It was excellent.''

"Let me gather up the rest for you."

She scampered to the kitchen like a bat out of heck. Lulu dashed eagerly for the front door. She didn't like being there. I stood there in the empty dining room and looked around at the bare walls. I decided I didn't like being there, either.

Marjorie reappeared, pie box in hand and a sparkly smile on her young face. It was as if she'd inhaled something in there. She led me to the door, where Lulu waited.

"Do you like Harry Connick, Jr.?" she asked.

"I think he should be stuffed in a trash compactor. Preferably while in the act of singing."

"Oh." She reddened. "Then I guess you wouldn't . . ."

"I wouldn't what?"

"Nothing." She lunged for the door and opened it. "Good night. See you at tomorrow's run-through."

"I wouldn't what?"

She swallowed. "I happen to have these two tickets to see him at Carnegie Hall on Saturday night. And I thought that now that we're working together, if you were a fan of his we could . . ."

"Are you asking me out on a date?"

"Oh, heavens, no," she gasped, horrified. "Like I said, I simply thought that if you liked him we could . . . but since you don't . . . oh, never mind. Good night, okay?" She bit her lip, supremely stung.

I sighed inwardly. I'd left her hanging out to dry. A gentleman doesn't do that. At least he's not supposed to. "I'd love to, but I'm afraid Lyle occupies most of my nights these days. I'll have to let you know, okay?"

"Okay," she said coolly.

"If you get a better offer, take it."

"I will, believe me."

I smiled at her. "Good night, Marjorie."

Grudgingly, she smiled back at me. "Good night, Stewart."

"My mother calls me Stewart."

"Does that mean you don't want me to?"

"I'll let you know about that, too."

Lulu glowered at me the whole way down in the elevator.

My phone was ringing as I came in the door. Tommy Meyer. "You don't want this shit, man. Don't want it." His voice was thick, his words slurred. He was drunk. "Don't go near it. Stay away, y'hear?"

"Stay away from what, Tommy?"

I heard shrieks of laughter in the background. Raucous, dirty laughter. Women, two or three of them. A glass shattered.

"Where are you, Tommy?"

"My wife . . ."

"What about her?"

"She's so ugly I wouldn't fuck her with *your* dick."

"Especially if you got a good, close look at it."

"Stay away, Hoagy," he warned. "Stay away." I heard a muffled noise, then the phone went dead.

I undressed. The phone rang again a few minutes later.

"Did my partner just bother you?" Marty sounded alert and sober. Also worried.

"No."

"He didn't call you?"

"He called me. But he didn't bother me."

"Oh." Marty was silent a moment. "Look, I apologize, Hoagy. Tommy goes through these periods where he sort of loses it. I'm trying to say he has a drinking problem. He knows it, and he's working on it. But Lyle doesn't know anything about this, and sensitive he's not. What I mean is—"

"He won't hear about it from me."

"You're okay, Hoagy," he said, greatly relieved.

"I haven't been okay since they decided to bring back bell-bottom trousers."

"Good line. Can I steal it?"

"It's yours. Do you always clean up after him?"

"Partners have to do a little bit of everything for each other," Marty said heavily. Then he hung up.

I went to bed. I dreamt I was on *Wheel of Fortune.* In fact, I was nailed right to the wheel. Merilee, in a sequined maternity gown and bouffant hairdo, was spinning me around and around. Lyle was throwing knives at me. They were made of rubber, these knives, and they tickled. Every time he hit me I laughed. So did Lulu, who brayed like a donkey. I laughed again and again. It was so easy to laugh. I was laughing my ass off when the phone woke me.

"Get your skinny butt in here, Hoagster." Lyle, in his command mode.

I peered at my clock on the nightstand. It was nine-thirty. "A wake-up call really isn't necessary, Lyle."

"Yeah, it is. Somebody just bombed the set."

Five

It was the set for the Japanese restaurant to be exact, the one where Rob and Deirdre were going to eat on their revised first date. All gone now—the shoji screen walls, the tables, the bonzai planters nothing more than a heap of smashed, charred sticks awash in fire extinguisher foam. One wall of the kitchen had also burned. It too was bathed in foam. Firemen were clomping around. Also a detail from the bomb squad and a couple of uniforms. Lyle, in his mask and gloves and caftan, was bellowing at all of them, demanding to know who knew what and did what and why. Most of the cast and crew were over by the bleachers, drinking coffee in stunned silence. The Boys and Annabelle. Katrina. Leo. Chad and Fiona. Amber and The Munchkins. Lulu sniffed delicately at the edge of the debris, the cops eyeing her. One cop in particular.

Not that Detective Lieutenant Romaine Very looked like a cop. Very was a short, muscular, deeply tanned street kid in his twenties with soft brown eyes, wavy black hair, an earring, and a degree in Romance Languages from Columbia. He wore a tank top of purple nylon, canvas trail shorts, knee socks, and a pair of all-terrain hiking boots. On a cord around his neck was a pair of mountaineering shades with round, mirrored lenses and leather nose shields. He looked like he was all set to scale the Chrysler Building. He stood there watching Lulu for a moment, hands on his narrow hips, biceps rippling. Then he came over to me with his chin thrust

defiantly in the air. It was Very who'd handled the trouble
when I got mixed up with Cam Noyes. We'd parted company
with a truce, but it wasn't one that would stand up to trouble. This qualified as trouble.

"Yo, what's happening, dude?" he asked, nodding his
head rhythmically as if he heard his own hip-hop beat. The
man had a serious intensity problem, as in he had too much
of it.

"Good morning, Lieutenant. Anyone injured?"

He shook his head, his jaw working on a wad of gum.
"Where you at with this?"

"The usual."

He made a face. "That would be, what, pissing people
off and withholding evidence and generally making things a
whole lot shittier than they have to be?"

"That about covers it," I replied.

He gave me the once-over. I'd switched to the oyster
gray herringbone suit of featherweight silk that I'd had made
for me at Strickland's. With it I wore a lavender broadcloth
shirt and powder blue mallard bow tie. "Still living large?"

"Jumbo, as always."

"Where you been, Hollywood?"

"Abroad."

"Cruise?"

"No, I rented a house in the south of—"

"Check, I'm asking you is the father Tom Cruise?" he
said sharply.

"And you, Lieutenant?" I growled. "They have you on
the bomb squad now?"

He glanced over at the wreckage. "Still on homicide. I
was just street hiking by on Seventh when I heard the commotion. Stopped to see what was coming down. I gotta hike
everywhere these days," he complained miserably. "Can't go
near my bicycle for three more months. Can't run. Can't do
my sit-ups. Can't lift anything heavier than a pencil. It really
sucks."

"What happened? Were you wounded?"

"Naw, I got my hernia fixed. They cut me wide open, dude. Hurt like hell. Dig, I could tell you stories—"

"Now wouldn't be a good time."

"Whatever. Doc said I can walk as much as I want, so I do ten, twelves miles a day. But I'm still turning into pudding."

"And here I was thinking you looked cuter than ever."

Lyle noticed me there with Lieutenant Very. He came barging over, his eyes icy blue slits. "Still think I'm imagining things?" he demanded angrily.

"I never thought you were imagining things, Lyle. If I had I wouldn't be here. When did it happen?"

"A few minutes after nine." He shot a look down at Very, who was listening and nodding. "I was in my office with Katrina when I heard these two *booms*. Whole fucking building shook."

"Couple of blockbusters," Very informed us, chomping his gum.

"Exactly who are you, pal?" Lyle demanded coldly.

"It's Very," he said, sticking out his hand.

Lyle recoiled from it in horror. "It's very *what?*"

"Detective Lieutenant Romaine Very," he said pleasantly. "It's my name. An honor to meet you. I'm a big fan of yours."

"What's a blockbuster, Lieutenant?" I asked.

"A homemade fragmentation grenade, dude. Homeboys call 'em cluster fucks. First you dip a firecracker in melted wax, then dip it in BB's. When the wax dries it holds onto the BB's. Each one's equal to a quarter-stick of dynamite when it blows. And any eight-year-old can make 'em."

"Horrifying thought," I observed.

"I'm down to that," Very agreed, looking around at the wreckage. "We're not talking fun and games here. We're talking first-degree arson."

"Who's doing this to me, Hoagy?" Lyle demanded,

clenching and unclenching his fists. "Who's *doing* this to me?"

"There's the picketers for starters," I suggested.

They were back out front two hundred strong that morning, along with the fire trucks, bomb squad van, police cars, and press. I'd had to throw a few elbows to get in the door. Lulu had bared her teeth, a sight known to terrify reporters of all ages.

"I don't see that, dude," Very countered. "Their whole thing is about deploring sex and violence."

"Which makes them all the more suspicious."

"Nah, there's no way one of 'em could get past Tyrone at the front desk." Lyle heaved a huge sigh. "It was one of mine," he said heavily. "One of my own fucking people did this to me."

"Why would they want to do that?" asked Very.

"Because they want me *gone!*" Lyle roared, quivering with rage. "Off the air! *Ruined!*"

Very gaped at him. Lyle did take some getting used to. "Who was here when it happened, Lyle?"

"Everyone," he replied bitterly. "Except for Bobby, who's always late on Tuesdays, and you. The Munchkins were getting tutored. The Boys and Annabelle were punching up the script. Leo and her girls were running off the new pages—"

"What about here on the floor? Where was the crew?"

"Downstairs having their morning coffee and flirting with the girls."

"So nobody was in here when it happened?"

"Nobody. We all came running up here together."

"How long a fuse does a blockbuster have, Lieutenant?" I asked.

Very shrugged his shoulders. "As long or as short as you want to make it."

"Could someone have sneaked up here, lit them, and then made it back downstairs before they blew?"

Very's eyes flickered at the steel stage door. "What's that? Twenty, thirty seconds?"

I nodded.

"Easy." He glanced at the heavy chronometer on his tightly muscled wrist. "I'm outta here. Shit to do." To Lyle he said, "Nice meeting you, Mr. Hudnut." To me he said, "Maybe we'll get together at your place for a brew. Do some catching up."

"Sounds good. You can help me move some furniture."

Very winced. "Still making with the jokes, huh?"

"Feelings. Nothing more than feelings."

"Whatever. Dude?"

"Yes, Lieutenant?"

"Stay with me." And with that he went strutting off.

Lyle watched him go. "Friend of yours?" he asked sourly.

"More of a nodding acquaintance, as it were."

"Well, whatever he is, I don't want you—"

"I know, I know. You don't want me to talk to him."

"Right," Lyle affirmed.

"Wrong. I talk to whoever I want, whenever I want. If you don't like it I can quit right now, Lyle. It's entirely up to you." I was getting a little tired of his bullying.

"Whoa, wait a second," Lyle said appeasingly.

"Do you want me to quit?" I demanded.

"Well, no. I just—"

"Fine, then let's drop the subject, shall we?"

Lyle crossed his huge arms. "Fine," he said tightly.

We stood there in brittle silence, watching the cops and firemen pick through the debris. Lulu was still sniffing. This was her being helpful.

"What does this do to this week's show?" I asked.

"Little enough. We'll rebuild the kitchen. The rest we'll improvise. That's one thing we know how to do around here."

"So it won't screw you up?"

"Nah."

"Then why was it done?"

"I just *told* ya!" he screamed. "Somebody wants to *fuck* me!"

"Calm down, Lyle."

"That's easy for you to say. Nobody's trying to ruin you."

"You're right. I have only myself to blame for that."

Lulu had found something in the rubble. She was slowly inching it along the wet cement floor toward me with her large black nose. I went over to her and examined it.

"What's she's got?" Lyle demanded.

"Just a cigarette butt." Not that it was a common butt. It was a dark brown Sherman. I pocketed it and patted Lulu and told her she was a good girl. She snarfled at me to let me know she already knew that. For this she expected an anchovy.

"Damned crew's been smoking up here again," Lyle grumbled, shaking his huge red head. "I *told* 'em not to smoke on the set! Do they listen to me? No! Does anyone? *No!* I'm not running this show. Everybody just does whatever the fuck they want. They wanna smoke, they smoke. They wanna blow me up, they blow me up." He was shaking now, sweat pouring from his brow. "They're *all* fucking me! Every single one of them. Fucking me. Fucking me!"

Katrina came up behind him now. Today she wore a strapless floral bubble dress cut to midthigh and white spike heels. "Uh, Lyle . . . ?" she squeaked tentatively.

"What!" Lyle raged blindly.

She shrank from him, terrified. "N-Nothing."

He got hold of himself. "Oh, geez, I'm sorry, baby," he apologized, running a gloved hand over his face. "I didn't mean to . . . what is it?"

She tossed her frizzy blond mane. "It's just that I was thinking, since everybody's so bummed out, maybe we could—"

"Here's your herbal tea, Lyle," Naomi interrupted, handing him a steaming *Uncle Chubby* mug. Another P.A. trudged along two steps behind her with an armload of blue-paged scripts. She handed me one. One of the strongest memories I have from my stint on the staff of *Uncle Chubby* is someone handing me a new version of the script.

"Gee, thanks, kid." Lyle brightened considerably as he took the mug from Naomi, who today wore gym shorts and a short-sleeved jersey cropped an inch above her navel. "Hey, what's that perfume you got on?"

"I'm not wearing any, Lyle," she replied coyly.

"All little ol' you, huh?"

She giggled. "Uh-huh."

"Well, don't change a thing," he said, winking at her.

Katrina missed none of this. Coldly, she watched Naomi head off, tail swishing. Then she turned to Lyle, bewildered and hurt.

"You thought maybe we could do what, Trina?" Lyle asked, sipping his tea.

"Lunch for everybody," she replied, in her cotton candy voice. "We could get Big Mama Thornton's to bring over chili and stuff, and we can all eat together in the rehearsal room. It'll promote a spirit of togetherness, and maybe boost morale."

Lyle made those popping noises with his lips. "Whattaya you think?" he asked me.

"Can't hurt."

"Can't hurt is right," he agreed, warming to the idea. "Go for it, baby. Have Leo take care of it."

"Leo!?" Katrina called.

She was over by the bleachers talking to Phil, the stage manager. She heard Katrina—she flinched. But she ignored her. Katrina's nostrils flared, and she began to chew on the inside of her mouth.

"Yo, Leo!?" bellowed Lyle.

"Yes, Lyle?" Leo came right over, an unlit Sherman behind her right ear.

Lulu coughed and anxiously nudged my ankle with her

head. She gets a little overeager on occasions. No sense of timing. I suggested she cool it.

"I'd like to do lunch for the whole gang today, Leo," Katrina informed Leo stiffly. "From Big Mama Thornton's."

Leo's eyes were on Lyle. Katrina she refused to look at.

"Chili and corn bread," Katrina went on. "Some cole slaw, sodas, and a little beer, but not too much. Please have everything ready in the rehearsal room at twelve-thirty. We'll need paper plates, plastic forks, spoons—"

"What, no tablecloths?" Leo cracked.

"Tablecloths would be nice, too," she shot back.

Leo stood there fuming.

"Okay, Leo?" Lyle asked her.

"Whatever you say, Lyle," she replied gruffly. "What do we tell the news media about the bombing?"

"Why, are they outside?" he asked, his voice filling with dread.

"In full force," she replied.

"Tell 'em nothing," he ordered. "We got no idea why it happened, no idea who did it. Make sure no one else talks to them, either. I want a tight lid on this. And I don't want them in here with their cameras, understand?"

"What do I tell Marjorie?" Leo asked. "She's called twice already."

"Tell her I'm busy," Lyle snapped.

"But she wants to know how we're going to deal with it," Leo pressed.

"We'll deal with it," Lyle said, with mounting impatience. *"Us,* not her." And with that he went barreling off.

Leo started away as well.

Katrina stopped her. "Leo, I want Naomi Leight fired from the show."

Leo whirled and looked down her nose at her. "No chance," she said witheringly. "She's my best girl."

"I want her dropped," Katrina ordered. "Today."

"You don't have the power to make personnel decisions, Katrina," Leo huffed, sneering at her. "Only Lyle does. Take it up with him, why don't you?"

Katrina's cheeks turned blotchy. "Don't challenge me, Leo. You can't win."

"You've got that wrong, Katrina," Leo snarled. "I can't lose." Then she marched off.

Katrina stood there chewing on the inside of her mouth some more. "I'm going to ask you something, Hoagy," she said, heaving her chest at me. A sure way to get a man's attention. "And you'd better not lie to me."

"I wouldn't dream of it, Katrina."

"Did Lyle eat with you last night?"

"Eat with me?"

"He positively reeked of garlic when he got home. The smell of it was oozing from his pores when he came to bed."

"Sounds romantic."

She stood there glaring at me, the tigress trying to guard her prize cub. And failing miserably. She was angry and she was scared. Toxic combination. "And where did you take him afterward? He didn't get home to the Essex House until three. And he was *so* exhausted he fell right to sleep. Didn't even . . . well, you know . . ." She ran her pink tongue over her lips.

"We talked, Katrina. All we did was talk." Until eleven. I didn't know where he went after that, although I had a pretty fair idea.

So did she. "Lyle isn't very strong," she informed me, a strain in her itty-bitty voice. "Not like you and me. He's someone who needs constant watching. I thought you understood that. I thought I could count on you."

"I'm his collaborator," I said. "Not his keeper."

"If you're going to be a bad influence on him you're not going to be anything—except gone."

"Suits me. Do you want to tell him or shall I?"

She narrowed her eyes at me. "Are you trying to insult me?"

I shook my head. "When I insult you there won't be any doubt about it."

She hissed and called me a bad, bad name. Bounced right off of me. When it comes to insults I'm coated in kryptonite. Then she ootsie-fooed off on her high heels.

I joined the writers in the front row of the bleachers. Lyle was pacing before them like a high school basketball coach, running his hands through his curly red hair while he collected his thoughts. Tommy looked positively decrepit after his night of drinking—at least a full year older. Marty looked rested and fit and at least a full year younger. Bobby was still among the missing.

"Who was that major babe you were talking to?" Annabelle wanted to know. "I'm like, ow-mommy mommy, have him bathed, oiled, and brought to my tent."

"He's Very."

"He's *edge.*"

"No, that's his name. Romaine Very. He's a cop."

"I'd like to undress him with my teeth."

"Jesus Christ, Annabelle," muttered Lyle. "Get your fucking hormones outta the gutter, will ya?"

"Sorry, daddy-waddy." She rolled her black button eyes mockingly.

"As if that greaseball Lorenzo isn't bad enough. What is it with you and low-class gorillas anyway? Hairy knuckles make your pants itch?!"

"It was just an observation," she objected heatedly. She was genuinely pissed. "And I'm, like, Lorenzo's *not* a—"

"Can we talk about my show now?!" Lyle broke in. "Do you mind?!"

She said nothing more, smoldering.

Lyle resumed pacing, all energy. "Okay, here's what we're gonna do. We go back to the pool hall. But we play down the gambling angle. Deirdre doesn't hustle the milkman. Just shoots pool with Rob. Give the two of 'em their scene together, the same way we were gonna do it in the

Japanese restaurant. Only do it in the pool hall, okay?'' He clapped his hands together. "Better get on it." He started off for the living room set. The fire department was leaving, the crew drifting back to work.

"Wait, what about the network?" Marty called after him.

"What about 'em?" Lyle demanded.

"Shouldn't we clear it with them first?"

"What the hell for? It was the gambling they had the problem with, not the pool hall."

"She mentioned the pool hall, Lyle," Tommy pointed out dryly.

"No, she didn't," Lyle insisted. "She was cool with it. Am I right, Hoagy? Tell 'em I'm right."

"She mentioned it, Lyle."

He gave me The Scowl. "So what if she did? You guys gotta learn how to handle a network. You clear it with 'em *after,* not before. Otherwise, they'll interfere in every single thing ya do. She'll find out tonight at the run-through. She'll have to swallow it because it'll work fine and because it'll be too late to change it. Leo!?" he bellowed. "Get the pool hall back from the warehouse!!"

"Right, Lyle!" she called out.

"Let's rehearse! Time's a wasting!" He looked around the sound stage. "Where's the Chadster?!"

"Here, Lyle," Chad piped up, from the living room sofa, where he sat reading over the script.

Lyle marched over to him, rubbing his hands together. "Okay, pal. Today, *you* drive this car," he declared loudly. "Let's you and me get to work—just us two."

"Great!" exclaimed Chad, grateful for his master's attention.

I stayed there with the writers. "Bobby still in Boston?"

Annabelle nodded. "He flew up there late last night. He'll get in before lunch."

"Were you three together when it happened?"

"Yup," said Marty.

"I don't suppose one of you stepped out for coffee just before it happened."

"Nope," said Tommy.

The three of them seemed quite unfazed by the bombing and the devastation. I guess they were so used to Lyle's eruptions that nothing could shake them.

"Any idea who did it?" I asked.

Marty: "Don't look at me. Loud noises scare the shit out of me."

Tommy: "Me, either. I haven't tossed a live grenade since I was six."

Annabelle said, "Maybe Lyle's not wacko after all."

"Great punchline," cracked Tommy. "But what's the setup?"

"Seriously," she said. "What if someone really is out to destroy him?"

"Then I wish that individual would come forward," Tommy intoned solemnly. "Because I'd like to buy him or her a brand-new luxury automobile."

"Where were you when it went boom?"

"Right here," Fiona Shrike replied, gurgling.

Right here was her dressing room, where Lyle's ex-wife sat perched, cross-legged, on her love seat with her shoes off. She wore linen pants of a shade the catalogues would probably call asparagus, and a loud, baggy Hawaiian shirt that made her seem even more fragile than she was.

"Doing what I'm doing right now," she added, clawing at the cuticles of her left hand with the nails of her right. She was already in need of two new Band-Aids. Busy morning.

"Which is what?" I asked, averting my eyes. I don't like to see people draw blood, especially their own.

"Trying to learn this awful script." It lay open on the love seat next to her.

"You were alone when it happened?"

"I concentrate better when I'm alone." She patted the sofa. "Have a seat if you'd like."

I sat. The glass coffee table set before the love seat was heaped with fashion magazines and mail and different drafts of the script. A stick of fruity head shop incense burned in a ceramic holder. Lulu stayed outside in the hall. Incense clogs her sinuses. The door to Fiona's much-coveted private bathroom was discreetly shut.

"Don't like this week's show?" I asked.

Fiona tilted her head forward so her hair shielded her fine-boned face. "What's to like? It's not funny. It's not intelligent. It's not . . . anything."

"According to Lyle, it's the most original, most brilliant half-hour in the history of series television."

She let out a girlish snicker, covering her mouth with her hand. "The truly amazing thing about Lyle is he believes it, too. The man has an endless capacity for self-delusion."

"Bobby thinks it's just a device Lyle employs to psych everyone up, himself included. He thinks Lyle knows, deep down inside, that *Uncle Chubby* isn't that good."

Fiona shook her head vehemently. "Bobby doesn't know Lyle. Trust me, Lyle *believes* it. Once, when we were leaving the theater after a Woody Allen movie—I forget which one— Lyle turned to me and said, 'Woody's not as good as I am.' And he meant it. He was completely serious. See, Lyle has no perspective. In order to have perspective, you have to be tethered to reality."

"And Lyle isn't?"

"Lyle isn't tethered to anything," she replied. "He's a man who has no core. At least, that's what Noble thinks."

"And what do you think?"

"I think he's a born liar," she said with quiet bitterness. "And that he believes his own lies."

"Can we talk about your early college days? When the two of you first met at N.Y.U.?"

"Sure, only they're *my* college days, not Lyle's. He was

never enrolled there. Or anywhere. I grew up in Scarsdale. My father was an insurance executive. I had an extremely boring, antiseptic upbringing. My house was clean, quiet, and safe. *I* was clean, quiet, and safe. And I didn't want to be. I got interested in the theater when I was in high school, and I talked my parents into letting me go to N.Y.U. drama school. Mostly, I wanted to escape to Greenwich Village and be *artistic.* Write sensitive poetry, drink espresso at Café Figaro. And I did, too. I found a cute little apartment on West Twelfth Street. I wore peasant blouses and jeans and no bra, not that I've ever needed to wear one. I listened to Joni Mitchell. I marched in antiwar marches. I worked part-time in a record store on Bleeker and had sex with a lot of guys who I was friends with, which was no big deal then. If you liked someone," she recalled a bit wistfully, "you slept with him. Only it never seemed particularly special or meaningful. Not sex, not school, not my life." Fiona shuddered, so convulsively she shook the love seat. "I wasn't sure why."

"And then you met Lyle?" I suggested, to nudge her along.

She nodded, hugging a throw pillow tightly to her chest. "In line at the Bleecker Street Cinema. I was by myself, waiting to see *La Dolce Vita,* and Lyle was working the line. He was a street performer in those days—Fucko the Clown, he called himself. He wore a big red wig, red nose, and white-face, and he carried a drum. He'd bang on it and crack terrible jokes and badger people until they'd give him a quarter so he'd go away. He was gigantic and brash and loud. He was eighteen years old."

"Did you think he was funny?"

"I thought he was horrible. You know what Lyle Hudnut's first words to me were? 'I'd like to stick my tongue up your ass.' That's what he said to me. And then he honked his nose. I ignored him completely. I mean, I was absolutely appalled. Then a few days later I was in acting class and this big, redheaded guy who was sitting in that day kept, well, grinning at me. Like he knew me. I didn't recognize him, naturally, since he wasn't wearing his Fucko the Clown makeup. After class he came up to me and said, 'I'd still like to.' I said, 'You'd still like to what?' And he said, 'Stick my tongue up your ass.' Well, I really let him have it. I told him you do *not* talk to a girl that way—it's sexist and demeaning and crude. To which his response was: 'I'm just being honest. Maybe you'd like me better if I lied.' I said, 'It certainly couldn't hurt, because right now I don't like you at all.' And do you know what? He got so hurt he started to cry. Genuine tears rolled down his cheeks. We ended up having coffee together, and from that moment on Lyle Hudnut was a major part of my life." Fiona paused, gulping for air. "Lyle was . . ." She shuddered again, this time practically lifting the entire love seat up off of the floor—I'm talking Linda Blair in *The Exorcist* here. "He was a wild man. A total free spirit —impulsive, reckless, spontaneous, and wonderfully liberated. He threw himself full-tilt into everything he did, as if he were alive for that moment and that moment alone. He had no past and no future. Only *now.* And because of that, he made *now* so much more vivid and exciting than anyone I'd ever known. He was utterly mad, of course, but for this repressed little twenty-year-old girl from Scarsdale, aching to bust out, he was a dream come true. He had this huge motorcycle, a Triumph, on which he zoomed around the city with total disregard for anyone's safety, particularly his own. No helmet. I'll never forget the first time he took me for a ride. I'd never felt so terrified in my entire life. Or so alive."

"Was he still living at the Chelsea Hotel?"

"No, he shared a basement apartment on Perry Street with a large, ugly rat. It cost him a hundred a month. No kitchen, no heat—it was disgusting. Food wrappers and dirty clothes everywhere. I hated to go there. It *smelled.* For that matter, so did he. Lyle was totally lacking in what you would call basic personal hygiene in those days. He didn't shower or brush his teeth regularly. He wore the same clothes for days and days at a time. He was, well, *scattered*. He hardly ever knew what day of the week it was. Or even what month it was. He was always broke. For money he did his clown thing and delivered pizzas on his bike. What he really wanted to do was act, so he was sitting in on classes at N.Y.U. and hanging around the off-off-Broadway scene, auditioning for every workshop and showcase that came along. He had no agent, no training, no clue. He was merely one of those thousands of people, young and old, who exist on the edge of the theater world, and on their dreams of glory.''

"How did he seem to you?"

Fiona frowned. "Seem?"

"His mood. Was he angry?"

She considered this a moment. "He was very hostile toward authority, but who wasn't? It was '72 and Vietnam was happening.''

"And what about his parents?"

She glanced at me briefly. "Anything in particular you're wondering about?" she asked guardedly.

"He says he told you about his shock therapy. You and no one else.''

She nodded. "I wondered if that's what you were getting at. It's actually going in his book?"

"It is.''

"He told me all about it one night in bed. He said his parents did it to him, and that was why he hated them so much. Naturally, I . . .'' She tipped her head forward once more to hide her face. "I didn't believe a word of it. Still don't. I just think he was trying to impress me by portraying himself as this dangerous, romantic rebel who society had failed to tame. One thing you should understand about Lyle, Hoagy, is that he's always searching for villains in his life. For enemies. The truth is, he has none—other than himself. My own opinion's that he simply took too much acid when he was a teenager and it made him a little crazy. In a good kind of way, of course.''

"Which kind of way is that?"

"He held nothing back. Not one thing. That made him . . ." She tossed her hair back with a violent shrug. "He was incredible in bed. The best lover I've ever had. Though I'd appreciate it if that didn't make it into his book. It would come as a real source of shock and disappointment to Noble."

"Consider it forgotten."

"You're not like other ghostwriters," she observed, raising an eyebrow at me.

"I'll take that as a compliment."

"Is that because you've had your own dirty laundry aired out in public?"

"He held nothing back," I repeated, to get her back on Lyle's track, and off mine.

"Yes." She looked at me a moment longer, then abruptly went back to tearing at her cuticles. "That also made him an amazing actor. I was in awe of him. Because he wasn't afraid of anything. That's what holds most of us back. Fear. Lyle had none. No inhibitions whatsoever. I also thought he was terribly sweet underneath. He wasn't. Underneath, he was a cauldron of rage. But I didn't know that then. Or maybe I did. Maybe I was fooling myself. Maybe we always do when we love someone."

"You can drop the maybe."

"After a few weeks, he gave up his place and moved in with me. And we were a couple."

"How did your parents react to him?"

"He refused to meet them," she replied. "Wouldn't go out to Scarsdale with me. And if they were coming in to see me, he'd actually leave the apartment and not come back until they'd gone. It was years before he finally met them, and he was real surly and unpleasant toward them. My dad thought he was just horrible. . . . They gave us a washer-dryer combo for the apartment when we got married. We'd been living there together for three years by then. Lyle thought it was *the* most absurd gift. A symbol of everything that was wrong with middle-class society. He wanted to throw it out in the street. He never got over my parents giving us that."

"What did you think of it?"

"I *asked* them for it," she replied with a snicker. "Beat going to the laundromat."

"Did he have any contact with his own parents?"

"They were totally excluded from his life. He never phoned them or wrote. He wouldn't even invite them to the wedding."

"Did you ever meet them?"

"Just once, a couple of years after we were married. We were living in the apartment on Bank Street then. Things were just starting to click for us. Lyle was on *Saturday Night Live.* I was getting steady theater work. We were finding our way in life. But it really kept bothering me how much Lyle hated his folks. I loved mine. I wanted him to love his. So I got it in my mind that I was going to bring about a reconciliation. I called them and invited them to town to visit us. They were *thrilled.* I didn't tell Lyle they were coming. I figured if I warned him, he'd freak. Anyway, when they walked in . . . the blood completely drained from his face. And he started screaming at me: 'How could you *do* this to me?! I thought you *loved* me! How could you do this?!' He punched me in the mouth, Hoagy. Hard enough to break a tooth and bloody my lip. Then he ran out the door like a child having a temper tantrum. Naturally, the Hudnuts were horrified. They fussed over me, got me some ice for my mouth. They were terribly upset. So was I. That was the only time Lyle ever hit me. It was a long time before I forgave him. I don't think he ever forgave me."

"What were Herb and Aileen like?"

"Well, they didn't fart in public," she joked. "If that's what you're wondering."

"It's not." Out in the hallway, Lulu seconded that with a

sour grunt. She sounded remarkably like Elliot, Merilee's former pig, when she did that. I missed Elliot. Or, more precisely, the sandwiches.

"They were parents." Fiona paused, reaching for the words. "Surburban, dull, totally unhip. But perfectly nice people. Herb wore a tie and wing-tip shoes, and he kept rattling on about their train trip in, and the cab ride down—he was obviously very uncomfortable. Aileen seemed frightened by the whole experience. Dazed, almost. It *was* rather surreal. I mean, I'd been living with their son for five years and they'd never met me before and now here I was flat on my back, bleeding from the mouth, and they're trying to apologize for their son decking me."

"Can you remember what they said?"

"That it was a nice try, and they appreciated that I'd made the effort."

"Anything about Lyle?"

Fiona frowned and began pulling at her left thumb, hard, as if she were trying to yank it out at the socket. This was a new one. "She said that Lyle had been his own little man from the time he was two years old. That's what she called him—his own little man. She said he always knew what he wanted and that once he'd decided he couldn't be budged. Not ever." She released her thumb. "They didn't stay long. And that was the only time I ever saw them."

"Did the subject of shock therapy come up?"

"I just told you—that never happened."

I nodded, glancing through my notes. "I understand you were drama school classmates with Marty Muck."

She brightened. "That's right. Marty was extremely funny and quick. And a gifted writer, even then."

"How did the Suburbanites come about?"

"Well, improv was just sort of the thing to do," she replied. "For actors, it's basic training. How you learn to reach inside yourself, to use your body, to interact with other performers. You know, the teacher will say: Okay, Hoagy, you've just gotten a phone call that your son was killed in a car accident, and now you have to tell your wife. It's totally spontaneous. You just never know what will come out of anyone, especially yourself. It can be really moving or angry or scary. Of course, our emphasis with the Suburbanites was on funny and crazy. Because we all were. We were classmates, except for Lyle, and we all hung out together—Steve Sweet, who is out in L.A. now writing for Jay Leno, Tory Modesto, who just had her own HBO comedy special, Marty, Lyle, me . . ."

"Tommy Meyer?"

She shook her head. "Tommy had terrible stage fright. Couldn't get up in front of an audience. He wanted to be a serious playwright. He and Marty were always working on some play. The rest of us were constantly improvising sketches together. We'd laugh and laugh. These days, if you're funny, you break in by doing stand-up on the comedy club circuit. In those days, you cut your teeth in an improv group. Like Second City in Chicago, which produced John Belushi, Danny Ackroyd, Harold Ramis, half of the original *Saturday Night Live* people. There were improv groups all over the country then. In L.A. there was The Committee. In Boston there was The Proposition, which Jane Curtin came out of. Typically, they'd perform a few standard sketches. Then they'd take audience suggestions and come back after intermission and have at them. Sometimes they paid off, sometimes they didn't. It was live. That gave it a real edge. To a degree, that's what has made *Saturday Night Live* work to this day. . . . Anyway, that's the sort of thing we talked about doing. We developed a stable of characters. Lyle's best was Commander Fuck, who was the self-styled Liberace of professional wrestling. He and Steve had a whole ring routine they did together. Marty did a bartender who turns into a rooster every time someone says 'on the rocks.' Tory did a reporter from *Rolling Stone* who is conducting an interview with Johnny Puke, the oldest living Grateful Dead roadie. I did this sadistic school nurse, Nurse Hertz, who lived to inflict pain on little girls with menstrual cramps. Oh, and Lyle and I did Katherine Hepburn and John Wayne dropping acid together for the first time on the set of *Rooster Cogburn.*" Fiona craned her neck, a là Hepburn. "Dahling, your *teeth.* They've become *worms.* The most dahling, dahling worms." She let loose with Hepburn's cascading trill of a laugh. It was a drop-dead imitation. Her John Wayne wasn't bad either: "And *you,* Katie, are the spitting image of a Comanche warrior name of Howls-at-the-Moon, with whom I once had anal intercourse one cold night along the banks of the Missouri." Fiona let out another laugh. Her own this time. "It was really silly stuff, but we were kids. Lyle would try anything for a laugh, and he'd get one as often as not. He was quite clearly our star."

"And your leader as well?"

This seemed to amuse her. "I'm sure he feels he was. He's always felt he carried us. But Marty's really the one who put it all together. It was Marty who approached St. James Infirmary, this basement jazz club on Hudson, and talked them into letting us go on on Sunday and Monday nights, when the musicians were off. There was no cover, just a two-drink minimum. We got a split of the take, which was maybe fifty dollars a night for all of us at the beginning. Later on, when we'd developed a following, we each made about two hundred a week. Not much, but we could survive, which was more than a lot of performers could say."

"How did the character of Chubby Chance come about?"

Her face turned to stone. "I'd rather not get into that."

I tugged at my ear. "You were there, weren't you?"

"I was just along for the ride," she said, turning vague. "Talk to The Boys. They're really in the best position to fill you in." She broke off, gurgling. "Lyle was far and away the neediest member of the group. He had this insatiable hunger for the audience's attention. If there's one thing you should understand about Lyle as a performer it's this: He was in it for love. For him, the audience was there to give him the love he was denying himself from Herb and Aileen. To dote on him, fuss over him, adore him. He was so desperate to impress. That's what drove him as a performer. I think, more than anything, he was just very immature. He had to be the center of attention, onstage or off, like a spoiled child. If we had people over for dinner, say, and the subject turned to something he didn't know anything about, like the war or Vonnegut or the new Albee play, he'd get really restless and surly. Don't forget, he never went to college, and he had a very limited range of subjects he could talk about. His favorite was *him*. He loved to talk about how talented he was."

"He still does," I observed. "What else did he want? What was he after?"

She glanced down at her cuticles. She'd drawn fresh blood. She lunged for a Band-Aid on the coffee table and began dressing her finger. "He worshipped the *National Lampoon* crowd, which was *the* hot, hip crowd of young talent in New York. They did the magazine. They did *National Lampoon Radio Hour,* featuring people like Billy Murray. They did *Lemmings,* the satire of Woodstock that Tony Hendra put together off-Broadway. Belushi was in that. So was Chevy Chase. Lyle desperately wanted to be a part of what they were doing. He used to hang around the magazine offices trying to pitch them ideas for articles and radio scripts. But it was a very closed, very elitist group, and he couldn't crack it. It took something very extraordinary for that to happen. It took *Saturday Night Live,* which positively exploded on the scene. That was in the fall of '75. John and Chevy became instant stars. Huge stars. And it so happened that Lyle could do an absolutely uncanny impersonation of John—particularly John doing his samurai warrior bit. It was truly devastating. So we worked it into this insane sketch about the day John Belushi flips out and *becomes* the samurai warrior *while* he's at the doctor for a prostate examination. Marty played the doctor. It was totally over the top—"

"Or bottom," I suggested. "As the case may be."

"But the audiences went crazy over it. And before long word reached John that there was this kid down in the Village who did an incredible imitation of him. One night, he and a few of his friends came down to see us perform. After Lyle did the bit, John jumped up there onstage with him, totally bombed, and pretended he was going to sue him. I'll never, ever forget the look on Lyle's face when he realized John Belushi liked what he'd done."

"What was it?" I asked.

"It was triumph," Fiona replied. "It was as if in that moment, on that stage, Lyle had been *born*. After the show, John asked Lyle to join him for a drink. They ended up partying through the night, and from then on John kind of took him under his wing. He put him on *Saturday Night Live* as the Warrior of Christmas Past in the *Samurai Christmas Carol.* He was Lyle's best man at our wedding. He even insisted on springing for our honeymoon. John . . . John was this crazed master of disaster, a drugged-out wild man, a night wanderer. He'd go from club to club to club, never wanting the party to end. For him, Lyle was a new partner in crime. Someone who'd drink and smoke and snort with him until dawn. He was also someone who hero-worshipped John, although John was every young comic actor's idol in those days. Because he was a volcano of talent and because he was living out every show-biz fantasy imaginable. John wanted to be a movie star, so he did *Animal House.* John wanted to be a rock 'n' roll star, so he and Danny invented the Blues Brothers. John was on the cover of *Newsweek.* John was blazing the trail that Lyle hoped to follow. I saw less and less of Lyle once the two of them became friends. John would just call up at three in the morning and say . . ." Swiftly, she became Belushi—busy eyebrows, gruff bellow, the works.

" 'Hey, is Lyle there?' " She was a singular mimic. Just as swiftly, she reverted back to herself, shudders and all. "He treated me like I was Lyle's mother. Lyle would grab the phone from me and say, 'I'm there,' and out the door he'd go. I wouldn't see him for two days." Fiona shook her head ruefully. "It's probably a cop-out to say that John Belushi ruined our life together, because it wasn't working out too well anyway. But he certainly didn't help."

"Why wasn't it working out?"

"Lyle was the world's worst husband," she replied, with rising anger. "He absolutely refused to deal with any of the day-to-day realities of adulthood, like paying bills, buying groceries, cleaning house. He had a real rock 'n' roller's view of life—he regarded its mundane details as something for other, lesser people to worry about. People like me. He expected me to clean up after him, wash his clothes, feed him. Well, I wasn't his mother and I told him so, but it just never sank in. With Lyle, if there was a problem *I* was the one who had it, not him. As far as he was concerned, everything was cool. He had zero respect for me and zero comprehension of my feelings. None. He did whatever he felt like doing, whenever he felt like doing it. We could be in the middle of a romantic evening at home together, making love in front of the fire, and if John called him—wham—he'd be out the door. He treated me like shit, Hoagy. He did really mean things to me."

"Like sleeping around?"

She flushed slightly. "Again, as far as he was concerned it was totally cool behavior. He couldn't believe I was being so uptight and possessive." She shook her head. "It was hopeless. It really was. We saw less and less of each other. Our schedules were so different. He'd party all night, sleep all day. I was never a big partier. And then we hardly saw each other at all after the Suburbanites split up."

"Why did you?"

"It was time to end it, that's all," she replied offhandedly. "We were each getting involved in our own careers.

Marty and Tommy had full-time jobs in advertising. I was playing an ambitious little slut on *Guiding Light,* and then I did a Sam Shepard play for Joe Papp, *Curse of the Starving Class."*

"Did that play make any sense to you? From the inside, I mean."

She frowned. "Not really. Why?"

"Just checking. And Lyle?"

"Lyle got picked by CBS to be one of the performers in *Nuts,* their rip-off of *Saturday Night Live.* They launched it with great fanfare—Fridays, after the late news—and cancelled it after three weeks. Their affiliate stations refused to carry it."

"Too controversial?"

"Too stupid. But Lyle went right from that into the sitcom version of *Animal House* that ABC did. He played John's part, Bluto. That took him out to L.A., so I didn't see him at all for a couple of months. He did come back to New York when it got cancelled, only by then I was leaving town to be with the national company of *Chapter Two.* So we were apart again. When *Chapter Two* finished up its run in California, my agent suggested I stay out there for a while. She thought I could get some sitcom work. I asked Lyle to join me, but he insisted there was too much happening here in New York. Actually, he sounded thrilled that I was staying there. It meant he was free to snort coke until all hours and sleep around without me there to nag him. I got some guest shots right away. I played Judd Hirsch's love interest for a couple of weeks on *Taxi.* And then Jim Brooks hired me to do his new sitcom pilot. Michael Keaton and I played newlyweds. That's when Lyle changed his mind about coming out. Not that I had anything to do with it. John and Danny were doing *1941* for Spielberg, and John said to him . . ." Again with the eyebrows. " 'Hey, come on out and be a movie star with me.' Lyle had a tiny part in it. He played a traffic cop. All I ever saw was his suitcase. He was on the set all day with John, and hanging out all night with John. And then . . ." She gave a spasmodic shudder. "One night I came home from the studio after rehearsal and there he was in my bed with some teenage punk floozy. There was coke and tequila on the nightstand, and the whole bedroom reeked of sex. I—I freaked. I'd had it. I was not going to be treated that way by anyone. I threw his clothes out onto the front lawn and told him to get out. I never wanted to see Lyle Hudnut again. I came back here a few weeks later when my pilot didn't get picked up. Lyle stayed in L.A. until John went to Chicago to do the Blues Brothers movie. That left Lyle all by himself in L.A., and broke. So he came home to Mommy. Begged me to take him back. I did, of course. Because I had such a low opinion of myself, and because I still loved him."

"And how did it work out?"

"Perfectly," she replied. "We never saw each other." She let out a sad laugh. "I went back to the stage, which I guess is really my first love. I did *A Day In Hollywood/A Night in the Ukraine,* which gave me a chance to work with Tommy Tune. I really had to polish my singing and dancing, so I was busy all the time. Lyle got picked by Lorne Michaels to join the cast of *Saturday Night Live* as one of the replacements for John and Danny. So he was at Thirty Rock around the clock. Sunday was the only day we had together, only he was usually unconscious after partying all night after the show. Angry, too. *Saturday Night Live* was just an extremely painful and disillusioning experience for Lyle."

"I can't remember—did he do Uncle Chubby in it?"

She glanced away uncomfortably. "He did his wrestler, Commander Fuck, who he had to rename Commander Buck, and very little else. That's because he had to compete head-on with Billy Murray and the other stars for airtime. It was a very competitive, very political kind of creative environment, and Lyle didn't do well in it. He didn't get along with the writers—I understand he once even punched the head writer, Alan Zweibel. And he didn't like playing straight man for anybody else. He's not a team player. Lorne dropped him after one season. I think, in the long run, it proved to be a valuable experience for Lyle, because it taught him how important it is in television to have clout. But it was a bitter and demoralizing experience for him. He went into a deep, deep funk after he was dropped. Convinced himself he was a failure. Convinced himself he'd never succeed. It was always somebody else's turn to break out—Billy Murray, Eddie Murphy, Billy Crystal, John Candy, Martin Short. It was never his. I kept telling him to be patient—your turn will come. Only it didn't. In fact, the phone had stopped ringing. His career was stalled. Mostly, he just got stoned a lot. He'd sit there in the dark by himself for hours staring at cartoons, not talking, not eating, not sleeping. He was like a zombie. Very down. It went on for weeks, months. I was worried about him. I couldn't get through to him, couldn't reach him, couldn't help him. I—I felt so powerless. It was truly awful. It was John who finally pulled him out of it—by dying. If John Belushi hadn't OD'ed out in L.A. in '82, I honestly don't know what would have happened to Lyle. His death really shook Lyle. Snapped him out of whatever he was in. Gave him a renewed sense of purpose. He even promised me he'd become a better husband."

"And did he?"

"I told you—he's a born liar, remember?" she retorted bitterly. "What he did do was get back in touch with Marty and Tommy. They'd gotten very successful writing commercials, but they were bored with it and looking for a diversion. And a diversion is one thing that Lyle has always been. The three of them took to sitting up nights together drinking coffee and shpritzing, like in the old days. The upshot of it was that Lyle began to test out the Uncle Chubby character as a stand-up act at Catch a Rising Star. He'd come out on stage as Chubby, sweater and all, and start telling these filthy bedtime stories. The audiences loved it. So did Lorne, who decided to give Lyle a second chance as part of *The New Show,* a prime-time comedy hour he was launching for NBC with Dave Thomas, John Candy, and a bunch of the others. Marty and Tommy took leaves from the agency to write for it. The show . . . it was a disaster. It had zero concept. But it was the best thing that ever happened to Lyle. It launched Uncle Chubby. From there he did Carson and Letterman. He did the HBO special, the album, the concert tour . . ." She trailed off, sighing. "And the old behavior patterns staged a roaring comeback. The staying out all night, the coke, the women, the whole Belushi rock 'n' roll star fantasy. On top of which he started to get incredibly nasty. You know, the 'I'm hot and you're not' syndrome. He told me I was a real drag. He told me I was holding him back. I said fine, Lyle, I'm not going to hold you back anymore. And we split up—this time for good. I went back out to L.A. to get away from his aura and to heal myself spiritually. I did six weeks on *St. Elsewhere* playing a woman who thinks she's a cabbage moth—they nominated me for an Emmy for that. I did a sitcom pilot with Nell Carter where we play twins who were separated at birth. I fell in love with a writer for a while. . . ."

"I'm truly sorry to hear that."

"I'd been back in New York for a few weeks when Lyle phoned and asked me to do this pilot with him. My initial reaction, I must confess, was no way. But the more I thought about it, the more I kept thinking I was letting my emotions get the best of me. Not many sitcom pilots get taped here in New York, and this one had a real shot at getting picked up as a series. He and The Boys had even written Deirdre with me in mind. So I said yes, even though I was afraid it meant I had some neurotic, self-destructive need to be victimized by Lyle."

"Do you?"

"It was pretty horrendous at first." She was, wringing her hands so tightly I was afraid she'd crack a small bone. "Not the show, which was a huge hit from day one. But Lyle was just coked to the gills. One week he got so bombed on tape day that he couldn't make it out of his dressing room. We had to send the audience home. Happily, Noble had come into my life by then, and he helped me to draw the line between my professional and my personal selves. I learned to just do my job and leave. Not get involved. I looked upon Lyle as my director and my costar, not my ex-husband. And Marjorie Daw made things a lot easier for me, too. It was she who now had the privilege of playing mommy for him. Only, Lyle misjudged her. Marjorie's no marshmallow. That day when he passed out in his dressing room, she refused to cover for him. She got right on the phone to God and told him all about it. God went ballistic. Told Lyle if he didn't clean up his act he'd shut him down and sue him for breach of contract. Lyle, to his credit, toed the line after that. But he never forgave Marjorie for putting her own career first—ahead of *him*. As far as he was concerned, that was unforgivable. He still hates her for it."

"He keeps referring to everyone around here as his family. Does he genuinely believe they are?"

"He does," Fiona reflected. "Because they give him what he requires of a family. They're devoted to him. They laugh at his jokes. Feed him when he's hungry. Wipe his nose when it runs. They need him. The only thing they can't give him is love. Which is terribly sad, because that's the one thing Lyle wants most out of life. Except you can never love Lyle enough. There isn't that much love. If you ask me, this isn't so much his family as it is his asylum. All that's missing is the cure. He's not getting any better."

"You told me yesterday that he's not a happy man. Why isn't he?"

"Can we get real here?"

"Don't let me stop you."

"Lyle wants to be a megamovie star like Belushi was. He wants to be idolized, and he's not. That hasn't happened for him. He's Uncle Chubby, a TV sitcom star, period. To him, that's not true stardom. True stardom is box office—people shelling out money to see you. True stardom is what John had. This . . ." She glanced around at her small dressing room, gurgling. "This is a semicute eight o'clock network show. That's all it is—Lyle's chest-thumping to the contrary. And that's just not enough for him. He's not satisfied. In fact, he hates it. Yet it's all he has. He has no other life. No other career. No family, real or otherwise. Just Chubby. That's why he tried to kill himself when they pulled us off the air. . . . Lyle is a very proud, very insecure man. His ego is huge and fragile. He genuinely believes he should be John, and he can't accept that he's not. He gets frustrated. It boils up inside of him. I think that's what he was doing at the Deuce Theater. Venting his frustration."

"He feels he was set up that day by one of the family."

Something flickered in her eyes. "I know he does," she acknowledged reluctantly. "He told me so at the time."

"Did you believe him?"

"Of course not."

"Do you now? After what's happened this morning, I mean."

She shook her head. "I'm sure they'll find out it was just one of the protestors. No one is out to *get* Lyle, Hoagy. Him saying so is just Lyle being Lyle. He always has to overdramatize. Like him saying he's better than Woody Allen."

"Or him saying his parents forced him to have shock therapy?"

She smiled at me. "Now you're catching on."

I tugged at my ear. "I'm not so sure I want to."

"That's beside the point. You're along for the ride now, Hoagy. He's got you hooked."

"What makes you say that?"

"You're human, aren't you?"

"There are different schools of thought on that question."

"Lyle is an irresistible force," Fiona Shrike asserted. "Everyone who comes up against him *has* to know. They can't help themselves."

"Has to know what?"

"What makes Lyle run," she replied simply.

"You lived with him for fifteen years. . . ."

"Off and on," she acknowledged.

"What's the answer?" I found myself leaning toward her. "What does?"

"Don't ask me." She shuddered. "I hardly know the man at all."

My own tough luck—I ran smack dab into the Chadster on my way back to my office. He was coming out of the bathroom. Lyle's personal bathroom. A major no-no in Lyleland. And, me, I'd caught him at it.

Chad's initial reaction was total panic. The man looked exactly like a little kid who'd just been nailed shoplifting. Then he turned on the charm, which meant some heavy working of the dimp, followed by a manful, conspiratorial wink. "Our little secret, okay?"

I glanced about. The alcove outside of Lyle's suite was deserted. In fact, everyone in the place seemed to have vanished, except for Naomi, who was busy working the copy machine on the other side of the main office. She may or may not have seen him.

"It's like I've always said," I replied. "Where a man takes care of his business is his own business—provided he closes the door."

Chad grinned at me gratefully. "Thanks, man."

"Don't mention it."

"And I did close the—"

"I said, don't mention it."

Chad lingered, moving in closer to me. "Is this place a dump or what? The Jane Seymour miniseries I did last spring for NBC, they gave me my own air-conditioned trailer. I had a shower, a microwave, a fridge stocked with any kind of bottled water I wanted—Evian, Pellegrino, Apollinaris, Perrier, Henniez, Ty Nant—"

"How nice," I broke in, before the big clod could name every brand known to waterdom. I backed away.

He kept coming. "Seriously, have you *seen* the men's room out there?"

"I took a brief tour."

"Totally unacceptable. I had a long, long talk about it with my agent last night, and he backed me one hundred percent. He told me, Chad, you're a *star*. Stars piss wherever they want, whenever they want, and no director can say otherwise. I mean, how petty can you get? He told me to just go ahead and use Lyle's." Chad glanced at me nervously. "But just in case Lyle is that petty, thanks for keeping quiet."

"I trust you'll do the same for me."

He frowned. "How so?"

"I'm breaking the law as well—I'm not supposed to be speaking to you."

Chad leaned a broad shoulder against the wall, carefully smoothing his thinning blond hair. "Some directors are like that. They try to be in charge of everything. Can't be done. You have to delegate, or you end up shortchanging some aspect of the production."

"Such as the cast?"

"Exactly. I had to *force* the man to give me some direction. I shouldn't have to. Christ, that's his *job.*"

"Where were you when the bombs went off this morning?"

Chad hesitated, thumbing his granite jaw. "I was in my dressing room," he replied, working the dimp.

"Alone?"

He cleared his throat uneasily. "No, I was running lines with . . . with Amber. She has some fantastically interesting ideas for Rob. Such as making him a guy whose fiancée left him at the altar. So now he's, y'know, seriously gun-shy about women. Gives him a real attitude." He glanced at me hopefully. "Don't you think?"

I left that one alone. Because I know actors. The political ones—and Chad Roe was a political one—often lobby their cause this way. If I said I liked it, he'd run and tell the next person that it was *my* fantastically interesting idea. By the time anyone bothered to figure out who the original source was—Chad Roe himself—it would be in the script. "Where is everyone?" I asked, looking around at the empty office.

"The food's here," he replied. "We're all eating together today. Katrina's doing. You coming?"

Before I could answer him Leo came marching across the office toward us clutching a tray of food. She sat with it at her desk outside of Lyle's office and began to eat.

"I'll catch up with you," I told Chad.

Mercifully, he headed off to lunch.

Leo leafed through some papers while she ate her chili and cole slaw. Me she ignored.

"Doesn't look terrible," I observed.

She grunted noncommittally.

"Why aren't you eating with the others?"

"I happen to be kind of fussy about the company I keep," she replied impatiently, looking down her nose at me. "Did you want something, Stewart Hoag?"

"To warn you, Leo. You ought to be more careful."

"About what?"

I removed the Sherman butt from my pocket. "Where you smoke these," I said, laying it on the desk before her.

She peered down at it, then up at me. "So I sneak a smoke now and then. So what?"

"So someone might get the wrong idea—the police, for instance."

Not to mention Lulu, who was eyeing her balefully.

Leo muttered a curse under her breath. "I was right here

when those bombs went off," she informed me angrily. "Ask any of my girls. Go on, ask them!"

"Now, now, Leo," I admonished her. "You and I both know you could have slipped away for a few seconds without them noticing." I poked at the butt on her desk. "Hell, you do it all the time, don't you?"

"Go fuck yourself," she snarled.

"If you insist. But, frankly, I'm starting to get tired of it."

"You're a son of a bitch, Stewart Hoag!" she cried. "A fucking son of a bitch!"

She wasn't wrong, I reflected, as I walked away. Neither was Very. This *was* what I did—pissing people off, making a nuisance of myself. And why not? Everyone ought to be good at something.

Naomi was still at the copy machine running off copies of the script. She gave me a dirty little grin as I approached her. I know it made me feel dirty to be on the receiving end of it.

"You said if there was anything you could do for me . . ."

"Absolutely, Hoagy," she assured me, hungry to please. She was all tight curves, dark, moist crevasses, and treachery. "Just name it."

"It's about you and Lyle."

She froze. "Excuse me?"

"If you two are going to keep getting it on behind Katrina's back, you'll have to do it without my blessing. I will not cover for him. I will not be used that way. That's one of the places where I draw the line. Will you tell Lyle that? Can you do that for me?"

I left her standing there with her mouth open and her eyes boring holes in the back of my head.

The rehearsal room had been transformed into a commissary, with the accent on festive. Elmore James was making with the slide guitar magic on a boom box. There were red-checkered tablecloths on the tables. Waitresses from Big Mama Thornton's were on hand to dish up the grub and work the beer keg. Of course, Lyle, being Lyle, was personally ladling out the chili for cast and crew alike. He was all decked out in a puffy white chef's hat and apron, his manner jovial as can be. Katrina was helping him, though she wore no puffy hat or apron. Practically the whole gang was already in there eating and strictly observing the production hierarchy code, which is: thou shall not mix. Television production is about the last structured society I know of, aside from the military and the insect community. The crew ate together at their own table, the P.A.'s and runners at theirs, the day players at theirs. Casey and Caitlin were at the kiddie table with their tutor. Chad and Fiona were making polite conversation at their star's table, Fiona picking at cole slaw and corn bread, and looking profoundly bored. A line snaked out into the corridor. I took my place at the end of it behind Amber, who was chatting gaily with Gwen, the costumer. They abruptly stopped talking when I did. I was beginning to take that personally. Gwen moved along.

Amber gave me a rather haughty, disapproving once-over. She had traded in her jodhpurs for a khaki safari jacket and trousers, Willis and Geiger by the look of it. "Niles says hello," she said to me. "My ex-husband. I mentioned I was working with you."

"I hope he had nice things to say about me."

"He said you were the Racquet Club loon, actually," she replied tartly, a smile creasing her leathery face.

"Someone had to be. I understand you were running lines with Chad when the bombs went off."

Amber flared her nostrils at me. "Whoever told you that?"

"He did. He said you were full of good ideas."

"The poor dear's confused," she assured me coolly. "I was alone in the kids' dressing room, reading, when it happened. They were having class in the rehearsal room."

"And Chad?"

She shrugged. "I have no idea."

Well, well. One of them was clearly lying. Was it Amber, because she didn't want Lyle to hear she'd been coaching Chad behind his back? Or was it Chad, because he *hadn't* been in his dressing room when the bombs went off? Hmm. The line moved forward. We moved with it. Got our trays and plates and forks, all of plastic. I don't believe I've ever eaten a good meal with a plastic fork, and I don't believe I ever will. Lulu inspected the contents of the serving table and padded back to me, grousing. No catfish.

"It must be frustrating for you," I suggested to Amber.

"What must be?" she asked.

"Wanting to be creatively involved here, and not being allowed to—yet, that is."

She shot a look over at Lyle, who was merrily serving Gwen. "You've heard something?" she murmured hopefully.

"I hear lots of things. The trick is making sense of them."

"If you need any help I can be an interpreter," she offered. "Anytime. I mean it."

"I just may take you up on that, Amber," I said warmly. Or what passes for warmly from me.

"Do."

Lyle and Katrina were all smiles and jokes while they served her. As I waited my turn I discovered Bobby Ackerman standing in line behind me, looking even more angry and intense than usual. Possibly his session hadn't been a roaring success. He was unshaven and disheveled, his hair matted and uncombed. He was gazing at Katrina. The kid had it bad.

"How was Boston, Bobby?" I asked.

"F-Fine," he replied, blinking, blinking. "Troubling, b-but fine."

"Step right up, Hoagster!" Lyle called out heartily.

Katrina was still pissed at me. Wouldn't even make eye

contact when she dropped a hunk of corn bread on my plate with a pair of tongs.

Lyle's blue eyes were twinkling. "Hope ya like it hot, pal," he exclaimed, ladling a big scoop of chili into my plastic bowl. "We got the three-alarm special." He lowered his voice to a stage whisper. "And wait'll you taste it—*yum!*"

Katrina heard him, of course. "Pinky, did you eat some of this?" she demanded, in her Kewpie-doll voice.

"Absolutely not," he lied, with total conviction. "I meant, I *hear* it's great."

She shook her tousled blond locks at him. "You *must* stay on your diet. What am I going to *do* with you?"

"You could take me into my dressing room and spank me," Lyle cackled, pinching her bottom.

"Pinky!" she gasped, swatting his hand away. "You're being *baad!*"

Bobby stood there staring at him with undisguised hate. He looked like he wanted to stab the man in the neck with his fork. Maybe that was why they opted for plastic cutlery.

Katrina glanced nervously around the room. "People seem real happy, don't they?" she squeaked.

"You bet, cookie," Lyle said reassuringly. "Great idea. A real lift after this morning. Right, Hoagy?"

"Absolutely," I agreed heartily. Or what passes for heartily from me.

Katrina just glowered at me as I moved on down the line.

Chad spotted me right away. "Join us, man," he called to me from the stars' table—a grand gesture this. "I saved you a seat."

"Writers' conference," I apologized, as I sat with The Boys at their table.

"Sure," growled Tommy. "Go ahead and use us as an excuse for—"

"Ducking that bozo," interjected Marty.

"Thanks. Don't mind if I do." Bobby joined Annabelle at

the junior writers' table. Lulu curled up under me with a low, unhappy moan. She can be a real pain when she doesn't get what she wants. Something she picked up from me. "Stay away from what, Tommy?"

He stared at me blankly. "Huh?"

"Last night on the phone you warned me to—"

"Don't pay attention to anything I said last night," he muttered, shooting an uneasy look at his partner. "That was just me having a party."

"All right." I spread my napkin in my lap. "How's the chili?"

"Good," replied Marty, spooning some into his mouth. "Most unusual taste."

"I think it's kerosene," said Tommy, smacking his chalky lips.

I sampled it. It was indeed hot, but well above average. Made with slow-cooked cubed beef instead of hamburger meat. Pinto beans. Tomatoes, but not too many. Onions, garlic, cumin. And something else I couldn't quite place. Ground coriander, possibly. The cornbread was dry and flavorless. Good cornbread is a rarity. Merilee always made hers in a smoking-hot cast iron skillet with buttermilk and hunks of bacon in it. I missed it. It's often the little things one misses most when someone leaves your life.

"I was talking to Fiona about the Suburbanites."

"Ah, the bad old days," cracked Marty, sipping from his plastic cup of beer.

"She said I should ask you how the character of Uncle Chubby came about."

"That was tactful of her," Tommy said bitterly.

"One might also say diplomatic," agreed Marty.

"So how did it?" I asked.

They both glanced across the room to make sure Lyle was out of earshot.

"He stole him from us," Tommy said flatly.

"Care to tell me about it?"

They exchanged a look.

"We'll give you the facts," Marty said carefully. "Lyle will no doubt give you a different version of them. . . ."

"If he hasn't already," broke in Tommy.

"But ours is the real story."

I nodded. In my business I am often treated to six or eight entirely different versions of the real story, each one of them entirely believable. As for the truth, well, the truth is that there is no real story. There's only one individual's self-interest bumping up against another's. That's why you shouldn't ever believe anything you read in the newspaper, with the possible exception of Calvin and Hobbes.

"I met Fiona in drama school," Marty recalled. "I was still kind of torn at that point in my life. Part of me wanted to perform. Part of me wanted to write. Tommy and me, we started writing together when we were still in high school. Comedy routines, sketches, one-act plays. We've been writing together for, Christ, it must be—"

"Twenty-five years," said Tommy. "Which makes us—"

"Old fuckers," concluded Marty, shaking his head.

I ate my chili, wondering what it must be like to write with someone else for so long. Their brains must have become a single mutant organism by now, neither one complete without the other. Step right up, ladies and gentlemen, and see the incredible Siamese twins of shtickdom.

"For a while," Marty continued, "the two of us had been tummeling this idea for a stage play. Kind of a *Man Who Came to Dinner* vehicle, only the uninvited guest isn't this world-famous author, he's—"

"My Uncle Maxie," said Tommy, picking up the ball and running with it. "My mom's kid brother, who used to periodically descend on our household when I was a little boy. Maxie was this totally exotic, Runyonesque character. He hung out at the racetrack, he drank cheap whiskey, he fucked hookers—my kind of guy, in other words. My father hated him, because he never had a real job and because he was a major leech. Ate up all our food, ran up huge phone bills. He'd stay for weeks at a time, driving my father crazy. Only he couldn't throw Maxie out—my mom adored him. One year they got in this huge fight over him, with the result being that Maxie had to pull his weight if he was going to stay. That meant baby-sitting for me and my little sister. And, believe me, Maxie was the baby-sitter from hell. He'd have his floozy girlfriends over. He'd entertain us with these incredibly filthy jokes he picked up in the navy. The man was totally cool. He made me who I am today."

"Wait, I thought you said he was totally cool," cracked Marty.

"Anyway," Tommy went on, "Marty and I were talking about doing this play based on him, told from the little boy's point of view, when—"

"Fiona brings her new boyfriend, Lyle, into the Suburbanites," said Marty.

"What was your first impression of him?" I asked.

"First impression?" Marty's eyes were on Lyle across the room. "I thought he was a total scumbag. That's one good thing you can say about Lyle. He isn't one of those guys who became a shit after he got successful. Lyle was always a shit. A fake hippie. Mr. Peace and Love. Mr. Spontaneous. Always talking about how we were all brothers, man. Total bull. He was strictly out for himself. From day one he was hyping himself, always going on and on about how talented he was, and how untalented everyone else was. He had this nasty way about him, this smirk. He was strictly a taker. The others were certainly taken by him, especially Fiona. Christ, she was in love with the fat fuck. Me, I thought he was a schmuck. Repulsive, too."

"The guy never bathed," explained Tommy. "And let's face it—he was a big guy who sweated a lot. Zowie, did his feet—"

"The others wanted to vote him into the group," recalled Marty. "I didn't want to, but I went along. Because he was so damned good—almost as good as he thought he was. I couldn't deny that. When it came to improv Lyle was better than Steve, Tory, and all of us put together. You'd say to him, okay, you're a fresh-caught bass in the bottom of a rowboat. And, zot, the man's flopping around there on the stage floor. All you needed was the lemon and tartar sauce."

Lulu promptly sat up, salivating freely. I explained to her it was just a figure of speech. She stretched back out with a harrumph.

"He was huge, he was physical, and he held nothing back," said Marty. "A dynamite performer."

Tommy: "And a miserable fucking human being."

Marty: "He had a total absence of consideration for the rest of us. If you're in a group, you put the group first. That's what it's all about. It's a team. You support each other. Play straight man for each other. Take turns. Not Lyle. To him, the rest of us were rivals for the audience's attention, period. He did whatever the hell he felt like doing. He hogged the stage. He grandstanded. He'd even run out in the middle of somebody else's bit and piss all over it. If we called him on it, he'd just smirk and say, 'Hey, I got a laugh, didn't I?' That's all that mattered to him—whether *he* got a laugh. It was totally bush. Like with his Belushi imitation. There was no real point to that stupid sketch. It was just Lyle showing off. But he was so talented that he got away with it. The audiences loved that bit."

"As did Belushi, I understand."

Marty rolled his eyes. "After he became friends with John he was totally impossible."

"So impressed with himself," added Tommy, with dry dismay.

"Everything was Beloosh this and Beloosh that. And Lorne and Gilda and Chevy and Candy Bergen and Carly fucking Simon. He was totally obnoxious about it. He gloated. He boasted. And he made it real clear he no longer considered the rest of us worthy of him. What he said was, 'I've outgrown you people.' Before he could say another word, Steve walked. So did Tory. She couldn't stand Lyle. He was constantly hitting on her, even though he was living with Fiona. And that was the end of the Suburbanites."

"Fiona made it sound like you were all ready to go your separate ways," I countered.

"She's just being diplomatic again," Marty said. "We would have stayed together if we felt good about what we were doing. Lyle made us feel worthless. We broke up because he broke us up."

Tommy: "And Marty and I told him if he ever tried to use Uncle Chubby without our permission, we'd sue his fat ass."

"Yes, getting back to Uncle Chubby . . ."

Marty nodded amiably. "One morning we're all sitting around the Pink Teacup shpritzing ideas for new material and we got to talking about Tommy's Uncle Maxie and how we were going to write a play about him."

"Right away, Lyle's eyes light up," Tommy remembered. "And he says, 'Hey, this guy would make a far-out character for a sketch.' "

"Translation: 'He'd make a far out character for *me*,' " said Marty.

"Right away we said no," continued Tommy. "Very firmly, I might add. We told him we already had plans for him."

"Translation: Back off, Jackson," said Marty.

"And he didn't?"

"The shithead used him on stage that very night," Tommy replied angrily. "At intermission, someone in the audience tossed out a one-line idea—Mr. Rogers stoned. Next thing we know Lyle comes out as my Uncle Maxie, totally zonked, and he sits down in a chair and starts improvising this incredibly filthy bedtime story. The audience went berserk. It was fucking hilarious," he admitted sourly. "Especially when Fiona jumped into his lap and started saying stuff like, 'And then what happened, Uncle Chubby?' And, 'Ooh, what *are* you doing with your finger, Uncle Chubby?' And there you have it—Uncle Chubby was born. Lyle's attitude has always been that we all collaborated on it. Marty and me contributed Uncle Maxie. The audience contributed the Mr. Rogers angle. He, Lyle, brought him to life. And Fiona named him. That's what he says. We say he appropriated our character without our permission. He even wanted to take Chubby with him when the Suburbanites broke up."

"But we were damned if we were going to let him do that," Marty said. "Maybe we couldn't prove that Chubby was ours. We had nothing on paper. Nothing copyrighted. But he was certainly the property of the Suburbanites, not Lyle Hudnut. That much he understood, and had to respect. Mostly because of Fiona, who sided with us. She told Lyle she'd never speak to him again if he tried to take Chubby away from us."

"So he backed off?" I asked.

"Temporarily," allowed Marty. "When he got hired for *Saturday Night Live* he tried to get us hired, too. He made out like he was doing us this great favor, when the fact is he just wanted to get his hands on Uncle Chubby. But Lorne Michaels wasn't that interested in taking on a team of personal writers for Lyle fucking Hudnut, so Uncle Chubby fell by the wayside."

"Did you two ever write that play?" I asked.

Tommy shook his head glumly.

"Too bad," I said. "Sounded like a good idea."

"Do you really think so?" He brightened considerably. Practically came to life.

"I do. Particularly told from the kid's point of view."

Tommy was silent a moment. "Yeah, well, real life sort of got in the way," he said with weary resignation.

"We didn't hear from Lyle again until after his close personal friend Beloosh OD'ed," Marty recalled.

Tommy: "Actually, it was Fiona who called us."

Marty: "She said Lyle was incredibly down. Depressed, his career in the toilet . . ."

Tommy: "My attitude was, hey, lemme at the flusher."

"But we agreed to meet with him," said Marty. "We did it for her, not him. We did it strictly for Fiona." He looked at her there at her table, eating with Chad. "For her, we'd do anything."

"Why is that?" I asked.

Marty poked uncomfortably at the remains of his chili. "She didn't say anything?"

"What about?"

"Fiona and me . . ." He cleared his throat. "We were living together when she met Lyle. She was my girl. Lyle stole her from me. I—I guess I was just too tame for her. She wanted someone reckless and dangerous. Someone who'd make her feel like she was living fast and hard. Someone who'd treat her like dirt. She wanted Lyle, and she got him. Broke my heart." A faint, wistful smile crossed his lips. "But it never changed how I felt about her."

So that's what Annabelle meant when she said Muck and Meyer's attachment to the show cut deeper than money. Marty had an even stronger reason for hating Lyle than I realized. Much stronger. I set down my fork and shoved my half-eaten lunch to one side. I wasn't as hungry as I'd thought. "So you got together with him?"

"We sat down with him," Marty acknowledged. "And I'll tell you—Fiona wasn't kidding. He was a changed man. Someone who'd been taken down a few pegs. He was subdued, morose, shaken."

"It was pretty satisfying," Tommy recalled happily.

"We knew going in exactly what he wanted," Marty said. "And he wasted no time getting to it: He asked us if he could try Chubby out as a stand-up routine. We let him—again, strictly as a favor for Fiona. We even banged together some material. No money changed hands. The man was simply trying out an act at Catch a Rising Star, and we were simply helping him out. Anyway, as you know, it flat-out clicked. Lorne hired him for *The New Show,* and this time we were brought along as writers. We quit the agency, and we never went back. Neither did Lyle. Uncle Chubby just took on a life of his own after that. He's a modern cultural phenomenon."

"Or at least he was," Tommy reminded him.

Marty nodded. "You'd have to say the jury is out on him right now."

"Who owns the rights to the character?" I already had a pretty good idea what the answer was.

Marty sighed. "Lyle does. As far as the world is concerned, he created Chubby, he owns Chubby, he *is* Chubby."

"You don't share in any of the licensing royalties?"

"Not one penny," Tommy answered tightly, shifting in his chair. He looked pained and unhappy. Even more so than usual. "We hired lawyers. Tried to get him to give us our fair share. It would have been the classy thing to do. But he wouldn't. Because he didn't have to. We never registered anything with the Guild. Never protected ourselves legally. It's strictly our word against his. As far as he's concerned, he's taken good care of us. He got us started in TV. He put us to work here. Christ, we each made four hundred thou last year from this damned show. We've got nothing to complain about."

"I can think of several million reasons," I suggested.

"No, you don't understand," Marty argued, with surprising vehemence.

"Then help me."

"This show," he declared, "this is us getting what's ours. We get our salary, we get episode fees, we get residuals. Christ, when *Uncle Chubby* goes into syndication we'll have money coming in for years. That's why we stick around. If we leave, Lyle gets it all. We won't give him that satisfaction. So we stay. He treats us like shit, day in and day out. And we take it, day in and day out. Because we're the ones who are sticking it to him." Marty broke off and made a face. "Hey, Tommy?" he said, glancing down at his bowl.

"Yeah, Marty?"

Marty burped. "I don't feel so good all of a sudden."

"That makes two of us." Tommy looked exceedingly unhappy now.

"Correction, gentlemen," I said, staggering to my feet. "That makes three of us."

Six

I watched the six o'clock news sprawled limply on my back on my sofa with a damp washcloth on my head and a tall glass of Pellegrino water in my hand. I had been downing Pellegrino for the past hour, so as to replenish my precious bodily fluids. I didn't know which brand Chad Roe was home drinking, and I didn't give a shit.

In all, fifty-one of the fifty-four members of the *Uncle Chubby* family had become violently ill about fifteen minutes after sitting down to our festive catered lunch. We barfed our guts out, if you must know. And I'm afraid you must. The lucky three who hadn't were Katrina Tingle who, unlike Lyle, had stuck devoutly to her macrobiotic diet, Fiona Shrike, a vegetarian who had eaten only the cole slaw and corn bread, and Naomi Leight, who was still working the copy machine in the office when the early birds had started dashing for the johns. She had not considered this a glowing review.

Lulu, of course, was feeling mighty superior. In fact, she was gloating.

If Chad thought the men's room was bad before lunch, it was positively revolting afterward. Crowded, too. Lyle still wouldn't let anyone else use his. His was germ-free, after all. Also *ocupado,* the big fella flopped down on his knees, praying to the porcelain gods while Katrina dutifully held his head and wiped his mouth for him. I'd call that true love. I caught a glimpse of this intimate scene because Lyle insisted I visit him in there—when I was capable of it.

The man was boiling. Partly because it was his own damned fault he got sick—he wouldn't have if he hadn't sneaked some chili. Mostly because the production, which was already stretched plenty tight because of the revisions and the blockbusters, had to be shut down for the rest of the day. That meant a solid half day of rehearsing and rewriting were lost, as well as the evening run-through.

"I don't know how the fuck I'm gonna do it," Lyle groaned, rocking back and forth on his knees. "I don't know *how* I'm gonna have a quality show ready to tape by Friday."

"Don't you worry, Pinky," Katrina squeaked soothingly. "We'll be fine."

"The fuck we will!" he raged. "It can't be done, I tell ya! I promise ya one thing—I'm bringing the goddamned health department down on that rat-trap for serving us spoiled food. Christ, of all the rotten luck."

"It wasn't luck, Lyle," I informed him from the doorway, where the doorjamb was keeping me vertical. "And the food wasn't spoiled."

He peered up at me, his eyes menacing blue slits. "What are you saying?"

"I'm saying our symptoms aren't consistent with food poisoning. No diarrhea, I'm happy to report."

"He's right, Pinky," whispered Katrina.

"I'm saying I tasted something in the chili," I went on. "Something that wasn't ground coriander. Something that has made all of us sick enough to foul up production, just like bombing the set this morning fouled up production. I'm saying you're—"

"I'm getting *rat-fucked*," growled Lyle, his anger mounting. He was starting to shake all over. His face was purple. "Royally."

A huge sob of animal rage came out of him. It was almost a Tarzan yell. Blindly, he hammered the tile floor with his giant fists, once, twice, three times, smashing downward with the force of two ten-pound sledges. And then he blew for real. Trashed the place. He attacked the sink first. Yanked the damned thing right off of its pedestal. Water spewed in geysers from the broken pipes. He raised it over his head, chest heaving, and hurled it with such colossal force at the mirror that he shattered it and the mirror both. Then he went after the urinal, pulling it mightily from the wall, kicking it, punching it, raging at it. The man was out of control, a cyclotron gone amok. A 6.7 on the wig-o-meter, easy.

And then he stopped. Just stood there, panting, surveying the wreckage as if someone else had done it.

"Get the plumber up here right away," he commanded Katrina, who was watching him in utter horror. "I want this place functioning and spotless by nine A.M. tomorrow, understand?" She nodded obediently. Then he turned to me, his thick lower lip stuck out petulantly. "Somebody else has been using this john. I *feel* it! I *know* it!"

Mr. Sensitivity. Me, I oozed on down the road for home. Changed into my shawl-collared silk target-dot dressing gown from Turnbull & Asser and my tattered mukluks. An old work ritual. Writers tend to be superstitious. People who are frightened usually are. I tried to rough out the first two chapters, only I couldn't make it work. Too many questions. So I did some phone work instead. Spoke to my cousin Tommy in New Haven, among others. Tommy has been exceedingly helpful to me in my second career. Don't tell him that or he'll start charging me. He's a psychiatrist. Also the only member of my family who will speak to me. I don't know if there's a connection there or not. After I got off the phone with him, Marjorie Daw phoned to say how glad she was she hadn't come by for lunch—she'd intended to but got called into a meeting at the last minute. She asked if she could bring me anything on her way home from work. I made the mistake of saying, such as? She made the mistake of saying such as a container of her homemade Wisconsin-style cream-of-corn chowder. And that took care of the rest of the afternoon.

The six o'clock news played up that morning's bombing

of *The Uncle Chubby Show* set big-time. Anything to do with Lyle was still hot. Although there were no facts to support it, the coverage left a clear impression that the bombing somehow had to do with the presence of the protestors out front. This because the reporter delivered her stand-up out there surrounded by them screaming and waving their signs. Visuals. Just one of the not-so-subtle ways television distorts the news.

They did not report the chili incident. This because they didn't know about it. Lyle didn't want "his kids" to know he'd been sick. So the police were not called. Knew nothing about it. At least not officially. Romaine Very knew. I phoned him before I left the office. Even left a Styrofoam container of chili downstairs for him with Tyrone—for purposes of analysis, not consumption. Very acted somewhat put out, but he agreed to check it out. And stop by later.

I was lying there watching Merilee's favorite show, *Jeopardy!*, when I was buzzed from downstairs. Very, I assumed. I buzzed him in, not bothering with the intercom, which hasn't been operational since the days when Pat Paulsen was considered presidential timber. I opened my door, turned off the TV, and waited for him.

Only it was Katrina. She'd changed from her sedate office ensemble into a pair of skintight Gianni Versace leopard-skin jeans and a black suede baseball jacket, which she wore zipped to the neck. She stood in the doorway with her hands stuffed in her jacket pockets, looking around the place. It doesn't take long. Then she focused on me, or rather about a foot to the right of me. Her eye seemed to get worse as the day wore on.

"You don't live very well," she squeaked, tossing her frizzy blond mane.

"Just passing through. This is strictly temporary."

"How long have you been here?"

"Nineteen years." I made room for her on the easy chair, which involved shooing Lulu out of it. "Have a seat."

Before she did, Katrina unzipped her jacket and draped it over my desk chair. She was wearing a sheer, shimmery bodysuit under it, the sort that a woman might wear with a silk camisole underneath. Or, if she were feeling particularly frisky, a black satin bra. Katrina wore neither of these things. She wore absolutely nothing. Her immense, gravity-defying breasts were just *right there,* the nipples a pale pink and the approximate circumference of a 7 Eleven Big Gulp cup. I stared. I couldn't help it. They looked as if they might honk if I squeezed them. Or squirt me in the face. Or . . . oh, never mind.

"I just wanted to make sure you were okay," she said, choosing to sit next to me on the couch. "I've stopped by to visit a few of the others."

"That's very considerate of you."

"It's the least I can do. I feel so badly. What I really want to do is take you home and give you crabs."

I tugged at my ear. "Excuse me?"

"I make them with spices from the Maryland shore. That's where I'm from originally. Best thing in the world when you're not feeling well."

"I don't doubt that for a second."

She smelled of lily of the valley, a heavy, cloying scent vaguely reminiscent of a Frank E. Campbell funeral parlor. It made me drowsy. Lulu went over to her and sniffed at her, whimpering weakly.

"What's wrong with her?" Katrina wondered, petting her.

"She's hungry," I replied, trying not to stare at her hooters. Katrina's, not Lulu's.

"I can feed her for you," she offered.

"Please don't. We're a team. If I suffer, she suffers. Besides, she was gloating earlier."

"Dogs don't gloat," scolded Katrina.

"Believe me, she gloats. Has Lyle calmed down?"

"Oh, yes, he's lots better. He can be a little scary when things . . . boil over. But afterwards, he's fine. For him, letting go is a really healthy thing."

"I'm not so sure his plumber would agree."

"Plus, he had a good, heart-to-heart phone conversation with God, and that made him feel a lot better. See, Lyle wanted to push back the taping a week so we'd have time to do things right. God said no, because that would mean we'd have to push back our air date, too, and we're a big, big part of premiere week. So then Lyle suggested we bump Rob Roy Fruitwell back to a later episode, so we can give him the attention he deserves. But again God said no. . . ."

"I thought you said Lyle feels a lot better."

"Because God agreed to cover the overages," she explained patiently. "We'll have to tape over the weekend. That means paying the crew monster overtime. Costs us a fortune. The network never kicks in on that. They consider it the supplier's problem. But God said he'd foot the bill. That's a major, major show of support. Lyle really needed to hear something like that. We'll tape on Saturday. We'll still have to rush, but at least it's doable. There's a writer's meeting tomorrow at nine. Marjorie will be there."

"Okay."

She shot me a nervous sidelong glance. "Actually, Lyle doesn't know I'm here." She chewed fretfully on the inside of her mouth.

"Why are you?"

"I told you—to see how you are."

I nodded. "Me and a few of the others."

"None of the others," she confessed in a soft, intimate voice. "Just you. I was really upset about that little tiff we had on the set this morning. You were absolutely right—it's not your job to baby-sit Lyle." She let out a sigh, hooters heaving. "I think I've figured out what our problem is."

"We have a problem?"

"We're too much alike."

"We are?"

"We both have trouble trusting anybody. Because we've both seen the bad side of other people."

"You mean there's a good side to other people?"

"I have one," she asserted, her eyes meeting mine. Almost. "And so do you. I want us to like each other, Hoagy. We're on the same side. Lyle's side. We should be friends. We should be . . . close." She put her hand on my thigh.

I glanced down at it. Her fingers were gently caressing my dressing gown. She was no Kewpie doll, this one. She was smart and she was tough. Also pissed off at Lyle for fucking Naomi Leight behind her back. Was this her way of getting even? I took her hand and held it. She let me. She even leaned into me so that her right breast rested on my arm. It was surprisingly heavy. "I'm glad you feel that way, Katrina. Because I do, too."

"Oh, good," she whispered, her breath moist on my neck.

I was very warm all of a sudden. Her body heat. Lyle wasn't kidding. She was a woman to perspire to. "It must not be easy. Being in a relationship with him, I mean."

Her steamy thigh pressed against mine. "Oh, it's not. He's so, so weak. Like a little boy. And he isn't in the habit of thinking about someone else's feelings. Not like you are."

"Is there something you wanted to tell me, Katrina? Something you didn't want Lyle to know you'd told me?"

She looked at me blankly. "Like what?"

"Has he ever hit you?"

"Oh, no. . . . Well, not really."

"It's not a gray area, Katrina. Either he has or he hasn't."

"Last spring," she admitted, gingerly fingering her jaw. "Only he wasn't hitting *me,* per se. He was hitting God. For cancelling him."

"And did *you* consider cancelling him?"

She lowered her eyes. "It's only happened that one time."

"And if it happens again?"

"I'm not a punching bag, if that's what you're wondering," she said defensively. "I have too high an opinion of myself to let anybody do that to me."

"Good." I squeezed her hand. "May I ask you something else?"

She ran her fingers lightly through my hair. "You can ask me *anything*."

"Why did you doctor the chili?"

She hadn't seen that one coming. "What are you talking about?" she demanded frostily, dropping my hand.

"The catered lunch was all your idea. You specified chili. You even helped serve it. You and Lyle. Only Lyle got sick, and you didn't. Why did you do it, Katrina?"

She shook her head at me in bewilderment. "Are you for real?"

"As seldom as possible. What did you use, anyway?"

"You're crazy!" she cried, her eyes blazing at me. "The food was sitting there in the hallway outside the rehearsal room for five or ten minutes while we were setting up the tables. *Anybody* could have put something in the chili. And, besides, why would I even *want* to, huh?! What possible reason would I have?" She gazed at me uncertainly. "What is this, some kind of test?"

"No, this is me trying to figure out what the hell's going on."

My phone rang. I took it in the bedroom. It was Pam, Merilee's most British housekeeper.

"Greetings, dear boy," she exclaimed cheerily. "I trust you are well."

"That would be something of an exaggeration, Pam." I flopped down on my unmade bed. "And you?"

"I myself am ginger peachy. But, alas, poor Vic . . ."

"Something's happened to Vic?"

"It has indeed. This frightful business between you and Merilee. Oh, he's putting up the bravest of fronts—men will be men and all. But he's taking it terribly hard."

"Look, Pam, if you're calling about Lulu . . ."

"Merilee needs her, Hoagy. The poor dear is inconsolable. Weeps at the drop of a hat."

"Good."

She was silent a moment. "This isn't like you, Hoagy."

"It's the new me."

"Oh, dear, I was still trying to fathom the old you. I do wish you'd reconsider, Hoagy. It would be the decent thing to do. You've always been decent."

"That was the old me. I'm sorry, Pam. Also appalled. If she needs Lulu this badly you'd think she'd have the courtesy to ask me herself."

"But she doesn't even know I'm calling," Pam insisted hurriedly. "It was entirely my own idea."

"Do you and Vic rehearse your lines together, or what?"

She was silent again. "I haven't the slightest idea who the father is, Hoagy."

"I wasn't asking," I growled.

"I only know Merilee's spirits are terribly, terribly low. No one visits. No one rings up. I—I'm worried about her. A woman needs her strength at a time like this."

I could hear Katrina stirring around in the kitchen. "Look, Pam, I can't talk right now, okay?"

She gasped, horrified. "You've a *woman* there, haven't you? A bleached blonde—with a monstrous pair of cow udders on her."

I found myself glancing out the window. "Are you perched on the roof across the way with a pair of binoculars?"

"I am not," Pam replied witheringly. "I simply know men—too bloody well." And with that she hung up. I think she was disappointed with me.

Katrina was putting down canned mackerel for Lulu. "You didn't have any other pet food," she squeaked. "I thought she *might* eat this stuff."

"She'll do fine," I said, watching her wolf it down. The smell of it made me light-headed, but I held my ground.

"The poor thing was whimpering," Katrina explained.

"That's one of the things she's best at."

"I really should go," she said. "Lyle misses me."

"I understand Leo misses you, too."

"Why, what have you heard about the two of us?" she asked casually.

"That she cared about you."

"We were friends," Katrina stated. "If she thought we were anything more than that, she got the wrong idea."

"Sure you didn't help her?"

"Positive," she replied coldly. "If I had my way I'd shit-can her. She's such a negative presence. But Lyle won't allow it. They work too well together."

"So I hear."

She came over to me and reached for the belt of my dressing down and held it in the palm of her hand. She stood very close to me, her nipples grazing against my chest, her eyes fastened on my mouth. I think. "You're going to hear a lot of negative buzz about me," she said softly. "Don't believe it. Ninety percent is envy. Because of how I look. And because I have Lyle. You have to understand how much everybody there resents me."

"Bobby doesn't," I pointed out. "In fact, he's crazy about you."

"How sweet," she said, her eyes flickering with surprise. Or that may have been her computer filing away the data for future use. "It's like I told you when we met, Hoagy. I always get what I want."

"That must be nice."

A faint smile crossed her lips. "Oh, it is. It's very nice."

"You'll have to tell me how you do it sometime."

"I show better than I tell," she said, leaning in closer. Now her nipples were climbing inside my dressing gown. "I'm beginning to think you and I have a future."

"And what about Lyle?"

"Maybe all we have is a past."

"You change your verb tenses awfully fast," I observed.

"Some things I do fast. Other things I do real slooow. . . ." Just in case I was missing her point she ran her tongue seductively over her lower lip. "You can help him, you know," she whispered.

"Can I?"

"Well, the word's out that you're definitely *in* with Miss Priss," she pointed out.

"Am I?"

"You can help him," she repeated, a bit more desperately.

"And if I can't?"

She didn't bother to answer that one. Didn't need to. It was obvious. She was looking to hold onto what she had, with or without Lyle. Ready to change sides. Ready to change men. Ready for anything. Or at least ready to let me think she was.

"I felt something happen that first day, Hoagy," she squeaked, tugging gently at my belt. I wished she'd stop doing that. "The second you and Lulu rang the doorbell."

"I was the one who rang it. She just stood there doing nothing." Like she stood there now, stuffing her face on cat food.

"I felt someone important walking into my life," Katrina confessed. "Someone who could see right inside my soul."

"You're mistaken there. My vision isn't nearly what it used to be. In fact, my ophthalmologist is talking bifocals."

"Don't tease me." She pouted. "I'm laying myself wide open. I'm out there."

"I'm out there, too, Katrina." Not that I knew what the

hell that meant. I only knew it was what she wanted to hear. And that she might eventually prove useful to me. Strictly in a professional sense, you understand.

She let out a little squeal of pleasure and threw her arms around me. "I'm so glad we had this talk, Hoagy," she exclaimed, hugging me tightly. "I feel so much better about us now." She planted a warm, wet kiss on my neck. Then she zipped her zoomers safely and snugly back inside her jacket and left me there, wondering.

There was so much to wonder about. Had Katrina doctored the chili? Bombed the set? Stolen Uncle Chubby's sweater? She did have a key to the wardrobe cupboard. What about the Deuce Theater? Had she set Lyle up? Why would she do that? Why would she do any of it? What possible reason could she have for wanting to destroy *Uncle Chubby*? It made zero sense. Besides, Lyle had said the two of them were together when the bombs went off. He could vouch for her. . . . He could not, however, vouch for Fiona. No one could vouch for Fiona, and she hadn't eaten the chili either. Was she responsible for all of this? Was this her getting even with Lyle? I wondered. Just as I wondered about Naomi, who hadn't touched the chili and who was screwing Lyle. How did she figure in? And what about Chad Roe? He'd lied to me about what he was doing when the bombs went off. Either he'd lied or Amber Walloon had. Of course, they'd both gotten sick from the chili. . . .

I stood there, wondering. Not for long, though. My buzzer sounded again, and this time is was Very, in his shorts and hiking boots, extremely out of breath. Sweat streamed down his face and neck. "Evening, dude," he panted. "Dig, wasn't that Katrina Tingle I just saw wiggling on down the street?"

"It was."

He nodded. "Thought I recognized her from this morning. She don't exactly blend into a crowd."

"Especially with her jacket off."

"I'm down to that. You poking her behind Hudnut's back?"

"Not exactly."

He peered at me suspiciously. "Meaning you're not poking her? Or you are but he's hip to it?"

"None of the above."

He mopped his face with a bandanna. "Whew, gotta cop me a squat."

"Don't let me stop you."

"Street hiked up here from Soho—a solid hour at warp speed." He settled carefully into the easy chair, wincing. "Damned hernia. Son-of-a-bitch surgeon cut me open like a fish. I could tell you stories about—"

"Now wouldn't be a good time, Lieutenant. Get you a beer?"

"I could handle that."

I opened him a Bass, and after a moment's deliberation, one for myself. We drank, Very nodding to his own rock 'n' roll beat. Lulu stuck her head on his bare knee. He patted her. "That surgical mask Hudnut wears. What's up with that?"

"He's risk averse." I took a seat on the sofa. "Or so he claims."

"Yo, he picked the wrong city to live in."

"Yo, he picked the wrong universe to live in."

"Got the lab results on the chili," he informed me, gulping down his beer.

"That was fast."

"Rushed it through."

"And?"

"And you was right, dude. There was a foreign substance in it, category nontoxic. Ever hear of ipecac?"

"Syrup of ipecac? Sure. Parents keep it around in case their midget human life forms swallow something they shouldn't."

"That's the stuff. Guaranteed to induce projectile vomiting in fifteen to twenty minutes."

It was my turn to wince. "Projectile and vomiting are two words I don't need to hear together in the same sentence for a few weeks, Lieutenant. If you don't mind."

"Sorry, dude." He drained his beer. "Mind if I suck down another one? Worked up a major thirst."

"Help yourself."

"Mind getting it for me? Hard for me to get up once I'm down. See, he slashed right through my lower abdominal muscles and—"

"I'll get it, I'll get it." I fetched it for him, though I'd appreciate it if you wouldn't mention that to anyone. "So that's what was in the chili? Syrup of ipecac?"

"No."

I frowned. "But you just said—"

"Stay with me—Syrup of ipecac would never work. Too strong a flavor. Shit tastes like—"

"No need to go into details."

"Plus the adult dosage is two tablespoons. To knock out fifty-plus people you'd have to dump something like two quarts of it into the chili. No way you wouldn't notice it. What this was, dude, was fluid extract of ipecac, which ain't exactly lavender honey either, but it's fourteen times stronger than the syrup. Couple of ounces in the pot and—coo-coo-ka-choo—you're all taking a guided tour on the Chunk City Express. The chili, being highly spiced, disguised the taste."

"Can you buy fluid extract over the counter?" I asked.

He shook his head. "According to the lab, you can't buy it anywhere. 'Should no longer be found in any pharmacy,' was how they put it." He peered at me suspiciously again. "What's going down, dude? First the blockbusters, now this. What's happening over at that place?"

I shrugged. "Just the usual fun and games that occur

when you put a group of highly creative, sensitive psychotics together in a pressure-packed environment."

He stared at me, jaw muscles tensing. "Not what I had in mind, dude."

"What did you have in mind, Lieutenant?"

He took a gulp of his beer. "Look, maybe we better clear the air in here."

"I can open a window," I offered. "Katrina's perfume was—"

"That's not what I meant," he snapped impatiently. "Last time around, you free-lanced on me. Held out on me. *Boned* me."

"And you forgave me."

"No, I didn't," he stated firmly. "I chalked it up until next time. Well, guess what? It's next time. And we're playing it different. A free-flowing exchange of ideas and information. For starters—"

"Are you going to deputize me?"

He rolled his eyes in exasperation. "No, I'm not going to deputize you."

"How about Lulu?"

She snuffled excitedly. She's always wanted to carry a badge.

Very glowered at me. "No offense, Hoagy, but I talk better when you don't."

"Sorry, Lieutenant. What did you have in mind?"

"Crime prevention," he replied. "It's like this: I could sit back and wait until this gets hotter."

"Hotter how?"

"Hotter like maybe next time it's a toxic substance in the chili. Or there are a whole bunch of people on the set when it gets bombed. Then everybody will say, hey, how come this crazy fuck was walking around? How come the police didn't see this coming? I don't want that shit to happen, Hoagy. Okay? This is me trying to nip it in the bud. I'm being straight with you. I'm asking you to help me. And you can help me. By telling me what you know.''

"And if I don't?"

"I'll still respect you in the morning," he replied calmly. "But if this shit does get hotter, and somebody maybe turns up dead, then you'll know you had a chance to stop it from happening, and you didn't. And that'll be on your conscience, if you got one, until the day you die.''

"Get you a putty knife, Lieutenant?"

"Huh?"

"Laying it on a tad thick, aren't you?"

He started to say something, but he stopped himself. Drained his beer and handed me the bottle, wincing. Quietly, between his teeth, he said, "Yo, somebody isn't joking here, dude. You know it and I know it. So stop dancing with me and get me another beer and three Advil and tell me what the fuck's going down, will ya?"

I got him his beer and his Advil. "How tight are you with the Public Morals Division?"

"Vice? About as tight as I care to be. Why?"

"Know somebody over there?"

"Why?" he repeated.

I told him why. I told him about how Lyle believed he'd been a target that day at the Deuce. That it was no routine sweep. That the press got there too soon. That someone had tipped them off. "Can you find out what went down that day, Lieutenant? What the vice squad was doing there?"

"I can ask. Only, why wasn't this pursued at the time?"

"According to Lyle, there was a desire on everyone's part to put it behind them."

"And now there isn't?"

"It would certainly appear that way."

I filled him in on the rest. The bombing and the chili he already knew about. He didn't know about the sweater being stolen. Or about the network trying to ease Lyle out of his own show. I told him about The Boys, who wanted to take over, and Bobby, whom Lyle loved to torment, and Annabelle, whose boyfriend Lyle had slagged. I told him about Lyle's ex-lovers, Amber and Marjorie, and about Naomi, his new one. I told him about Leo, who may or may not have been Katrina's ex, but who certainly hated her like one. I gave him a few leads—things he could check out that I couldn't. I gave him plenty. Not everything. But plenty. He listened intently, jaw working his gum.

"Satisfied?" I said, when I was done.

"Not supersatisfied," he replied. "But it's a start." He got to his feet, slowly, and stood there a moment, biceps rippling, knee quaking. "Listen, you really don't know?"

"Don't know what, Lieutenant?"

"Who the father is. Not that I mean to get up in your business . . ."

"You're up in it, all right."

"Want me to find out for you? I can ask around. Discreetly, of course."

"Why would you want to do that?"

He shrugged. "Because we have a relationship, that's why. You help me, I help you."

I tugged at my ear. "I appreciate the offer, Lieutenant. But it so happens I'd rather not know who the father is."

He raised his chin at me, eyes flashing. "Ignorance is bliss, huh?"

"Ignorance is hell. But knowledge is worse."

He considered this a moment, nodding, before he said, "Afraid of what you'll find out about yourself, aren't you, dude?"

"Whatever do you mean, Lieutenant?"

"I mean you're afraid if you know who the cocksucker is you'll want to grab him around the throat with your bare hands and squeeze the life out of him. I mean you're afraid you're just like all the rest of us—capable of losing it."

"I've already lost it."

"Oh, yeah?" he blustered. "When's the last time you punched somebody's lights out in anger?"

"Does immediate family count?"

"No."

"I'll have to think about it."

Very stood there grinning at me. "You go ahead, dude. You just go right ahead and think." Then he let out a short, harsh laugh and barged out my door into the steamy New York night.

I undressed and slid into bed and lay there. I didn't have to think about it long. I knew exactly when I'd last thrown my last punch in anger, and who I'd thrown it at. It was Chapin Lumley, summer of '62. He'd stolen my Tom Tresh rookie card and wouldn't give it back. So I clocked him one right on the nose. I couldn't believe how much it bled. Or how hard he cried. We were never friends again after that. Chapin Lumley. Congressman Lumley now . . . I lay there thinking about what Very had said. What *would* I do when I found out who Dada was? Would I go far, far away? Would I stay and fight it out with him? Or would I just get on with the rest of my life, such as it was. Or wasn't. It was over with Merilee. For good. That much I knew. It was time to let it go. So why couldn't I? I lay there in the darkness with the air conditioner droning and Lulu snoring softly on my head. I lay there, wondering why she had done this to me, just like I wondered why almost every night. And got no reply at all. Eventually, I slept. I dreamt I was laid out on an operating table with my private parts exposed. And wouldn't Dr. Freud have a romp through the tall grass with that one. The surgeon stood poised over me, scalpel in hand, only it was Lyle behind the mint-blue mask and he suddenly seemed much more interested in breaking my arm. He twisted it in ways it wasn't supposed to twist, pinned it behind me, torturing me. I yelled from the pain. That made him mad, so he attached a wire to my head. I immediately heard this ringing noise. Ringing . . . Ringing . . .

It was my telephone, jolting me awake. My arm was killing me—Lulu had it pinned underneath her. These things happen sometimes in the night. The phone was still ringing. I squinted at my clock. It was a little past three. I answered it.

"How could you, Hoagy?" she sobbed.

My heart began pounding at once, which is what it always does when I hear that proper, feathery teenage girl's voice that is hers and hers alone. "What do you want, Merilee?"

"Oh, how *could* you?" She wept, grandly and tragically. Never forget that Merilee Nash is an Academy Award-winning actress. I don't. "You *know* how vulnerable I am right now."

"Merilee, it's three o'clock in the—"

"And with a sleazy bimbo, no less. A cheap bottle blonde with hooters out to Hoboken." She let out a long, plaintive moan. "I honestly thought I raised you better than this."

"You raised me, Merilee," I conceded. "And you lowered me."

"Is that what this is about? You getting back at me? And don't bother to deny it, Hoagy. Pam told me. I *know*."

"You know what?"

"That you've taken your beeswax elsewhere," she said gravely. One of her quaint little expressions.

"Fairly good idea under the circumstances, wouldn't you say?"

Long silence from her end. "Hoagy, couldn't we . . . ?"

"Couldn't we what, Merilee?"

She sniffled. "Couldn't we talk like two normal people?"

"I don't believe either of us qualifies."

"Just for a minute, darling?" she pleaded. "Like the old days?"

I sighed. "All right, Merilee. If you wish."

"Hoagy?"

"Yes, Merilee?"

"Hello."

"Hello yourself."

"How was France?" she asked, with forced gaiety.

"Not terrible."

She waited for me to say more. When I didn't, she said, "And how was your day?"

"Fine, if you enjoy projectile vomiting."

"I myself vomit every morning."

"I know. Vic told me."

"I wish he hadn't. I hate to see your illusions about me shattered."

"I have no illusions left about you, Merilee."

She drew her breath in. "That was a mean, horrible thing to say, Hoagy. Pam warned me that you'd turned somewhat acrid."

"Let's just say that I put one and one together and it added up to fool."

Lulu edged closer to the phone, whimpering at it. She always knows when it's her mommy. Don't ask me how.

Merilee gasped girlishly. "Oh, is that my sweetness?"

"No. Just the bedspring."

"Why, is *she* there?"

"Who, Merilee?"

"The bimbo. Is she in your bed at this very moment? Her tanned, taut limbs wrapped around you, her pungent animal scent smeared across your bare chest like a—"

"Merilee, have you been reading Jackie Collins again?"

"I have not."

We were silent a moment.

"I need her, Hoagy. I need my Lulu. It would just be for a couple of weeks."

"Well, you can't have her."

"I'd take good care of her. I'd even make her her favorite tuna casserole, with melted Gruyère on top."

"She's not interested." Actually, she was dripping doggie drool on my hand just at the mention of it. But Merilee didn't need to know that.

"I miss her, Hoagy. I miss *us.* Oh, God, I've made such a terrible, awful mess of everything. The newspapers are calling me a slut. My parents won't even speak to me anymore. Mother said she doesn't understand me."

"Does anyone?"

"This wouldn't be happening to me if I were a man."

"Yes, I believe that's correct."

"You know what I mean, sir," she said angrily. "I made a personal choice to have this baby. I *want* this baby. It's something I'm very happy about. But people won't let me be happy. They have to make me feel crummy and cheap, as if I ought to have a scarlet *A* pinned on my chest. They have to ridicule me, invade my privacy—"

"You're public property, Merilee. You belong to them."

"I don't belong to anyone," she retorted sharply. "It's my body. My baby. My business—no one else's." She paused. "But the worst part, Hoagy, is how I've treated you. I've hurt you."

I left that one alone.

"You're not in my corner anymore, are you, Hoagy?" she asked softly.

"I'm not even in your area code, Merilee."

"If I could undo all of this, I would. Truly. This isn't how I wanted it. I wanted it to be private and dignified and—" She broke off. "Only something else entered into it."

"Not to mention someone."

"That was *your* choice," she charged.

"Was it?"

"You told me you never wanted children. Or midget human life forms, or whatever the devil it is you call them."

"I know I did, Merilee."

"You hate children."

"They are, after all, people."

"There's a reason, Hoagy. Why I've kept the father's identity a secret. A good reason."

"I'm not interested in what it is, Merilee. Or in who it is. I may be the only person in America who isn't."

"You honestly don't care?"

"I honestly don't care."

"You mean if I told you his name it would mean nothing to you?"

"Nothing."

"I think you're full of horseradish, mister." Those were strong words, coming from Merilee Nash. Didn't get much stronger. "Don't you even want to know whether it's going to be a boy or a girl?"

"Why would I want to know that?"

She made that little noise of hers that she makes when she's trying not to cry. "We've had our little booms and busts before. Sometimes they've been your fault. Sometimes they've been mine. But we've always survived them, Hoagy. Because we're friends. Friends understand."

"Friends don't shit on each other."

"I'm sorry, Hoagy. I'm very, very sorry. I don't know what else I can say."

I took a deep breath, let it out slowly. "You can say good night, Merilee."

I hung up the phone and went into the living room, my chest aching. I poured myself two fingers of Macallan and drank it down. I poured myself another and put on some Garner, sat in my easy chair drinking and listening to the Little Elf play "Stardust." Lulu padded in and growled at me to come back to bed. She'd seen my Mr. Norman Maine before, and didn't much care for the performance. I didn't blame her. It wasn't one of my favorite roles either. I told her to leave me alone. She did.

I don't remember finishing the bottle, or dropping off. I only know I was out cold in the chair when I got my wake-up call. Hazy sun was coming in the window, and my mouth felt like I'd been gargling a dead cat. It was Lyle. I was late for the nine-o'clock writers' meeting, but that wasn't why he was calling. He was calling to say that somebody had tried to kill him. They'd failed. They'd killed Chad Roe.

Seven

The man who was supposed to play Rob Roy Fruitwell was lying on the floor of Lyle Hudnut's personal john with his eyes and his fly wide open. It was a small bathroom, not well ventilated. There seemed to be a great deal of urine splashed about. I saw no blood. Romaine Very was standing over Chad's body with his nose wrinkled. Someone from the Medical Examiner's office was standing there with him, taking pictures with a Polaroid. A huge blond kid in uniform stood guard in the alcove outside the door. A pair of EMS workers and their stretcher waited with him.

Most of the *Uncle Chubby* staffers were huddled together out in the main office, pale with shock and horror. Several, including Naomi, were crying. Tyrone, the kid from downstairs, was comforting another young black man, who wore gray overalls and a utility belt, and who was utterly distraught. The above-the-liners—Lyle and Katrina, Leo, Fiona, the writers—were cloistered in Lyle's dressing room.

Lyle was sobbing uncontrollably. "It was meant for me," he moaned, his huge red head buried in Katrina's lap. "That poor son of a bitch. It was meant for *me.*"

Marjorie Daw was in there, too, looking crisp and clean and extremely grim.

Very nodded to the uniformed cop to let me in the john with him. Lulu stayed outside. She wanted no part of it.

In death, Chad looked frightened, and older. His hair was mussed, exposing his receding temples and bald spot. It would have upset him, exiting that way. I don't know why I thought of this. "How did it happen, Lieutenant?"

Very grimaced. "Somebody hot-wired it."

"Somebody hot-wired what?"

"The urinal, dude."

"The *what?*"

"Yo, take a look," he ordered me. "Go on."

It was a brand-new urinal, freshly installed since Lyle trashed the place the previous afternoon. Looked shiny and plenty nice. The only odd thing about it was the insulated gray extension cord that ran from its basin to the electrical outlet over by the sink. The sink was brand-new, too. The mirror above it was still out. Otherwise, the bathroom was completely back in business.

I turned back to Very and shook my head.

"It's a CIA golden oldie," he explained, chomping his gum. "Ideal for assassinating well-protected heads of state. They took out a dude down in Nicaragua with it twenty, thirty years ago. Don't matter how many armed men he's got guarding him—when he's gotta go, he's gotta go. Know what I'm saying?"

I nodded. "He's gotta go. But—?"

"How much do you know about electricity, dude?"

"Enough to be afraid of it."

"Okay, I'll keep it real simple. Check it out—your quote-unquote weapon is the drain cover there in the bottom of the basin. See it?"

Most urinals have some such grid or screen in the bottom of the basin to keep cigarette butts and chewing gum out of the plumbing. Often, they are made of plastic. This one was made of metal, and was attached to the extension cord that plugged into the wall.

"Dig, the cover's electrically charged, okay?" Very explained. "It's hot. Your target walks in, unzips his pants, and makes contact with it as soon as his pee hits the grid. Urine, as I'm sure a well-educated dude like you knows, is super-salty. An ideal conductor of electricity. As I'm sure you also know, electricity needs a return path to complete its circuit. It won't go in unless it can come back out again. So what you've gotta do is make your *target* the conductor. Do that and you've smoked him."

"And how do I do that, Lieutenant?"

"Clog up the drain under the grid," he replied. "Wad of paper towels will do it. Dump some water in on top of 'em. Your man's standing there with his stream of pee hitting the live grid, and suddenly he realizes, whoa, the basin's filling up too fast. Who knows why—maybe the last slob didn't flush it. So he says to himself, hey, I better flush it right now or I'm gonna get my Bruno Maglis all wet. So he reaches over and grabs the handle and zap, you've got him. Handle's metal—it's grounded. Soon as he touches it the electricity shoots right up his stream of urine into his dick and through his body. One minute the man's standing there with his life in his hands. Next minute he's lit up like Trump's Castle."

I felt my knees squeezing together involuntarily. I was not alone. Very and the coroner's man were standing funny, too.

"Normal building current is enough to kill someone?" I wondered.

"Dude's dead, isn't he?" Very glanced down at him. "Fifty-five volts will kill you. Normal building current is a hundred and ten, hundred and twenty. Plenty."

I nodded. "Whoever did this—"

"Whoever did this," interrupted Very, "is a sick fuck."

"No argument there. Only, how did our sick fuck learn to do something like this?"

"I take it you don't read the mercenary magazines."

"Not lately."

"There's all kinds of sleazy ads in the back—how-to pamphlets, booklets you can write away for. The soldier of fortune wanna-bes gobble them up." He sighed in disgust. "You can learn about this trick anywhere, dude. This and a million others that would make your hair stand on end."

"It's already standing on end. And how hard was all of this to rig up?"

"There's nothing here you can't buy at any hardware store. Whole thing can be carried in your pocket and hooked up in two, three minutes. Especially because they took a lot of shortcuts." He crouched by the basin, examining the murder weapon. "Check, they didn't bother with an on-off switch, which you'd ordinarily need for purposes of selecting your subject. This was just flat-out on—first to use it loses it. They also didn't bother to hide the extension cord. If we were talking about a professional hit on a high-security target, you'd have to take up these wall tiles and bury your wires underneath. I mean, Christ, no way a guy whose life is in danger is gonna pee into a bowl that has an extension cord sticking out of it. Surprises me that anybody would," he added, frowning down at Chad. "I mean, you'd think he'd notice it and wonder."

"Who notices?" I countered. "You go in and you use it. Plus, he was an actor."

"What the hell's that got to do with it?" Very demanded.

"There's a mirror over the urinal, Lieutenant. That's where Chad's eyes were. That's where any actor's would be."

He nodded grudgingly. "Maybe so."

"Besides which," I pointed out, "this is a construction site. The plumber's been working in here."

Very glanced down at his notepad. "Name of Byrone Hendrix. No relation to Jimi, but a close relation to Tyrone Hendrix, the kid who works the front door. His older brother. Employed by the building as a super. Does a little bit of everything."

"He works fast," I said. "This place was a total shambles yesterday afternoon."

"They keep a supply of sinks and urinals on hand at all times," Very reported drily. "Hudnut's known to be on the combustible side. This was the fourth time he's wrecked this place in two years. Byrone was here half the night. Only thing he didn't have was a mirror for over the sink. Was going to put that in this morning."

"Was the extension cord his?"

"He says no. Custodian cleaned up in here this morning at seven-thirty. The extension cord wasn't in place at that time."

"He's sure?"

"Positive. He used the urinal himself—and lived to talk about it."

The medical examiner was done with Chad, for now. The men from EMS were ready to move him.

"Yo, getting a little close in here," Very observed, popping his gum. "Stay with me, dude."

We went into Lyle's dressing room. There the air was fresher, and Lyle was still sobbing and babbling. The others sat with him in stricken silence.

"If only he'd followed my rules!" Lyle cried. "The poor dumb son of a bitch. Fuck me, if only he'd *listened!* If only . . ." He trailed off, noticing me. "It was meant for me, Hoagy! It was meant for *me!*"

The others looked up at me with undisguised hostility. I was not one of them. I was an outsider. Someone who had, somehow, brought all of this trouble with me. They had closed ranks against me. For now at least. All except for Marjorie. She gazed at me steadily, her back stiff, her lower lip clamped tightly between her teeth.

"Why couldn't he stay out of there?" moaned Lyle. "Why did he have to use *my* john? If he'd *listened* to me he'd still be *alive!*"

"And you'd be the dead one, Lyle," Katrina squeaked quietly.

"I wish I was," he claimed, his chest rising and falling. "I wish that was *me* on that floor."

"No, you don't," she said.

"It was *meant* for me. It was *supposed* to be me. Me, all over again. *Me!*"

This one Katrina didn't dispute. No one did. It just hung there in the air.

Tommy broke the silence. "Zowie, I've heard of dying with your pants down, but this is shocking."

"This is *not* a time for jokes, Tommy," Katrina said fiercely. "Poor Chad is lying in there and you're kidding around."

"Hey, I don't hear the man complaining," Tommy fired back.

"You're really sick, you know that?"

"Stop it, you two!" ordered Fiona, shuddering. "Please!"

"At least there was no blood," said Marty. "Better this than, I don't know . . . being attacked by a blunt instrument."

Tommy nodded. "Like his wit."

Katrina glared at him, but kept silent.

Lyle sat up abruptly. "Jesus, what about his wife? Did somebody call Brenda?"

"All taken care of," said Very.

"And what about the poor little Munchkins?" Lyle wailed. "Did Amber get 'em outta here?"

"Twenty minutes ago, Lyle," Leo said woodenly.

Amber. The mention of her name jogged my memory.

Lyle ran his hands through his hair. "The poor son of a bitch *cared*, y'know that? All he wanted was the same thing I want—a good show. An honest show. I was really starting to like him. I really, really was."

"He liked you, too, Lyle," Katrina soothed.

"I gotta talk to God," Lyle said impulsively. "We gotta figure out what to do about Rob. Get me God on the phone."

Very was staring at him.

"Don't worry about that now, Lyle," Marjorie said coolly. "It'll all work out. Somehow."

Lyle ignored her. "Leo, get me God. Right now."

Very motioned for me to join him out in the main office. I did. Everyone was still sitting there. They watched us carefully.

"I want to take a look at Roe's dressing room," he informed me quietly.

I led him to it. Lulu joined us.

As we walked Very said, "Check, does Hudnut actually think he can get hold of God on the fucking telephone?"

"He can and does. He means Godfrey Daniels, head of the network."

"Oh. My apologies—I was thinking he was maybe loco."

"You can forget the maybe."

"Was he on target about being the intended victim?"

"Very."

He glanced at me. "Yeah, Hoagy?"

I sighed. "He was very serious. That's his personal john. No one else uses it. At least no one's supposed to—his cootie thing. It was meant for Lyle, no question about it."

"What did he mean when he said, 'Me, all over again'? Did somebody try to take him out before?"

"Somebody tried to take out Uncle Chubby that day at the Deuce. To a performer that constitutes attempted murder."

Very stopped in the doorway to Chad's dressing room, nodding to his own personal beat. "Yo, this is starting to get major strange."

"No, it isn't, Lieutenant. It's been major strange for quite some time."

A portable garment rack stood just inside the door.

Chad's leather knapsack and a tan windbreaker hung from it. There was his Joe Weider pressing bench, his twenty-pound dumbbells, his full-size three-way mirror. There was a love seat, a glass coffee table, a bathroom scale. There was a dressing table with four different hairbrushes neatly lined in a row, along with two combs, a tube of styling gel, hair spray, hair tonic, a hair dryer, a hand-held magnifying mirror, a tube of Retin A wrinkle cream, an electric razor, a battery-operated nose hair remover, tweezers, breath spray, dental floss, a travel toothbrush, and a tube of Rembrandt toothpaste, the kind that's supposed to make your teeth look whiter.

"Jesus, look at all this shit," marveled Very.

"Tools of an insecure trade. What are you looking for, Lieutenant?"

"Whatever," he replied, searching through the pockets of Chad's windbreaker. They were empty. "I don't get it, dude. If Hudnut's john was off limits, then what was the victim doing in there?"

"Being a star. He strongly objected to having to share a bathroom with the crew. He wanted his own. Fiona has one. Katrina as well. Lyle refused to build him one, and refused to share his, so Chad was sneaking in and using it behind his back. Just a petty little show-biz spat. Damned stupid, really, when you consider that it cost the man his life."

"Hudnut didn't keep it locked?"

"Lyle doesn't believe in locks, Lieutenant. None of the offices or dressing rooms have them."

Very began leafing absently through the scripts and papers heaped on the coffee table. "Who are we looking for, dude? Break it down for me. You know what goes on here. You know the people. I don't."

I tugged at my ear. "All right. For starters, we're looking for someone who has a rather wicked sense of humor."

"Humor?" Very's eyes glinted at me. "I don't see nothing funny going on around here."

"Nor do I, Lieutenant. But you must admit that Chad's

murderer is no bludgeoner. There was a definite flourish to this. A sense of theatricality, of publicity value—the papers will go crazy with it. Face it, that was a singular way to take out someone whom you really, really don't like." And *so* sexual, too. A woman, no? One of Lyle's exes? There were certainly a number of those to choose from. "You're checking the bathroom for fingerprints?"

He nodded. "Guarantee you it'll turn up clean. We're talking one smart perp here. Yo, I'm with you so far, dude. So dish me this: Who really, really doesn't like Hudnut?"

"Everyone who knows him, pretty much. The man is an equal opportunity offender."

"That include his girlfriend, Katrina Tingle?" he asked, peering at me.

"It does."

"He fucks around on her?"

"He does."

"Who with?"

There was a sound out in the hall. Somebody passing by, within earshot.

"Who with?" Very persisted.

"I'll let you know, Lieutenant, if it becomes important."

Very shook his head at me with disgust. "Now you see, that's just the kinda shit you're always pulling that pisses me off. It's not up to you to decide what is or isn't important. It's up to *me*. I'm the judge, not you. Got it?"

"Let me explain something to you, Lieutenant. I'll keep it short and sour. If people around here think that every little thing they tell me is going directly to you, then guess what? They won't tell me every little thing. In fact, they won't tell me anything at all."

"Maybe so," he admitted, his knee quaking impatiently. "But I got a murder investigation to run."

"And I have a book to write, and feelings to specialize in. I also happen to work much better on my own—I'm a little shy that way. So if you'll excuse me, I'll leave you to it."

I started for the door. Lulu didn't budge from the love seat. She knew I wasn't going anywhere. I stopped in the doorway. "Exactly what time did Chad get zapped, anyway?"

"Nine-twenty-three," Very replied, chin thrust at me defiantly.

"And who was here?"

"Everyone was here. Except for you."

"Including Marjorie Daw?"

He nodded. "She got here at nine for the writers' meeting. Yo, she's some kind of long, tall cutie. Legs up to her neck."

"Bakes a mean pie, too." And was she handy as well? Did they teach her how to hot-wire urinals and build homemade grenades back home in Rhinelander? Did they teach her how to kill? "Where was the writers' meeting?"

"In Muck and Meyer's office. They were all in there when Chad got it."

"Who found him?"

"One of the production assistants."

"Naomi Leight?"

"How'd you know?"

"She's just one of those players who has a nose for the football."

"She the one boffing Hudnut?"

I didn't answer him.

"Thought so." Very grinned at me triumphantly. "She says she was sitting at her desk outside of Hudnut's office. Heard a thud. Chad touching down. She knocked, and when no one answered she went in and found him there."

"Did she see him go in?"

"She saw nobody go in there. Says she was at her desk by eight-fifteen, first to arrive, but she allowed as how she does a lot of running around. Starts the coffee, works the copier, shit like that. So she wouldn't necessarily have seen him. Or our perp, for that matter. Me, I figure our perp rigged it before she even got here—right after the janitor finished. But that's strictly theory at this point. I still need to shake Tyrone loose—he's the one who'll know if anyone else was around." Very paused, scratching his head. "Of course, there's also an inside door that connects the john to Hudnut's dressing room. Another means of access. But Naomi swears she saw nobody go in or out of the man's dressing room either—until he got in at ten minutes til nine. At nine sharp, he went to the meeting. She saw nobody else go in there between nine and when Chad got waxed."

"Is it possible that someone else saw something?"

"No one's come forward yet, but I'll know more in a few hours."

Chad's copy of the script lay open on the coffee table, notes and questions scrawled in the margins. There was a manila envelope filled with eight-by-ten publicity photos of Chad working the dimp. There was a fat black leather address book. There was a lined yellow legal pad on which he'd scribbed a list of eight things to do on this day:

1. *Don't nosh—Rob cares about nutrition*
2. *Listen for the laugh*
3. *See the camera*
4. *"Be the terrific guy you are"*
5. *Positive, positive, positive!*
6. *Each day I get a little bit better*
7. *Smile, smile, smile!*
8. *Clear the air with Hoagy—friends don't tell each other lies*

Very stabbed at the last item with an index finger. "You two were pals?"

"I guess he thought we were." I suddenly felt a tremendous sadness wash over me.

"What's this lie he's talking about?"

"Yesterday, I asked him where he was when the bombs went off. He said he was in here running lines with Amber Walloon."

"And?"

"She told me they weren't. In fact, she told me she wasn't in here at all."

Very grimaced. "Why didn't you tell me this last night, dude?"

"Because both of them got sick from the chili," I replied. "And because I thought she was the one who lied to me. I figured she just didn't want Lyle to know she'd been giving Chad direction behind his back. He's very into control."

"I see," Very said skeptically.

"But, clearly, it was Chad who lied to me, not her." I tugged at my ear. "Which means either that he was the one who bombed the set—highly doubtful, considering his current status among the nonliving—or that he was doing something else that he didn't want anyone to know about."

Very considered this. "Could be the two of them were fucking in here."

"Could be," I acknowledged, glancing down at the love seat.

Lulu, keen huntress, was suddenly showing an uncommon interest in the love seat herself. Something tucked under one of the cushions. She burrowed under there nose-first, snarfling and snorting with reckless abandon. I picked up the cushion. There was a spray can under there.

"What is that?" asked Very.

"It's our answer, Lieutenant," I replied, reaching for it. "Hair dye. You spray it on your head to cover over your bald patches. Chad had one, and he was extremely self-conscious about it. That's what he was doing in here when the bombs went off. He was painting his head. Didn't want me or anyone to know. The poor fucker."

"Yo, why didn't he just get a toupee?"

"Because he didn't want to walk around with a dead animal on his head. Believe me, it'll make perfect sense to you in another ten or twelve years."

"They say you get smarter as you get older," Very ventured.

"No, you don't. You just get older."

"I'm down to that," he agreed. "Dig, when the doctor told me I had to get cut open I—"

"Don't start telling me about your damned hernia operation again. I'm not in the mood."

He stared at me. "You cool with this?"

"As can be." I bent down and scratched Lulu's ears. "Well, that's one mystery solved. Good girl, Lulu."

She beamed at me happily. Then started barking.

"Why's she doing that?" Very wondered.

"She still wants to be deputized."

Very looked around at Chad Roe's dressing room. "Y'know, dude, it's not too late."

"For what, Lieutenant?"

"For crime prevention. We still got a chance."

"How do you figure that?"

"Because, check it out, whoever was after Hudnut this morning ain't gonna be content with waxing the wrong party."

"Meaning they'll try again?"

"Count on it," Very affirmed. "Uncle Chubby's in danger —major league."

"You'll protect him, of course."

"Men on him around the clock, for sure. But that's not our best bet, talking prevention. Best is to catch our perp *before* he pulls any more of this shit."

"Were you able to talk to Vice?"

"No time. But now I'll make the time." Very stuck a fresh piece of gum in his mouth and put on the mirrored mountaineering sunglasses that were around his neck. I could see my own reflection in them. I looked worried. "Stay with me, dude," he said.

"I'm with you, Lieutenant. I'm with you."

Which wasn't totally true. Very took off from the studio a few minutes after that, leaving behind two uniforms to question people in Katrina's office, and a matched pair of hulking, bullet-headed plainclothesmen around to keep an eye on the place. One was assigned to Lyle, the other to the outer office, where he was parked on the sofa with his nose buried in *Daily Variety.* As for me, I ran into a major tussle of my own. Or I should say Lulu ran into one. And it wasn't pretty.

It seems that Rusty, the lovable canine star of *Uncle Chubby,* was on call for rehearsals that morning, and in the confusion immediately following Chad's death no one bothered to tell his trainer, Skip, to go home. Or to tell me that Rusty was on the premises. So there I was strolling up the hall toward my private office, Lulu ambling peacefully along beside me, when suddenly a rottweiler possessing approximately the same musculature and temperament of a young Lawrence Taylor came rocketing down the hall toward us, a feral growl coming from his throat and saliva dripping from his gleaming fangs. He left his feet a full ten paces short of us and simply flew the rest of the way, landing directly atop Lulu with most of her in his mouth. It all happened so fast that Lulu didn't have a chance. Not that she would have had a chance even if she'd been given an hour's warning and a fully loaded TEC-9. All she could do was let out a strangled yelp before she disappeared in a fierce blur of snarling dog flesh, the two of them rolling around and around on the rug, Rusty tossing her about like she was a throw pillow with ears. It was pretty horrifying. I know I was certainly horrified, and you can imagine how Lulu felt. Skip came sprinting down the hall at once to pull the vicious beast off of her before *Uncle*

Chubby suffered its second fatality of the morning. As it was Lulu had one torn ear, a bloody mouth, two chipped teeth, and great big bites of hair and flesh missing from her back and from under her left eye, which was already swollen half shut. She was also covered with saliva and whimpering from shock and terror.

"Geez, I'm so sorry!" cried Skip, who was barely able to restrain Rusty by his collar. The dog smelled blood and wanted to finish the job. "I had no idea there was another dog around."

"She doesn't like to think she is one." I tried to pick Lulu up and hold her, but she wouldn't let me. She was too ashamed of herself for getting stomped so badly.

All of this commotion brought Leo, the office general. Annabelle, the pet specialist, scurried along one step behind her.

"Okay, wait," the tiny writer exclaimed. "I'm, like, they didn't hit it off. Am I right?"

"It was over in one round," I replied.

Skip quickly hustled his sadistic bully of a star out of there. A veterinarian arrived in minutes to patch up Lulu in the makeup room. He reported no serious damage, just superficial bumps, bites, and bruises. Still, he had to give her a S-H-O-T, and by the time he was done with her she looked a little like a tattered stuffed animal. Her left eye was swollen completely shut, her ear wrapped in a bandage. She definitely looked even more mournful than usual. He left me a bottle of antibiotics to give her.

Leo stayed behind with the patient and me. "She can stick around for the rest of the day, Hoagy, but that's it. Rusty needs to be here. She doesn't."

"I understand," I said heavily. "And it's no problem. I've flown solo before. It's been a while, but I'm sure I still know how."

Leo softened. "Is there somebody she can stay with?"

"I don't want to talk about that."

"I'm sorry, Hoagy," she said gruffly. She seemed almost human at that moment.

"Not nearly as sorry as I am."

Lyle called everyone together for a family council meeting at noon around the big table in the rehearsal room. The whole family was on hand, with the exception of The Munchkins, who'd been sent home with Amber. And Lyle and Katrina, who were late. No free catered lunch today. Just fresh pots of coffee and tea, but if you think anyone went near them, you're crazy. No one dared go near Chad's empty seat at the table either. It was somber and tense in the rehearsal room while we all waited for the royal couple to show. Word was that Lyle had heard from God about the network's plans for the future. Word was the news wasn't good.

"We're g-getting pulled," sputtered Bobby, blinking furiously. "I b-bet that's what this is about."

"God can't take us off the air a second time," argued Marty. "It'll make him look too wishy-washy."

"But why leave us on?" countered Tommy, tugging at his tuft of white forelock. "They wanted Rob in the show, or else. Call me crazy, but with Chad dead we got no Rob."

Marty mulled it over. "Maybe until we can recast. Maybe that's the plan."

"And how long will that take?" I asked.

"Months maybe," Tommy replied. "Hardest thing in the business is finding a forty-year-old leading man who can play comedy and who isn't already in his own show."

"There's only a handful of them out there," Marty agreed. "The network-approved list is real short. All of the fall shows are in production already, so that means most of them are tied up. And if by chance someone *is* available he has to accept third billing *and* be willing to move to New York."

"Face it, partner," Tommy concluded glumly. "We're doomed until some of the new fall shows get cancelled."

Marty nodded. "Doomed."

Annabelle came hurrying in the door, slightly out of breath. She settled with us. "I'm, like, I've been working the phone to the coast, only *everyone's* stonewalling me. They all said the same thing—we don't know. I'm, like, no way!"

"D-Doomed," echoed Bobby.

"Where *is* that fat fuck?" demanded Tommy, glowering at the empty doorway.

"Hear we're losing our official Team Chubby mascot, too," Marty said to me. "Bummer."

"That it is," I agreed. Right now she was resting uncomfortably in my office, under the desk.

"Can we get her something to cheer her up?" asked Tommy. "A squirting dog biscuit? Maybe a video to watch? She got a favorite movie?"

"I'm afraid not." Actually, she does have one—*The Incredible Mr. Limpet,* that 1964 classic in which Don Knotts turns into a fish. But it's too embarrassing to mention. "I'll tell her you were concerned. I'm sure she'll be touched."

"Won't be the same around here without old Lulu," said Marty.

"I'm, like, what are you going to do with her?" asked Annabelle.

"I don't want to talk about that."

Tommy shifted in his chair, bones creaking. "Don't know about you, partner, but I haven't taken a leak all morning."

"I may never take another leak for as long as I live," confessed Marty. "They're gonna have to hook me up to one of those plastic bags."

"Imagine how Lyle m-must feel."

"Sorry, Bobster," snapped Tommy. "My imagination isn't that sick."

Katrina came in the door first, looking tense and drawn.

Marjorie followed, her face a careful, noncommittal blank. Then came Lyle, gloved and masked. His police guard remained in the doorway with his arms crossed, a big hall monitor in a cheap suit.

All eyes were on Lyle as he sat. "I've spoken with God," he began. His voice was hollow and shaky. "And I'm gonna be totally up front with you, because we're all family in this room. God wants us to shut down production for a few weeks, effective immediately." There was an instant rumble of protest, curses, and mutters all around. Lyle held up a gloved hand for silence, and he got it. "What he said was he'd like us to take stock. Give ourselves a chance to find another Rob. Give the police a chance to do their thing. And then, when everything's back to normal, we premiere midseason." Another rumble of protest. Again Lyle held up a hand for silence. "I went to the mat with him. I said no way, I'm *not* sending my people home. We are all artists here. Our work is how we deal with our grief. Chad . . . Chad was one of ours. We have to do something for him. We have to do a show—as planned, on schedule, on the air, dedicated to Chad fucking Roe. The best show we've ever done. That's what we gotta do," Lyle declared, his eyes filling with tears, "because that's how artists say good-bye to each other. And you can't, goddamn it, take that away from us! No one has that right!"

A rousing ovation erupted, everyone cheering except for Marjorie, who stared straight ahead, her cheeks mottling slightly.

"I won us a temporary restraining order," Lyle revealed. "God has agreed to fly in so he can assess the situation in person before he commits one way or the other. He's on his way here right now. It is my hope, my *belief,* that we'll be able to change his mind—assuming he has one." That drew laughter. "Until then, we're on hold. Feel free to go home once you've been questioned by the cops. Or hang out here if ya want. Whatever ya feel most comfortable doing. This is a day for us to deal with our own personal feelings of loss and grief." He paused, making eye contact with people around the table. "If you want to know how I'm going to be dealing with mine, I'll be huddling with the writers over the script. Because I intend to tape on Saturday, as scheduled. That's my plan—no matter what God says. I'll pay for this episode out of my own pocket if I got to, but one way or the other we are taping this week. We owe that to Chad." He heaved a huge sigh, ran his fingers through his red curls. "Before I let ya go, there's one more thing I want to get out in the open. . . ."

"Holy shit, Batman, he's gonna whip out his wienie again," whispered Tommy.

Annabelle kicked him. He kicked her back.

"It's no secret that there's some weird, bad shit going on around this place. Somebody . . ." Lyle glanced over his shoulder at his police guard. "Somebody wants to destroy me —poor Chad, he was just in the wrong place at the wrong time. It's also no secret that this somebody is one of the people in this very room." He looked slowly around the table, his eyes lingering with cold suspicion on a number of those people. On Leo. On Fiona. On Annabelle and Bobby and The Boys. Suspects, one and all. Everyone's eyes followed his, wondering about them, wondering. . . . "Well, whoever you are, I have some bad news for you: I will *not* be pushed out! I will *not* be scared off! I will *not* run! I will *not* hide! This is *my* show and *my* family and *I'm not going anywhere!*" For this Lyle got a thundering ovation. Phil, his stage manager, even turned it into a standing O, which Lyle lapped up in grateful silence, tears streaming down his cheeks. "I was . . ." He trailed off, blubbering. "I was thinking of an old saying this morning: 'Tough times don't last, but tough people do.' I think that describes all of us who are here today. We're tough people. We're gonna get through this thing—together. Nobody can tear us apart. Which reminds me—Chad's death is gonna be page-one news. Reporters will try to stir it up. Get dirt, gossip, whatever they can out of ya.

Some of 'em will even offer ya money. It's what they do. Here's how we handle it—we don't talk. Not to anyone. Any and all comments about Chad's death are to come out of Marjorie's office, by way of me. She is the official spokesperson for this show. Her and no one else. No one, I repeat *no one,* is to have any contact with the press. I find out that you have and you're off the show, understood? Questions? . . . No? . . . Okay, you're excused. Writers, please remain."

Everyone began to file out, Fiona pausing to gurgle a few private words of comfort in Lyle's ear. "We're behind you" was all I could make out.

Annabelle shook her big, lacquered hair. "I'm, like, this is blah-blah-blah, am I right?"

"Blah-blah-blah?" I said.

"Insane."

"You expected normal?" scoffed Tommy.

"What's insane?" asked Marty.

"Us writing a show," she replied. "We don't have a Rob. We're off the air. . . ."

"Vintage L-Lyle," Bobby declared, bristling with intensity. "As l-long we're writing a show, then there *is* a show. The p-power of positive self-delusion. The man ought to write a book about it."

"He is," I reminded him.

Marjorie rose and glided over to the coffeepot, the first to set foot near it. The lady was not lacking for nerve. I joined her.

"And how is the official spokesperson holding up?" I asked, pouring coffee for her.

"Okay, I suppose." She looked paler than normal, and there were dark smudges under her large, liquid green eyes.

"Still, you must be seriously disappointed."

"About what?"

"God coming to town."

"Why should that bother me?" she asked, raising her cup to her lips.

"You're not actually going to drink that, are you?"

She looked down at it warily.

"This show is your turf," I pointed out. "God's invading it. Not what I'd call a ringing vote of confidence."

She set the cup aside. Not so nervy after all. "It's Godfrey's decision to make, not mine. I don't feel the least bit upset that he's coming. All I feel is . . ." She hesitated, then plunged on. "I feel fed up. I've had it with the TV business. What I want to do is run home to Wisconsin, have three or four kids, and spend my time baking cookies and taking them to soccer practice."

"What kind of cookies?"

A faint smile crossed her lips. "Sounds silly, I guess."

"Utterly. Have yourself a husband all picked out?" I asked. And it was the wrong thing to ask.

Her eyes locked onto mine. There was challenge in them. There was invitation. And there was something else—a jolt of attraction. Strong one. She felt it. I know I did. "I'm working on that," she answered me huskily. Then she strode back to her seat.

Me, I poured myself a cup of coffee, black, and took a big slurp. It didn't kill me. No such luck.

Lyle clapped his huge, meaty hands for attention. "Okay, here's the deal, gang," he announced, as he and Katrina moved down to the writers' end of the big table. "We take the initiative. We prove to God that we're prepared to do a show without Rob. That we *have* a show without Rob."

"But we haven't," Marty pointed out.

"We do, too," argued Lyle. "Same story, new twist—the schmuck stands Deirdre up. Doesn't show for their date."

Tommy shifted in his chair. "Who fixes the dishwasher?"

"Nobody," replied Lyle.

"But Chubby's g-got parts strewn all over the kitchen floor," Bobby protested.

"So he bullshits her," Lyle pitched. "Tells her the repairman had to order a part or something. Typical Chubby lie.

He's making it up as he goes along, hoping it'll somehow work out.''

"That plays," Tommy admitted grudgingly. "Only we don't have a second act without Rob.''

"We do, too," insisted Lyle. "Chubby takes her to the pool hall himself. Because he wants to cheer her up and because—''

"He's hoping to win the repair money from her," Marty said.

Lyle nodded. "So he can call the guy tomorrow and get it fixed, okay?''

"Wait, what do we do with The Munchkins if they're both out?" asked Annabelle.

"We fuck the kids," Lyle snapped irritably.

"Tonight, a very special episode of *The Uncle Chubby Show,*" intoned Tommy gravely.

"Shut up, Tommy," snarled Katrina.

"We c-could park them with Mrs. Dennison," Bobby suggested. "The neighbor with the g-giant—''

"Okay, fine," accepted Marty. "But what do we *do* at the pool hall?''

Lyle said, "A whole bunch of real nice brother-sister shit about how much they mean to each other. Until the milkman shows up, and she finds out what really happened to the forty bucks. She gets pissed, but she forgives him. We top it off with our bedtime story and we fade out. Perfect, right?'' he exclaimed, daring someone, anyone to contradict him. "Perfect!''

No one said a word. All eyes were on Marjorie, who sat there thinking it over, her long, slender fingers forming a steeple under her chin. "I don't think it's strong enough, Lyle," she concluded.

Lyle gave her The Scowl. "Who died and made you queen?''

"This is our return episode," she continued, undeterred.

"We need a show that people will be talking about the next morning at work. Something truly special."

"I suppose you'd be happier if we had robots in it!" he fumed, sneering at her.

Marty: "Seems kind of thin to me, too, Lyle."

Tommy: "Me, too."

"I'm, like, yeah."

"It's n-not about anything."

"I suggest," stated Marjorie, "that we wait until God gets here before we—"

"Well we're *not* gonna wait for God!" Lyle waved his arms and roared. "We're gonna go with *this* show. *Now!* Because I say so! It's *my* fucking show, and I say we're going with it! We *have* to show God that we're carrying on, business as usual. If we don't he'll be in our faces morning, noon, and night, all season long. If he wants us to recast Rob down the road, that's cool. We can do that. But in the meantime, we carry on!" Again he clapped his hands together. "Okay, now everybody beat it. Get to work. Except for you, Hoagy," he said, turning his gaze on me. "I need to talk to you in private."

Marjorie and the writers filed out, Muck and Meyer grousing at each other under their breath like two old-timers on a shuffleboard court. Katrina remained behind with Lyle and me.

"I said *in private,* Katrina," he said stiffly.

"But—"

"Beat it, you stupid cunt!"

She ootsie-fooed angrily out the door, Lyle's guard eyeballing her every curve. And there were many. The white leather halter dress she was wearing was very tight and very short.

"You're all class, Lyle," I observed quietly.

Lyle ran a gloved hand over his face. "Geez, you'd think people would be more sensitive," he moaned.

"To what, Lyle?"

"Me. My needs. Support is what I need from them right now. Not some stupid argument over Act Two. Christ, somebody's trying to fucking *kill* me!"

"That's true, Lyle. Somebody fucking is. And you were lucky—this time."

He shot me a worried look. "What, you think they'll try again?"

"I do."

Lyle glanced across the room at his guard, then back to me. "This detective," he said, lowering his voice. "This Very person . . ."

"What about him?"

"He got any leads yet?"

"That takes time, Lyle."

He began to pace. "Who's doing this to me, Hoagy? Who wants me gone?!"

"I don't know."

"You have *no* idea?"

"I have plenty of ideas."

"Share 'em with me."

"Not now."

He gave me The Scowl. "When?"

"When they've started to take shape. Right now they're just a big blob of ooze. Kind of like our book."

He paced some more, his lips making those crisp, flatulent noises I'd come to know and not love. "Naomi says you know about the two of us. Who told you?"

"No one had to. Discreet you're not."

Lyle didn't disagree. "She says you were pissed about—"

"Being used as a cover so you could screw her behind Katrina's back? I was."

He shrugged his big shoulders. "You were just handy is all. Seemed like a nice, tight fit."

"So to speak."

"She's a bright kid. I'm just trying to give her a leg up in the business."

"So to speak."

"I won't do it again if it bugs you."

"It bugs me."

He smirked at me. "What, you don't approve of me giving her some?"

"Your sex life is your business."

"You got that right," he said defiantly. Then he slumped into a chair. "Can't help myself, Hoagy. Women are like a compulsion with me. A need. I hope you can understand that. I hope you're not gonna stay mad at me."

"What do you want me to do, Lyle? Slap your hand? Tell you that you're a baaad boy? What do you want?"

"I want you to like me," he replied meekly.

"We're collaborators, not friends."

"I want us to be."

"Not possible—not unless you make some big changes."

"Like what?"

"Like stop shitting all over people."

"You mean Katrina?"

"I mean everyone, Lyle."

He shrugged. "It's like I told you—I'm just honest, that's all."

"You're just a schmuck, is what you are. Why do you think somebody's trying to kill you?"

His face darkened. "Geez, you don't think it's *Katrina*, do you?"

"Could you blame her?"

He thought about that a moment, visibly distraught. "No, I guess not," he admitted. "Maybe . . . maybe you've got a point. Maybe I'm not the easiest person to be around. But I'm gonna change, Hoagy. I'm gonna take something positive out of this. I swear I am." He looked up at me beseechingly, a big, unruly kid starving for approval. "Okay?"

"Okay, Lyle," I said, not sure if he meant it or not. Possibly he was just shaken by Chad's death. Or telling me what he thought I wanted to hear. Who knew? I didn't. The man was a riddle. Always.

His blue eyes twinkled at me now. "Gonna pitch in on the script with us?"

"Can't today, Lyle. Things to do."

He frowned at me. "What things?"

"The book, of course."

"What if I need you? Where will you be?"

"I'll be working at home."

"What's wrong with your office here?" he demanded.

"I'll be working at home," I repeated.

He peered at me suspiciously, sensing I wasn't being totally straight with him. Dumb he wasn't. "Okay, if you say so." He struggled to his feet. "Only, it runs both ways, Hoagy."

"What does, Lyle?"

"The shit. You ever lie to me and you'll be sorry. I'll find out, and you'll be sorry."

"Watch your step, Lyle," I said cheerfully.

"You, too, Hoagy," he said, not the least bit cheerfully. There was nothing but menace in Lyle Hudnut's voice. "You, too." Then he barged out the door, his police guard tagging along two steps behind him.

Vic came downstairs to meet us. I waited for him outside under the awning with Lulu cowering between my legs, swathed in bandages. Passersby glared at me angrily. They assumed I'd been abusing her. So did Mario, the daytime doorman, who kept curling his lip at me. He'd never liked me. Which was okay. I'd never liked him either. Three paparazzi were camped out by the curb in the hot sun, waiting for Merilee to show herself. Me they didn't bother with.

"Wow, get a load of her," droned Vic as he came out the

front door. He still had his apron on over his polo shirt and slacks. Rather frilly one, too. A smaller man couldn't have pulled it off. "Must have been some tussle."

"It wasn't exactly a fair one. He was much bigger and he bit below the belt." I picked her up gently and said a few things to her I won't bother to repeat here. Then I handed her over to Vic, along with her collapsible Il Bisonte travel bag. "Some things she'll need—salve, pills, change of bandages, her various sinus medications, her *Flipper* chew toy. . . . Also a jar of anchovies. She prefers them chilled."

"I remember," he assured me, cradling her in his big arms. She pawed feebly at his hairy wrist. "Nice gesture on your part, Hoag. Merilee's elated."

"I had nothing to do with it," I said gruffly. "Lulu just got herself banned from the studio, that's all."

"Sure, sure," Vic agreed gently. "Mother's touch is what she needs. Works out well for everybody. Except for you, I guess."

"You kidding? First good night's sleep I'll get in years."

Lulu let out a low, pained moan. I scratched her under her right ear, the good one, to let her know I didn't mean it. She licked my hand to let me know she knew it.

"You're welcome to visit her, Hoag," Vic offered. "Any time, day or night."

I thanked him. Then I mumbled something about having to run and I headed off quickly down Central Park West. No sense dragging it out. I don't know if she tried to tear herself out of Vic's arms and come limping after me. I like to think she did, but I didn't look back. It was best not to.

I was halfway down the block when I heard Merilee calling to me, her stage-trained voice booming out over the din of cars and busses. Of course, if she were appearing onstage right about now they'd have to clear out the orchestra pit and the first seven rows of seats just to accommodate her stomach. I wasn't prepared for just how huge she'd become. Not just her stomach either. Her hips were as wide across as the avenue. Her tush, which had once resembled a ripe, firm peach, was now riding like the back end of an old Buick—an old Buick toting two tons of sandbags. She made her way down the sidewalk toward me in slo-mo, as if she were moving through Jell-O, so bloated she could barely waddle, the photographers circling her like angry flies as they snapped her picture and shouted questions at her. Merilee Nash is not a petite woman. She's six feet tall in her size-ten bare feet, big-boned and broad-shouldered. But she's also one of the two or three great natural beauties in the entire film world. And that was pretty hard to imagine right about now. Her long, shimmering golden hair was unkempt and greasy, her fine patrician face puffy and flushed, her skin broken out all over. Her glasses had slid down to the end of her nose, which was running. The jumbo-size, somewhat damp, gray sweatsuit she was wearing gave her an unappetizingly larval appearance. On her swollen feet she wore sneakers without laces.

I didn't recognize this person. This person was not Merilee Nash. I stared. Couldn't help it.

She caught me. "I look just like a Queens housewife named Gert, don't I?" she panted, swiping at the dirty hair that was smeared across her sweaty forehead. "All I need is a hair net, fuzzy slippers, and a cigarette stuck in my lip."

"You've never looked lovelier, Merilee." I gave her my linen handkerchief.

"You, mister, are full of baked beans," she sniffed, mopping her face with it.

"I've missed your quaint little expressions."

"I've missed *you,*" she said shyly.

The photographers were snapping both of us now, and yelling at me.

"HEY, STEW, WHO'S THE DADDY?!"

"PUT YOUR ARM AROUND HER!"

"YOU TWO GETTING BACK TOGETHER?!"

"SAY DA-DA!"

Vic left Lulu in the arms of Mario and came after them. He meant business, too. He'd thrown down his apron. He stepped in front of them, his tree-trunk arms spread wide, and began herding them toward the gutter, their curses and protests bouncing off of him. This was Vic doing his job. The man is a human snowplow. He pushed them right out into Central Park West in front of oncoming traffic. They had to cross over to the park to avoid being hit. He stayed where he was, standing guard over us at a discreet distance.

"When are you due?" I asked her.

"Two more weeks," she replied wearily. "Personally I think I'm going to explode before then." She glanced back at her building, where Mario stood under the awning with Lulu. "I wanted to thank you for her. It's awfully damned decent of you, considering what I've put you through."

I shrugged. "The truth is I had no choice."

"Horseradish. You could have boarded her."

"She got worms the last time I did. She still hasn't forgiven me."

"I promise you I'll take good care of her."

"I know you will, Merilee."

"I'll make her a big plate of asparagus with hollandaise sauce first thing."

"She doesn't eat asparagus."

"I do—all the time. Hot, cold, pureed. Morning, noon, and night. Can't get enough of it."

We stared at each other a moment.

Until she looked away and said, "God bless Alex Trebek. *Jeopardy!* is all that's left between me and total mental meltdown."

"Now there's a horrifying thought."

"It gets worse. I'm even . . . promise me you won't laugh . . ."

"I won't laugh, Merilee."

"I'm seriously considering getting into soap operas. I keep hearing they're actually better than prime time."

"Can't be any worse."

Her brow creased fretfully. "Poor Mister Hoagy. You're not having much fun these days."

"Or nights."

Her eyes suddenly filled with tears. "Sorry, I cry all the time," she blurted out. "Doesn't mean anything." She dabbed at her eyes with my handkerchief. "Is that a new suit? I don't remember it."

It was the pure white linen I'd had made for me in Milan. "It is. Like it?"

"Oh, God, Hoagy," she blubbered. "You're such a sight for sore eyes I'm going to start sobbing uncontrollably. Please go before I made a huge fool of myself in public."

"I'll take that as a yes."

She laughed through her tears. We stared at each other some more. Until she broke it once again. "It's all gone, Hoagy. Isn't it?"

"What's all gone, Merilee?"

"The love." She swallowed. "You don't love me anymore, do you?"

I leaned over and kissed her damp, flushed forehead. "Take good care of yourself, Merilee," I said. Then I walked on down the block with a lump in my throat and that same ache in my chest. The rest of me was just plain numb.

Eight

When's Lyle getting here, young fella?"

They were older than I expected. Closer to eighty than seventy. Not far from feeble. And they were by no means ogres. Of course, that was easy for me to say. They were Lyle Hudnut's parents, not my own.

Herb Hudnut was a scrawny, defeated little man with a chicken neck, big ears that stuck straight out, and a full head of white hair that was combed flat, except for a schoolboy cowlick. He smelled of Vitalis. He had a striped knit shirt on over a white T-shirt—not a look I recommend—blue polyester slacks, and heavy black Florsheim wing-tips with white support hose. He was very fidgety. Kept moistening his lips and reaching nervously for the pocket of his shirt, as if he had something valuable in there and he wanted to make sure it was still there. Near as I could tell he had nothing in there. He had an old, faded tattoo on the back of his left forearm. His hands shook.

It was Aileen who Lyle took after the most. She was big and she was hefty. Must have outweighed Herb by fifty pounds. She had the same jack-o'-lantern face as Lyle, the same chin half submerged in a puddle of jowls, the same pug nose, the same shrewd, twinkling blue eyes. There were still a few streaks of rust in her curly, steel gray hair. She wore a lime green pantsuit, ventilated white nurse's oxfords, and crimson polish on her nails. Her hands were big and meaty like Lyle's. They clutched stubbornly at the white vinyl handbag on the sofa beside her, as if she were afraid to let it go. Kind of like Herb and his shirt pocket. She was smoking a cigarette and watching me carefully. She seemed much sharper and more alert than Herb. Tougher, too. My guess was she always had been.

Both of them were anxious. They thought they were about to see their son for the first time in a long, long time. I had let them think this. On behalf of Lyle I had booked them a suite for the night at the Mayfair Regent Hotel on Park Avenue, which I think is the nicest of the smaller luxury hotels. I thought it best not to put them in the Essex House. There was no telling who they might run into there. The Mayfair also happens to do a superior high tea. I'd told them I'd be there for tea—with Lyle. The cart sat there beside us heaped with china pots and eight different teas and plates of sandwiches and cakes.

"When's Lyle getting here, young fella?" Herb repeated, his voice whiny and apologetic, and tinged with working-class Queens.

"Are you folks happy with your suite?" I had to speak up. Both were slightly deaf.

"Everything's just fine," Herb replied, looking around at the sunny, elegant sitting room. The sofa and club chairs were grouped before an ornamental fireplace. On the coffee table between us sat the baskets of fruit and flowers I'd had sent up. "All seems kinda on the grand side for just us two. Single room woulda been hokey-dokey. How much is this costing Lyle, anyways?"

"Not to worry. He can afford it."

"Bet he can." Herb chuckled proudly.

"We was just so excited when you called us, Mr. Hoag," said Aileen, stubbing out her cigarette. "Lyle hasn't contacted us in so long." Her voice was fluttery and high-pitched for such a big woman, and had a peculiar singsong quality to it, as if she were reading a nursery rhyme. If you listened hard you could hear Uncle Chubby's bedtime story voice in it.

"Y'see, he still has a whole lot of childhood anger toward us. My, my, we know we made mistakes. All parents do. Mine sure did. But there comes a time when you have to let go of whatever grudge you hold."

"And Lyle just plain hasn't," said Herb, moistening his lips anxiously. "Up till now."

"It's been years since he spoke to us," confessed Aileen.

"We always watch him on TV, of course," Herb said.

"My, my, he's gotten so heavy," said Aileen. "Just like Daddy did. Daddy weighed just over three hundred pounds when he passed away. Poor thing had to have a custom-made casket."

"So when's he getting here?" Herb asked, yet again.

I poured us Irish breakfast tea through a silver strainer and offered them sandwiches. Herb declined. Aileen tried the salmon. Then I sat and crossed my legs and said, "He's not coming."

They exchanged a look. "Change of plans?" asked Herb hopefully.

"I'm afraid I've lured you folks here under false pretenses. The truth is that Lyle doesn't know anything about this."

She shot me a sidelong scowl. *The* Scowl. It sent prickles up my neck. "What the heck is this? You said on the phone you was some kind of associate of his."

"I am. And I need your help. Desperately."

Aileen shook her head at her husband. "I knew it was too good to be true. I *knew* it." She bit into her sandwich.

"I needed to speak to you two in private," I explained. "And I didn't think I could get away to Bay Shore without arousing Lyle's suspicion. I'm sorry if I got your hopes up."

"That's just what you did, young fella," said a crestfallen Herb, his hands shaking so badly his teacup rattled in its saucer. In another couple of years he'd be ready to be a waiter at Ratner's. He set it down on the coffee table. "What kind of help you mean?"

"Lyle's in serious trouble. Somebody's trying to kill him."

Aileen's eyes widened. "Kill him? What the heck for?"

"That's what I'm trying to find out."

"What are you?" asked Herb. "Some kind of detective?"

"I'm his collaborator. I'm helping him write his life story."

Aileen pointed a pudgy finger at me. "Sure. You're the fella who used to be married to what's-her-name. The one who got herself pregnant."

"That's me."

"It's disgraceful what she did." Aileen's sandwich was gone. She reached for another. "And I used to like her movies, too. Especially that outer-space one where they shaved her head. She looked so cute without her—"

"I'm trying to help Lyle," I broke in. "So are the police. Only there are certain things he won't talk about. I can't help him unless I have all of the facts. I need the facts."

"Facts about what?" she asked.

"About whether or not he had shock therapy. About what's wrong with him—if anything."

They exchanged a frightened look. My heart beat a little faster.

"Maybe," Herb suggested carefully, "he don't want you to know."

"I have to know."

"But if the boy don't want you to, it's not really our place to—"

"I have to know."

"What's this got to do with somebody trying to kill him?" asked Aileen.

"Maybe nothing. Maybe everything. I can't tell—without knowing."

They were silent a moment.

Aileen broke it. "This isn't some dirty filth for people to

read about in the checkout line at the supermarket, y'know. This is our personal heartbreak."

"A family matter," agreed Herb, nervously fingering his shirt pocket.

"I know that. And nothing will go in Lyle's book unless he wants it to. I'm on Lyle's side. You must believe that."

"Why the hell should we?" she demanded, turning hot on me. Lyle had her temper, too.

"Now, simmer down, hon. We have no reason to tussle with this young fella." Herb patted her knee reassuringly. "How do we know we can trust you, Mr. Hoag? That's what we're wondering."

"You don't know." I leveled my gaze at him. "But you can. I'm trying to help Lyle. He needs help. Just like . . ."

"Just like what?" Aileen demanded, leaning forward.

"Just like he always has," I said quietly.

They exchanged another look.

"Has it occurred to you," Herb said slowly, "that maybe there are some things Lyle doesn't know himself? And that he's better off for it?"

I nodded, though it's been my experience that, when someone close to my celebrity says those words, they're the ones who'd be better off, not my celebrity. "That's a chance I have to take. *We* have to take."

Aileen reached for her cigarettes. "Is Lyle happy?"

"Well, someone's trying to kill him, like I said."

"But how are his spirits?" asked Herb.

I sipped my tea. "He says he's never been happier. And Lyle tends to believe what he says, whether it's true or not."

"Is it true?" she asked.

"I'd have to say no."

"Any women in his life?" She lit her cigarette and kept it cupped in her palm, like a night watchman patrolling on a windy night.

"Several."

"One in particular?" persisted Herb.

"Yes."

"Nice girl?"

"She certainly has plenty to offer."

"And is he seeing a good man these days?" asked Herb. I tugged at my ear. "Good man?"

"A doctor," she said, drawing on her cigarette.

"Do you mean a psychiatrist?"

Neither of them responded to this. They just sat there, waiting me out. The elderly can be exceedingly patient.

"He's not seeing anyone," I replied. "He says he's into self-therapy."

"Dear God," murmured Herb, paling visibly.

Aileen poured him more tea, dumped four packets of sugar in it, and made him drink it down. When his color began to return she said to me, "Just exactly what has Lyle told you about his boyhood?"

"That he was a rebellious kid. A rockhead, as he put it. Constantly fighting with the other kids. Getting into trouble at school."

Aileen cleared her throat. She was clearly ill at ease now. "Anything earlier than that?"

"His earliest memory is biting the mailman."

"He was three," she recalled dejectedly. "But we'd already been through so much with Lyle by then, Mr. Hoag. Night and day, day after day, from the moment we brought him home from the hospital. He cried constantly, see. Screamed with red-faced anger twenty-four hours a day. Cried when he was hungry. Cried when he was full. Cried when he was wet. Cried when he was dry. That child would not be pacified. Rocking him didn't help. Holding him didn't help— he pulled away from me if I so much as tried to touch him. I tried music, long rides in the car . . . Nothing worked. He would not sleep. Cried all night long, every single night. Occasionally, he'd pass out for an hour or two out of sheer exhaustion. But soon as he woke up he'd start in screaming again. He wore both of us ragged, Mr. Hoag. And frustrated me to the point of tears. I just didn't know what I was doing wrong. I tried everything, believe me. But he just wouldn't stop."

"What did his pediatrician say?"

"That he wasn't sick," she replied. "That he wasn't in pain. That he was just . . . angry." She flicked her cigarette ash into the ashtray with a red fingernail. "I began to have fantasies about checking into a hotel all by my lonesome and taking a hot bubble bath and just *sleeping* for two whole days. That's how tired I was. Finally, when Lyle was four months old, the doctor gave him something so he'd sleep."

"So all three of us would," Herb chimed in.

"Liquid phenobarbital, wasn't it, Herbert?" she said to him.

He nodded. "Poor boy was on medication before he could even walk."

"And after he could walk?" I asked. "What happened then?"

"He ran around the house like a little demon," Lyle's mother recalled, in her singsong voice. "Crashing headfirst into tables, chairs, walls. Herbert had to make him a little foam helmet with a chin strap so he wouldn't knock himself out. If the weather was nice I'd let him out in our little yard, and he'd just run around and around in a circle until he collapsed, limp, from exhaustion. Then I'd carry him inside and put him to bed. That was the only time Lyle'd ever let me hold him."

"Was he hyperactive?"

She put out her cigarette and sampled a tea cake. "Doctor said no. Said Lyle was healthy and normal—just full of steam. As a baby, he had no way to let off his steam, other than to cry. Or run into things. When he got to be two or three, he began to turn it on the grown-ups around him."

"Such as the mailman?"

"Such as Aileen," Herb replied darkly, glancing at her.

She brushed at a crumb in her lap, growing more and more uncomfortable. Then she shifted her bulk on the sofa, wheezing from the effort. "Herbert needed me full-time down at the store in those days. We couldn't afford to have a woman stay with Lyle, so I brought him with me." She shook her head at the memory. "He was a holy terror, Mr. Hoag. Chasing our customers out with his screaming. Mixing up all of the piles of clothes in the back room, hurling them around, stomping on them. Once . . . Once I even caught him back there making pee-pee on all of the dress shirts. He ruined hundreds of dollars in shirts. I—I just had to keep him at home. So Herbert got an older woman to help out at the store and I stayed home with Lyle. It was . . ." She reached for another cake. "It was living hell. I—I can't even begin to tell you."

"Try, Mrs. Hudnut. Please."

She gazed off at the window. "He'd get this smirk on his face. What I used to call his Holy Terror look. And there'd be no dealing with him. If I wanted him to sit down and eat his lunch he'd throw his food on the floor. If I wanted him to take his bath, he'd hide from me—for hours sometimes. If I wanted to take him to the park, he'd want to stay home. If I *had* to stay home, like if the TV repairman was coming, he'd want to go to the park. And if he didn't get his way he'd holler, scream, kick. . . . None of this sounds too terrible, I guess, but it was so *constant.* Every single thing was a fight with Lyle. And I—I *swore* he was willful. Purposely tormenting me. He wasn't, of course. How could he be? He was only two, three years old. A baby. But he was so . . ." Her eyes filled with tears. Herb reached over to take her hand. She yanked hers away roughly.

"When did you start beating him, Mrs. Hudnut?"

She didn't flinch. Just swiped at her eyes and sniffled. After a moment, she glanced imploringly over at Herb, her face etched with pain and guilt. His was, too. I waited them out, saying nothing more. They were ready to unload. I knew it and they knew it. Because they wanted it off their chests. And because they had nothing to lose at this point in their lives. Their relationship with Lyle couldn't get any worse.

"My problem was I took it personal," she finally said, her voice quavering. "I took his behavior as a personal rejection of *me*. All I ever wanted was for him to be a healthy, happy little boy. I wanted to help him. I wanted to love him. I *did* love him. But with Lyle, there was never enough love. He'd just wring you dry. One day I just couldn't take no more of him, Mr. Hoag. I lost it. Once. Just that once. But it was horrible, what I did to him. He was just a *baby*." She shook her head. "I've regretted it every single day of my life. The shame's never left me. I just thank God he don't remember it."

"Remember what, Mrs. Hudnut?"

She ducked her head. "I—I threw Lyle down the basement stairs when he was two. Threw him on his head. Hard. I tried to kill my baby. I—I just couldn't stand any more of him! Not another second! At first he didn't move at all. Just lay there on the cement floor. I thought he was dead for sure. Then his arms and legs began to twitch a little. But he wouldn't come to. I—I came to my senses and called his doctor. Told him Lyle tripped and fell down the stairs. He called an ambulance. At first, they was afraid he had a fractured skull. But it was just a concussion. He was okay in a few days." She paused, reaching for her tea. "I just thank God we didn't have no gun in the home."

"We do now," Herb pointed out.

"I know, Herbert," she said patiently. "But we didn't then. That's my point."

"Do you think you would have used it on him?" I asked her.

"I know I would have." She reddened, her eyes avoiding mine. "That's a terrible, awful thing for a mother to admit. But it's true . . . At first, I—I kept the truth from Herbert. Told him Lyle fell. Then I—I locked myself in our room for

weeks and cried my poor eyes out. I was so ashamed. I finally
told him the truth when I couldn't stand it no more."

"What did you think, Herb?"

"I thought she needed help," he replied, tight-lipped.
"So we went to see her doctor. She didn't want me to go
with her, but I insisted."

"And what did he put you on, Mrs. Hudnut? Miltown?"

"How'd you know that?" she demanded, startled. "Lyle
tell you?"

"Hardly. In fact, Lyle recalls surprisingly little about you.
Except that you had to lie down a lot. It's Herb whom Lyle
remembers most. Herb saying, 'Your mom is tired, Lyle.' Herb
saying, 'Your mom's not as strong as we are, Lyle.' Of course,
that's a rather typical family pattern, given the nature of Lyle's
illness." They didn't react. Didn't so much as blink. I took
that as a green light, and kept right on going. "It all fits,
actually. What Lyle told me about his childhood, I mean. He
merely glorified it a little. Gave it a heroic spin. But there's
really nothing heroic about it all. It's a sad story about a little
boy who was hostile and incorrigible, who kept getting into
fights with the other little boys, who had a lot of trouble
with authority figures, who felt persecuted and pressured.
Trapped was the word he used. This little boy got harder and
harder for the public school to handle. His doctor prescribed
Thorazine. But it didn't help much. Eventually, he ended up
in a residential treatment center. He showed some progress
there, enough so that he could go to the public high school,
only he got into trouble with drugs. That's often the case
with kids like Lyle. And then a major episode presented itself.
That's often the case, too. An episode that Lyle can't or won't
talk about. An episode that was serious enough to prompt his
doctors to administer electroconvulsive therapy. I'm told that
ECT came about from studies that found that people like Lyle,
people who suffer from manic-depression, seem to show a
marked improvement after undergoing a seizure."

Herb stopped me. "They never said that to us at the

child guidance center. They never said Lyle was manic-de-pressive."

I nodded. "They're very reluctant to pin those labels on children—for fear it's a stage they'll outgrow. They don't want to stigmatize them. But with Lyle it wasn't a stage, was it?"

"No, it wasn't," Aileen said quietly. "They made the diagnosis later—when he was in high school."

I poured myself some more tea. "When a child turns up manic-depressive like Lyle, the professionals look at what kind of family environment caused it to happen. They look at the parents. At the genes. These days, they feel it *is* a gene, passed along from generation to generation. They look for a parent who's, say, a depressive. Or a grandparent. Not that it's necessarily so obvious. Depressives often self-medicate. Mask their symptoms. Their illness might, for example, present itself as a drinking problem."

Aileen reached for her cigarettes. "You're describing my daddy, Mr. Hoag," she said, lighting one. "He got drunk every Saturday night and beat up Mommy. When he got tired of hitting her, he'd hit *me*. He was a rough, tough, two-fisted workingman. And he had his moods. That's what Mommy called them—his moods. Real black and angry, they was. He'd go off on his drunken toots. Get in fistfights down at the corner tavern. Disappear for one night, sometimes two. God knows where he was—a brothel, jail, the gutter. We never knew. He'd show up all bloody and sorry. Mommy would wipe his face and send him off to work. Then she'd go to church and pray for him. But nobody ever gave a second's thought to how he was. Nobody said, 'That Frankie O'Reilly, he's a depressive.' No sir. Not in Elmhurst, Queens, in the thirties. All they said was, 'Watch out for Frankie O'Reilly when he's been drinking.' And he wasn't the only one in the neighborhood they said it about, believe me."

"And how about in your case, Mrs. Hudnut?"

She gave me The Scowl over her cigarette. "I got his

temperament. It's true. Mommy used to say to me, 'Aileen, you're just like your dad—born under a gray cloud.' But I never had no trouble with alcohol. Sure, my girlfriends and I liked to have fun. We'd take a drink now and then, dance with the boys. Maybe I drank a little more than the others did. Why not? It made me happy. I liked being happy. I liked a good time.''

"First girl I ever met who could drink me under the table,'' Herb kidded, winking at me.

"Still could if I cared to, Herbert,'' she sniffed. "But I was never a drunk. Just a social drinker. And I stopped cold when I was carrying Lyle. I wanted to be a good mother. I wanted it more than anything in the world. But I just . . . I just . . .'' Her voice became choked. "I could . . . not . . . please him.''

"So they started you on tranquilizers?''

She stared down at her meaty hands. "First Miltown, like you said. To improve my spirits. And it did help some. Only, the doses kept getting bigger, and the stuff they gave me more powerful and . . . Half the time, I was in this never-never land. Just sort of floating. Felt real strange, but real comfortable, too. And after a while, it was the only way I knew how to feel.''

I nodded. This was what Fiona had meant when she said Mrs. Hudnut had seemed dazed to her, that day at the apartment.

"I was hooked on them pills for over twenty years, Mr. Hoag,'' Lyle's mother stated matter-of-factly. "Seconal. Dalmane. Valium. Quaaludes. . . .'' She blew some cigarette smoke up in the air. "The kids used to take Quaaludes to get stoned. My doctor *prescribed* them to me. I was an addict—plain and simple.''

"Not that she knew it,'' Herbert pointed out in her defense.

"No, sir,'' she agreed. "Not until I went in for my gall bladder in . . . when was that, Herbert?''

He sat there fidgeting while he tried to remember. "I think it was '77. Carter was president."

She said, "It's common procedure for 'em to make note of the drugs you're on. The surgeon was the one who said to me, 'Madam, you got yourself a problem.' "

"And do you still?"

"I haven't taken anything stronger than aspirin in over ten years, Mr. Hoag," she replied, stubbing out her cigarette. I guess she didn't consider nicotine a drug.

The air was getting stale from her smoke. I got up and opened a window, filling the room with the sounds of East Sixty-fifth Street. Then I sat back down. "Did Lyle know that you were drug dependent?"

"Lyle was never able to see past his own anger and pain," she replied. "He couldn't understand someone else's."

"The subject never came up in family therapy?"

Aileen glanced at her husband. "We figured it was best to keep it between ourselves."

He took her hand. This time she let him. "It's like Aileen said, young fella. All we ever wanted was for Lyle to be healthy and happy. To have pals, play sports, do well in school. Only, it never seemed to work out for him. That boy was always getting in fights with the other kids on the block. He was a bully. And big for his age. They were scared of him. I could see it in their eyes. Their fathers came to our door on more than one occasion to tell me I oughta control him better. And then, once he started school, we was always getting calls at the store from the principal about something or another that he'd pulled." Herb shook his head sadly. "I kept telling him: 'Lyle, ya gotta learn how to get along with other people in this world.' But he just couldn't."

"Were you ashamed of him?"

Herb recoiled at this. "Now why would you ask something like that?"

"Because Lyle believes you were," I replied. "Above all else."

Herb looked down at the carpet. "Look, neither of us enjoyed getting bawled out by the neighbors, or hauled down to the school to pick him up. Who would?" He moistened his mouth. "But *ashamed?* Nah, that was never how we felt."

"Concerned," declared Aileen. "We was concerned."

"Sure, sure," agreed Herb. "And anxious to help him. When they recommended that family therapy stuff, we tried it. Didn't help, but we tried it. When they told me to make more time for him, I came home every day at four. Had Celia, the gal who worked for me, close up the store. I tried, Mr. Hoag. Dammit, I tried. I remember saying to him, 'We just want ya to be happy, son.' But he was never, ever happy. Me, I like to tinker. Keeps me out of trouble. My therapy, I guess you'd call it. I tried to share that with him. Get him interested in ham radio. Only he got that Holy Terror look of his, and then he turned on me."

"Burned down your ham shack."

"That's what he did," Herb confirmed. "I think that was the first time we realized, down deep inside, that our Lyle wasn't like the other boys."

"Were you frightened?"

"Wouldn't you be?" Herb fired back angrily.

"I felt a lot of guilt, too," Aileen said regretfully.

"Guilt?"

She stared at me. "You don't have no children of your own, do you?"

"No, I don't."

She nodded to herself with satisfaction. "I didn't think so. Y'see, when things turn out bad with your child, you tend to blame yourself. Figure you should have done something more for him, or less, or different, or—"

"Do you still feel that way?"

"My, my, yes," she replied. "When he got himself arrested at that pornographic movie house, that was my first reaction. Feeling guilty. Because he's still troubled, and because I couldn't ever help him."

"We hoped and prayed we'd hear from him during that whole mess," Herb said. "It's at a time like that when a man needs his family, the people who love him. We were here for him. Only he wouldn't turn to us. He bears us a real grudge. Sure, we made some mistakes, like Aileen said. But we loved that boy, and we still do. He's not a bad person, y'know. He's never hurt anyone else. Just himself."

"He's always been hardest on himself," she agreed.

I let them have that one. They needed something to hang onto. They had so little, other than helplessness. I said, "After the ham shack incident you sent him to the Allen School."

"Somehow, we found the money," recalled Aileen. "Whatever it took. Allen was a more nurturing environment than the public school. They gave the kids a lot of individual attention and counseling. Plus it was a real positive place. Lyle did good there. His grades picked up. We got glowing reports on his progress. He really seemed to be turning the corner. He was going through puberty right around that time. It was our hope—our dream—that he was outgrowing his childhood demons. Doctors said it was possible. They were plenty encouraged themselves. Saw no reason for him not to enroll in the public high school, not so long as he maintained his therapy sessions and his medication. Of course, we was thrilled to have him home again. He'd changed quite a bit. Had that long hair. Listened to his loud rock 'n' roll and used a lot of slang we didn't understand. Still, we was happy. And he seemed to be, too. Herbert fixed up the garage for him, so he'd feel he had a place that was his. We let him go his own way. Crossed our fingers is what we did." Her face dropped. "But he fell right in with the bad kids in the neighborhood. And they got him started on drugs."

"That all started at Allen, actually."

"Did it?" Herb was surprised. "We never knew that."

Aileen said, "We knew his grades was getting bad. He stopped going to class. Even started skipping his appointments with his analyst. He'd just hole up out there in his room for days at a time, stereo blasting, kids coming and going at all hours. It was those drugs. Those damned drugs."

"I understand he got caught selling them at school."

Herb nodded dejectedly. "Shouldn't have come as any surprise to us—after all we'd been through with him. But it did. Guess I just never thought I'd be fishing a member of my own family out of jail. They were willing to put him on probation. And the high school agreed to take him back so the boy could get his . . . his . . ." Herb was suddenly having trouble talking. He swallowed and stared down at his veiny hands, which were shaking even worse now.

Aileen cleared her throat uneasily. "Just what did Lyle say to you about what happened after that?"

"He said that you folks were ashamed to be the parents of a drug dealer," I replied. "So you came down hard on him. His exact words were, 'I was a bad boy, and bad boys get punished.' He claims you had him institutionalized. And that you forced him, against his will, to undergo electroconvulsive therapy. Because you'd had it with his rebel ways. Because you wanted him to toe the line. And because . . . and because you hated him."

"Oh, my, no!" she cried, shaking her head. "My, my, no."

Herb got up and went over to the window, where he blew his nose into a large handkerchief. He stayed where he was a moment, staring out the window. I'm better at reading faces than I am backs of heads, but I'm fairly certain the old man was struggling not to cry in front of me. He took a deep breath and came back and sat down, his jaw clamped tightly shut. Aileen took his hand and squeezed it. Both looked shell-shocked.

"What did happen?" I asked them gently.

"Not that," he replied huskily. "But my God, if he believes that . . ."

"He does."

Herb swallowed. "Then he has every reason in the world to hate us like he does." He turned to his wife. "Christ, that explains so much."

She said nothing. Just stared straight ahead, stone-faced.

"Please tell me what happened," I said.

"He didn't stop taking those damned drugs, is what happened," Herb told me. "Those psychedelic drugs of his. The LSD, the mescaline, those crazy darned Mexican mushrooms or jumping beans or whatever the heck they were. Playing with fire, he was. A boy in his unstable psychological state. Didn't stop him, though. No, sir. He just kept taking more and more of 'em. H-He even went to school high as a kite on 'em."

"One of the custodians found him," Aileen said softly. "He was up on the roof of the gymnasium, threatening to jump. It was after school. Most everybody had gone home for the day. He'd been up there for hours. A bum trip, they called it. We almost lost him that day. He so wanted to die. Luckily, the police was able to restrain him. His doctor hospitalized him. He thought Lyle would be better in a day or two, soon as that damned drug was out of his system. Only . . . Lyle didn't come out of it, Mr. Hoag. It was no bum trip. In fact, the LSD had little to do with it. Other than maybe hastening it."

"Hastening what, Mrs. Hudnut?"

"Lyle was in the middle of a m-major clinical depression," she replied, her voice choking. "He totally withdrew from the world. Wouldn't talk. Wouldn't eat. All he'd do was sit in his hospital room in the dark and cry for hours at a time. Or sleep. He slept eighteen, twenty hours a day. He was like a different person. That Holy Terror look of his was gone. All he had was this dull gaze. It was like a light had gone out inside of him. He had no interest in anything or anyone. No idea of pleasure. No idea of the future. College, adulthood—none of it meant anything to him. All he wanted to do was die. They had to keep his belt and his shoelaces away from him. No sharp objects or utensils. They tried everything to help him. Heavy doses of Thorazine. Therapy. But he wouldn't respond. He'd gone down a black hole. He was a sick, sick boy. Weeks went by, six long weeks, before the doctors ever discussed giving him the shock treatments. Frankly, we was horrified by the whole idea. Sounded to us like something from out of *The Snake Pit.*"

"We were very, very reluctant," Herb agreed.

"But they assured us it was a safe, legitimate medical procedure," she went on. "And that in certain cases like Lyle's it had been proven to be a help. They were very straight with us about the memory loss, too. They warned us."

"But their feeling about it," recounted Herb, "was, hey, this boy is in a hopeless depression. May never come out of it. This may pull him out. So what if he has a spotty memory? Small price to pay, considering the alternative. The two of us went home and slept on it. Slept, hell. We talked all night, holding hands in bed like a couple of scared kids. In the morning, we told 'em to go ahead."

"They gave him a series of eight treatments," Aileen told me. "And he *did* respond, thank God. Started showing an interest in things again. He said he missed his records, his Grateful Dead records. And he wanted the current issue of Rolling Stone and—"

"And a pepperoni pizza." Herb smiled faintly. "With extra cheese. I went and got him one. He ate the whole damned thing all by himself. Let out a belch you could hear clear out to Orient Point. Right then I knew the boy was gonna be hokey-dokey."

"Those shock treatments saved Lyle, Mr. Hoag," Aileen argued. "Without 'em, we'd have had to institutionalize him permanent. With 'em, he was well enough to come home in a couple of weeks."

"What was his memory like?"

"Spotty," Herb conceded.

"He didn't remember a thing about the six weeks," she explained. "He remembered the bummer, as he called it, but not the rest—it was like he'd been in a coma. We considered giving him the details, but why remind him? It was a blessing in disguise he didn't remember. Doctors agreed with us."

"As I understand it, much of that memory loss is supposed to come back gradually over time. Did it?"

They looked at each other.

"We wouldn't know, young fella," replied Herb. "He hasn't spoken to us in over twenty years, remember?"

"Was he hostile toward you when you brought him home?"

"Not in the least," said Herb. "He seemed grateful. Happy to be home. Happy to be back in school. We was real proud of him, too, day he got his diploma."

"Said he wanted to take up acting here in New York," Aileen recalled. "Performing was something he really enjoyed in school. About the only thing he talked about doing with himself. We was wary of it. Didn't think he was up to it. Plus he was barely seventeen. And New York is, well, New York. But the boy was insistent. So, we spoke to his doctors about it, figuring they'd say no."

"But to our great surprise, they didn't," said Herb. "They thought it was positive that Lyle had something he wanted to do. New York didn't scare 'em, neither. They said, he's gonna have to learn to sink or swim on his own no matter where he is. They advised us to let him go. So we put him on a train for Manhattan. Gave him some money." Herb scratched his chin. "I don't remember how much. . . ."

"It was twelve hundred dollars," Aileen declared crisply.

"He phoned us from his hotel when he got settled," Herb went on. "The Chelsea, it was. Some kind of residential hotel. And he wrote us pretty regular for a while. About the acting classes he was taking. Friends he was making. But then he stopped writing, and our letters to the Chelsea started coming back to us unopened. Seems he'd moved on, and left no forwarding address. And that was the last contact we had with him.''

"Except for that one time Fiona invited us to visit 'em,'' said Aileen. "My, my, what a horrible day that was. He *struck* the poor little thing, ran out of there like a crazy man, looking at us with so much *hate*. We didn't know why. We never, ever knew why. Until now . . .'' She heaved a huge sigh. "You opened our eyes, Mr. Hoag. And for that I thank you.''

"Both of us do," Herb added sincerely.

"And I thank you,'' I said. "For your cooperation, and your candor.''

"Is there any chance we'll get to see Lyle?'' Herb asked, moistening his mouth anxiously. "I don't mean today. But sometime soon, maybe?''

I sat there looking at him. He was such a sorrowful little old man. I didn't ever want to be so sorrowful. Or so old. I didn't ever want to have children. I took to my feet and smoothed my trousers. "I hope so,'' I said. "I realize that's not much, but—''

"You couldn't be more wrong,'' Herb assured me cheerfully. "Hope is a lot. Hope is plenty. Yessir. We haven't had hope for a long, long time.''

Aileen started to reach for her cigarettes but stopped herself. I don't know why. "Mr. Hoag?''

"Yes, Mrs. Hudnut?''

Her eyes were on the carpet. "What'll you tell Lyle? Will you tell him about those six weeks? A-About what I did to him when he was a baby?'' She looked up at me imploringly, a mother's love and pain scrunching up her soft, round face. "What'll you tell him?''

I started looking around the room for Lulu, until I remembered she wasn't with me anymore. I went and got my hat. Then I went to the door. Then I said, "I honestly don't know."

Because I didn't.

One of the hardest positions I ever put myself in as a ghost is when I manage to find out something important about my celebrity that he doesn't know about himself. Something his loved ones never told him—for a variety of reasons. Some selfish. Some not so selfish. But all of them painful. You can't hurt other people when you write a novel. You can piss them off, disappoint them, bore them. But you can't hurt them. It's different with a memoir. A lot different. With a memoir, you can hurt them bad.

I chewed on it as I strolled across Central Park toward home. True, Lyle's parents had handed me gold. The stuff that best-sellers are made of. This definitely rated the cover of *People,* which is for tell-alls what the cover of *Rolling Stone* is for rockers—*I made it, Ma, top of the world!* Good for the book, no question. And that was all that mattered—what was best for the book, right? Or was it? What about the people involved? What about what was best for them? Lyle Hudnut already hated his parents, blamed them for everything that had gone wrong in his life. If he found out his mother tried to kill him when he was two, he would only hate her more. Want to expose her in print. After all, here was *proof* of Aileen's evil. Here was Lyle's chance to bury them, once and for all. I had no doubt he would see it that way. None. But was that fair to them? Was it right? And what about his six weeks down that black hole of depression? *Did* he remember it? Was I dealing with fabrication and denial, as Vic had suggested, or had Lyle's memory actually been erased? If so, would it help him to find out now, after all these years, why he'd undergone shock therapy? Or would it only hurt him? Would he be able to deal with it? The man was already plenty unstable. Plus somebody was trying to murder him. Could he handle this on top of it? I chewed on it. I had a job to do: Help the world understand a major television star named Lyle Hudnut. But at what cost? Would it be worth it if it tore him up inside? Who the hell was I to decide this? What right did I have to say what one human being should or should not know about his own life? I was not a loved one. Or friend. I was not his shrink. I was just the guy whose name would be found at the bottom of the title page, under the words "As Told To."

Sometimes I'm overpaid for what I do. I admit that. This time wasn't one of those times.

It was a warm evening, the air soft and hazy. There was still a lot of activity in the park. The paths were filled with joggers and Rollerbladers, the baseball diamonds crowded with office softball teams playing with great intensity and ineptitude. I paid them little attention. It was the others I was noticing. The guys who were tossing sticks for their ebullient, arfing retrievers. The couples who were pushing their babies along in carriages. They were the ones I kept noticing. Everywhere I looked I saw them. It was a genuine laugh riot how many dogs and babies were out in Central Park that late summer evening. Just to round out the hilarity, the path I was on brought me out of the park directly across the street from Merilee's building. Amazing how that happens. I sat there on a bench, looking up at the eight windows. Lights were on up there. Lulu was up there. *She* was up there. Everyone was up there. Except for me. I was sitting on a park bench all by myself, getting soot and chewing gum on my linen trousers. I took a deep breath and let it out very slowly. Then I went and found a pay phone.

I met Very at The Blue Mill down in the Village on Commerce Street, where neither the menu nor the decor has changed one bit in my lifetime. I was already deep into my second martini, heavy on the olives, when he came charging in, muttering about all of the goddamned reporters who'd kept him on the goddamned phone. I ordered calves' liver with bacon and onions. He went for the trout almondine. Lulu's favorite. Our waiter, Pete, was nice enough not to ask me where she was. Just brought me another martini, and a Rolling Rock for my nodding acquaintance.

Very gulped down half of it from the bottle before he puffed out his cheeks and demanded, "Ever try to come up with a delicate way of saying that a guy died while he was taking a piss?"

"What did you say, Lieutenant?"

"That Roe was electrocuted in the washroom—while in the process of using the urinal. Let 'em figure it out for themselves. Yo, it's not like your basic pisser has a wide assortment of uses. You don't wash your socks in it. You don't brush your teeth in it. . . ."

"Did you call it an accident or murder?"

He gestured for another beer. "Didn't say one way or the other, dude."

"Why not?"

"Because you got to watch how much you give the New York press corps."

"Why?"

His dark eyes flashed at me impatiently. "Because no matter how much you give them, they always figure you haven't given them everything."

"Because you haven't," I pointed out.

"Because I can't, dude," he insisted. "Not if I want to keep it sane. Yo, even if I'm totally one-hundred-percent straight with them they'll still go ahead and invent shit—shit that's even more lurid and frightening than what really went down. That's their job. My job is to contain it, just like I would a riot. I don't confirm. I don't deny. I tell 'em only what I *know*. Facts. They already know about the bombs. By tomorrow some unnamed staff source will have tipped them off to the chili deal." Pete brought him his beer. Very drank some down, and added, "Let 'em draw their own conclusions."

"But you *know* Chad was murdered, Lieutenant."

"I know shit," he retorted. "I *think* he was murdered. I have concluded he was murdered. But I don't know it. No one's been charged. I got no suspects. There were no fingerprints at the scene. . . ."

"Wiped clean?"

"As a whistle. I got bubkes, dude. Just an ultrascared intended victim, Hudnut, presently tucked in for the night at the Essex House on Central Park South with the bodacious Katrina Tingle. I got me a man in the lobby and a man in the hall outside his room. I got me Hudnut among the living—for now. Otherwise, I got shit." He removed a small notepad from his back pocket, glanced through it. "Yo, we finished questioning the office personnel about an hour ago. Breaks down like so: The custodian mops down the john at seven-thirty, and sees nobody around yet. Office lights are out. Now, dig, it's *possible* our perp's waiting there in the dark for the dude to leave so he can rush in and rig the urinal. If so, he's been hiding there all night. And we're semifucked. People don't have to sign out downstairs when they leave, and Tyrone can't be expected to remember every face that went by. Still, we can check out everyone's whereabouts last night if we have to. And we may have to." He shook his head, disgusted. "Okay, Tyrone arrives downstairs at the front desk at five after eight. He says nobody could have got in before he got there. Building's locked, and *Uncle Chubby* folks don't get front door keys, for security reasons. So we can forget that particular angle."

"Unless someone made a key," I pointed out.

"Don't complicate this, dude. It's already bad enough."

"Sorry, Lieutenant."

"According to my homey, Tyrone, the earliest arrival was Naomi, who got there about eight-fifteen, just like she said. Leo Crimp, the producer, got in next. She gets in every day at eight-thirty, he says. Then Bobby Ackerman got in at eight forty-five. He was the first writer to arrive."

I tugged at my ear. "Hmm. That's interesting."

"Why's that?" he asked, peering at me.

"And then who?"

He examined his notes. "Hudnut and Katrina. At ten before nine, like Naomi said. Katrina went into her office, Hudnut went into his. Annabelle Gamba, Marty Muck, and Tommy Meyer trickled in over the next few minutes. Marjorie Daw got there at nine sharp. Writers' meeting commenced immediately in Muck and Meyer's office, Hudnut and Katrina sitting in. His john and his office were vacant for the next twenty-three minutes until Chad Roe, schlemiel of the century, got waxed. Which would be your prime time to wire it, you'd think. . . ."

"But?"

"But nobody saw anyone go in the man's office or his john that whole time."

"Someone was in a position to?"

He nodded, brightening. "Leo. She was at her desk right outside that whole time doing paperwork. Dig, she even saw *Roe* go in there. Says he just winked at her and went right in. She immediately went and got herself some coffee. Claims she didn't want to be around in case the meeting broke and Hudnut found the dude in there—she figured Hudnut would go ballistic at her for allowing it. So that's why Naomi was the one who found the body. But, dig, Leo swears she saw nobody go in there until Roe did. Twisted, huh? I mean, how do you figure it?"

"One of two ways," I replied. "Either she really didn't see anyone go in, like she says, or she did and she's not talking—either because she had something to do with it herself or because—"

"She's protecting the guy who did it," said Very grimly.

Our food arrived. The liver was tender and moist. I won't order it anywhere but The Blue Mill. There's nothing worse than overcooked liver, and there's nothing easier to overcook.

"Why do you assume it's a guy?" I asked, as I ate.

"Just do." He frowned. "You don't?"

"A number of the people who hate Lyle are women."

"You mean like Leo?"

"I mean like Leo."

"Say she's being up front with us. Say nobody went in there during those twenty-three minutes. Who are we looking at, dude? Naomi?"

I shook my head. "Naomi has every reason to want Lyle alive right now."

"Then who? And how the hell did they do it?"

I mulled it over as I ate. "Exactly how long was Bobby there before Lyle got in?"

Very checked his notes. "Five minutes."

"Long enough to rig the urinal," I suggested.

"I'm down to that," he agreed. "And interesting you should bring up Bobby, on account of I like him for it—he got in early, he's known to be good with his hands and . . ." Very rifled through his notes. "We got something else on him. One of your leads. Dig, y'know when the bombing went down yesterday morning? And Bobby was on his way back from his shrink in Boston?"

"What about it, Lieutenant?"

"He wasn't. He doesn't see Dr. Helfein on Tuesdays anymore. Hasn't for almost a year. Bobby told him his schedule wouldn't allow it. He only sees the good doctor on Saturdays and Mondays now."

"So where was he yesterday morning?"

"Dunno yet. I only know he wasn't on the Boston shuttle. According to Tyrone, Bobby didn't show up at the studio until just before lunch. Still . . ."

"Perhaps he did and Tyrone missed him."

"Right on. Although Tyrone swears he never left his desk. And there's only the one way in." Very finished his trout and pushed his plate away, smacking his lips. "Still, Bobby's not being straight, and his whereabouts during the bombing are unknown. Interesting, huh?"

"Very."

"Yeah, dude?"

I sighed. "It's very interesting."

"You want interesting," he continued, leafing through his notebook, "try on Lorenzo Peritore, former *Uncle Chubby* cameraman and present significant other of Annabelle Gamba. Possessor of a pharmacology degree from Fairfield University. Current status: unemployed. I checked this particular dude out myself and, dig, he copped a major 'tude with me. He was hostile, rude, and ultrauptight. Hates Hudnut. Claims the dude really fucked him, career-wise, when he axed him. We're talking major bitter here. Also major bum. Dude's hanging out at home in the middle of the day drinking beer, watching Sports Channel. But he denies knowing anything about how that fluid essence of ipecac ended up in the chili. Says he hasn't worked in a pharmacy in over four years. I ask him real polite if he'd mind showing me his tax returns for the past four years. Dude practically shits in his pants. Starts hollering get a warrant, get a subpoena, get a court order, but until you do, get out."

"Are you planning to?"

"You got that right," he confirmed. "Dude cops a 'tude with me, he's hiding something."

"Could be he just didn't like you, Lieutenant."

"Could be he helped his sweetie pie spike the chili and who knows what else," Very countered. "Yo, I'm going back —Lorenzo's a prospect. But you know who looks even better for it?"

"Do tell."

Very smiled at me. "Tommy Meyer. He's my main man. We're talking one major strange dude here. I mean, we ran down some shit about his . . . lifestyle you won't believe."

"I'll believe it."

"During the week he lives right around the corner from the infamous Deuce Theater at a real shithole on West Forty-third, the Rutledge Hotel. We're talking one small step up from a welfare hotel. Check it out, dude's pulling down fifteen-twenty grand a week, has a nice house in the 'burbs, a wife, kids . . . What the fuck he's doing at the Rutledge? He's getting his jollies, is what he's doing. Likes to bring hookers up to his room from the street. Black ones, the older the better. His fave is Dolly Mae Bramble, age thirty-six, which in hooker years is like a hundred and twelve for you and me. Pays Dolly Mae fifty bucks to let him dress up in her clothing. Then she spanks him while he gets off in her underwear. Which he keeps."

"My, my." I was sure glad Lulu wasn't around to hear this.

"Dolly Mae thinks Tommy's name is Floyd, and that he's a sporting goods salesman. She described him as one of her regulars. He even gave her a Christmas present—silk lingerie, red. And dig this: She says he hangs at the Deuce all the time. She's gone in there with him late at night to watch the flick and do him."

I tugged at my ear. "Interesting."

Very finished off this beer. "Wait, it gets better. I talked to one of the guys in Vice who made the Hudnut collar."

Pete came by to clear our table. I ordered cheesecake and coffee. Very went for the lemon meringue pie.

"And what did he say, Lieutenant?" I asked.

"That they were responding to a complaint," he revealed. "Superspecific one, too. I got a look at the paper on it —call came in at twelve-thirty P.M. from a woman who identified herself as Lillian Young, assistant manager of the Deuce. She said that these two guys had showed up the day before on their lunch hour with a pair of hookers and started getting it on with them in their seats—moaning, carrying on, disturbing the other customers. The manager asked them to either get a hotel room or show a little bit more consideration. One of the men got superabusive. Threatened to beat the shit out of the manager if he didn't get lost. Really scary dude, she said. A large, heavyset man in his forties with curly red hair. The second man, also in his forties, she described as slender and gray-haired, with a sickly complexion and—get this—a tuft of white in his hair."

"Tommy Meyer."

Very nodded. "Anyway, she said they left without incident but now they were back again, making a racket with a new pair of hookers, and would someone please come over and handle it. So they take a ride. When they get there they discover no assistant manager named Lillian Young and no slender man in his forties with a white tuft of hair. But they do discover a large, heavyset dude with curly red hair sitting by himself in the back row watching *Of Human Blondage* and quietly doing a yankel on his frankel. Since he matches the description, they ask him, politely, if they can have a word with him outside. He immediately starts cursing them and carrying on."

"That's our boy."

"So they reel him in. Soon as they get him out to the lobby they realize who they've got. But check this out—the press is already out there waiting, and they *already know* that our beater is Hudnut."

"Meaning someone did tip them off in advance, like Lyle says."

"Had to," Very confirmed. "And that someone wasn't Vice, because it was in motion before they knew what hit them."

I tugged at my ear. "Meaning someone must have followed Lyle to the theater, then phoned the police pretending to be this Lillian Young, and then phoned the press to alert them about what was coming down."

"That plays," he acknowledged. "And our man Tommy

folds into it real neat. Reads Meyer all the way to me. Especially when you trip on what our Caller I.D. turned up—call originated from the *Uncle Chubby* production offices."

"Whose office?"

"Yours," he replied. "Which, according to Leo Crimp, was vacant at that time."

I dug into my cheesecake. I wasn't disappointed. "Didn't your friend in Vice find any of this just the tiniest bit weird?"

"Didn't give a shit. The thing is," he explained, sampling his pie, "they got what they came for."

"So to speak. About this Lillian Young. What did she sound like?"

"An older woman, Caucasian."

"Was any such woman employed at the Deuce?"

He checked his notes. "There were no women employed there. None."

"And what about Dolly Mae Bramble?"

"What about her, dude?"

"Is she acquainted with Lyle?"

"Knows him from the tube. But she says she's never had a date with him. And doesn't know of any girl on the street who has."

I sipped my coffee. "There's one thing I don't get, Lieutenant. If Tommy Meyer *did* set Lyle up, then why did he go out of his way to ID himself as the second man? That makes no sense."

"Agreed," grunted Very. "No sense."

I sat back in the booth. "Still, you're making definite progress, Lieutenant."

Very unwrapped a stick of sugarless gum and stuck it in his mouth. "The fuck I am. When I'm making progress, things start to get clearer. That ain't what's happening here. Gimme some relief, dude. I can't even figure out what I'm looking at anymore."

"You're looking at a loose cannon, Lieutenant," I said. "Lyle Hudnut is controversial, he's volatile, and he's probably insane. The network would like to see him gone. That's why they brought in Chad. A number of the man's loyal followers would like to see him gone, too. For suspects, you're looking at the network's envoy, Marjorie Daw. She's desperate to keep *Uncle Chubby* on the air. She also happens to despise Lyle. They were lovers, and the man broke her heart. Speaking of broken hearts there's also Amber Walloon, who wants to take over as director, and Fiona Shrike, who used to be married to him and still hasn't gotten over him, in my opinion. You're looking at The Boys, Muck and Meyer, who would love to run this new, Chubbyless show, and who hate Lyle for stealing the Chubby character from them years ago. He also stole Fiona from Marty back when the three of them were struggling young actors." I broke off. I'd jogged my own memory—Marty had been an actor. I kept forgetting that. "You're looking at Annabelle Gamba, who hates Lyle for firing her boyfriend, Lorenzo. And at Bobby Ackerman, your basic soul in torment, who blames Lyle for much of that torment. You're also looking at Leo Crimp, who doesn't necessarily want Lyle gone but who definitely hates his guts. It seems the man stole Katrina from her."

Very's jaw froze. "Katrina goes both ways?"

"She says not," I replied, signaling Pete for a calvados. Very declined. "She claims she and Leo were just friends. I don't know. I only know that Leo believes she was wronged. You also have Katrina herself to consider. She's pissed at him for screwing Naomi Leight behind her back, although this would appear to be a fairly recent development." Pete brought me my calvados. I sipped it. "That's what you're looking at, Lieutenant."

Very was silent a moment, head nodding, jaw working his gum. "Can we shorten the list, dude? Cross anybody off?"

"Leo's out of a job if Lyle's gone," I advised. "She likes that job. I doubt she'd tear up her meal ticket no matter how pissed she is."

"Same with Katrina, right?" he ventured. "She needs the dude. Without him there, she's history."

"Not necessarily, Lieutenant."

He frowned. "Why not?"

"Because Lyle told me Katrina is his sole beneficiary. He's left everything to her in his will. True, she has no motive for rat-fucking the show, or easing Lyle out of it. But she has a huge one for killing him. If Lyle's dead she *owns* it. She and Panorama, the studio that bankrolls it."

"And what's it worth?"

"About a hundred million dollars when it's sold into syndication after this season. She'd clear a third of that after Panorama and the distributor take their cuts."

He let out a low whistle. "You mean thirty mil?"

"Plus his beach house in East Hampton and whatever else he has socked away. All for her. Unless, of course, she has a partner."

He frowned. "Like who?"

"Like Leo," I suggested. "Possibly they only pretended to break up. Possibly they've planned this whole thing together, everything from Katrina seducing Lyle to Leo—the lone sentry outside Lyle's bathroom—hot-wiring his urinal."

"What, you mean like *Thelma and Louise* times twelve?"

"You have to consider all the possibilities." Of course, that wouldn't explain Katrina coming up to my apartment to tug on my belt. Unless that was to throw me off.

"Christ, the press would *cream* for that one." Very thought it over a moment longer before he concluded, "You're supremely twisted, dude."

"Tell me something I don't already know."

"Yo, who do *you* like for it?" he wanted to know. "Which one of them?"

I sipped some more calvados. "Why does it have to be one of them?"

"Meaning what?"

"Meaning what if they're all in it together? It's what makes the most sense, if you stop and think about it."

"You mean some kind of palace coup?" he asked skeptically.

"Precisely," I replied. "A planned operation designed to rid *Uncle Chubby* of its despised leader. Each one of them carrying out a different facet of the plan. You've got Tommy Meyer for the Deuce Theater setup. For Lillian Young, the voice on the phone, you've got Fiona, who's a gifted mimic. She was also alone at the time of the bombing—easily could have tossed them without being seen. Likewise Amber Walloon, who is pals with Gwen, the costumer, and therefore good for stealing the Chubby sweater from its locked wardrobe cupboard. Bobby, who is handy, makes the bombs and hot-wires the urinal. Annabelle's honey, Lorenzo, scores the ipecac. She slips it in the chili—"

"But most of them got sick on the chili," he pointed out.

"So they got a little sick—big deal," I countered. "It's not as if they were swallowing poison. And what better way to throw off suspicion. They want the man gone, Lieutenant. They tried to bury him last spring, but he bounced back on them. So when production resumed, they tried to scare him with bombs and shutdowns. No use. The man won't be budged. So they tried to kill him—only they killed their great white hope, Chad Roe, by mistake. An ironic twist of fate. It adds up, Lieutenant. They're all in on it—except for Katrina and Naomi."

"What about Leo?"

"They'd have to include her if they wanted to get away with hot-wiring the john."

He thought about it. "Dunno, dude," he said doubtfully. "It's a reach."

"It's not, Lieutenant. Not if you know them. They're all cowards. Not one of them even has the nerve to talk back to the man, let alone murder him. So they band together. It's perfect."

"It talks good," he admitted. He shook his head. "But it doesn't happen. Not in my experience. I mean, sure, the secretaries get together in the lunchroom all the time and plot some crazed Mongolian grudge-fuck for their boss. They fantasize about it. They dream about it. But they don't *do* it. One person does it. Someone who is cold-blooded and mean and bent. We're looking for one person. What about Marjorie Daw?"

"What about her?"

"Think she's involved?"

"I honestly don't know."

Very grinned at me. "You want yourself some of that, don't you, dude?"

"What makes you say that, Lieutenant?"

"Yo, I'm a detective, remember? I notice things."

"What things?"

"Like how something happens to you when her name comes up. You get this dopey look on your face."

"Oh, that. It comes from working on a sitcom. I've noticed it myself in the mirror when I shave."

He was still grinning at me. "They say there's no better way to help you forget."

"Who's *they?*"

He shrugged. "I dunno. *They.*"

"Well, I'm not interested in her."

"Whatever you say, dude." He shifted in the booth. "Me, I've had trouble getting interested in women period since my surgery. It's not the equipment. Hell, no. I can get vertical. It's more like . . . why bother, y'know? Dig, when I got the news I was gonna have to get cup open, I fainted dead away —right there in the doctor's office. You ever faint?"

"It's been known to happen."

"Well, not me. Not ever. I mean, I'm a guy who's stared down the barrel of a loaded handgun and lived to tell about it. And there I am, out cold on the floor, being revived by a seventy-year-old internist named Bert Greenbaum. It was fucking humiliating. And, Christ, the shit that was running through my head. I could tell you stories—"

"Now wouldn't be a good time."

"Sure, sure." He signaled for the check. "My treat, dude. You've brought a real dose of fresh."

"I am something of a vinegar-and-water douche."

Pete brought the tab. Very gave him his Visa card. He went off with it.

"I also intend to live up to my end of the bargain," the lieutenant added. "The one where you help me and I help you."

"With what?"

"With who the da-da is."

"I told you I didn't want to know, Lieutenant," I growled.

Pete returned. Very signed the check and we went outside. It was quiet on Commerce. The Cherry Lane Theater next door still hadn't let out. The air was freshening a bit. It was almost breathable.

Very inhaled it deeply. "Dude?"

"Yes, Lieutenant?"

"Don't shit me, okay? Shit somebody else—other people, your readers, anybody you like. But don't shit me. Now I got the identity of Miss Nash's Lamaze partner for you. This one the press doesn't have. I had to pull some strings to get it. Do you want his name or don't you?"

My heart was beating faster as I stood there. Very was staring at my hands. I glanced down at them. My fists were clenched.

"Well, do you?" he demanded, his knee jiggling impatiently.

"Give it to me," I said, between clenched teeth.

"Whew." He made an elaborate show of wiping his forehead. "Welcome to the human race. You better chill, though, on account of—"

"I'm perfectly chill."

"You can't take him. Dude's got a neck as big around as your chest. His name's Vic Early."

I felt my body uncoil. "Vic's her bodyguard."

"Yo, Princess Stephanie and *her* bodyguard went and had—"

"Vic's just helping out—in lieu of the biological father." Very frowned. "You sure?"

"Positive. But it was a good try, Lieutenant." I patted him on the back. Solid muscle. "I appreciate it."

Very knelt and tightened the laces of his hiking boots. "It's not like I'm done yet. I got other avenues. Plenty of 'em. You'll see."

"I'm sure I will."

"I'll find out."

"I'm sure you will."

"Later, dude."

"Good night, Lieutenant."

We went our separate ways. Very headed east, street-hiking across Manhattan for home. Home being Brooklyn Heights. Me, I moseyed a hundred yards over to Hudson to hail a cab. While I waited for one, I had this strange feeling somebody was watching me. I looked around but saw no one. In fact, the street was rather deserted for ten o'clock. But I couldn't shake off the feeling. Possibly my nerves were on edge.

The apartment felt empty and smaller without Lulu. It felt dead. Not that she's the ideal roommate. She's messy, moody, stubborn. She has deplorable eating habits. She snores. She drools. She smells like a hound. She's allergic to twenty-seven different forms of airborne plant and tree ef-fluvia. Did I mention she snores? But she's also alive. Now nothing in the place was, unless you count me. And me I'm not so sure about. I flicked on the air conditioner and checked my phone machine. Three messages, all from Lyle. Demanding to know where I was and why I wasn't home writing like I'd said I'd be. I washed out Lulu's bowls and dried them and put them in the cupboard with her mackerel tins. I swept up the kitchen floor. I took off my shirt and tie and put on some old Lightnin' Hopkins. I thought about getting out my mukluks, but I didn't feel much like writing that night. When I was younger I worked whether I felt like it or not. That's what it meant to be a professional, I told myself. I don't think I know what a professional is anymore. I don't think anyone else does either. And I'm positive they don't care.

I got all of my shoes out of the closet. Lined them up there in front of the sofa and went to work on them. I always polish my shoes when I get the blues. I don't know why. Maybe because I have something to show for my effort when I'm done. I so seldom do otherwise. I never let anyone else touch my shoes. Because they don't know what they're doing, and because I get the blues pretty often. I brushed off the loose dirt first, and saddle-soaped the shoes that needed it. Most of them did. New York is hard and dirty on shoes. While the saddle soap dried, and Lightnin' sang "Sometime She Will," I did my suede balmorals and moccasins. I never use a suede brush—much too stiff. I use an old Oral B ultrasoft toothbrush, and a pencil eraser on grease smudges. When the saddle soap was dry I wiped it all off and applied a thin layer of Meltonian shoe cream, neutral, to each pair. Then I went to work on them with a horsehair brush until they glowed. It was past eleven by the time I was done. I undressed and got into bed and lay there, staring at the ceiling. I was dead tired but I couldn't sleep. I missed Lulu too much. I tried putting a pillow over my face, but it didn't smell like dead fish and it didn't suffer from any upper respiratory problems. So I just lay there a while, feeling totally alone in the world. Before I finally turned on the light and picked up the phone and dialed it.

She answered on the first ring.

"About Harry Connick, Jr.," I said. "I can sometimes be—"

"I know exactly what you're going to say, Hoagy." As always, Marjorie Daw sounded crisp, calm, and prepared. "You don't think it would be such a good idea for us to see each other socially. It's not that you don't like me. You do. You think I'm really nice, bright, attractive. . . . But you're absolutely, positively *not* looking to get involved right now. And, besides, you—"

"I hate Harry Connick, Jr."

"You hate Harry Connick, Jr. It's perfectly okay, Hoagy. I understand. Really, I do."

"What a relief," I said. "Marjorie?"

"Yes, Hoagy?"

"That wasn't what I was going to say."

"It wasn't?" A tiny hint of eagerness crept into her voice. "What were you . . . ?"

"I was going to say that I can sometimes be found at the Café Carlyle after midnight when Bobby Short is in town, and when I'm not in the greatest of spirits." I paused. "Sometimes."

She was silent a moment, sorting through this. "Is he in town?" she asked, very carefully.

"It happens he is."

"Are you in the greatest of spirits?"

"It happens I'm not."

She waited for me to say something more. Something a bit more definite. Something. Anything. When I didn't she said, "Well, okay, Hoagy. Thank you for . . . for letting me know this."

"You're welcome, Marjorie. Good-bye."

I put down the phone and stared at it a moment. Then I went and showered. I stropped grandfather's razor and shaved, doused myself in Floris, put a dab of something greasy in what was left of my hair. I dressed in my double-breasted ivory dinner jacket and pleated black evening trousers, my starched white broadcloth tuxedo shirt with the ten-pleat bib front and wing collar, my black silk bow tie, and grandfather's pearl cuff links and studs. Then I caught a cab across town to the Carlyle Hotel.

I don't exactly know what it is about the Café Carlyle, that living pastel monument to Manhattan's elegant yesteryear, that last bastion of high-stepping sophistication. Maybe it's the sharp brine of the caviar and the tart, cold, crispness of the Dom Pérignon. Maybe it's Bobby, so refined and ageless there at his piano playing Porter and Gershwin like no one else can. Maybe I just like to get all dressed up. I don't know. All I know is that when all else fails me, the Carlyle cures me. Bobby was singing "Just One of Those Things" when she came in, looking impossibly tall and slim and cool. She had on a strapless minidress of peach-colored silk with a paisley scarf thrown over one bare shoulder, white stockings, mules, a bit of lipstick, no jewelry. Heads turned as she made her way across the room toward me like a serene swan, her chin held high. She slid into the banquette beside me without so much as looking at me. Her scarf made an electric noise against her skin as she slipped it off of her uncommonly slim shoulder. I poured her some Dom Pérignon.

She reached for it, gently stroking the champagne flute's stem with her long, slender fingers. "I have to tell you something," she said, leveling her gaze at me. "That was the strangest invitation I've ever gotten from a man."

"I told you—I'm not like other men."

"I can't tell you how glad I am to hear that." She gave me an approving once-over. "You look awfully nice in evening clothes."

"You look awfully nice, period. Too bad you don't have green eyes."

She frowned. "But I do have green eyes."

"That's right, you do." I smiled at her.

She got busy with caviar and toast, reddening. "I wasn't sure whether you really wanted me to come or not," she said, after taking a delicate bite and swallowing it. "And if so, when? Tonight? Tomorrow night? I didn't know."

"Why did you come tonight?"

"It so happens I wasn't in the greatest of spirits myself. And I thought your invitation might have something to do with Lyle."

"What about Lyle?"

"Does it?"

"No, it doesn't."

"Good." She smiled at me. "Actually, I thought I scared you off before with all of that talk about Wisconsin and cookies and soccer practice. That's . . . not really what I'm after. Not right now, anyway."

"What are you after right now?"

She didn't answer that one. Just gazed at me steadily. I gazed back at her.

And then Bobby took over. He'll do that. Slammed into his untemp rendition of Gershwin's "I've Got a Crush on You." Then kept right on going with "Street of Dreams" and "Body and Soul." He sounded especially good that night. Marjorie listened to him with intense concentration, her lips pursed, eyes half shut, hands folded neatly before her on the table. Her shoulders swayed slightly to the beat. I liked the way she listened.

After he finished off with "As Time Goes By," she took a sip of her champagne and said, "Okay, you win."

"In what way?" I asked, ordering us another bottle.

"Harry Connick, Jr., is strictly pretend. Bobby Short is for real." She looked around the room admiringly. "Actually, it's not just him. This whole place—it's like going back in time and finding it to be exactly how you imagined it would be. I like it here, Hoagy."

"Good. I was going to ditch you if you didn't."

Her eyes searched my face over her glass. "You used to come here with her, didn't you?"

I nodded. "It's true. Lulu and I have spent many evenings here."

"That's not what I meant."

"I know it's not."

She looked away. "I'm in the middle of reading *Such Sweet Sorrow.* . . ."

My second one, about the poisoned marriage between a famous writer and a famous actress. Partly autobiographical. And totally a bust. "It's a rich novel. There's something in there for everyone to dislike."

"Well, I'm really enjoying it. I mean it. You're a brilliant writer, Hoagy."

"Correction—I was."

"What happened?"

"If I knew that, I'd still be brilliant." I helped myself to some more caviar. "I'm surprised you were able to find a copy of it."

"My secretary called your publisher."

"They're still in business?"

"How much of it is reality and how much is fiction?"

"You make it sound like there's a difference."

"Are you always so sarcastic?"

"Only when I'm in a bad mood."

"And when you're in a good mood?"

"I'm still not a very good deal. For one thing, there's this whopping excess baggage allowance to consider."

She stared at me some more. "You're not over her, are you." It wasn't a question.

I sipped my champagne. "I'd like to be."

"But you're not."

"I'd like to be."

"Why did you call me tonight, Hoagy?" she asked gravely.

"I've never had a woman bake me a pie before. It did something strange to me. What did you put in it, anyway?"

She was having none of that. She wanted a serious answer. And she was willing to sit there gazing at me, until I gave her one.

"I called you tonight because I was alone. And I didn't want to be."

She gave me a knowing nod. "And right away you thought of good old Marjorie." A bitter edge crept into her voice. "Because she happens to live right around the corner, and because she happens to be so excruciatingly available. Decent figure. Good legs—"

"Great legs."

"So you figured—go for it. Maybe you'll get lucky. Does that about cover it?"

I tugged at my ear. "I'm just trying to get back to basics, Marjorie."

"What's that supposed to mean?"

"It means I'm looking for someone I can trust."

"No, you're not," she argued. "You're looking for someone you can lay." She shook her head at me angrily. "I was wrong about you. You're *exactly* like other men." She reached for her scarf, slid out of the banquette, and stalked out.

I sat there for a moment, staring at my glass and thinking about how Lulu was starting to look better and better as a late-night companion. Then I threw down some money and went after her.

She was two blocks down Madison by the time I caught up with her, her stride long and purposeful. She wouldn't stop when I called to her.

"Will you please hold up a second?" I asked, grabbing her by the arm.

She yanked free from my grasp. "Why should I?" She sniffled. She'd been crying.

I handed her a fresh linen handkerchief. She used it, shivering slightly. The breeze had picked up, turning the night air blessedly clear and crisp.

"There's something I wanted to ask you." I glanced sky-
ward. It was so clear I could see stars. You rarely can in
Manhattan during the summer. "Would this be an Alberta
Clipper?"

She let out a short, humorless laugh. "I *don't* want to
talk about the weather."

"What do you want to talk about?"

"I don't want to talk at all."

"What do you want to do?"

She didn't say anything. She didn't have to say anything.
Not the way she was looking at me.

We hurled ourselves at each other. There was nothing
tender or sweet about it. No violins. No cherubs. Just two
lonely, love-whipped people clamped hungrily together there
on Madison Avenue, trying to devour one another. Some kids
passing us in a Saab convertible broke out in applause.

She came up for air first. "I—I don't know what I'm
doing," she gasped, holding my face between her hands.

"That's okay," I panted. "I'm a grown man—I don't
know what I'm doing either."

"But it doesn't make any sense," she protested, half-
heartedly.

"Now you're catching on."

We kissed some more. A tiny bit gentler, though not a
whole lot. Before she took my hand and said, "Let's go back
to my place. I want to make love to you." She got quite
specific about how she intended to do it, too. A blow by
blow description, as it were. Things I couldn't imagine her
learning about in Rhinelander, Wisconsin. Or in network programming. Maybe she picked them up from Lyle.

Now there was a horrifying thought.

It was past one, and there were no cabs in sight. We
walked down to Seventy-second Street in hopes of catching
one speeding crosstown. We waited in the street across from
Castle Ralph, the retail monument Sir Ralph Lauren built to
himself. I didn't mind the wait. Her lips were on my neck.

One of those big new Chevy Caprices, the ones that look like baby whales, finally came cruising by us from the park, heading east. I hailed him. He blinked on his brights in response, then turned around and started back toward us. I extended my right arm. Quaint old custom. An old-time cabbie once taught me that a true pro will pull up so that his fare doesn't have to move that arm an inch to open the passenger door handle. You don't find many drivers that good anymore. These days they overshoot you, or stop short of you. These days they make you come to them. Our baby whale driver didn't even slow down at all.

He speeded up. Floored it. Came roaring right at us with his brights on as we stood there in the middle of the street. And he wasn't stopping. That wasn't his plan at all. He was going to run us over. It was so sudden, so unexpected, that we barely had time to realize that we were dead. I froze. Marjorie screamed. Then I pushed her.

Nine

All we had was a split second. No time to think. Only time to survive. Or to try. The way any living, breathing animal would instinctively try. I shoved Marjorie as hard as I could toward the curb. Then I dove the other way, into the middle of the street. He came barreling right between us like a big yellow four-door bowling ball, missing us both. He screeched to a halt, jammed it into reverse. He had me. I was a dead duck out there in the street, flat on my stomach. But we weren't alone now. There were a couple of pedestrians on Madison. Cars had stopped at the signal. Witnesses, all of them. So he took off toward the park instead, burning rubber all the way. I managed to get his medallion number before he disappeared into the night. Then I struggled to my feet.

Marjorie was sprawled in the gutter, smeared head to foot with some of New York City's filthiest, blackest wetness. She was scraped up pretty badly, too. Her knees bled through her torn stockings.

"You okay?" I asked her.

She nodded, her eyes wide with fright.

I helped her to her feet. She trembled, leaning on me heavily. Me, I had no one to lean on.

"D-Do you believe that asshole?" she gulped. "What was he trying to do?"

"Kill us," I replied simply. Or, more exactly, one of us—me. It hadn't been my nerves. Someone had been measuring me when I was on Hudson Street earlier that evening. Waiting for the right time and place. He'd found it, too. Almost. She was staring at me. "Are you serious?"

"I am." I dusted off my knees. My trousers were torn. Morris Kanter, my tailor, would have a small fit. "You may find this difficult to believe, Marjorie, but not everyone likes me."

She let out a laugh. Relief, mostly. "You saved my life, Hoagy."

"I would have done it for anyone—except maybe Oliver Stone." One of her shoes was out in the street, smashed flat. I went and got it for her. Staring at it in her hand, she began to tremble. I said, "C'mon, we'll get you checked out over at Lenox Hill."

"No, no. I'm really fine." She looked down at her besmirched and bloodied self. "All I want to do is get into the shower—and burn these clothes."

I hailed us another cab. This one overshot my outstretched arm by ten feet. But at least he didn't try to flatten us.

Marjorie headed straight for the bathroom when we got to her place. I headed straight for the liquor cabinet. It was in the cupboard over her refrigerator. One bottle of everything, most of them full, most of them good brands. It was as if she'd read a book on how to stock a bar. No problem finding the Courvoisier—the bottles were arranged alphabetically. So were the spices in her spice rack. Her kitchen was as bare and devoid of personality as the rest of her apartment. No snapshots of her college roommate's new baby stuck to the refrigerator door. No wall calendar with engagements and family birthdays marked on it. No lists, no coupons, no gaily colored oven mitts, no nothing. I found two glasses and poured out two stiff brandies and drank them both. Then I refilled them and took them out to the living room. The phone was on the floor next to the sofa. I sat and phoned Very at home and woke him up.

"Whoa, you're getting close, dude," he concluded, instantly alert. "Must be you struck a nerve."

"I sure wish I knew which nerve."

He took down the medallion number of the cab—5P77 —and said he'd phone it in. He said that the letter, being high up in the alphabet, meant it had been a fleet cab, rather than an owner-operated one.

"Driver must have been watching the Carlyle, waiting for you to come out," he mused aloud. "You didn't see who it was?"

"He had his brights on."

"What makes you so sure it was a he?" he demanded.

"Touché, Lieutenant. It could have been a woman."

"Was there anyone else in the cab? A fare?"

"I don't believe so. I think the driver was alone."

"And what about you, dude?"

"What about me?"

"Were you alone?"

"I was not."

"Marjorie Daw, am I right? I *am* right." He chuckled, immensely pleased with himself. "Way cool. At least we can cross her off our list of suspects now."

I glanced at the hallway. She was still in the shower. "Yes, I suppose we can."

"Where are you, dude?"

"Her place."

"Want protection?"

"No, I think I can handle her."

"Yo, I meant—"

"I know what you meant, Lieutenant. And I'll be okay."

"Cool. I'll come by the studio in the morning. See if you can stay out of trouble until then."

"What's your second choice?"

He laughed. "Dude?"

"Yes, Lieutenant?"

"Enjoy."

I hung up and drained my brandy. She came out a moment later, scrubbed all clean and pink, her cropped blond hair slicked back, smelling of almond bath oil. She had on a sparkling white terry cloth robe. Her long, slender feet were bare. Her raw knees still oozed blood. She was clutching antibiotic ointment and bandages.

She limped slightly as she made her way over to me. "I was just thinking . . ."

"Always dangerous."

"How can you be sure it was you? What if it was *me* the cabbie was trying to run down?"

"No one has any reason to kill you," I replied, looking up at her. "Do they?"

She looked away. "Why, no. I just . . . You're right. Why would they?" She started to say something more, but changed her mind.

I took the first-aid things from her. "Here, let me."

"I can do it," she insisted.

"Sit." I pulled her down onto my lap. She was a feather compared to Merilee, even in her leanest of times. Feel free to tell Merilee I said so.

I stretched her long, smooth legs out onto the sofa and smeared ointment on her wounded knees. She winced but didn't cry one bit. Just sat there sipping her brandy and watching me warily. I could feel her green eyes on me, feel the tension in her slim body. I could feel something else, too. Our feverish hunger for each other was gone, the spell broken. It was lying somewhere out in the middle of Seventy-second Street with tire marks all over it. Her good sense had taken over. Or maybe mine had. I don't know. I only know we were back where we'd started—strangers who hardly knew each other. And we both knew it.

I bandaged her up, wondering why it was all of the women in my life were wearing gauze these days. "Look at it this way. At least you're in the clear with Lieutenant Very now."

"You mean I wasn't?" She seemed startled.

"No one was. And no one is—except for you."

She lingered there in my lap. Until I smiled at her. Hastily, she got up and sat as far away from me on the sofa as she could. Sat there in silence, inspecting her bandaged knees.

"It's not ever going to happen, is it?" she finally said, quietly.

"What's not?"

"You're never going to be over her."

"I'm never going to be over her."

She sighed and glanced up at the ceiling plaintively. "Oh, well. At least you're honest." She got up and came over to me and kissed me on the forehead. Then she padded down the hall and closed her bedroom door softly behind her. She didn't bother to say good night.

I sat there a moment, finishing her brandy. Then I rinsed out the glasses and turned out the lights. Then I went home. I don't know if a big yellow cab followed me. I don't know if anyone followed me. I didn't care.

I didn't sleep very well.

In the morning God arrived from California.

Ten

We sat down with him around the big table in the rehearsal room at nine o'clock sharp. God was big on punctuality. Lyle and Katrina were there, Katrina decked out in a sober leopard-pattern *bustier* and hot-pants ensemble. Marjorie, Leo, and The Boys were there. So was Jazzy Jeff Beckman, vice president of television production for Panorama Studios, who had flown in from L.A. with God. Fiona, Annabelle, and Bobby were not there. I was. There was coffee. There was pastry. There was a plainclothesman guarding the door. There was a great deal of tension, and no cheer. None. Zero.

The morning papers had pounced on Chad's death. "ZAPPED!" screamed the banner headline in the *Daily News.* "PISSED!" cried the *Post.* Both were calling it murder, just as Very predicted they would. And both were right on top of the "mysterious food poisoning incident" as well, the *News* describing *The Uncle Chubby Show* as being "the victim of a crazed psycho-killer out for revenge or blood or both." The *Times* didn't bother with the story, since it happened locally. But the tabloids played it up big, so big it crowded the photos of Merilee and me standing together on Central Park West all the way back to the People pages, where the *Post* identified me as "former literary lion Shelby Haig." Out in front of the studio, TV crews from *Hard Copy, Inside Edition, A Current Affair,* and *Entertainment Tonight*—the four horsemen of TV journalism's apocalypse—were spilled out into the street with the Citizens for Moral Television, clamoring for more dirt. God had had to fight his way through the mob to get inside the building. As a consequence, he was in a bad mood. I didn't know God well enough to know if he had a good one.

Godfrey Daniels was a lanky, sandy-haired man in his early thirties with a chilly manner and a face like concrete. He said very little, and revealed even less about his true feelings or his intentions. Merely sat there, oozing self-importance. He wore thick, rimless glasses, and when listening to a pitch he propped them up just above his eyebrows, like a pair of welder's goggles. When he spoke he affected a faint English accent, the result of a year of postgraduate studies at Oxford. Somehow, a myth had arisen that he'd been a Rhodes scholar-athlete, a myth he did nothing to deny. Actually, he had been one of the top amateur golfers in California when he was at Stanford. But it was television, not golf, that was in his blood. His father had been one of the producers of *Gomer Pyle*. And a close friend of Grant Tinker, who gave Godfrey his first job. Godfrey dressed casually but expensively in a Charvet striped broadcloth shirt open at the neck, glen plaid linen slacks, and tasseled Ferragamo loafers. A pale yellow Sea Island cotton cardigan was thrown over his shoulders. Sweaters were his trademark. He always wore one, never a jacket. His detractors, and they were many, called him The Empty Sweater. When they weren't calling him God.

Jazzy Jeff Beckman, Lyle's financial partner, was an edgy, pimply little ferret in his late twenties with a flattop crew cut and the softest, pinkest hands I'd ever seen on a man. Jazzy Jeff wore a denim shirt and flowered silk tie and khakis, as well as the lingering symptoms of Bell's palsy, a stress-related disorder where the nerves on one side of the face go numb, causing it to sag—somewhat like a Dick Tracy character. And causing him to dribble saliva out of that side of his mouth. He had to keep dabbing at it with a napkin, and had trouble speaking. Which was no problem. Like God, he was there to listen.

And Lyle was there to pitch. And pitch he did. He went

high and hard with the same patched-together retread of his that he'd shpritzed the day before, the one where Chubby takes Deirdre to the pool hall himself. Heavy on the brother-sister bonding. Heavy on the meaning of family. Heavy on the social relevance thing, too. Up came those six million hungry kids again, and the sixteen million without health coverage, Lyle wielding the statistics like a club, daring God to turn his back on those poor, sick, hungry kids, *his* kids. Lyle pitched sans mask and gloves, and he was surprisingly nervous. Kept talking faster and faster, like a salesman who is about to have the door slammed in his face. Still, it was a good pitch. Lots of enthusiasm. Lots of laughs.

Not that God ever laughed. Not once. The programming wizard merely sat there slumped in his chair, glasses up on his forehead, listening. Never once did his facial expression change. Jazzy Jeff laughed once or twice, politely, but mostly sat there wiping his drool and watching God for a sign. Marjorie Daw kept watching God, too. She was extremely deferential around him. Did not speak unless spoken to. She wore a navy blazer and white gabardine slacks over her bandaged knees, and seemed even more poised and alert than usual. Me she wouldn't look at.

God didn't react at all when Lyle was done. Just continued to sit there, blank-faced, all eyes in the room upon him. Until, abruptly, he flipped his glasses down onto his nose and turned to Jazzy Jeff. "How do you like it?" he asked the little studio veep.

"Cute," Jazzy Jeff hedged, dabbing at his mouth. Actually, what he said was "Oot-groot," but I'd never stoop so low as to make fun of someone with a speech impairment, even a short television executive. I'm just trying to give you a feel for the room. Part of my job.

"It's marvelously cute," God agreed, his voice genteelly clipped. "It's about heart. It's about warmth, family values—everything we're looking for at eight o'clock."

"I knew you'd like it, pal." Lyle was beaming. "Because it's about who we are. And wait'll I tell ya what happens in the second show—"

"But we're mothballing you until we can recast Rob," God broke in brusquely. "We'll hold your slot for you until then. I'm here to give you my word on that, Lyle. We're good for at least three weeks—we've got the Mac Culkin back-to-school special, the American League Championship Series . . . Worst-case scenario, we can even slide in a couple of your slam-dunk shows from first season to get your viewers wet for you. Right?"

Lyle gaped at him in stunned disbelief. It was obvious that God had already made up his mind before he left L.A. He'd simply listened to Lyle's pitch as a courtesy. He had no intention of going ahead without a new Rob Roy Fruitwell. None. Zero.

"Major bonus for your writing staff, as well," God continued. "Gives you time to get your first six-pack in Emmy shape. Meanwhile, we look for Rob. It won't be easy. Chad was such a perfect fit. But we'll find our man. Maybe someone will shake out after the first-wave cancellations. If not, we can always—"

"Time out here!" Lyle blustered, his anger mounting. "This is the show I wanna do, Godfrey. I'm taping *this* show *this* week. And I feel *very* strongly about it."

God said nothing. He had already spoken. He would not get down in the trenches with Lyle. Instead, he shot a look at Jazzy Jeff.

Jazzy Jeff wiped his mouth. "How do you feel about Tony Curtis, Lyle?"

The Boys froze. I think Tommy Meyer even stopped breathing.

"What's Tony fucking Curtis got to do with anything?" Lyle demanded, glowering at him.

"Man's looking for a series," Jazzy Jeff replied. "Looks

great, feels great. Any reason Rob couldn't be a tiny bit older?"

"He's seventy years old!" Lyle roared, his face turning red.

"Sixty-nine," Jazzy Jeff countered. "And it's not as if Fiona's twenty-something."

"Tony would perk up our older demographics immensely, Lyle," added God. "Let's face it—it's the seniors who are sitting home at night watching us. And older women, they remember Tony when he was a real matinee idol."

"Mr. Tight Pants," agreed Jazzy Jeff, nodding.

"He's seventy!" bellowed Lyle. He was sweating and shaking now.

"Sixty-nine," said God.

"And can he play comedy," Jazzy Jeff enthused, drooling. "I saw him on cable just the other night in *Some Like It Hot* with Marilyn Monroe. Drop-dead funny. And Tony was hysterical in it."

"That was thirty-five years ago!" Lyle shouted.

"People loved him in that bloopers special he did for us just last season," God countered.

"He tested so well we signed him to an overall deal," added Jazzy Jeff.

"Which you're looking to burn off by dumping him in my show!" hollered Lyle, enraged. Katrina patted his arm, trying to calm him. He slapped it away. "Absolutely not, Godfrey! No way! No, no, *no!* I refuse. You guys are outta your fucking minds. Tony Curtis?! Un-fucking-believable! I mean, shit, why don't we just go all out and hire Elvis, huh?! She can fuck his *ghost!*"

God stroked his chin thoughtfully. "I love that. That's a slam-dunk eight-o'clock show. It's *The Ghost and Mrs. Muir,* only hipper."

"Slam dunk," agreed Jeff. "If only we could find the Hope Lange of the nineties."

"Farrah," said God with cool certainty. "It's perfect for her."

"And Ryan can play Elvis," Jazzy Jeff burbled excitedly. "Real-life husband and wife—what could be more perfect? What resonance! What doability!"

"And Ryan won't even have to lose any weight," cracked Marty.

"Just remember to name her character Diana," Tommy advised drily. "So you can call it *The King and Di.*"

God stared at him. "I love that."

"Slam dunk!" cried Jazzy Jeff. "And I've got the perfect husband-wife writing team on the lot. She's even *from* Tupelo."

God pointed a finger at Jazzy Jeff. "We have to talk about this on the plane home."

"Definitely," agreed Jazzy Jeff.

Lyle just sat there in pained, miserable silence. They were so caught up in their idea they'd forgotten all about him.

Me, I just felt fortunate to be there. I was actually seeing the creative process happen—the birthing of a prime-time hit. I felt lucky. Ill, but lucky.

Lyle seized back the floor. "I won't do my show with Tony Curtis!" he screamed, pounding the table like a huge, unruly, child. "I won't! I won't! I *won't!*"

"Okay, then how about Richard Lewis?" offered Jazzy Jeff, effortlessly changing direction.

"The comic?" Lyle seemed thrown by this one. His fat lower lip started to quiver with agitation.

"We found him tremendously appealing in *Anything But Love,*" God reported. "We feel he has untapped leading man potential."

Jazzy Jeff nodded. "Untapped."

"But he's a *comic,*" Lyle protested.

"Is that a problem?" asked God.

"Of course it's a problem," he argued. "You can't have

two comics in the same fucking show. We'd bounce right off each other. Somebody's gotta be the straight man. And Rob's the straight man."

"Richard has the range to play straight," God assured him. "And he and Fiona will be electric together."

"Sparks," said Jazzy Jeff.

Lyle gave God The Scowl. "Has Fiona's agent been leaning on you?"

God frowned. "Why would you say that?"

"Because she and Richard Lewis have the same fucking agent, that's why!"

"I'm simply trying to help, Lyle," God said placatingly. "Chad was an ideal fit. We got lucky with him. We may not be so lucky this time. We may have to bend a bit."

"Bend how?" demanded Lyle.

"This isn't necessarily a negative, Lyle," God stated.

"Bend *how?*"

God shrugged. "I don't know how. You people are the creative—"

"BEND HOW!" Lyle screamed.

God sighed and pushed his glasses back up onto his forehead. "Perhaps Chubby needs to get out of the house a bit more. Get a job, get a girl . . . get a life."

Now Lyle panicked, his massive head swiveling around the table at everyone in bug-eyed fright. He looked like a cornered animal. He looked . . . trapped. For the first time since I'd met Lyle Hudnut I found myself feeling sorry for him. "You're . . . you're talking about a whole different show, Godfrey," he said hoarsely.

God said, "Not at all, Lyle. I'm merely suggesting that Chubby leave Deirdre alone with her kids from time to time. She does hardly any parenting, and we should give her that chance. The single mother thing is very hot right now. So is boomer romance. That's why we're so high on introducing Rob. We're talking about an engine here. This will give our engine the chance to run on six cylinders, instead of just four. Make it stronger, tougher. Give us a genuine ensemble of characters. Let's face it, most hit shows are ensemble shows."

Lyle snorted derisively. "We've been the number-one show in America for the past three seasons."

"And I want you to be number one for three more," God said reassuringly. "But to stay there we have to grow. We're talking about an organism here, Lyle."

"Gee, I thought we were talking about an engine," Lyle jeered, trying to bait him.

But God couldn't be baited. "Look at this as a challenge," he said smoothly. "Look at it as an opportunity to make something positive and good out of an unfortunate situation."

Lyle glared at him. "I don't want Richard Lewis."

"Fine," conceded God. "Cast whoever you want. It's your show." He glanced around the big table at everyone. "You people are the talent. We listen to our talent. And we support our talent, one hundred percent. That's why we're the number-one network. We believe in giving people the chance to do the work *they* want to do—their way. There are no sides here. We're all on the same side—your side." He paused, stroking his chin. "If it helps your thinking any, we're also searching for twenty-something appeal at eight o'clock. We'd kill for the next Luke Perry."

"Christ, who wouldn't?" said Jazzy Jeff.

"Maybe a *younger* boyfriend is the solution," God suggested. "Someone with poster appeal. Someone who can get us publicity—the *right* kind."

Lyle bristled but said nothing.

"We want what you want, Lyle," God said. "We want the same thing."

"And what's that?" growled Lyle.

"A stronger show."

"The show is perfect the way it is," Lyle insisted stubbornly. "Perfect."

"I couldn't agree more." Godfrey Daniels flipped his glasses back down onto his nose. "We just want it to be more perfect."

"I'm road kill," moaned Lyle, slumped behind his desk, hollow-eyed with shock and disbelief. "I'm dead meat. Over and out. Crow food. Dead, I tell ya. They don't want me no more."

He had fled for the privacy of his office immediately after God left the studio with Jazzy Jeff and Marjorie. His plainclothesman was stationed outside. Katrina was coiled on the sofa, sipping herbal tea and watching him with concern. I was sitting in an armchair watching him, too. This was a new Lyle, beaten and defeated. The bluster and cockiness had gone out of him. The defiance, the energy, the *life* had poured right out. He was like a freighter with a gaping hole in its bottom, sinking in deep black water right before our eyes.

"They don't want me no more," he wailed, one more time.

"They do so, Pinky," Katrina squeaked. "You heard God. He said he's behind you one hundred percent."

"That's the kiss-off," Lyle said despairingly. "Those are always their last words just before they chop your head off." Tears welled up in his eyes, spilled down his round cheeks. "I'm dead, I tell ya. Dead."

"And what are you going to do about it, fat man?" I demanded.

His head snapped back, as if I'd slapped him. "Huh?"

"You heard me," I said. "What are you going to do about it?"

"I'm gonna . . . I'm gonna . . ." He trailed off, ran a hand over his face. There was a spark in his eyes now. Tiny one, but it was there. "I'm gonna fight 'em, is what I'm gonna

The Man Who Cancelled Himself

do. It's my show. Mine. I'm *The Uncle Chubby Show*. Not Tony fucking Curtis. Not Richard fucking Lewis. Not Luke fucking Perry. *Me!*" He was coming back to life now, rising up out of his chair. *"Me!* I'll fight the bastards, that's what I'll do. My fans—I'll go right to my kids. My kids are with me. They won't let this happen to me. I can count on my kids. They love me. They . . ." He sank back down, the spark abruptly snuffed. "Fuck me, who am I kidding? I can't count on them. Or anybody else. Nobody gives a shit about me."

"I do, Pinky," Katrina insisted. "Hoagy does."

Lyle's eyes flickered at me. There was suspicion in them. I didn't know why. He heaved a huge sigh. "I hate having that fucking cop parked right outside my door."

"Sssh, he'll hear you," whispered Katrina.

Lyle snarled, "I don't care. I feel like I'm a fucking prisoner in here."

"He's protecting you, Lyle. Someone's trying to kill you, remember?"

"Let 'em," he snapped. "They'll be doing me a huge favor."

Katrina observed him, fretfully chewing on the inside of her mouth. "We should hold a family council meeting, Pinky."

"What the hell for?"

"To tell the staff that we're suspending production," she replied, finishing her tea. "How would noon be?"

Lyle shook his head. "I can't. Can't face all of them. No way. Just have Leo do up a memo. She'll know how to word it."

"But, Pinky, don't you think you ought to—?"

"Just do it, Katrina!" he barked. "And leave us alone for a while, will ya? I need to talk to Hoagy."

"Okay, Lyle," she muttered sullenly, starting for the door.

"And send Naomi in," he added.

She stopped in her tracks. "What for?"

"Whattaya mean, what for?" Lyle growled back at her. "I need her, that's what for."

"Why do you need her?" she demanded, crossing her arms.

He rolled his eyes, exasperated. "For *business*. Christ, Katrina, what's gotten into you?"

She hesitated, unsure if she wanted to get into this in front of me. Then she took a deep breath and plunged ahead, hooters heaving. "I'm only going to tell you this once, Pinky. So you better pay attention. Here it is: I've stood by you through thick and thin. And I'll continue to stand by you. Because I love you. But if you ever, *ever* shit on me, if you cheat on me, if you bone me, so help me you'll be sorry you ever got involved with me. Because I'll hurt you, Pinky. Worse than you've hurt me. I'll hurt you so bad you'll never stop hurting. Do you understand?"

Lyle glowered at her menacingly. "Sure, I understand ya. Now you understand me, cunt. Nobody hurts me. Nobody *can* hurt me. And *nobody* tells me what to do!" He pounded his chest with his fist. "I'm Lyle Hudnut! I do whatever I want, whenever I want, *to* whoever I want! Got that?"

She threw her teacup at him. Hit him, too. In the shoulder. Then she stormed out, slamming the door behind her so hard that Magic Johnson's picture fell off the wall.

Lyle rubbed his shoulder, cackling. "God, she's a pistol. Gets me hard as a rock when she's like that. My boner's about to lift this whole desk right up off the floor."

I tugged at my ear. "What about that heartwarming 'I'm gonna change' speech of yours, Lyle?"

He smirked at me. "Who are you trying to be, my conscience?"

"Thank you, no. I already have a full-time job." I sat back and crossed my legs. "What's on your mind, Lyle?"

"Nuttin'. Just needed to get me some." He anxiously reached into the credenza behind his desk and pulled out a plastic sandwich bag half filled with white powder. Coke. He dumped a heap of it out onto the Lucite-topped desk, stuck a length of *Uncle Chubby* drinking straw into his left nostril and began to make like a Dustbuster, snorting every last bit of it up.

"Where did you get that?"

"I still got my sources." He came up for air, sniffling. "Never know when you might need some. And I need me some. Gotta stay one step ahead of the panic."

"That won't do you any good, Lyle."

"Yeah, well, lemme tell ya something, Hoagster. That's a whole lotta bullshit. I feel mo' better already." And he already looked plenty glazed. "Want some?"

"No, thanks."

There was a discreet tapping at the door. Lyle hurriedly stashed the bag away, wiped the desk clean, wiped at his nose with the back of his hand. Then he said come in.

It was Naomi. "You wanted to see me, Lyle?" she asked, styling for him there in the doorway. The blue knit jersey dress she wore that day was particularly tight.

Lyle gazed at her hungrily. "Sure did. Come on over here, kid," he commanded, holding his arms out to her.

She glanced at me uncertainly.

"It's okay," he assured her. "Hoagster knows all about us. Come to Papa."

She flounced over to him and plopped down into his lap, and the two of them began to suck some serious face. Lyle ran his big mitt up her bare leg and under her dress. Until she let out a gasp. She stuck her tongue in his ear. He moaned. I can't begin to tell you how glad I was that Lulu wasn't around for this.

"You look at that duplex on West End?" he asked her, breathing heavily.

"It's darling, Lyle," she purred, wriggling around in his lap. "Only it's *way* too much for me on my salary. And the down payment is—"

"You let *The Uncle Chubby Show* take care of the down payment."

"But I just heard the show is being—"

"Don't you worry about that. You always got a job with me. You just keep on doing what you do best." He whispered something in her ear. She let out a dirty giggle. "Now go call the realtor and tell her you're taking it."

"If you say so, Lyle," she said, her eyes gleaming with naughty delight.

"I say so. I sure as shit do."

She scampered out. He watched her go, stoned and horny. Then he turned and gave me The Scowl. "Don't look at me that way."

"Which way is that, Lyle?"

"Like you just sucked on a pickle for half an hour."

"I was weaned on one. What happens now, Lyle?"

He shrugged. "Dunno. Guess I'll fuck 'em both till I get tired of one of them. Why, you want Katrina?"

"I meant with the show."

"Oh." He ran his hands through his curly red hair. "Fuck if I know. I mean, shit, Chad's starting to look better and better. I could *work* with the guy. Or at least *around* him. But this . . . this is scary fucking shit. No telling what we'll end up with—whole fucking show could end up on a PT boat by the time they're done with it. Totally different show. Totally different. Totally." He broke off, sniffling. "Fuck it. Doing a show's always a fight. Even if you're number one. Every day it's a fight. You never stop fighting. That's TV. It's about survival. It's about getting yours. I spend ninety percent of my time pushing this big huge boulder up the side of a mountain and the other ten percent of my time trying to figure out why the fuck I bother. Fuck it, maybe I should just quit."

"And do what?"

"Hang out at the beach," he replied comfortably. "We can finish our book. I can do another album, go on tour, shoot a movie. Who knows, maybe I'll even take up golf. I mean, shit, it's just a lousy sitcom. Who needs it?"

"You do. This show is your life. These people are your family."

"Says who?" he demanded.

"You did, as I recall."

"Aw, who needs it?" he said once more, though with much less conviction. Because he was blowing smoke and we both knew it. The man wouldn't walk away. Couldn't walk away. This was his home. This was his . . . what was it Fiona called it? His asylum. Yeah, that, too.

He clapped his hands together. "So where are we with the book?" he asked, turning businesslike.

"You feel like working?"

"Why not? Now's as good a time as any."

"Very well." I reached for my notepad. "I learned some not uninteresting things about you yesterday."

He frowned at me, puzzled. "Who from?"

"Your parents. I met them for tea."

His response was varied and rich. First came surprise. A widening of the eyes, tightening of the mouth. Then came embarrassment. He reddened, and couldn't make eye contact with me. Then came rage. Clenching of fists. Quickening of breath. Flaring of nostrils. And then, finally, came the brakes —the supreme effort to hold onto his self-control. All in a span of less than three seconds. "W-Why'd you do that, Hoagy?"

"There were some things I wanted to ask them."

"What about?"

"Global warming, the trade deficit, lasting peace in the Middle East. I booked them into the Mayfair. You treated them to *Guys and Dolls* and dinner at The Post House. Most generous of you. They went back this morning."

"You shoulda said something to me about this yesterday, Hoagy," he said quietly, between his teeth.

"Why is that, Lyle?"

"You *know* why," he growled menacingly.

I tugged at my ear. "Sorry, my mistake. I didn't think you'd be interested in seeing them."

He let out his huge *hoo-hah-hah* of a laugh. "You got that one right!" he cried jovially. I was forgiven. Possibly he was too stoned to stay mad. "So how are the old fucks?"

"Seemed well. They asked how you were."

"What'd you say?"

"That I didn't know."

"Why'd you say that?"

"Because I don't. I did say someone was trying to kill you."

"Why'd you say that?"

"Because someone is."

"I'm fine," Lyle declared. More for his own ears than mine. "I *will* get through this thing. I *will* survive. Somehow." He peered at me. "What'd you find out from 'em?"

"That you were put on liquid phenobarbital when you were four months old—to stop you from crying all of the time. That means we can trace your history of drug dependency all the way back to the crib. Not a terrible opening for the book."

"Geez, *great* way to open the book!" exclaimed Lyle. "Those sadistic fucks. How could they *do* that to me?"

"Your doctor prescribed it. They thought they were doing the right thing."

He sneered at me. "What, now you're taking their side?"

"I'm not taking anyone's side. I'm merely telling you what they said."

He narrowed his eyes at me suspiciously. "What else? Any other juicy shit they did to me I don't know about?"

I had considered this one carefully. Agonized over it, in fact. Because it goes against my nature to withhold something. Especially something as significant as Aileen Hudnut trying to kill Lyle when he was two. But it also goes against my nature to bury someone. And I'd be burying her but good if I disclosed—if *we* disclosed—what she'd done to Lyle forty years ago. It would put the old woman through hell. Also destroy whatever slim chance of reconciliation they might have. It would hurt, not heal. And I didn't wish to be a part of that. Was it my decision to make? Maybe not. But they'd asked me to make it, so I was making it. This was one secret I was going to keep from Lyle Hudnut. I cleared my throat and looked him in the eye. "They did it to themselves, is more like it."

"Whatta you mean?" he asked, frowning.

"I mean, Lyle, that Aileen was drug dependent herself for many years—addicted to an assortment of tranquilizers."

He stared at me in disbelief. "Aileen? A *druggie?!*"

"She was. All those times you remember Herb saying she was lying down, she was actually having problems of her own. Problems they shielded you from, as most parents of that generation did. Your mother suffers from depression, Lyle. As did her father."

Lyle rubbed his hand over his face. Then he jumped to his feet and began to clomp heavily around the office, shaking his head. "This is . . . this is unreal. No wonder I'm such a fucking nut. I come from a whole family of fucking nuts. And they *hid* it from me. All these years they *hid* it from me." He stopped and glared down at me. "How'd you get it outta them?"

"Everyone ought to be good at something."

"Man, you sure as shit are." He rubbed his hands together with gleeful pleasure, began to dance a little jig around the room. "We are gonna *nuke* those sanctimonious old shits. *Yesss!* What else you got? Gimme more, Hoagster. Gimme more!"

I looked up at him. "Have you been completely candid with me, Lyle?"

He tensed instantly. "Why, what'd they say?"

David Handler

"Their version of the events leading up to your shock therapy is markedly different from yours."

"Well, you gotta expect that," he said, waving it off mildly. "You don't think they'd admit the truth, do ya? They're covering their butts, pal. But the facts don't lie. They had a son who was a bad ass. A son who dealt drugs. A son who—"

"Tried to commit suicide by jumping off the roof of his high school gym." I gave it to him hard.

And he took it hard. Like a boot in the balls. From Raoul Allegre. All of the air went out of him. His face went completely white. He hovered over me a moment, making those farting noises of his with his lips. Then, slowly, he sank onto the sofa, somewhat like the Goodyear blimp *Columbia* touching down. "That was . . . no big deal," he whispered. "I'm sure . . . I'm sure whatever they told you about it was total bullshit."

"You didn't tell me anything about it, Lyle."

"Because it was *no big deal,*" he repeated, sticking his chins out at me. He'd reverted to the bully boy. "Aren't you listening to me?"

"I'm listening. I just don't hear you saying anything."

He hesitated, his chest rising and falling. "Look, about this book . . ."

"What about it?"

"A positive spin on things wouldn't do me no harm under present circumstances," he reasoned. "If ya know what I mean."

"How about if you leave the spin up to me, Lyle. And just tell me what happened."

"Why should I?" he demanded.

"Because if you don't I'll quit."

He looked at me, incredulous. "What, just like that?"

"Just like that. There's no in-between with collaborators, Lyle. Either you're prepared to take me into your confidence or you're not. If you're not, then I don't want to have any-

336

thing to do with the project. So let's have it—the whole story. Or I'm out of here."

"You're serious, aren't you?"

I didn't bother to answer him.

"Well, okay then," he said reluctantly. "If it's that big a deal." He kicked off his Birkenstocks and stretched his mammoth self out on the sofa.

I sat there in my chair with my notepad, waiting. Celebrities often fall into the patient-shrink thing with me. Sometimes I think I ought to just get a degree like Cousin Tommy did. His hours are better than mine. And no one ever tries to run him over.

"It was an acid thing," he began, gazing up at the cracks in the ceiling. "That's all it was. They built it into something bigger. But it wasn't, I tell ya. I flipped out, that's all. Dropped some bad acid, and bummed."

"Describe it."

"I don't know if I can. To someone who's never dropped, I mean."

"Lyle, you're speaking to a man who once spent the whole night convinced his entire body was clad in Mylar. I was unable to move a single muscle for nine hours. Couldn't even speak."

"Really?" He grinned at me, amused. Then his face dropped. "Then maybe you remember how . . . sometimes you could sort of lose your normal perspective."

"That was sort of the whole point, wasn't it?"

He swallowed. "I guess I—I just opened up one of those doors that you're better off keeping shut."

"Which door are we talking about?"

"I mean, if you ever actually *think* about what happens to you after you die . . ."

"Oh, that door."

"It's pretty fucking depressing—even when you're *not* tripping. And when you are, well, it gets you to wondering what the point of any of it is. And, wow, before you know it you can't think of a single reason to stay alive. No matter how hard you try." He lay there recalling it, pudgy hands resting on his belly. "I dropped at lunch, on a full stomach. Figured I wouldn't start peaking until school let out. But I was wrong. It was potent, potent shit. Orange sunshine it was. And I started coming on to it right away. By the time final period was over, I was really tripping my brains out. . . . Had to get away from people. There were just so many *people* everywhere. I felt so—so . . ."

"Trapped?"

"Yeah, trapped. Kids crowding the halls, the exits, the gates, *everywhere*. I just *had* to get away from them, y'know? Sure ya do. You been there. I—I went up on the roof of the gym to chill out. We used to go up there all the time at lunch to sneak joints. Only this time, some janitor saw me up there and freaked. He called the cops. They called my parents. And *they* right away stuck me in the hospital. Christ, it was just the *acid*. Y'understand what I'm saying, don't ya? I was fine soon as I came down the next day." He trailed off, brow furrowed. "Okay, maybe it was two days before it was totally outta my system. I can't remember exactly. The point is I was fine, soon as I got my head straight. But Herb and Aileen, that wasn't good enough for them. They couldn't deal with it. They had to make it into something wrong. Something *bad*. So they had me jumped. I was fine, and they fried me, those evil fucking—"

"You weren't fine, Lyle," I said quietly.

He turned his head to look at me. "What'd you say?"

"I said you weren't fine. There's more to it than that. Something you don't remember. Something that was . . . that was wiped from your memory. Or maybe you've just blocked it out."

His eyes searched my face. "What is it? Tell me, damn it!"

"It wasn't one or two days, Lyle. It was six weeks. You sat in a darkened hospital room, sobbing, for six weeks. You went into a bottomless pit of depression that the doctors couldn't bring you out of."

He shook his head violently. "No way. Uh-uh. No!"

"Yes! They tried drugs, therapy, everything. Nothing worked. You were hopelessly suicidal. Diagnosed as manic-depressive. The shock therapy wasn't some willful act of social repression by your parents. It was the doctors trying to save you. And they did."

He jumped to his feet and started thumping around again, greatly agitated. "N-No way. That never happened."

"It happened."

He stood there over me, hulking, his fists clenched. "You believe them over me, don't you?" he said with quiet rage.

"I believe something happened that you don't remember. And I don't believe they'd make this up."

"They would, too!" he screamed, the veins popping in his fat red neck. "They're liars! They're *lying* to you!"

"Why would they?"

He let out a harsh laugh. "To cover their asses, that's why," he replied, sneering at me. "Just like I told ya before."

I tried the reasonable approach. "Okay, fine. You don't have to believe them, Lyle. We can go out to the hospital where it happened, get the names of your doctors, track them down. I'm sure some of them are still in practice. We can look up your medical records. We can look up your—"

"Records are bullshit!" he roared. "Nuttin' more than people rewriting history. I don't believe records. I believe what I know, and I know what happened. You hear me? I *know* it!"

So much for the reasonable approach. I got up and went over to the window. I parted the leopard-skin drapes. Not much to see. Just the dirty air shaft, but it was something. The outside world. Real. I could feel his eyes on me. I turned to him and said, "Lyle, I realize this is hard."

"You realize *shit!*" he raged, storming over to me. "My

own parents are making up stories about me! And you believe 'em! And I have no way of proving that they're total fucking liars! None!"

"They're not liars, Lyle." I went chest to chest with him. He wasn't much taller than me, but he was so much wider. I grabbed him by his meaty shoulders. "Do you hear me? They were coming clean. They were astonished to discover you blame them for authorizing the ECT. It shook them, Lyle. Really shook them. Because they've never, ever understood why you hate them the way you do. They were only trying to save you, Lyle. You've got to understand that. You've got to let them off the hook."

"Never," he insisted. "I can never do that." He shook himself loose from my grasp and flopped back down in his desk chair. "Never."

I stood there a moment, looking down at him. "Why don't we get in touch with some of your doctors?" I suggested gently.

He waved it off. "I don't remember any of their names."

"Herb and Aileen will."

A derisive snort.

"Want me to find out their names for you?"

He looked at me curiously. "You'd do that for me?"

"I would."

"Does this mean you're my friend?" Like a child he said it.

"It does not."

He frowned. "Then why are you doing all of this? What's in it for you?"

"A memoir with my name on it. I'm somewhat old-fashioned when it comes to books. I believe they should be about something. Even if not many people in publishing agree with me anymore. What do you say, Lyle? Shall I call them?"

He stared at me. "I don't know. Could you . . . ?" He trailed off, swiveling his chair around so that he faced the window, his back to me. "Leave me alone for . . . for a while, okay?'' he asked, voice choking with emotion. "I—I need some time to think about this.''

"Okay, Lyle.''

I gathered up my things and started for the door. He was already sobbing by the time I closed it softly behind me.

Leo was hurriedly searching through my desk drawers, her fingers deft and nimble. She was not alone there in my office. Two very large and very alive lobsters were bobbing around on the floor in a big clear plastic bag filled with greenish sea water. Maine lobsters, direct from our editor's posh summer home in Ogunquit. The Merchant of Menace had sent them to me that morning when he got word of Chad's death. His note said, "I hate to be greedy, but how do you do it?'' No reply was expected, which was just as well. I don't know how I do it.

I stood there in the doorway watching Leo and wondering what she was searching for.

Until she noticed me. If she was startled she was much too cool to show it. Just adjusted the Sherman parked behind her right ear and barked, "I was looking all over for you, Stewart Hoag.''

"I seldom hide in my desk.''

"Came in to leave you a copy of the memo,'' she said stiffly, offering me one from the sheaf she was clutching.

It was addressed to all *Uncle Chubby* staff, informing them that production was to be shut down for a minimum of two weeks, effective immediately. The writing and office staff would continue working, but the cast, crew, and all other staff were dismissed until further notice.

"Also to tell you that Fiona wants to see you,'' she added.

"Any particular reason?''

"She just said it was important,'' Leo answered dubiously.

I tugged at my ear. "Care to make a deal, Leo?''

She gazed down her nose at me. "What kind of deal?"

I sat in my chair. "I don't tell Lieutenant Very I found your Sherman butt in the bomb rubble if . . ."

"If *what?*" she demanded icily.

"If you tell me who it was that used Lyle's john just before the Chadster got himself zapped."

"I saw nobody."

"Your desk is right outside of Lyle's suite. You claim you were sitting there just before it happened. Never left—until Chad went in there. That means you saw who did it. You had to. You don't want to tell Very, that's fine. Tell me."

"I saw nobody," she repeated, louder this time.

"I'm afraid I don't believe you, Leo."

"I couldn't care less what you believe!" she bellowed angrily. "Or what you do! I've got nothing to hide. You want to tell your cop friend about that butt, you go right ahead and tell him! And while you're at it I really wish you'd go fuck yourself!" And with that she brushed past me in the tiny space and stormed out, keys jangling on their chain.

Annabelle came scurrying in a moment later, wide-eyed. "No way! I'm, like, what was that about?"

"That was just me wearing Leo down. The woman's nuts about me. I can tell."

Annabelle glanced down the short hallway, and lowered her voice. "Can we cop some face time? I'm like, deep into the shit thing."

"All right."

She glanced around my tiny office. "It's not the same without Lulu, is it?"

"It certainly smells a lot better. What kind of shit thing, Annabelle?"

Before she could reply there was a tremendous commotion out in the hallway. And then the two blond Munchkins came hurtling in, all energy and noise.

"We found you!" cried Caitlin, excitedly hugging Annabelle.

"You found me!" sang out Annabelle, as she embraced both of them. All three were about the same size.

"We get to go home," said Casey.

"I get to see my kitten," said Caitlin.

"And I get to see my Tony," added Amber, who stood planted there in the doorway in her jodhpurs and riding boots. "Cast officially dismissed."

"I'm, like, lucky you." Annabelle sniffed. "We worker bees have to stay here and write."

"You and Lorenzo must come out this weekend," Amber insisted. "We can unwind by the pool, putter in the garden. The kids would love to have you."

"Yeah!" they chimed in.

"Sounds awesome," said Annabelle. "I'll let you know."

"Please do." Amber treated me to the aristocratic flared nostril bit. "I hope you'll still be around when we return from hiatus, Hoagy."

I treated her to my best grin bit. "Why, do you know something about my future that I don't?"

Amber immediately got very uncomfortable. "Why, no. Not at all," she said hastily. "It's just that people are always coming and going so fast around this place. That's all I meant. Really. It was just something to say."

"I see," I said, not believing one word of it. I wondered what she'd heard about Lyle's future, and from whom. Possibly Fiona had heard it as well, and that was why she wanted to see me.

Amber turned back to Annabelle. "Call us."

"Like, I will," Annabelle promised.

Then she and The Munchkins departed.

Annabelle shut the door behind them, which made the tiny, airless office even tinier and more airless. "Just for a second, okay? I'm, like, it's about your cop friend. The babe."

"Very."

"Fer shure," she acknowledged, licking her lips. "But

I'm, like, he's in Lorenzo's face, okay? About whatever got put in the chili, okay?"

"It was fluid essence of ipecac. Not available over the counter."

"Lorenzo hasn't worked in a pharmacy for years."

"Then he has nothing to worry about."

"Yeah, he does," she countered, tossing her lacquered big hair. "They wanna beam on his tax returns."

"So?"

She lowered her eyes. "So there's, like, something maybe a little nonkosher in them, okay? Like when he's hard up, he shoots a little blah-blah-blah, okay?"

"Blah-blah-blah?"

"Porn. Hey, somebody's got to do it, and they pay real money. Only it's not a union deal, which means he gets paid under the table, and his union isn't hip to it."

"Is the IRS?"

"Of course," she said defensively. "You think he's some kind of crook?"

"I'm trying to figure out what to think."

"I'm saying he could get thrown out of his union. That's what I'm saying. You got to help him, Hoagy," she pleaded, grabbing me by the lapels with her tiny fists. "He's the one great love of my life. I'll *die* if he gets in any kind of trouble. I won't eat. Not a morsel of food will pass these lips. I'm a desperate woman, Hoagy. I'm, like, begging you. Please help him."

I extricated myself from her grasp. Linen wrinkles so easily. "And what *doesn't* the IRS know about?"

She reddened. "What makes you think there's—?"

"I have to know, Annabelle. If you want me to help you."

After a moment's hesitation she caved in. "Okay, okay. So, like, maybe he's done some other shit he hasn't reported. Chump change, strictly to make ends meet. I'm talking eating here."

"Such as what, dealing drugs?"

She gasped in horror. "No, never. I swear. No drugs. Not ever. Strictly legal stuff. But the IRS could wax him over it. The penalties alone would—"

"What does he do?"

"He drives a cab."

"Ouch. That was not a good answer."

"I'm, like, it's the truth."

"I'm, like, it's still not a good answer."

"Will you help him, Hoagy?"

There was a knock at my door, somewhat timid. She reached over and opened it. It was Bobby. He was unshaven, and he looked like he'd slept in his clothes—on the floor of Penn Station. He also seemed greatly agitated. He was blinking furiously and trembling. He clutched a script, his knuckles white. "You g-got a minute, Hoagy?"

"He's all yours," Annabelle answered. "Just remember, Hoagy. This woman's heart is in your hands. Not that I'm trying to pressure you."

"No, of course not."

She scurried off. Bobby closed the door behind her. It was a morning for closed doors.

"What's on your mind, Bobby?"

He smiled at me, or tried. It came out more like a grimace. "How are y-you enjoying the sitcom business?"

"It's not dull."

"Still, you m-must be anxious to get back to your novel."

"I'd be a lot more anxious if I had the slightest idea what it was."

"Yeah, b-but at least you'll be doing what you want. A free man."

"You just keep right on believing that, Bobby. What was it you wanted?"

"It's this c-cop," he sputtered. "This V-Very guy. He's been checking up on me. As if I'd every t-try to hurt anybody. It's absolutely n-nuts. It's insane. It's—"

"It's thoroughly justified under the circumstances, Bobby. You told everyone you were in Boston seeing your shrink the morning of the bombing. You weren't. In fact, you haven't seen him on Tuesdays for quite some time."

He ducked his head. "I-I know," he admitted. "But I had n-nothing to do with bombing the set. Or killing Chad, or any of it. You have to b-believe me."

"Why should I?" I said roughly. "You've been lying to everyone about your whereabouts. Plus I have no idea what you *were* doing."

He tossed the manuscript onto my desk. "This."

I glanced down at it. It was *The Human Dramedy,* a play in two acts, by Robert Jay Ackerman.

"My n-newest," he explained. "I've been writing it l-longhand on the plane, flying back and forth every weekend. T-Tuesday mornings, I type it up in my apartment. Okay, s-so I lied to people. But it was the only way I could set aside a little work time for myself. T-To preserve my sanity." He swallowed. "It's p-partly based on this show—it's *The Front Page,* except about a p-prime time sitcom, and with a tragic side. Amber's b-been giving me notes all along. Go ahead and ask her. She's read it."

"I'd like to read it, too."

"You can't." He snatched it back from me possessively. "Not yet. It's not done. But this is what I was d-doing the morning of the bombing. I was home writing. You have to tell Very, Hoagy. He has to know—I'm n-no killer."

"You are, however, extremely good with your hands."

"So are lots of people."

"Like who?"

"Lots of p-people," he repeated vaguely.

There was another knock on the door.

Katrina. She was crying, eyes red, nose running. And her chest was heaving, which was cause for tremendous awe and wonderment. At least it was for Bobby. He stood there gaping at her zoomers as they thrust back and forth through the doorway at him in her scant little *bustier.* I thought the poor kid was going to swallow his tongue.

"I'm sorry to bother you, Hoagy," she blubbered, barely noticing him. "But I just have to talk to you. Right away."

"N-No problem," Bobby assured her hastily. "No problem at all." He slipped past her in the doorway, somehow, and fled down the hallway.

She lingered there, sniffling. "I've just been sitting in my office sobbing like a baby girl," she squeaked. "I don't know what to do."

I gave her my linen handkerchief. I get them by the dozen. Then I ushered her in and closed the door behind her. There was barely enough room in there for the two of us, and the two of them. The smell of her lily of the valley perfume hung heavy in the air. Right away, it started to get a lot warmer.

"What's wrong, Katrina?" I asked her, my cup abrim with concern and kindness.

"I have to know, Hoagy. I just have to."

"Know what?"

"What went on in there after I left. Between Lyle and Naomi."

"Nothing went on, Katrina."

"Then why did he ask to see her?" she wondered plaintively. "Was he just trying to make me jealous or what?"

"Nothing went on, Katrina," I said, a little less convincingly this time. A lot less convincingly.

"You're lying to me!" she cried. "I know you are. I can tell. He's dicking her behind my back, isn't he?"

I gathered her hands in mine. They were hot to the touch. I looked deeply into her red-rimmed blue eyes, the left one gradually drifting from my gaze. "Look, the truth is I don't want to get caught in the middle of this."

"Why not?" She whispered it, breathlessly. Her eyes, or eye, searching my face.

"Because it's not part of my job description, okay?"

No, it wasn't okay. She needed to hear more. She edged closer to me, her hot hands squeezing mine tightly. I could feel her breath on my face, and her breasts pressing against my chest. Her mouth seemed to grow softer and heavier, her lips flowering. The cunning and sensual beast in action. "Are you sure that's the only reason?" she asked, her cotton candy voice throaty and intimate.

"Of course. What other reason would there be?"

She gave me an up-from-under look. "I don't know. You tell me."

An invitation. This one even less subtle and more humid than the last one. If I wore glasses, they'd be steamed up. She was feeling threatened now. Seriously threatened. From all sides. She was vulnerable. She was eager. Or so she wanted me to believe.

Yet another knock on the door. Now who, Rusty? I let go of Katrina's hands and opened it.

Marjorie.

She looked somewhat less poised and composed than usual. Ill at ease, in fact. And when she spotted Katrina there next to me wiping her eyes, she turned positively chilly. "Oh, I'm sorry. I didn't realize you were occupied."

Katrina gave her an equally chilly look back. Then she squeaked, "Excuse me," and brushed past Marjorie and out the door.

Marjorie watched her go, back arched, claws out. "I thought you'd left with God."

"Clearly," she observed tartly.

"That was nothing. Just me doing what I do."

"I'm not so sure I like what you do."

"That's only because you don't know enough about it. When you've had a chance to examine it from all sides, up close, you'll be positive you don't like it."

"I came back to sound out Lyle on his feelings about this morning's meeting." She turned stiff and networky on me.

"Only he wouldn't see me. He's hiding in his office. Unless he's gone. Has he gone? Do you know?"

"I don't know." I smiled at her. "How are the knees?"

That was the wrong thing to ask. All of the color drained from her face. She came in and shut the door firmly behind her. Then she faced me, wringing her hands. "Look, I'd rather people around here not . . ." She trailed off. Her eyes avoided mine. "I don't want them to know about what happened last night. Between you and me."

"Nothing happened. You went to bed, I went home. Remember?"

She stood there wringing her hands some more. Then she sat down in my chair. Then she noticed the lobsters there by her feet and jumped right back up again. She was very skittish. "Godfrey just said something very disturbing when he and Jeff were getting into their limousine."

"Oh, what was that?"

"Jeff said, 'I can't believe we have to pay rent on this whole building when we have three perfectly good sound-stages sitting empty on the Panorama lot.' And Godfrey replied, 'Don't worry, Jeff. You won't have to for long.' "

"Meaning what?"

"One of two things," she replied glumly. "He's planning to either move *Uncle Chubby* to Los Angeles or cancel it outright."

"I see," I said, wondering if this was what Amber had heard on the rumor mill.

"Which is a lose-lose scenario for me," she said fretfully. "And the fact that Godfrey hasn't shared his plans with me can only mean one thing—I'm out of the loop. Perhaps because he feels I've been too closely associated with Lyle. I don't know. I only know that I may be out of a job."

"Is that why you're so upset?"

"What makes you think I'm upset?" she demanded, her eyes stubbornly avoiding mine.

"It's about last night, isn't it?"

Reluctantly, she gave me the briefest of nods.

"Want to talk about it?"

"No," she said curtly.

"Nothing happened, Marjorie," I reminded her.

"You keep *saying* that!" she cried, erupting suddenly. "And you're so full of shit!"

"You finally noticed, huh?"

"*Sex* didn't happen, but all of the feelings did. I didn't sleep more than thirty minutes all night, Hoagy. I had to get up in the middle of the night and put in my bite guard, because I was clenching my jaw so tight. I'm angry, okay? I'm angry that you called me. I'm angry that you got me interested in you. I'm angry that it's not ever going to happen between us. Maybe I'm just not very sophisticated about these things. I picked up the newspaper this morning and saw the picture of you and her together and *that* made me angry. Everything about you makes me so angry I could punch you!"

"How do you think I feel?"

"I actually don't care!"

"I'm sorry, Marjorie."

"I don't want you to say you're sorry."

"What do you want?"

She leveled her large, liquid green eyes at me. I felt a jolt, this one all the way down to my toenails. "I want all of this to make some kind of sense," she replied gravely.

"The things that matter most in life never make any kind of sense. Sorry to be the one to break it to you."

She gazed at me. "Are you saying this matters to you?"

"I'm saying I didn't sleep last night, either."

She seemed surprised by this. "Really?"

"Really."

She looked away. "I-I threw out my Harry Connick, Jr., tapes this morning."

"You won't regret it."

"I don't regret any of it. After all . . ." She gave me a quick, fleeting smile. "Nothing happened, remember?"

"Like it was yesterday."

She kissed me once, lightly, on the mouth, and opened the door. "Thanks again, Hoagy."

"For what?"

"For Bobby Short. And for saving my life."

"You're welcome, Marjorie."

She hurried out the door before either of us could say anything more.

I stared at the empty corridor thinking it was probably just as well it wasn't going to happen. She was too normal for me. I wasn't accustomed to dealing with someone who expected life to make sense. Merilee . . . Merilee *would* have punched me. And then we'd have ended up on the floor together with the lobsters. Then sworn our undying love for each other. Then broken up for three months. Not this. This was weird.

I was starting down the corridor toward Fiona's dressing room when Tommy intercepted me outside The Boys' office. "Hoagmeister, just the man I wanted to see."

Inside, Marty was dodging a reporter's questions over the telephone. "I can't speak to you on or off the record, John. You'll have to go through official channels. Try two, or four, or seven . . ."

Tommy closed the door and stood there, shoulders hunched, blocking my path. "Chuckles have any news?"

"No news."

"Then what did she want?" he asked, raising an eyebrow at me.

"None of your business."

"You banging her?"

"What do you want, Tommy?" I said impatiently. "No, wait. Don't tell me. I'll tell you. It's about my friend Very, who is not, by the way, my friend. He's been asking about you at the Deuce Theater, where you are a regular customer, and been snooping around at your hotel. He's even been talking to one Dolly Mae Bramble, whose clothing you enjoy wearing. And jerking off into.''

Tommy's chalky complexion turned green. He glanced about furtively but no one was within earshot.

Me, I didn't care if they were or not. "I don't know why Very's been doing all of this," I continued. "I have nothing whatsoever to do with it. Or him. But if I speak to him I'll tell him that you don't know anything about Lyle's arrest or Chad's murder or any of it. You're completely innocent. You just happen to have a drinking problem, a dysfunctional marriage, and incredibly skeegee personal habits. Does that about cover it, Tommy?''

Tommy gulped, momentarily speechless. "Well, yeah. That covers it, Hoagmeister.''

"Fine. Now if you'll please excuse me, I have someone to see. And don't ever call me Hoagmeister again.''

The main office was crowded with people saying good-bye to one another. I passed through them to the dressing rooms. Very had sealed Chad's door shut. Fiona's door had no seal on it, but it was shut, too. I tapped on it and went in before she had a chance to say come in.

Not that she would have said come in. Or get lost. Or anything else, for that matter.

She was sprawled out on the love seat with a throw pillow tossed casually over her face. I removed it. She was staring right at me. Someone had smothered her with the pillow. She wore an oversized linen shirt and a man's striped necktie. Her tie was askew, but otherwise she looked fine. If you can call dead fine.

I stood there a moment, wondering why she'd wanted to see me. Why it was so important. Why it had cost her her life. Why I hadn't gotten here ten minutes sooner. Whether she'd still be alive and shuddering if I had. I wondered a lot of things. Then I called Very.

Eleven

Why didn't they kill *me?!*" moaned Lyle. "Why did they have to kill Fiona?! *Why?*"

He was howling hugely and painfully in the corridor outside of her dressing room. The man was distraught, he was grief-stricken, he was terrified.

Marty wept openly. He was so upset he even threw himself into Lyle's arms. And Lyle was so upset he let him. The two of them hugged each other tightly, tears streaming down their faces.

Very was inside Fiona's dressing room with the door closed. The rest of the family stood out in the hall, silent and numb with shock. Tommy, Annabelle, and Bobby. Leo. Katrina. Naomi. Amber and The Munchkins, who hadn't left yet. Everyone was there. Everyone except Marjorie, who wasn't anywhere.

"There's no *Uncle Chubby* without Fiona," Lyle sobbed. "I'm folding the show. We're history. She *was* the show. I give up. I tell ya, I give up."

"But we've got to do something, Lyle," protested Marty. "Give her something—a tribute."

Lyle's eyes lit up. "A tribute!"

"Her best bits," suggested Marty.

"Her best bits!" Lyle echoed excitedly. "We'll give her a special episode. Our way of saying good-bye. Our way of—" He broke off, the grief overtaking him again. He looked around for someone else to hold onto. Both Katrina and

Naomi were right there, anxious to offer him comfort. When they weren't shooting poisonous looks at each other. But it was Leo who he lunged for. "She loved you, Leo!" He wept, hugging her tightly. And surprising the hell out of her—the Sherman behind her ear went flying. "She loved all of us!" Then he released his producer and focused on me. "Why Fiona, Hoagy? I wanna know why!"

"That all depends, Lyle. What did she know?"

He frowned at me, bewildered. "Know about what?"

"She had something she wanted to tell me. Something important. What was it?"

"How the fuck should I know?" he cried. "I'm getting my mind blown here and you're asking me questions!"

"Because we need answers."

He started turning red. "This is too much!" he raged. "Way too much. I can't take anymore of this. I can't. I just can't." He was quivering now, sweat pouring from his face. He looked like he had just before he trashed his bathroom. "I'm gonna blow, I tell ya! I'm gonna blow!"

"You're *not,* Lyle," I said, raising my voice at him. "Do you hear me?" He didn't seem to. His eyes looked right through me. I turned to Katrina and said, "Take him to his office. Try to calm him down."

She took him by his clenched fist. "C'mon, Pinky," she squeaked gently. "Come on, honey. Let's go have some herbal tea, okay?"

He didn't answer her, but he let her lead him away, like he was a giant, docile child. Naomi, the odd woman out, watched the two of them go, her beady eyes icy with jealousy.

"Have you seen Marjorie?" I asked her.

"She left," Naomi replied sharply, glaring at me. I'd chosen Katrina over her. She would not forget this when she became queen.

"When did she leave?"

"Right after she was in talking to you."

"How do you know she was in with me?"

"She doesn't visit any of the other writers, except for Annabelle. And I can see Annabelle's door from my desk. She wasn't in with her."

I tugged at my ear. "You don't miss much, do you?" I observed, eyeing her.

She eyed me back. "I try not to."

Fiona's door opened. A most grim Very motioned for me to join him in there. I did. He wasn't alone. Fiona was still there on the love seat, staring. Someone from the Medical Examiner's office was there taking pictures of her. They're always taking pictures. The plainclothesman who'd been parked outside of Lyle's office door was there, too, looking real unhappy. He closed the door behind me.

"Yo, this is not cool, dude," Very muttered, jaw working his gum. "This place is a war zone."

I gazed down at her. She looked so frail and tiny, almost childlike. But people, like mice and cockroaches, always look smaller when they're dead. "Did she put up any kind of a fight?"

"Not so you'd notice." He shot a look down at the coffee table, which was neatly piled with magazines and scripts. "Nothing strewn around. Nothing kicked on the floor. Her clothes aren't torn. No visible scratches." He took one of her lifeless hands in his and examined it. "Chewed her nails down to the quick, so I doubt we'll find much under them, if anything." He dropped it, nodding to himself rhythmically. "My guess is it was over in a flash—the lady got overpowered."

"Meaning we're talking about someone strong?"

He looked her over, his right knee quaking. "She weighed ninety, ninety-five pounds, tops. Any dude in the place would have the power."

"Would a strong woman?"

"Yeah. A strong woman could have done it."

"Not much flair to it," I observed.

"Flair?" Very stuck his chin out at me. "What the fuck you talking about, flair? Dead is dead."

"Lieutenant, Chad's murder had a certain dash to it. This was just quiet and brutal."

"So?" he demanded impatiently.

I shrugged. "So nothing. I'm just thinking out loud."

"No offense, dude, but I think better out loud when you don't. *Motherfucker!*" He slammed his fist into his palm. "We even had a man here!"

"I was assigned to watch Hudnut, Lieutenant," said the plainclothesman, hanging his head in shame. "Not her."

"I know that, dammit," Very told him.

"He was in his office, so that's where I was," he persisted stubbornly.

"I know. I'm not blaming you, okay? But I'm still gonna get toasted over this. The papers will smoke me! I'll be directing traffic outside of the Holland Tunnel by the time this is over."

I nodded sympathetically. Cops worry about critics just as much as writers do. And hate them even more. "You didn't notice anyone heading in this direction?" I asked the plainclothesman.

"There was millions of people coming and going," he answered gruffly. "No way I could keep track of all of'em. Even if I was trying to. And I wasn't."

"Pretty cheeky, if you think about it."

"What's cheeky?" snapped Very, with mounting annoyance.

"Coming in here and murdering Fiona while a policeman's parked right out there in the office. That takes guts."

"Yeah, well, your average psycho killer is not, as a rule, short on guts, dude," Very fumed disgustedly. "Just social fucking correctness." He puffed out his cheeks with exasperation. He started to say something more, but he stopped himself. And we went to lunch.

"Why Fiona, dude?"

We ate around on Twenty-ninth Street at Vernon's Jerk Paradise, a Jamaican barbecue place. We both had the jerked pork, and washed it down with glass after glass of Vernon's own tropical fruit punch. Jerk is so highly spiced it makes your forehead bead up with sweat and your lips burn. But it's well worth it. You'll just have to take my word.

"She knew something, Lieutenant. Something she wanted to tell me."

"And who knew that?"

"Leo did. She's the one who passed me the message."

"Uh-huh. Anyone else?"

"I have no idea."

"What happens to the show without her?"

"Nothing good. At least not as far as Lyle is concerned. He's already on thin ice with the network. He and Fiona were still a strong unit together, the core of the show, the franchise. Without her, he's even more vulnerable. There's no telling what the network will decide to do now. They could recast Deirdre. They could revamp the show. They could cancel it outright. It's anybody's guess."

"Yo, what's *your* guess?" he growled impatiently. Possibly, his incision was itching again.

I answered, "We're talking about show business, Lieutenant. If you can imagine it happening, if it makes sound, rational sense and it's good for all parties concerned, then that's not what's going to happen." I sipped my fruit punch. "Only God knows what will happen."

"Which God are we talking about here?" Very asked.

"The one who wears tasseled loafers."

"I see," he said glumly. "You got anything for me, dude? Anything at all?"

"A string of denials, mostly." I told him what Annabelle, Bobby, and Tommy had asked me to tell him. "And you, Lieutenant? What have you got?"

"Some info on that cab tried to run you down last night —which may cut our man Lorenzo a little slack. Not that he's off the hook, mind you. Cab was stolen, like I sorta figured." He glanced through his notepad. "Got jacked from outside a twenty-four-hour bagel place on Houston Street and West Broadway. Cabbie haunt. Dude double-parked out front, ran in to pick up a coffee to go. Was in there thirty seconds, tops. Came back out, it was gone. Not that this means we're looking for some prime-time jackboy. Bozo left the engine running, on account of he had the air-conditioning on. Counterman said a lot of'em do that, because they're in and out so fast, and because they're fleet drivers and they don't give a fuck what happens to the cab."

"Did anyone see who took it?"

Very shook his head. "Not the cabbie, not the counterman, not nobody."

"And what time did this happen?"

"A little before ten."

Very and I had separated outside The Blue Mill around ten. Our killer must have tailed me to the restaurant from my apartment, then walked over to Houston Street and stolen the cab while we ate. Then he—or she—followed me home, angling for a good, clean shot. No witnesses. Possibly I'd have been murdered in my bed if I hadn't come back out and headed over to the Carlyle to see Bobby Short. After which that good, clean shot did present itself. Almost.

"We know Katrina Tingle stayed home all evening," Very revealed. "On account of we had a man parked outside Hudnut's suite at the Essex House. She never went out. Hudnut neither—man took a hot bath and sacked out early. We also know that Marty Muck was home with his wife. So was Tommy Meyer."

"Tommy was with Marty's wife, too?"

Very sighed. "With his own, in the 'burbs. I think we maybe shamed the dude into going home. We're still trying to nail down the whereabouts of the others when it happened." He drained his fruit punch, pushed his plate away, and took out a fresh stick of gum. "Yo, dig on this, dude." He chomped thoughtfully. "Somebody tries to kill you—to shut you up, most likely. Fails, goes after Fiona Shrike. And succeeds. Could be the two of you struck the same nerve, and that's why she got it and you almost did."

"What's your point, Lieutenant?"

"Maybe you already know what she knew. Could be you have the key to this whole fucking thing, and you just don't realize it."

I tugged at my ear. "That may be true, Lieutenant. But I have no idea what it is."

"Our perp don't know that," Very pointed out.

"Meaning I'm still in danger?"

He nodded. "Afraid so, dude. I'm putting somebody on you tonight."

"That won't be necessary, Lieutenant."

"Yeah, it is. I don't want to lose you."

"Why, Lieutenant. I'm touched."

"Don't be. My interest in you is strictly professional. You're my best hope for a break—which I sure as hell could use right about now." He knuckled his eyes wearily. "I'm a hurting puppy here. Got bits and pieces all over the place. Got a list of suspects as long as my arm. Bottom line—I got bubkes. I need a break, dude. A pry bar to wedge this sucker open. I need somebody, something, *anything.*" He shook his head. "No way I been able to keep up my end of our bargain, which I apologize for. I was hoping to sweat Merilee's doorman a little, but I haven't had the time."

"I understand. It's quite all right."

He leaned forward over the table, wincing slightly. "So how did it work out last night?" he asked, lowering his voice. "You and Marjorie Daw. She help you forget?"

"I'm afraid all she did was help me remember."

His brow creased with concern. "Geez, dude. You got it bad."

"Lieutenant, I've got it terminal."

I didn't go straight back to the laugh factory. I strolled uptown on Eighth Avenue to Forty-second Street instead. Took the walk that Lyle took that fateful afternoon last spring when he felt trapped. When it all came crashing down around him. I strolled. It wasn't far. Nothing in Manhattan is. It was hot and sticky out. The humidity was back, the air thick and gray, the street tar soft under my feet. Rain was in the forecast. A tropical depression, Marjorie would no doubt call it. I wondered if I would always think of Marjorie when it got hot and sticky. Or it rained. Or got cold. Or would she merely recede into the back of my mind like they all did, compared to Merilee. I strolled. At Thirty-first I hit the vast backside of Penn Station, one of the two great buttholes of modern American architecture. The other, the Port Authority Bus Terminal, was on my left up at Fortieth Street. In between there were pawnshops and discount stores selling boom boxes and beepers and sneakers and more sneakers. Guys were unloading trucks everywhere. Sidewalk peddlers were selling stolen jewelry, toasters, toys, bootlegged videotapes. Music was playing. Calypso music, Indian music, rap music. Vendors sold greasy meat pies. Incense was burning. Men sat on folding chairs smoking cigarettes and sucking from tall cans of Bud with straws, killing the summer afternoon. At Forty-second Street I made a right, heading east.

In many ways, Forty-second Street is not what it once was. There is much less of it than there used to be, thanks to a vast, stalled urban redevelopment project that has left a lot of the porn theaters and hooker hotels boarded up. The hot-sheets trade has moved to places like Queens Boulevard and Jersey City, where rents are cheaper. A lot of the movie houses have simply succumbed, casualties of the home video revolution. Frankly, the whole place has about as much life now as downtown Hartford on a Saturday night. Yet in many ways, Forty-second Street hasn't changed one bit. It's still the best place in the city to buy an out-of-town newspaper, a hash pipe, a Spiro Agnew Halloween mask, a specimen of plastic vomit, or a deck of playing cards featuring photographs of men and women having sex with a variety of farm animals. And there are still some peep shows and topless bars and X-rated movies to be found there. The Deuce, for instance, was showing *When Harry Ate Sally.* Glamorous, full-color marquee photos were plastered everywhere. Plenty of seating room. Step right up, gentlemen. . . . Okay, so, it's not Sutton Place. It's dirty. But no dirtier than many neighborhoods, and cleaner than some. Mostly, it just seemed kind of tired and harmless to me as I walked along. Of course, it was two in the afternoon, and I wasn't looking to buy anything or anyone. I didn't even know what I was doing there. I didn't see anything, or anyone I knew—other than that same old bag lady who sits on the sidewalk out in front of Herman's, feverishly scribbling incoherent gibberish on a long yellow legal pad with a pen. She has long silver hair, very dirty, and she's been writing away for as many years as I can remember. As I stood there looking at her the same thing occurred to me that always occurred to me: I was no different than she was. Just blessed with a bit more clarity. On a sporadic basis. I bent over and gave her ten dollars. Then I went back to the studio.

Fiona's dressing room was sealed now. Her body had been taken away. A fresh plainclothesman was parked outside of

The Boys' office. Inside, Lyle was huddled with Muck and Meyer, The Kids, and Katrina. They were quite up, a party atmosphere. There was laughter all around. Pizza, too, although Lyle wasn't having any under Katrina's watchful eye.

"Hey, there ya are, Hoagster!" Lyle called to me brightly, all twinkling blue eyes and jack-o'-lantern grin. Yet another complete mood swing. I was used to them now. They were the norm. "We're putting together a tribute show for Fiona."

"Nice idea."

"Thanks, I thought of it myself," he boasted.

Marty coughed. Tommy let out a short, rude laugh. Lyle frowned at them, astonished and hurt. Clearly, he had convinced himself that the tribute *was* his own idea, not Marty's. This was also the norm.

"Gang's all with me on it," he went on, rubbing his hands together eagerly. "We're putting together a list of her funniest bits. The hardest part's narrowing it down."

Marty read from his list. "So far we've got the flu show, the sleepwalking show, the mouse-in-the-house show, the big-toe-stuck-in-the-bathtub-faucet show . . ."

"I'm gonna introduce each clip personally," Lyle asserted. "Just me talking directly to the camera, reminiscing about Fiona and how much she meant to me. To all of us. We're gonna tape it this afternoon. No audience. Just our people."

"I'm, like, wouldn't it be sweet if The Munchkins introduced one of the bits?" suggested Annabelle.

"Nice touch," Lyle admitted grudgingly.

"How about the show w-when Rusty ate the cordless phone and it k-kept beeping?" sputtered Bobby.

"Perfect!" exclaimed Lyle. "Only let's not invite Rusty. I hate that flea-infested mutt."

"Gee, he says such nice things about you, Lyle," cracked Tommy.

"Where are The Munchkins at this very minute?" asked
Lyle.

"On their way home to Long Island," Annabelle replied.
"But Amber has a phone in the Range Rover."

"Have Leo call 'em and drag 'em straight back here,"
Lyle ordered Katrina.

"Yes, Lyle," she said obediently.

"And get the crew in. I wanna start filming my intros
right away. While my emotions are still raw." Lyle turned
back to me. "Wanna sit in on this?"

"Thanks, but I've got some work to do on the book.
Have you spoken to God yet about Fiona's death?"

"His plane's still in the air. Guarantee ya he'll come right
back on the very next flight. He loved Fiona."

"Gee, you'd think God could just order them to turn the
plane right around in midair," observed Tommy drily.

"It's a commercial flight," said Katrina, curling her lip at
him.

Tommy: "You'd think God would have his own plane."

Marty: "You'd think God wouldn't *need* a plane."

"Better." Tommy nodded.

"Would you two guys shut up?" Katrina cried.

"Y'know what?" said Lyle. "I don't care if the fucking
network even uses this tribute. I need to do it. And if they
don't wanna pay for it, that's cool, too. We'll throw ourselves
a giant party and we'll play it for everybody," he declared,
with mounting defiance. "We're doing it for ourselves anyway. It's for *us,* not for the public, not for God. Fuck God! Ya
hear me? Fuck God!"

He wasn't struck by lightning at that exact moment, but
there was a huge clap of thunder outside the studio. Shook
the whole building. Just a coincidence, I'm sure.

I went to my office and took off my jacket and shut the
door. Just me and the lobsters. I sat at my desk, chin on my
fists, my mind working overtime. Wondering, wondering. Did
I have the key. What *was* the key? What did I know that had

almost cost me my life, and had certainly cost Fiona Shrike hers? I sat there, turning all of it over . . . the Deuce Theater, the bombing, the chili, Chad, Fiona . . . It had to be there. That nugget of information that would somehow make all of it clear. It had to be there. But where was it? I didn't know. I couldn't find it. I just couldn't find it. A pry bar. That's what Very said he needed. A pry bar to wedge this thing open. But what kind of pry bar? And who to use it on? I sat there, wondering, wondering.

Until, bleary eyed, I got up and went to the john. Not Lyle's, mind you. I used the men's room outside the main office on the second-floor landing. It was disgusting in there. Wadded paper towels and cigarette butts scattered about, sinks filthy, rancid puddles on the floor before the urinals. And it smelled nothing like lavender, trust me. I splashed some cold water on my face and dried it with my linen handkerchief. There were no clean paper towels left. I ran a comb through what was left of my hair. None of this woke me up. Or stopped me from wondering.

I paused to look out the landing windows a moment before I went back inside the office. It had turned dark and nasty out. Lightning crackled. Thunder rumbled. Rain began to spatter lightly against the sooty windows, smearing the grimy glass so that I could barely make out the trash cans and duct-work down below in the air shaft. Then the lightning lit up the sky directly overhead, and this time I saw something. Something that explained a lot. Everything, in fact. Because suddenly it was terribly clear to me. All of it. So clear I couldn't believe it hadn't occurred to me before. But it was also sealed tight. No cracks. I needed a crack. As I stood there, watching the spatters of wet on the glass turn to sheets of warm, dirty rain, I realized that I had that crack. It was there. Had been all along. What I had to do now was drive a wedge into it—pry it open, nice and easy.

Only I was going to have to work fast.

When the tap on my door came, I took a deep breath and said, "Come in," and she did.

She was rushed. "What is it you wanted, Hoagy?" she asked, clutching a clipboard.

"Getting busy out on the floor?"

"Real busy. Crew's all here. Sound, lighting. We're going to start rolling in a few minutes. What's so important?"

"Close the door, Katrina."

She did. She had her hair tied back in a ponytail now, and her glasses nestled on top of her head. "Okay, but Lyle's going to freak if I'm gone for long."

"This won't take long." I stood up and took her clipboard from her and put it on the desk. I took her hot hands in mine. "I wasn't being totally straight with you before, Katrina."

"About what, Hoagy?" Anxiousness crept into her cotton candy voice.

"About Lyle and Naomi. I told you I didn't want to get involved because it's not part of my job description. And that's not the real reason."

She edged closer to me, squeezing my hands tightly. "What is?"

"I can't stand how he hurts you."

"What do you care if he hurts me?" she whispered, moistening her lips with her tongue.

"I care," I replied, "because I care about you. A lot. There it is—I've said it. It's out in the open, okay?"

She let out a squeal and jumped right into my arms, practically knocking me over. She was a big, healthy girl. "Okay!" she cried, squeezing me tightly, her zoomers squashed up against my chest. "Oh, God, Hoagy, I like you so much," she said rapidly and breathlessly. "Ever since that first day at the beach. I knew it right away. I *felt* it." Her mouth was on mine now, hers a blast furnace. "You felt it, too, didn't you?"

"I felt it, too."

"You're out there, just like me."

"I'm out there, all right."

She thrust her hips against mine, her pelvis grinding away. "Oh, God. You're so sensitive. Not like him. He's so self-centered and cruel. He hit me. He hurt me. You, you're a real feelings specialist."

"I am a feelings specialist. I don't know how real I am." This was me trying to rein her in. But it was no use. She was faster than a speeding bullet. More powerful than a locomotive . . .

She took my hands and guided them up under her *bustier* to her corn-fed assets. "Oh, yesss . . ." Her nipples did not honk when I squeezed them. But they did perk right up. And she did start to moan. Rather loudly, I might add. "Yesss . . ." Her eyes were shut, her head heavy on her neck. "We can have something special, Hoagy. I can make you feel so *goood.*"

"I don't think anyone can do that. But it's sweet of you to say so."

She gasped with delight. *"Sweet.* Nobody's ever called me that before."

"Nobody's ever known you before," I said, cringing inwardly. Because this made it official—bad, insincere dialogue had now crept into my life. I used to be able to contain it to my art. "But I have to know something first, Katrina. Something you alone can tell me."

"Anything, darling," she vowed. "Anything."

"Will you be totally candid with me?"

"Of course I will." She frowned at me. "Why, what's this all about?"

"It's about the two blockbusters and the three-alarm chili. It's about Chad and Fiona."

She gave me my hands back and tugged her *bustier* back

down with huffy propriety. "I had nothing to do with any of that."

"I'd like to believe you, Katrina. I really would. Trust is so important."

She softened. "Trust is everything between two people," she agreed. "Without trust you're nowhere. Only, I didn't do anything, Hoagy. I swear."

"But you do know something."

She gazed at me, bewildered. "I do?"

"I think so."

"What is it, Hoagy? Ask me anything. Go ahead and ask me."

I went ahead and asked her. I had to kiss her once or twice to get it out of her, and say a few more things to her I won't bother to repeat here, or you'll think even less of me. But I got what I needed. I felt shitty about it, but I got it. And that's all that matters, isn't it?

Well, isn't it?

Then she had to get back before Lyle missed her and started freaking out. And I had to make two phone calls, one of them to Very. I told him to get over there right away. And then, my pry bar in hand, I joined Lyle and the *Uncle Chubby* gang out on the floor of the studio.

Twelve

The control booth was hopping. Lyle's grizzled old assistant director, Sam, was parked at the console frantically barking orders into his headset. Same with the technical coordinator, sound man, and lighting man, who were seated alongside him, performing last-minute checks and repositioning their troops and hardware out on the floor. Leo sat behind them in the second row with a stopwatch, a fistful of pencils, and a logbook, ready to mark down shots. Naomi sat on one side of her, ready to assist as needed. Katrina sat on the other side, ready to be an executive as needed. Katrina glowed at me as I came in. Leo glowered. In the back row, Marjorie, who was strictly there to observe, glanced at me, then glanced away, her expression stony.

Lyle wasn't in there, but he was still a dominant presence. His round, pink face filled all four monitor screens on the wall before us. Four different cameras capturing him from four different angles as he sat on the living room set in Chubby's familiar easy chair, chatting with his stage manager, Phil, while he waited for the word that everyone was ready. He was all made up and in costume. Wore the Uncle Chubby sweater over a soiled-looking sweatshirt and baggy khakis.

The writers and everyone else were out in the bleachers, watching. Lyle's plainclothesman was out there, too.

I sat in the back next to Marjorie. "Have you spoken to Godfrey?"

She looked at me a long time, searchingly, before she

nodded, making a steeple of her long, slender fingers. "He was deeply upset. He has a big affiliates' meeting in San Diego this evening, but he intends to fly back here directly afterward, on the red-eye."

"Any idea what he intends to do?"

She smiled faintly. "I'm out of the loop, remember?"

"There are worse places to be."

"Are there?"

"Trust me—there are." I turned and watched Lyle up on the monitors, aware that she was staring at me, her green eyes shimmering in the booth lights. When I looked back at her, she hurriedly looked away.

Sam flicked the P.A. switch. "Okay, Lyle. Whenever you're ready."

Lyle cleared his throat and settled himself in the chair. His jaw became slacker, his expression a bit more dim-witted and sheepish. Shoulders softened. Chin melted down into his neck. He was *becoming* Uncle Chubby. A different person. The transformation was startling. It always is with actors.

Phil, wearing a headset, crouched in front of him holding a clapper that had "FIONA TRIBUTE" written on it in marking pen. "Quiet, please! Settle everyone!" he called out. "Are we ready now? . . . Five, four, three, two and . . . *action!*" He scuttled away, like a crab.

Lyle faced Camera Two, a subdued expression on his face. "Hiya, everybody. This is a special *Uncle Chubby Show* tonight. Heck, I guess you could almost call it the last *Uncle Chubby Show.* Life will never be quite the same for us around here. See, we've lost someone we all loved. A very special member of our own family, Fiona Shrike." He paused, turning slowly to face Camera Three.

Sam switched to Three with a snap of his fingers. "Move in, Three," he murmured into his headset, talking to the cameraman. "Snug it up, Junior. Snug it up." Lyle was now in extreme close-up—a talking head. "Perfect."

"When someone close to you dies," Lyle continued, "ya

like to gather your family and friends together and say a special good-bye to 'em. That's what tonight is all about for us. This is us saying, 'Good-bye, Fiona.' This—'' He broke off, his voice choking with feeling. "This is our eulogy. Fiona was a performer, a brilliant one, and the best way you can pay tribute to any great performer is to let their performances speak for themselves. Those of us who worked with Fiona, and loved her, feel a tremendous sense of loss. But at the same time, we feel tremendously fortunate. Because she's really not gone at all. Her performances are a legacy that will live on for all time. . . .''

And with that he introduced the first clip, from the *Uncle Chubby* pilot, when Chubby first shows up on his sister's doorstep and she flatly refuses to let him sleep under her roof. Lyle introduced two other bits as well, working off the top of his head—no cue cards, or notes—and nailing it all in one take. He seemed amazingly calm. This, too, was acting. Then he gave Sam the cut signal and reached for a bottle of mineral water and gulped some down. The bleachers erupted with applause. A heartfelt ovation from the troops. Lyle acknowledged it with only a brief, grim nod.

"Want to do another one from there, Lyle?" Sam asked him over the P.A.

Lyle looked around the set. "Nah, let's move to the kitchen.''

"Okay, moving to the kitchen, everybody!" Phil called out.

That meant a break. I took to my feet and I stepped out of the booth just as Amber and The Munchkins came rushing in the stage door, all three of them drenched from the rain, Amber still clutching her car keys. "I understand there's to be a tribute of some kind?" she said to me, clearly pissed by this sudden change of plans.

"You understand right. It's already happening.''

Phil spotted The Munchkins and whisked them right off to makeup, leaving Amber with me.

She heaved a sigh of annoyance. "We were planning a special family thing tonight. Now I've had to cancel. It's so impossible to have a normal life around this place, isn't it?"

"I'm sure Fiona would certainly echo that," I acknowledged. "If she could."

Amber's eyes flashed at me hotly. "I suppose you think I'm being selfish or insensitive or something."

"Or something."

Now I got the flaring nostrils bit. "I believe I could detest you without too much effort, Hoagy."

I tugged at my ear. "Me, I find it takes no effort whatsoever to detest people."

She made eye contact with Gwen, who started over to us.

"Excuse me, please," Amber said curtly. Then the two of them went off to see about The Munchkins' costumes.

The monitors suspended in the air over the bleachers were on now. So was the applause sign. The Boys were huddled together in the front row making notes about Lyle's performance, in case he wanted any. The Kids sat directly behind them. Lyle's plainclothesman sat off to one side, watching Lyle get ready on the kitchen set.

"Enjoying Lyle's tribute?" Tommy asked me.

"Are *you?*" I asked Marty.

"I am, actually," Marty replied somberly. "Very much."

"Chuckles watching in the booth?" asked Tommy.

"She is."

"She crack one smile?"

"Not so I noticed. But it's not one of your funnier tapings."

"True," Tommy admitted.

"I'm, like, did you talk to Very?" Annabelle asked me.

"I did."

"He have any n-news about who killed Fiona?" asked Bobby.

"He didn't."

Two more plainclothesmen were parked just inside the

big steel stage door now. Very had arrived. I felt my stomach muscles tighten. My heart was beating faster.

"You okay, Hoagy?" asked Tommy, peering at me. "You look funny."

"I just have a lot on my mind," I replied. "None of it good."

I crossed the stage floor to the kitchen set, stepping between two cameras and then over the coils of cables into the bright, hot overhead lights. A stagehand was brewing coffee in the electric coffee maker to lend a homey look. A mug sat before Lyle on the table, where he was parked. The stylist was touching up his hair. His makeup, which gave him a normal, healthy appearance on the monitors, glowed dull to the naked eye. His round cheeks resembled waxed fruit. He looked like he'd been embalmed.

"Heya, Hoagster," he exclaimed, beaming at me. "Book going good?"

"It's starting to heat right up." I sat with him at the table. The stylist scurried off.

"Been thinking over our conversation this morning," he said. "About my missing six weeks and the shock therapy and all. And I think you're a hunnert percent on target. I wanna get to the bottom of it. Let's go for it. Make some calls, maybe drive out there tomorrow and talk to the medical people. We can put the whole scene in the book, okay?" He looked at me eagerly. He was so anxious for my approval.

"That sounds real good, Lyle. Maybe . . ."

"Yeah?"

"Maybe we can stop off and see your folks while we're out there."

He stuck out his fat, red lower lip. "It'll be a plus?"

"A major plus."

He smacked the table with his palm. "Then let's do it," he declared decisively.

"Good man," I said, patting his hand. He didn't pull away. "What changed your mind, Lyle?"

"This whole thing with Fiona, I reckon," he replied. "I mean you can just lose somebody, pow, and whatever history you had together, whatever *life* you had together, it's gone. Forever. The folks won't be around much longer. I—I guess I'd hate to lose 'em without making some kind of peace with 'em first. I'll regret it for the rest of my life if I don't. The way I'm regretting things about Fiona. Shit I did to her. Shit I said to her. Shit I didn't say to her. Is any of this making any kind of sense?"

"It's making a lot of sense, Lyle. I'll call them this afternoon."

"Ready when you are, Lyle," Phil broke in.

I got up to leave.

"Hey, Hoagster?" Lyle called after me.

"Yes, Lyle?"

"Thanks."

"For what?"

"For everything. I mean that."

"You're welcome, Lyle."

I started back to the booth. Amber was seated in the bleachers now next to Annabelle. Very was standing just inside the door of the booth with his arms crossed and his right knee quaking.

"Welcome, Lieutenant. Glad you could make it."

"Ready when you are, dude," he said, jaw working his gum.

Everyone in there was watching us. Leo, Katrina, Naomi, Marjorie, Sam, and the others. It was extremely silent and still in that booth.

"They've been briefed?" I asked Very.

He nodded.

I turned to Sam, who was standing behind his chair. "Tape's rolling?"

"Tape's rolling," he replied, pulling the chair out for me.

I sat down in it. Then I flicked on the P.A. microphone.

Thirteen

Lyle?"

He grinned directly at me in the monitor. "What, you taking over, Hoagster?"

"That's correct. There is nothing wrong with your television set. I am now in control."

"Typical writer," he cackled, playing to the gang in the bleachers. They broke up.

"There's something I have to go over with you, Lyle."

He frowned. "What, right now?"

"I'm afraid so."

Lyle glanced at Phil, then back at me. "Can't this wait? We're in the middle of—"

"I'm afraid not."

He shrugged his shoulders. "Okay, pal. What is it?"

"Why did you do it, Lyle?"

Lyle swallowed. "Do what?"

"You engineered your own arrest at the Deuce Theater, Lyle. You brought about your own downfall. You did it all. You stole your own sweater, bombed your own set, spiked the chili, murdered Chad, murdered Fiona, tried to murder me. I know you did it, Lyle. And I know *how* you did it. But I don't understand *why*. I mean, is there some kind of plan here, or are you just totally out of control? I need to know, Lyle. We all need to know."

Lyle gave me The Scowl. "What is this, some kind of

prank? I don't think this is very funny. This is Fiona's tribute, know what I'm saying? Who else is in on this? Sam? Leo? What's going on in there? Did you people get wasted or what? What's going on?''

Very little, actually. They were just standing there behind me in a row, staring at the monitor. Katrina was biting on her lip and trying not to cry.

"Let's just cut this shit out, okay?" Lyle growled, his eyes darting nervously about the set. "I ain't in the mood for this."

"What are you in the mood for, Lyle?" I asked. "Would an Uncle Chubby story do? Okay, I'll tell you one. You just relax and enjoy, because it's a real whopper."

He glared at me, sweat forming on his upper lip.

"Once upon a time," I began, "there was a big, big television star. In fact, he was the Number One star in the whole country. But he was a sad, sad star. He felt trapped—he gets that way sometimes. He wanted to be free. So one day he decided to cancel himself. . . . Pretty ingenious of you, too, the way you set yourself up. First you phoned in the complaint to the police, posing as Lillian Young, the assistant manager of the theater. It was a snap—all you had to do was go into a vacant office and plug in your voice-disguiser telephone, the one you use to duck God when he calls you. You implicated Tommy Meyer to throw people off. In fact, Tommy had zero to do with it. His skeegee life-style simply gave you the idea, that's all. Then you tipped off the press in advance to maximize the exposure. You went to the Deuce *planning* to be arrested. And it worked like a charm. You were scandalized. You were destroyed. True, it was pretty humiliating. But it was worth it to you. Besides, a fallen star can always win back public sympathy with a couple of suicide tries. Fakes, both of them. You had no intention of killing yourself either time. You knew someone would find you. The day you hired me, Lyle, you said somebody tried to take Chubby from you, murder him. That person was *you,* Lyle. Why did you do it? Tell us why. Your family wants to know. Your family has a right to know."

Lyle was perspiring freely now, his makeup streaming down his face in rivulets. He looked like he was melting.

"Speak up, Lyle. Don't be bashful. That's not like you."

His chest began to heave. "You can't imagine what it's like," he said quietly, between gritted teeth. "Being chained to the same stupid character for your whole fucking life. Not allowed to be anyone else. Not allowed to do anything else. The same stupid little show, week after week after week. Stupid stories, stupid fucking little kids . . ." His eyes took in the set. "Trapped here, inside these three crummy walls. No way out. None . . ."

"Fiona was right about you, Lyle. She told me that deep down inside you hated Chubby. Because deep down inside you believed you were much, much bigger than this. You wanted to be Belushi. A movie star. An idol. Only, the public would never let you be someone else, anyone else. To them, you were good ol' Uncle Chubby, period. So you went on playing good ol' Uncle Chubby and watching the Billy Crystals and Dana Carveys achieve the big-time stardom you craved. And felt you deserved. And it ate you up inside. So much so that you decided to take matters into your own hands. You set yourself up—turned Uncle Chubby, his show, and all of his merchandise into poison. So you could be free of him."

"I had the right," Lyle insisted. "It's my life, my career. I didn't hurt anyone."

"What about all of the people who you threw out of work, Lyle? What about your family?"

He filtered that one out. "I had the right," he repeated stubbornly.

"Okay, maybe you did," I conceded. "Maybe killing Chubby *was* a victimless crime. Just like getting caught with your dick in your hand was a victimless crime. But you didn't leave it at that, did you? You couldn't. Because it backfired on you. For one thing, there was such a hue and cry from civil libertarians that the network *had* to bring you back. And you had to come back—because your agent couldn't get you a movie job. Not one. And because you were broke. You blew most of your money on those houses you gave your ex-girl-friends. Whatever you had left was quickly slipping through Katrina's fingers. Ten million on your beach house alone."

"Katrina's a magician," Lyle sneered. "She can turn money into shit."

I heard a scuffle behind me. Katrina, in tears, was trying to flee the booth. Very blocked her path.

"Besides, the really big bucks come from syndication," I added. "That meant one more season. So you came crawling back. You had no choice. Just as God had no choice in letting you. You agreed to tell all in a memoir, too. Again for the money. You wanted a best-seller. You wanted me. To rope me in, you told me someone set you up that day at the Deuce. You stole your own sweater to make it look like this someone was still after you. And to make yourself into an even bigger victim than the public thought you were. This was strictly you hyping your book. For the money. And for the attention. You need attention. Let's never forget that. And you need something else, Lyle. You need control. Total control. You just have to have your way. If you don't get it, well, we all have a pretty good idea what happens when you don't get it. . . . From day one this season, God wouldn't let you have it. Oh, sure, he knuckled under to public pressure. Brought you back. But on his terms. He wanted changes. He wanted Chad Roe in the show as a love interest for Fiona. He wanted to see more of them and less of the ol' Chubster. He wanted to ease you out. It was to the network's advantage. You're unpleas-ant, you're unstable, and you're expensive. Plus your image as a role model for kids—*your* kids—frankly sucks. It was to just about everyone else's advantage, too. Certainly The Boys, who'd get to run it, and Amber, who'd direct. The Kids could move up. Fiona could stretch. Lots of people around here would be happy with you gone. And that threw me off for quite a while, Lyle. Because I kept thinking you were the victim. I thought one of them was the perpetrator. Possibly even all of them together. I had it backwards. *You* were the perpetrator. You were rat-fucking your own show. Strictly to get your way. When God stuck you with Chad, you said fine, and then refused to speak to the poor guy. Wouldn't give him direction. Wouldn't let him use your john. You treated him like complete shit. Even went so far as to assign him to me, with my two hours of experience in the business, and then forbade me to speak to him. You treated his character the same way. Instructed The Boys to write him like a complete dick. Gave him woefully little to do in the season premiere. In fact, he was barely in it. Not that this escaped the network's notice. After the first cast reading Marjorie gave you God's verdict in no uncertain terms. We want more Rob, and we want the audience to like him. You didn't want that—it spelled the end for you, and you knew it. You bellowed and you roared, but it did you no good. Marjorie wouldn't budge. So you caved in. Devised a new second act where Rob and Fiona got some quality airtime together in the Japanese restaurant. Your idea. Then you turned right around the next morning and bombed the set, which 'forced' you back into using the one you'd originally called for, the pool hall. Again, your idea. Seize the initiative was what you called it, I believe. Once again this was you getting your way. Or trying. Somewhat extreme, but quite effective. Besides, no one got hurt, and the set was your own property. If you had to nuke it to get your way, hell, that's what creative differences are all about. Nice bit of publicity, too. Where did you get the blockbusters, anyway?''

On the monitor, Lyle grinned at me maliciously. "Made 'em myself for the Fourth of July. I was gonna do a whole fireworks show out at the beach for the kids in the neighborhood. Only none of their parents would let 'em come. On account of I was a *baaad* influence."

"I see. Well, they certainly did a job on the Japanese restaurant. But they couldn't do a thing about the calendar, could they? Time was not on your side. It was only Tuesday morning. The Boys still had the whole rest of the week to beef up Chad's character. And Chad had the week to grow into him. You didn't want that to happen. You didn't want Chad to be good. So you shortened the workweek—by spiking the chili. The catered lunch from Big Mama Thornton's was your idea. Not Katrina's. You put her up to it, encouraged her to suggest it in front of the gang so they'd like her and think she was contributing something to the show. But it was all your idea. She kept quiet about this, even though suspicion naturally fell on her. After all, she didn't touch the chili, and you did. You made a point of sneaking some so you'd get sick and throw suspicion off of yourself. But she refused to point a finger at you. She kept quiet. Just as she kept quiet about the fact that the two of you *weren't* together in your office in the moments just before the blockbusters went off. You lied to the police about that, and she covered for you."

"Ya got her to talk, didn't ya?" Lyle snarled angrily. "Ya got to her. I shoulda known. Never trust a cunt to keep her fucking mouth shut. But, hey, I needed an alibi."

I heard another commotion behind me. Very was restraining Katrina again. It was me she was after.

"Damn you!" she screeched at me. "You never meant what you said about you and me. I *believed* you and you were just *using* me!"

"I had to, Katrina. It was the only way."

"You were *pretending!*"

"Isn't that what we all do?"

"I hate you! I hate, hate, hate you!"

Marjorie was frowning at me. Poor child didn't know

what to make of me. I get a lot of that. And I'm not always proud of it.

I turned back to the microphone. "Katrina told me she knew you were responsible for those bombs, Lyle. And she suspected you were behind the chili, too. But she covered for you. Because you were her provider, her employer, her man. She figured you must have had your reasons for doing all of this. Besides, no one got hurt. Not really. Not yet . . . Where did you get the fluid essence of ipecac, anyway?"

Lyle answered, "Scored it three, four years ago from a Doctor Feelgood I used to go to on East Seventy-second Street. Found it in his supply cupboard. Thought it might be good for a prank someday." He ran his hand over his face, smearing his moist makeup. "He's in jail now."

"You don't say. Maybe you'll run into him."

"No way," he snapped defiantly. "I ain't going to jail."

"We'll see about that. Where was I? Oh, yes. By spiking the chili you shut down production for the rest of the day, stretching the schedule impossibly tight. You made a big hue and cry about this. Bitched, moaned, trashed your john. All for show. This was exactly what you had hoped for. This was you getting your way. Or trying. Because it backfired on you once again. God wouldn't let you have your way. Wouldn't let you bump Rob from the season premiere. Instead, he expanded your workweek. Agreed to pay for overages so you could tape over the weekend. Most generous on his part. In effect, he cornered you. Now you were trapped. Stuck with Rob. Stuck with the show that God wanted. And that's when things got ugly. Because *you* get ugly, Lyle, whenever people try to make you do something you don't want to do. When your father tried to get you interested in ham radios, you burned his place down. And you reacted violently once again. You're a sick man, Lyle. You have a serious illness. You have something else, too. A hidden gift. You told me Herb tried to get you interested in electronics. You told me how much you hated it. What you neglected to tell me was how gifted a pupil you were. I just found that out a few minutes ago, Lyle. I phoned Herb. He confirmed it. He said you were a wizard with electronics. That's why he was so sorry you didn't stay with it. He thought you had a real future in it. Needless to say, you've never lost your touch. And it served you exceedingly well when it came time to rid yourself once and for all of Chad Roe. It was you who hot-wired the urinal. It had to be you. Leo was telling the truth. She didn't see anyone go in your john before Chad did. No one *did* go in there. Which left only one possibility—*you.* You hot-wired it yourself in those few minutes you were alone in your office before the nine o'clock writers' meeting, a meeting which you insisted be held in The Boys' office. You entered your john by means of your own inside connecting door. You knew Chad was sneaking leaks in your john. Naomi ratted on him, no doubt. She misses nothing. You rigged it up, then went down the hall to The Boys' office to meet, and wait, knowing full well that Chad and no one else would eventually slip in there to use your urinal. And that when he did it would kill him instantly. You figured, correctly, that everyone would assume that *you* were the target, and that poor Chad was merely caught in the wrong place at the wrong time. But the truth is that it was Chad who was the target all along, not you. He was a threat to you. You wanted him gone. So you took care of him. Regained the upper hand. Not for long though. Because now God was all set to mothball you. Right away, you called a family council meeting. You vowed you would not let God take *Uncle Chubby* off the air. Because the show must go on—in Chad's honor. Because that's how artists say good-bye to each other. Because no one, not even God, has the right to take that away from you. Damned touching. And some performance, when you consider that it was *you* who fried the poor guy. Still, God did agree to fly in this morning to check things out firsthand. You figured once you had him here on your turf you could bully him and get your way. And all would be peaceful again in the land of Lyle. And

maybe it would have been, too, if I hadn't screwed things up.
You were suspicious of me when I cut out yesterday afternoon. You figured I was lying to you. And I was. The truth is I
was seeing your parents. You found out—from them. Herb
and Aileen called you after I left them yesterday to thank you
for your hospitality. Their way of reaching out a hand to
you.''

Lyle nodded grudgingly and growled, "They left a message. I wouldn't talk to 'em. No way I'd talk to 'em. Or trust
you, ever again. I warned ya. I told ya what would happen.
You went behind my back, Hoagster! You *lied!*"

"And *you* freaked. Because you couldn't control me.
And because maybe, just maybe, your parents told me what
really happened to you that day up on the roof of your high
school gym. Years ago, you made up a fiction about your
illness and your shock therapy, and you've lived with that
fiction ever since. Your memory came back. Sure it did. You
simply denied it. Denied the truth. Blamed your parents instead. Because it suited your self-image. And because it was a
helluva lot easier for you to swallow than your own severe
manic depression. You had every intention of putting this
fiction in your memoir, under the guise of truth. It was certain to win you some sympathy. Certain to win back those
fans you'd lost that day in the Deuce. They'd forgive you
now. Sure they would. You were a misunderstood, abused
teen. Zapped by evil, sadistic parents. They'd have to forgive
you. Trouble is, I found out the real truth about your suicidal
depression. And you figured I'd pressure you to reveal it.
Maybe even cash in and go public with it on my own. You
didn't want this. It was your life and your book. You wanted
complete control. Control you could feel slipping away. Because of me. Your lousy goddamned ghost, the overpaid
schmuck who was supposed to be helping you, not fucking
you. You had to get rid of me, and fast, before I could spread
the word around town. So last night you slipped out of your

suite at the Essex House. How did you manage to duck out on your police protection?''

Lyle cackled gleefully, puffing up at the memory of his cleverness. ''There was this one dumb shit outside the door in the hallway. Him I lost by going out the service door in the kitchen. I took the fire stairs down. They let out near the freight elevator. I went out the back entrance on Fifty-eighth. Cop in the lobby was watching the main entrance. He never saw me.''

Behind me, Very muttered something sourly under his breath.

''I told Katrina I felt like going to a movie,'' Lyle added. ''Told her I needed to be alone, and not to worry about me. She bought it. She wasn't happy, but she bought it.''

''Because she thought you were actually slipping out to see Naomi,'' I explained. ''And she feared she'd only drive you away if she hassled you. She figured it was best to let you get Naomi out of your system. She knew you were under a great strain, and that this was your way of dealing with it. She even covered for you. Told your police guard you were taking a bath when he checked in on you. Hell of an understanding woman, Lyle. More than you ever deserved.''

''I caught a cab to your place just in time to see you leaving for dinner,'' Lyle went on. ''I followed you down to The Blue Mill in the Village. Went and stole a cab while you was in there, only I couldn't get a clear shot at you after dinner so I followed you back home. Sat outside your building for a while. My alternate plan was to buzz you, go on up, and strangle you right there in your apartment.'' He held his fat pink hands up before him, fingers spread. ''Did feel kinda risky to me. A neighbor might see me or hear me. I was gonna chance it though. Only then you came right back out in a tux. I followed you to the Carlyle. Got my chance afterward, when you was practically slipping it to Marjorie right there on the sidewalk.''

I heard a pained gasp behind me. Marjorie.

"Sorry I had to come between you two, Hoagster," he apologized, sneering at me. "Not that you missed out on a whole lot. I mean, the fuck of the century she ain't."

Now it was Marjorie who was trying to flee the booth. Very wouldn't let her go, either.

"Only you didn't get me, Lyle," I reminded him. "You screwed up. Just as you screwed up by killing Chad. Because the sorry truth is that you were even worse off without Chad than with him—God made that clear to you this morning. He put you on the shelf. No telling what would happen to the show now. Or when it would happen. But one thing was clear: Fiona would play a big role in it. It would become more and more her show, and less and less yours. Which meant only one thing to you—Fiona had to go, too. She was a threat, so you killed her. She was your ex-wife and you killed her."

"AND I'LL KILL YOU, YOU EVIL SCHMUCK!!"

There was a commotion out on the stage. Marty trying to get at Lyle. The writer was hysterical. A cop restrained him.

"As it happens, Herb and Aileen always liked Fiona," I continued. "She'd been nice to them when you two first married, and they never forgot her kindness. So they phoned her yesterday while they were in town. To say hello, tell her they'd met with me—and tried reaching you. It was a short, pleasant conversation. But it scared the shit out of her. Because she knew precisely how you'd react when you found out I'd seen your folks behind your back. She knew you'd freak. She wanted to warn me. She wanted to tell me you knew about it. That's what she wanted to see me about this morning. But she never got the chance. You killed her before she did."

"I had to," he insisted.

"What were you going to do next, Lyle? Kill your folks, too?"

"I had to," he repeated stubbornly. "She made me."

"How?"

He didn't answer. Just stared at me, as if it were obvious. I guess it was, to him.

"Once again you had to be clever about it," I pointed out. "Since there was a plainclothesman parked right outside your office door. You had to slip out without him or anyone else seeing you, and you did. Because it so happens you have the only window in the entire place, and that this window has a nice, deep granite ledge—a ledge that runs along the outside of the building and connects up with the window at the second-floor landing. That's how you did it. You went out your window and came in the landing window. Then you unlocked the fire door to the dressing rooms, made your way unnoticed to Fiona's dressing room, smothered her with a pillow, and sneaked right back the way you came. No one saw you. In fact, as far as anyone knew, you were in your office the whole time. You told Naomi you didn't want to be disturbed. That's the message Marjorie got when she tried to see you. You did this for a very good reason—you weren't in there. The cop was guarding an empty office. Most ingenious, Lyle. You only made one mistake."

"What mistake?" he demanded, treating me to The Scowl.

"You forgot to clean up after yourself. You left your finger smudges all over the landing window. I saw them when the lightning lit up the sky outside the window. They were on the *outside,* Lyle. Meaning someone had opened the window from out on the ledge. That's when I realized what you'd done, and how you'd done it. But I still don't understand why. Not really. Not murder. Not over a television show." I paused and tugged at my ear. "Especially such a *stupid* television show."

He blew. "It is *not* a stupid television show! It's *Uncle Chubby!* The number-one show in America. And *I'm* Uncle Chubby. It's *my* show!" He was screaming now, pounding his chest with his fists. "Ya hear me, *mine!* I write it. I star in it. I direct it. I *am* it. *Me!* Nobody else. And nobody else has a right to take it away from me. Or change it. Nobody. That's *my* decision. My right!''

"And so you exercised your right?"

"That's it," he agreed quickly, tongue licking nervously at his lips. "That's it exactly, Hoagster. I exercised my right. Not for myself. Not for me. I did it for the show. To protect the show. I was fighting for the integrity of the show." He was speaking rapidly, breathlessly now. The words spilled out in a torrent. "You *have* to fight 'em. Because they're always trying to bring you down. Fuck ya. Make you compromise. A little here, a little there. They *ruin* you. Like with Chad. That was God fucking me. Trying to *ruin* me. He was a lox. Chad was a lox. And he *made* me use him. I said no way. I won't have him. Not in my show. He said, 'Oh, yes, you will, Lyle.' So I showed him. I—I took care of him. Couldn't play comedy if his life depended on it." Lyle cackled. "And it *did*. So I showed God who was boss. Not for me. I couldn't care less about me. I did it for my people. All my people." His eyes flickered around the soundstage. "You people who depend on *Uncle Chubby*. Who love it like I love it. Who love me like I love you. I didn't *want* to do it. But I had to. Same with Fiona. I didn't want to kill her. Christ, no. I loved her. But I had to. Because I love *Uncle Chubby* even more. And all of you who depend on it. I did it for you. I did it for *Uncle Chubby*. This show means more to me than anything, and anyone. Even more than Fiona. It's all that matters. Making it the best there is. My way. I did it for you people. I did it for you. . . ." He broke off, looking around at everyone, his eyes wild, his chest heaving. "Why're you all looking at me that way? Ya think it's *easy* being me? Ya think I *wanted* to kill 'em? No way. I had to. I tell ya, I had to. It was necessary. A necessary creative decision. I make millions of 'em a day. Millions. I didn't want to kill 'em. God *made* me."

"Which God is he talking about now?" muttered Very, who had moved right behind me.

Lyle was staring off into space now. "It was for my people. I did it for us. We're a family, don't you see? We're about caring. And love. We're about being *out there*. My family understands. Sure they do. And they forgive me. Because that's what families do. That's the great thing about them. That's why . . ." He trailed off midsentence, sat there in glassy-eyed silence. Didn't move. Didn't so much as blink.

Very took control of the microphone. "Okay, Mr. Hudnut, it's all over. The exits are covered. Please cooperate with us and we'll have you out of here with a minimum of fuss. Car's waiting downstairs in the loading dock. Freight elevator will take us directly to it. We don't want any more of a scene than you do. Okay, Mr. Hudnut?"

Lyle didn't respond. He'd withdrawn deep inside of himself, a low, tuneless hum coming from his throat.

"Wrap him up," Very commanded his troops.

They moved in. Lyle just sat there, frozen. He seemed completely unaware of what was happening around him. Until suddenly he sprang to his feet and dashed across the kitchen set and out the laundry room door. He moved surprisingly fast for such a big man. There was an emergency fire exit there behind the set. No one was guarding it. He barreled through the steel door and was gone, six uniformed cops in hot pursuit.

Very cursed under his breath. "Not to worry, dude," he said to me with a tight grimace. "We got men on the fire escapes downstairs. He can't go nowhere."

Katrina stood before me, tears streaming down her face and her lower lip quivering. She bit it, hard. Started to say something to me, but changed her mind. She slapped my face instead, a sharp, stinging blow. Then she ran into the comforting arms of Leo, who hugged her tightly and murmured, "There, there," in her ear, like a protective mother. Leo glared over Katrina's shoulder at me, a hard glint of triumph in her eyes.

Marjorie Daw was still frowning at me.

One of Very's men barged into the booth now and

pulled him aside, briefing him in rushed, frantic bursts. Very made a face, then motioned me to join them.

"Seems we got a small problem, dude," he said, with admirable cool.

"What is it, Lieutenant?"

"Hudnut won't give up. He's up on the roof, threatening to jump. He's asking for you."

"What for?"

"How the fuck should I know?" he snapped, losing that cool. "Go up there and talk to him, will ya? See if you can bring him down."

"Wait, aren't there people who are trained in this sort of thing?"

"Not time for that. He wants *you.* Move it!"

An ancient cast-iron spiral staircase took me up there, my footsteps resounding sharply in the dim, narrow stairwell. There was a steel fire door at the top, open, and two grim-faced young cops crouched just outside with their guns drawn in the warm, greasy rain. The city sounds were startlingly loud up there after being in the soundproofed studio. The air was so heavy and misty I could barely make Lyle out. He was just a hulking shape standing over by the edge of the roof, his back to us. There was a low ledge before him—the top of the building's facing. Nothing else, besides sky. The tar roof was slick and puddled.

He heard me splashing across it toward him and turned. "Hey, ya made it, Hoagster!" he called to me genially. He seemed completely relaxed and cheerful. "You two guys beat it, okay?" he ordered the cops. "Scram, or I'll jump! I mean it!"

They turned to me, eyes wide. They were big men and they had guns but they were scarcely out of their teens. I nodded to them. They gratefully retreated through the fire door, leaving us. I went over and shut it behind them. Then I started slowly back toward Lyle in the rain. "This isn't a very good thing to do, Lyle."

"Why not?" He gazed longingly down at the street six floors below.

The police had closed it off; blue-and-whites formed a barricade across it at either end of the building. Protestors and bystanders were bunched out in the street, waiting for something, anything to happen. And hoping they'd be lucky enough to be a part of it. It was at times like this that I hated people. In the distance I could hear a fire truck's horn blasting away. But it would take him several more minutes to get here in the rush-hour gridlock. Forever.

"Why not?" he repeated, insistently this time.

"You're a sick man, Lyle. You'll be hospitalized. You'll be helped. Your life isn't over."

He stuck out his lower lip at me. "Yeah, it is. I'm a performer, Hoagster. And I can never perform again, not ever. They won't let me on camera again as long as I live—except for maybe a Barbara Wawa interview, live, from my padded cell, in a couple of years. So, ya see, there's no point in going on. None. If a performer can't perform, he's dead. . . . This . . . This just makes it official." He gazed down at the street again. "They shoulda just let me go before—that day in high school. It woulda been so much better if they'd just let me go. Then none of this would ever have happened. I shouldn't have listened to 'em. I shoulda just gone ahead and jumped. Ended it, there and then. I'm sorry now that I didn't. Totally fucking sorry. Will you tell 'em that? Will you put that in the book for me?"

"If you wish."

"I do." He let out a huge sigh. "I . . . I guess maybe I still *believed* then. I guess that's the reason I couldn't do it." His features darkened. "But I don't believe anymore."

"In what, Lyle?"

"In anything." He turned around to face me, edging back against the low ledge. It barely reached the back of his knees. "Will you do something else for me? One other thing?"

"What is it, Lyle?"

"Will you push me?" He asked this as if it were nothing major. A small favor, like watering his plants while he was away for the weekend.

"No, Lyle. I will not."

"Please?" he begged.

"No."

"I-I can't do it by myself, Hoagy. I thought I could, but I can't. I don't have the guts. Help me, Hoagy. Please help me."

"Don't do this to me, Lyle. Or yourself."

"Put me out of my misery, Hoagy," he pleaded. His voice cracked with urgency and emotion. "It's my only chance. If I turn myself in I'll be an animal in a cage for the rest of my life. *Trapped.* You know I can't handle that. Show me a little compassion. Lemme go. Give me a push. One little push." His eyes flickered at the fire door. "C'mon, pal, we're all alone up here. No one can see us. No one will ever know, except for you."

"That's a fairly big exception."

"You're my only friend, Hoagy. The only one I can count on. You and no one else. Because you care about what's right. You *know* this is what friends do for each other."

I stood there. I didn't say I wasn't his friend. I didn't say anything at all.

He didn't quit. "Okay, if not for me than for the folks. Give Herb and Aileen a break. Don't put them through the trial, the publicity, the bullshit. . . . Do it for *them.*"

I held my hand out to him. "Come on, Lyle. Let's go downstairs."

"You lousy scumbag," he snarled, turning schoolyard bully on me. "You don't have the nerve to push me, that's what it is. You're a momma's boy. A fucking momma's boy. I *dare* ya to push me! Come on, momma's boy," he jeered, shoving me roughly in the chest. "Push me!"

"This isn't going to work, Lyle."

"Push me, momma's boy!" he taunted, shoving me once again. "Come on and push me!"

"Cut it out, Lyle."

"Hell, you're such a momma's boy you can't even control your own wife."

"Do me a favor and leave Merilee out of this, okay?"

He cackled at me. "Know why nobody can figure out who the father of her baby is? I'll tell ya why—'cause there isn't a guy in New York or L.A. who *hasn't* fucked her. I've had her. Christ, who hasn't? She's got a cunt on her like a swamp. I put it in her ass, momma's boy. That's right, I fucked your wife up the ass. Then I stuck it in her mouth. She liked it that way. She liked it so much she *moaned.* She called me her big daddy. She called me her big, bad—"

I punched him in the mouth. Hard as I could.

Which shut him up. And also rocked him back against the low ledge, dangerously off balance. At first, he chose life, waving his arms in desperation, his eyes wide with terror as he fought for survival. But then he suddenly stopped fighting. He hovered there for an instant. I didn't try to grab him, and he didn't thank me, or grin, or wink, or do anything like that. Errol Flynn he wasn't. He just hovered there in midair—cancelled, with no hope of renewal. And then he pitched over the side. I heard the screams down below. Then I heard him hit the sidewalk, a sound I'll never forget as long as I live. Somewhat like a watermelon wrapped in a wet newspaper, but not quite.

I stayed there on the roof in the rain, rubbing my hand.

Romaine Very arrived in seconds. "You okay, dude?" he cried out as he burst through the fire door, out of breath. I think he ran up the stairs, even though his doctor said he wasn't supposed to.

"Why wouldn't I be, Lieutenant?"

"No reason," he said quickly, frowning at me. "What happened to your hand?"

"Nothing. Just a little arthritis. Common among aging writers, particularly in damp weather."

He stood there, nodding to his personal beat. "Damn, I hate jumpers. They always leave such a mess behind." He waited for me to say something. When I didn't, he turned and looked at me. "You want to talk about this, dude?" he asked gently.

"Now wouldn't be a good time."

"Sure, sure. Only, see, I gotta file a report, y'know?" He came over and put his arm around me. Below, the sirens wailed. "How about I buy you a beer first?"

"I'm more in the mood for a single malt scotch."

"Whatever." He flashed a grin at me, began steering me toward the fire door. "Cool, dude?"

"Cool, Lieutenant."

"I'm with you, dude."

"Thank you, Lieutenant."

And then the two of us left the rooftop.

"Do you own a lobster pot?"

She was still frowning at me, standing there in her apartment doorway in a T-shirt and shorts. I could see the lights of the cars streaming up the West Side Highway out the windows behind her. "Do I own a what?"

"A lobster pot." I watched them bob around in their plastic bag.

She watched me. A long time, searchingly, before she said, "What did you do to Katrina?"

"I did my job. It can be ugly, like I told you."

"What did you do to her?"

"I used her."

"Did you sleep with her?"

"I let her think I was in love with her."

"Why?"

"I had to."

"You had to sleep with her?"

"I had to pry her open. She was the weak link. Lyle took her too much for granted. He shouldn't have." I paused. "And I didn't sleep with her."

She shook her head at me. "I'm not entirely sure I like you."

"I'm not entirely sure I do either."

We stared at each other a long time before she swallowed and said, "The answer is yes."

"Yes, what?"

"Yes, I do own a lobster pot."

"Excellent. I'd hate to see these go to waste. They're from Maine, you know." I handed them to her and said, "Enjoy." Then I started for the elevator.

She let me get almost all the way to it before she said, "Where do you think you're going?"

"Nowhere."

So I didn't. The lobsters were superb. In fact, all of it was. No, Marjorie did not help me forget Merilee, if that's what you're wondering. Or remember her. This wasn't about that. This was about proving to myself that I was still alive.

Much later in the night I dreamt that it was me up there on the edge of that roof, waving my arms, about to pitch over into the great wide open. I awoke screaming, drenched with sweat. Marjorie wiped me down with a cold cloth and held me for a while. Then she did some other things to me that I see no need to go into here. Although I can tell you she did not wear her bite guard. In the morning she went out early and got us fresh, hot onion bagels. We ate them out on her terrace. She'd picked up the morning papers, too. The *Daily News* went with a one-word banner headline: *"SPLAT."* The Post went the Van Halen route: "YOU MIGHT AS WELL . . . JUMP!" Lyle's death was such a big story even the *Times* covered it—

in the Metro section under the one-column headline "NOTED TV ACTOR DIES IN CHELSEA ROOFTOP PLUNGE." All three papers had the gory details about Lyle's death, Chad's death, Fiona's, all of it. Except for the early stuff. They didn't have Aileen trying to kill Lyle when he was two, or that he'd tried to jump once before in high school. They didn't have his six-week-long suicidal depression. They didn't have him in shock therapy. They didn't have any of that yet. I was the only one who had that.

It still happens. I still think about Lyle Hudnut and me up there on that roof. I still ask myself if I should have hit him. If I should have tried to save him as he teetered there. If I did right by him. I don't know. I don't know about Lyle either—if he could have helped himself from doing what he did. If any of us can. I'm not sure if I hated him or not. I'm not sure if he was evil, or if there even is such a thing as evil. To tell you the truth, I'm not sure of anything anymore. The new me grows a little bit dumber every day.

I guess I'm finally growing up.

Fourteen

You'll be pleased to know that *The Uncle Chubby Show* returned to its same Monday night time slot a few weeks later, slightly revamped. The Munchkins, tragically orphaned by the deaths of both Deirdre and Chubby in a car accident, were adopted by a childless black couple. The wife had been Deirdre's law school roommate. The show got a new title, *Our House.* But Casey and Caitlin, as the adorable Erin and Trevor, didn't change, and neither did good ol'Rusty. Neither did the house, for that matter. The black couple just moved right in. Ratings for *Our House* were strong. Not number one, like *Uncle Chubby,* but it premiered in the top fifteen and held its audience on a consistent basis. The critics weren't wild about it, but they were polite. God elected to keep the production in New York for the time being. It made for less of a disruption, and allowed it to hit the ground running. The Boys ran it and Amber directed it. Annabelle stayed on as a producer. A young black writer from Yale Drama School was brought in to replace Bobby Ackerman, who was busy seeing his play, *The Human Dramedy,* brought to Broadway by Mike Nichols. As for me, I didn't stay with *Our House.* Nothing about my experience on *Uncle Chubby* led me to believe I had a future as a feelings specialist, or wanted one. I also wasn't asked.

You'll also be pleased to know that *The Human Dramedy,* starring Joe Mantegna as a psychotic TV sitcom star, became the big hit of the Broadway season when it

opened in January. The *Times* hailed its young author, Robert
J. Ackerman, as "the Tennessee Williams of the MTV generation." The Bobster became the toast of New York, and was
frequently photographed at the chicest night spots and parties, usually squiring the new woman in his life, Katrina Tingle. Leo's triumph, it turned out, was short-lived. Katrina, as
Lyle's sole heir, did stand to be a wealthy woman when the
first three seasons of *Uncle Chubby* got sold into syndication
—and when Lyle's estate ever got untangled. But it would
doubtless stay snarled in victim lawsuits for a good long
while. Both Brenda Roe and Noble Gesture were demanding
their fair share. For the time being, Katrina was off to Hollywood with Bobby, who sold the film rights to *The Human
Dramedy* to Rob Reiner for $925,000, and was getting paid
even more than that to write the screenplay. Don't ask me if
the play was any good. Tickets were impossible to come by,
and I didn't try very hard. Don't ask me what happened to
Leo either. Or Naomi. I only know that they were both
dropped from the staff of *Our House*. And that we won't be
exchanging Christmas cards.

I worked feverishly on Lyle's book in the weeks following his death. The Merchant of Menace expected a lot for his
money and his crustaceans. Plus there was tremendous pressure on me to turn it around fast. Lyle's story was one that
seemingly everyone wanted to read. Especially after someone, I believe it was Leo, peddled a bootlegged copy of his
on-camera confession to *A Current Affair.* The tape of Lyle's
dramatic last moments quickly became as familiar to TV viewers as the Rodney King beating. A docudrama on his final
days was already in the works, with John Goodman being
talked about to play him. No word on who'd play me. Jeremy
Irons wouldn't be a terrible choice. Lyle Hudnut achieved a
special kind of infamy in death, the kind we reserve only for
the truly great or the truly sick. His albums and videos and
storybooks sold even better than they had before. There
were newspaper and magazine articles galore on his rise and

fall. Oprah and Sally Jessy and Phil devoted whole shows to
his death and how parents could explain it to their kids. *His*
kids. I was invited on all of them, and turned all of them
down. My phone rang constantly, reporters wanting to know
what Lyle was really like. I said I didn't know. They also
wanted to know what his last words were before he jumped.
There was a great deal of interest in that. I didn't tell them.
I've never told anyone, actually. I did speak to his parents a
few times in the days after his death. It seemed to make all
three of us feel better. It was Aileen who insisted I include
how she'd pushed him down the basement steps when he
was two. She wanted it all in the book. So it went in. Mostly, I
worked, writing for hours at a stretch, sleeping little, and
downing pot after pot of coffee as the days and the nights
melted into each other. There was no doubt in my mind that I
had a number-one best-seller.

A few late nights I wandered around the corner to Marjorie's. She welcomed me. We didn't talk very much about
what was going on between us. We didn't talk very much,
period. Just got lost together in her bed, two beasts starved
for something that neither one of us was genuinely capable of
giving the other. It didn't make any sense really, Marjorie and
me, but she didn't seem to mind that anymore. So I guess I
rubbed off on her a little. As soon as *Our House* got on track,
she got traded to the West Coast for two first-round draft
picks and cash. A promotion, actually. God put her in charge
of two-hour movies and miniseries. Even made her a vice
president, which made her very happy. It certainly didn't
take her long to pack up her things. We had dinner together
the night before she left. We promised we'd see each other
soon. We knew we wouldn't. We promised we'd stay in
touch. We knew we wouldn't do that either. But something
tells me I will end up on her Christmas card list someday.
When she finds Mr. Right.

I was working on the scene where Lyle first tried to pick
up Fiona in line at the Bleeker Street Cinema when Vic Early,

gentle giant, phoned to say he had something for me. I told him to come on over. It was Lulu he brought with him, although I barely recognized her. She was so fat from Merilee's rich cooking that she waddled like Winston Churchill, her belly brushing the floor. Clearly, I would have to put her on Weight Watchers. Either that or hire her out as a dust mop. She whooped when she saw me and tried to climb inside my shirt. She'd missed me. But not as much as I missed her. She still had a scab on her ear, but otherwise her wounds had healed completely. I hugged her and gave her an anchovy. Vic I gave a cup of coffee. He looked uncommonly exhausted, as if he'd been out carousing all night.

He gulped it gratefully, slumped into my easy chair. "It's a girl, Hoag," he announced in his droning monotone. "Merilee gave birth to a seven-pound, nine-ounce baby girl at four-seventeen this morning at the Manhattan Birthing Center."

I felt my chest tighten. I sat on the sofa with Lulu on my lap. "Mother and child doing all right?"

"Fine. Prettiest little girl you ever saw. Strong and healthy as can be. Merilee was in labor with her for fourteen hours, but she toughed it out like a real trooper. It's that Pilgrim stock of hers, I guess. You would have been real proud of her. I sure was. Never assisted at a birth before. It was an incredibly moving experience. I'll never forget it."

"Was the father on hand?"

Vic's face dropped. "No, he wasn't."

"How about her parents?"

"It was just the two of us."

"Glad it all worked out, Vic," I said. "And thanks for bringing Lulu back so quickly."

"Merilee insisted on it. A deal's a deal. She's taking the baby out to the farm soon as they're both up to it. She wants her breathing country air, not bus fumes. Which reminds me . . ." He reached into his pocket for an envelope. "I'm going shopping for a station wagon this afternoon. She wants a big, sturdy one. Anyway, this is for you." He handed me the envelope. "The pink slip for the Jag. She doesn't feel comfortable driving it anymore, not with the baby. She wants you to have it. It's partly yours, after all. From before the divorce. And because, well, because of everything she put you through these past months."

I bristled. "What, she thinks she can buy me off?"

"Not at all, Hoag. Heck, no. Just her way of saying she's sorry. Besides, she doesn't want some stranger driving it."

"I see," I said doubtfully.

"I thought about buying it myself, but it'd run me about two years' salary. It's in the garage around the corner from her place. Space is paid up for the rest of the year. It's yours now, Hoagy. Enjoy."

I stared down at the pink slip in my hand.

"You have a problem with this?" he asked, frowning at me.

"No, no. It's very generous of her. Uncommonly. Do thank her for me."

"I will." He got to his feet and put his empty cup in the kitchen sink. "Guess I'll go grab me a shower and a nap." He hesitated, pawing at the floor with his big foot. "She wondered if you'd stop by. When she gets home, I mean."

"What for?"

"To see the baby."

"I'd rather not."

"It would mean a lot to her."

"She'll barely know I'm in the room."

"I meant Merilee."

"So did I."

Vic scratched his stubbly chin. "No offense, Hoag, but I liked the *old* you better."

"So did I."

"She talks about you all the time, you know."

"She should have that checked out. It might be early senility."

"It would mean a lot to her," he repeated.

"It's still no, Vic. And if this is one of the conditions for giving me the pink slip you can have it back. I don't want it. I don't want anything."

He shook his head at me. "She told me you'd say that. Man, she knows you like a book."

"Written by someone else, no doubt."

"She wants to clear the air, Hoag. About who the father is. About everything."

"Why?"

"Because she doesn't want to go through life having you as an enemy, okay?" he replied. "Will you come? Please?"

I came.

The paparazzi were crowded onto the sidewalk in front of her building, hoping to get a picture of the Merilee and child. They had to settle for a picture of me. And Mario, the surly doorman, had to settle for letting me go up. Lulu curled her lip at him. My girl.

She was in the nursery. Long ago, it had been my study, the place where I spent endless hours thinking nondeep thoughts. Now it had pink wallpaper with little yellow duckies all over it. And an air purifier. And a crib. There was a midget human life form in the crib, asleep, its tiny fists clenched. Its hair, what there was of it, was blond, just like dear old mom. Who looked, I must report, positively lovely. Tired, no question. But radiant. She had on a pair of washed linen trousers, Arché crepe-soled suede shoes, and an oversized lavender sweatshirt of featherweight cashmere that had once belonged to me. Her waist-length hair was brushed out shiny and golden. Her green eyes gleamed with pride. She seemed to glow all over. I had never seen her glow that way before.

"Don't you think she's absolutely *the* most beautiful baby you've ever seen?" she whispered.

"I do." She smelled milky. Smelled like something else, too. I wasn't sure what, and didn't want to be.

"Want to hold her?" she asked shyly.

"I do not," I said, a bit louder.

Loud enough to wake her. She stirred and opened her eyes. They were green eyes. Merilee's eyes. And when she looked at me with them I felt the same jolt I'd felt the very first time Merilee looked at me, that night backstage after the Mamet play, two or three lifetimes ago. When she rocked me. When we *knew.*

She was a devil-child, that was it. Satan was her father.

Merilee picked her up and cradled her in her arms. She made a soft, gurgling noise. The baby, not Merilee.

"Have you decided on a name yet?" I asked.

"Tracy."

"As in Dick?"

"As in Tracy Lord, you ninny." The lead character in *The Philadelphia Story.* Merilee'd played her in London. It had been a happy time for us. For a while. "Like it?" she asked.

"Like it. And the middle name?"

"No middle name. I hate mine." That's true, she does— it's Gilbert. "All girls do, and I don't ever want Tracy to have anything in her life that she hates."

"Well, you're certainly starting her off on the right foot then."

"How so?"

"No father."

Her brow creased. She swallowed and put Tracy back down in the crib. "Let's go in the living room."

We went into the living room, with its signed Stickley originals and its windows overlooking the park. Manuscripts were piled on the coffee table.

"Planning to go back to work soon?" I asked.

"When I can. Tommy Tune wants me for *Eve,* the musical he's basing on *All About Eve.* He thinks I was born to play

Margo Channing. I still can't decide if that's a compliment or not."

She sat on the oak-and-leather settee. I took one of the two Morris armchairs. It was quiet. Pam and Vic seemed to have cleared out. They'd taken Lulu with them. It was just we two. We stared at each other.

She cleared her throat. "How is your girlfriend?"

"Girlfriend?"

She raised an eyebrow at me. "The one with the hooters."

"Ah." I tugged at my ear. "Three thousand miles away. It seems you've spoiled me, Merilee. As far as other women are concerned."

"I'm terribly sorry, darling," she said, though clearly she wasn't. In fact, she seemed immensely pleased with herself.

"She didn't have them, by the way."

"Have what, darling?"

"Hooters."

"Ah."

"And you, Merilee?"

"Well, they're bigger than they were. I'm lactating, you know."

"I meant," I said, nodding in the direction of the nursery, "how is your . . . sire?"

She sighed, grandly and tragically. "I'm afraid you've spoiled me, too, darling."

"I'm sorry, Merilee," I said, though I wasn't. "So you're on your own?"

"I am."

"Rather hard, isn't it? Being alone, I mean?"

"Hard," she agreed.

We sat in silence.

"You look terrific, Merilee."

"Bless you, darling. Actually, they're planning to make a movie about my life these days. They're calling it *Field of*

Creams." She sighed again. "Oh, horseradish, this tact business is really a bore. Can we just get it over with?"

"Get what over with, Merilee?"

"Me telling you who Tracy's father is."

"I don't want to know. I thought I made that clear before."

"Well, I want you to know!"

"Well, I don't care what you want!"

"Well, *I* don't care what *you* want! It's time you found
out the truth, mister, once and for all. No matter how much it
hurts. From my own lips. So . . . So . . . *here!"* She held
something out to me. Another envelope.

"What's that?"

"The father's identity," she replied.

"Why can't you just tell me?"

"Open it."

"Why are you—?"

"Open it!"

I opened it. There was nothing in it other than a pocket
mirror. A lousy, dime-store pocket mirror. Nothing written
on the back. Nothing on the face either. Just my own reflection. Plain old me . . . *me* . . . looking somewhat paler
than normal . . . looking a lot paler than normal . . . looking . . .

I was flat on my back on the living room floor when I came
to.

Merilee was kneeling over me with smelling salts, her
brow creased fretfully. "Oh, I'm so terribly sorry, darling. I
forgot what happens to you when you get a shock."

Like I told Very—it's been known to happen. "W-Why,
Merilee?"

"I'm not positive, darling. Something about the flow of
blood to the brain being interrupted by—"

"No, why did you do this?"

"Oh."

"Wait just a minute." I sat up, light-headed but none the worse for it. "How do I even know this is true? How do I know I really am the father?"

"They do have tests, darling. If you don't believe me."

"Why should I believe you?" I demanded.

"No reason," she confessed. "None at all. Except that it's the truth." She sat back on her haunches and gave me her up-from-under look, the one that gives me goose bumps. "Remember Thanksgiving? That uncommonly warm Indian summer day? I was weeding at the edge of the duck pond, and I slipped and fell in and you—"

"Came to your rescue, as it were. I remember."

She smiled wistfully. "That's when it happened, darling. I left for Fiji soon afterward, and . . . there's no one else, Hoagy. There never has been."

I swallowed and took her hand. "Merilee?"

"Yes, darling?"

"You've put me through nine months of living hell."

"Just like old times, wasn't it?" she asked sweetly.

"I don't believe I can ever forgive you for this, Merilee."

"It wasn't easy for me, either," she pointed out, pouting. "I suffered, too. Alone, I might add."

"That, Merilee, was your own choice. Why did you do this to me? To yourself. To *us?*"

"I didn't want you to feel obligated."

"Bullshit!"

"I'd appreciate it if you wouldn't use that kind of language in the house. Tracy might—"

"We would have worked this out, Merilee. I would have been here for you. You know that."

"I knew you didn't want a child."

"But we would have been together."

"You're a decent man, Hoagy. A gentleman. The last of a dying breed. And you would have done the decent, gentlemanly thing. I knew that. But I was the one who wanted her, not you. So I thought it was best to free you of any responsibility."

We gazed at each other, and I got lost in her green eyes for a moment.

"You're saying you did all of this for me?"

She ducked her head ruefully. "I guess it does sound like a load of applesauce, when you put it that way."

"Sounds more like one big publicity stunt. Who thought it up, your press agent?"

She stiffened. "That was low, Hoagy. That was beneath you."

"I'm not as tall as I used to be. You cut me off at the knees, remember?"

"I'm sick about that, darling. Truly I am. I'd never intentionally hurt you. You know that. But, well, I've never been one to do things in a quiet way either. I'm given to the dramatic gesture. There, I admit it, okay? And, well, it just got a little out of hand, that's all. The media, the speculation . . . I—I never meant for any of that to happen. I swear."

"Why the hell didn't you just set them straight?"

"How could I? No one would have believed me if I said the father was *you.* Not after all of those months of publicity. Merciful heavens, they would have thought I was crazy."

"You can hardly blame them, Merilee. But why didn't you at least set *me* straight?"

"Because I made a deal with myself, and I was determined to see it through. I regretted every minute of it, Hoagy. For myself, and for what it did to you. And, God, how I've missed you. Every second of every day. There's no one else, Hoagy. And there never will be. Just you. Only you." Her eyes searched my face. "Say something. *Please.*"

"I don't believe I can ever forgive you for this, Merilee."

"You said that already. Say something else."

"Very well, Merilee." I got to my feet. "I'll say something else. I'll say the last word: Good-bye."

I walked out of the apartment without looking back. Rode the elevator down. Elbowed my way past the photographers and into the park. I walked. I don't remember exactly where, or for how long. I was in too much of a daze. I know I sat on a bench, but I don't recall which bench. Or how long I sat on it. I only remember it was dark out when I finally shook myself and got up.

And went back upstairs to her. To them.